Pick Up Lines

A Kings Ranch Novel

Summer Adams

More Than Words- Extreme
Flowers- Miley Cyrus
Cold December Night- Michael Buble
Take My Name- Parmalee
Lover- Taylor Swift
Earned it- The Weekend
White Horse- Taylor Swift
What Was I Made For- Billie Eilish
Chasin You- Morgan Wallen
Haven't Met You Yet- Michael Buble
Everything- Michael Buble
Used to be Young- Miley Cyrus
Until I Found You- Stephen Sanchez
Make You Feel My Love- Adele
I'm Not The Only One- Sam Smith
Neon Star- Morgan Wallen
End Game- Taylor Swift
I'll Be Lovin You- Miranda Lambert
Die A Happy Man- Thomas Rhett
Seeing Blind- Niall Horan
Finally Found You- Enrique Iglesias
Love Me Like You Do- Ellie Goulding

To the Hot Dad
XOXO
Coco

CHAPTER 1
Mina

"Is this really it?" The mumbling had started weeks ago, but now Mina was a pro at it. She never seemed keen on saving her most pathetic thoughts for herself anymore.

Claire looked at her with her brows raised, begging for further explanation. Mina made a grand gesture with her hands as if regarding every shopper around them and trying to make it clear.

"I mean, is this it? Is this really what I have to look forward to?"

Standing in the middle of a Walmart aisle and herding their groceries along with the masses, Mina had stopped to take notice. She shrugged and lifted her hands, just like she learned in church as a little girl, and "lifted them up to the Lord."

Maybe she was, in a way. Perhaps asking God himself, in the middle of the bread aisle, is this the best I'm going to get? Her eyes darted right and left, scanning the patrons.

She wasn't being overly dramatic this time, though, because if these really were her only prospects for a future husband like she believed them to be, she wanted to hide in a hole until the end of time.

There were a couple of pudgy older men with bad taste in fashion and worse hair genes. A bodybuilder who seemed way too impressed with himself as he donned biker tights with a razor-back tank top that could rival the size she wore on her own petite five-foot frame.

An elderly man who looked like he could play some happy grandpa on an old-fashioned sitcom, and last, but certainly not least, a woman who would better go by the name Butch rather than Barb and seemed entirely too interested in Mina.

Given that she wanted attention from the opposite sex, she wasn't sure if she should be put off or proud of the unsolicited interest. However, her new lesbian admirer was giving her more attention than all the other men combined. She decided beggars couldn't be choosers, even if disappointment was a hard pill to swallow.

"Because if this is it, I don't think I'll ever have sex again."

Claire took a moment to look around, pursing her lips while sizing up the men surrounding them. The bright lights and linoleum floor only added to the grim ambiance of her new dating prospects, especially when Claire took so much time wading through the possibilities mingling with Mina's future.

Mina was well aware she was always hard on herself, and the sudden lull in their dire conversation seemed to sink her already wavering self-esteem.

Just because she had a kid and was in her late twenties, did that really make her damaged goods?

Is this my lot in life? To sift through the local Walmart for men? Or do I face the elements alone? Forever?

She let out an exasperated chuckle. *When did I become an inspirational speaker?* At this point, she was convinced that all the great loves were taken and the movies were full of shit. But to be fair, her thoughts were only on par with her life at this point.

A failed marriage left her with a soon-to-be ex-husband who loved vying for the attention of every woman in town. *The affair...*

"For fucks sake, Mina, we'll hit the dollar store every now and then too! But stop being so dramatic. We're in the bread aisle. We haven't even checked what the meat section has to offer."

A quick wink and a hip bump shook her from her own torment and helped them move on to their next destination.

She would have to stop with the theatrics and get a grip on reality, even if reality meant that Walmart might become a potential dating pool.

What should be the most wonderful time of the year was quickly turning into a shit storm, complete with a blizzard looming over all the mountain towns in the area. As if the entire county agreed with the dreadful turn her life had taken.

Mina hadn't dated since high school, and it was bound to be quite different. Playing sand volleyball and hitting up a Sonic between flirting with the football players didn't seem like it was in the cards for a twenty-eight year old divorcee with a kid.

Football players, good grief.

Back then, Mina was an entirely different person than she was now. She was the talk of the town and highly sought after.

Her sister had a steady boyfriend, and that made her the only single half of the only pair of twin sisters in the high school. Oh, how time could change things.

At this point, she was willing to admit that she was going to call it quits on the whole dating game for good, hopeless candidates or not. Yes, she could always try other ways of dating rather than saving it all for the finest that Walmart had to offer, but that would force Mina to come out of her introverted shell. A shell she grew to like once the town found out about the affair.

At this point, she would have better luck making an NHL

team than finding a man worthy of making her want to leave her house.

"Is it really true that someone called her a twat waffle?" Claire asked. Her smile was soaked in mischief, revealing just how happy it made her.

"Who do we know that would even use that word?" She could barely ask without giving in to a fit of giggles again.

The twat waffle she was speaking of happened to be the woman from the affair. Claire scanned the ingredients to different granola bars while Mina tried to think of anything other than her unstable future.

Three damn months after finding out, and she wasn't even fully divorced yet while he paraded his younger model around town like he had just traded in a truck. Her phone was constantly being blown up by an endless supply of calls and texts from friends and "friendlies" that wanted her to just "be aware" of what an asshole he was and where he was taking her out.

Everyone in town had seen them at one point or another. As if reporting it back to Mina would make any of it hurt or embarrass her any less.

She wished some days that she could just hide in a hole or move to a new place where no one knew about the scandal. Somewhere she could move on. But small towns have a way of keeping secrets or helping set them ablaze.

"They went even further than that," Mina added. "Whoever it was basically called her out as being a slut and a home wrecker."

Someone, a mystery to all, had gone online and made a fool of her ex by smacking a picture of the happy new couple on a gossip blog and then wrote a scathing little commentary to follow.

The picture seemed perfect for it, too. All smiles and squeaky-clean images like they had gotten all dolled up for a nice night out.

Too bad no one knew who the secret script was from. They lacked some details that made it clear it was no one super close to their circle of friends, but it was close enough to give everyone in town and anyone with internet access a glimpse into their sweet little love story.

A love story that brought a cheater and a home-wrecker together while his wife and child were put out in the gutter. Claire loved every bit of the harsh gossip. No one messed with her sister and got away with it.

"Oh my," she clutched her heart in mock horror, "the scandal." Her face quickly morphed to satisfaction as she leveled with her sister.

"They deserve all the backlash. I do, however, want to know who this mystery person is because they are officially my new best friend." For a split second, Mina could see the hurt and anger in her sister's eyes right before she tucked it away again.

Claire would never admit it, but she had to live through the scandal and pain it had caused as well. After all, he was a brother to her. She trusted him and loved him, only to be betrayed, just like Mina. They were all reeling from the shock of it all.

They scanned the rest of the aisle for kid snacks they may have forgotten and then walked on to the deli. Claire's features twisted more with each step.

"You know… you will get through this." She eyed Mina wearily before turning her attention back to the cart in front of them.

"It won't be easy, but you can do it. You have all of us in your corner, Mina. Always."

Mina fought the familiar burn in her nose as her eyes threatened to water. She knew her sister was right. Time had a funny way of making things seem a bit more bearable with the more space you gave, but she was still afraid.

What if time didn't help her broken and beaten heart? Because if time couldn't fix her heart and her trust issues, then she would be spending the rest of her days with nothing but time on her hands, alone.

One thing was for certain. Mina was positive she was part

of a handful of people in the world who had been graced with an unusually close and supportive family. The kind of parents her friends always loved to sit by during high school football games even though they were embarrassed to sit by their own.

Her parents were the type to buy a little cottage on the edge of town for her and her daughter to settle into and live comfortably until she could get herself back together. No questions asked. Her siblings regularly called to check in or popped over randomly to help out, and Claire's in-laws basically adopted her, too.

She had always known how lucky she was, but times like this either made a family stronger or highlighted the cracks. She was thankful her family decided to thrive under the pressure.

"We better get back. Goodness knows the kids are driving mom crazy at this point." The town nearby was only twenty minutes from Kings Ranch and boasted the only Walmart in the area. A good distance away from the scandal, but the few lingering stares she got throughout the store made it clear that Kings Ranch wasn't as far as she thought.

"Oh shit! I forgot to grab some tampons. I'll meet you up by the check-out counters."

Claire gave a knowing look, then sent her off with instructions to grab her a box as well. Apparently, Mina wasn't the only one who mumbled under her breath. She was pretty sure she heard Claire drop some choice adjectives about a certain friend coming for a visit.

The aisles were wide, and the way men avoided the menstrual section would make one believe that the condition was catching. However, the deserted state made her feel better about her considerably lacking appearance she had taken on these last few months. She wasn't in the mood to impress anyone since she thoroughly believed all men were scoundrels anyway.

She scanned the boxes for what she needed, noticing each picture on the outside was more annoying than the last.

She grabbed the goods and turned back to head for the registers, frustrated. The shitty prospects at Walmart would take a backseat to the tampon advertisers.

Why the hell do they need to make periods look so damn happy? As if hiking and biking are really what I want to do when I'm-

Her train of thought was cut off when a strong shoulder bumped hers and sent the contents in her hands flying to the floor.

Mother Fucker! John Cena just took out my shoulder.

"Oh my God, I'm so sorry. Are you okay?" The stranger's voice came quickly, accompanied by strong hands reaching out to try and right her after the assault on her shoulder. She was pretty sure she was at fault here, but her annoyance with life and the tampon industry wasn't about to let her take ownership of the situation.

She reached down after waving the hands off and got down onto the ground. On all fours and looking like a child trying to put a floor puzzle together as she scrambled and reached for her tampons, all of which were now in different directions.

Her hands stilled once she noticed a box of Durex XL condoms scattered into the mix.

"Totally fine." Was all she could muster while she avoided eye contact with the owner of the sexiest voice she had ever heard in her life. *When did voices become sexy?* Trying to will her hands into motion seemed far too difficult a task once the sexy voice squatted in front of her. Thick thighs and polished shoes accompanied his dark jeans. Of course, he had to be a damn gentleman and reach down to help her with the mess.

She continued her quest for further embarrassment as she knelt in front of him, blindly fumbling for boxes as corded forearms reached out and grabbed the two tampon boxes first.

Naturally, he had to be a muscular gentleman. She wasn't mad about it as she took in those forearms and cuffed sleeves until her eyes finally made their way to the only box left on the ground because his hands were a jumbling mess like hers.

Her mouth went bone dry once she realized she was left with no other option as she numbly reached for the condoms to return the favor.

She awkwardly pushed herself to her feet, avoiding eye contact while ideas on how to hand the muscular gentleman his condoms danced in her head. *What conversation would be the least embarrassing when making the exchange?*

Should she tell him she was buying in bulk for the church as they made the trade? Should she just make the exchange and run, no words necessary?

My God, what has my life come to?

She just wanted to get her tampons and get the hell out of there She already knew the church route would only work with a Costco-size box, but she was out of luck with two regular-sized boxes.

Baby Jesus, why did I have to grab boxes with the words SUPER on them?

It was time to face the music. She needed the tampons, and the muscular gentleman needed his condoms. His XL condoms…*God, you cruel bastard.*

Dragging her eyes up the tall frame, her sex-deprived body didn't miss his broad shoulders or the way his shirt stretched over his impressive chest. The man she nearly cussed out and who was now holding her tampons had to have a sculpted face and sea-green eyes. *Of. Fucking. Course.*

She immediately thought about what she was wearing. Had she brushed her hair this week? Was she even wearing makeup? The beautiful, gruff voice spoke up just in time to save her from herself.

"I think these are yours."

He had a smirk on his face that matched his devilish good looks. *Trouble with a capital T, and he knows it.*

He held out his hands full of the tampon boxes, and she started to wonder, *Do tampon boxes make me happy after all? If they just have him holding them up, their marketing strategy would be a whole lot stronger. Fuck the bikes, honestly.*

She was pretty sure anything this sinful-looking man advertised would become her favorite item on the market. His face was just that good to look at.

Vowing never to make eye contact again with the gorgeous tampon representative, she held out the XL condoms, her mind going down roads she hadn't let it wander to in quite some time.

She wet her lips, attempting to regain composure as well as play ignorant to his sinful looks.

"Yup…and this must belong to you," she added with a tight smile. She tried to force herself to act naturally, which was always the worst advice when nervous. It made her feel a bit better that he actually looked a bit nervous as they exchanged boxes. Her whole embarassing downfall didn't seem as humiliating when he bit his lower lip, nodding his head and chuckling to himself.

"Ha, yup. Gonna need those later tonight." The introvert in her just smiled nonchalantly and nodded along.

"Right…Well…bye." She was out of there before she could congratulate him on having a giant dick that needs the XL condoms or make a joke about them both having to use SUPER size things.

She was thanking her limited lucky stars for not allowing her nervous word vomit to spill out and make moving to a new state necessary.

As she hurried back to Claire, she didn't bother sneaking any last glances at the gorgeous lumberjack who almost broke her shoulder. But suddenly, she felt like the local Walmart just got a whole lot more interesting.

CHAPTER 2
Alexander

"Oh my God, Xander! Oh my God!"

The nameless blonde sprawled on her bed was on the edge and about to fall apart beneath him. Nameless was probably not the best word to describe her. This was his second date with her, after all, but he still had a hard time keeping names straight these days.

Dating in the twenty-first century could do that to a man. Dating apps and feminism made dating multiple women not only normal, but a right.

This was his third date this week with just as many women. No one wanted to waste precious time with one person for months only to find out they aren't compatible, but also suck in the sack.

Xander had never had trouble with the latter, but with women throwing themselves at him on dating apps, many of whom only wanted to keep it physical, it was hard to keep both heads on the same game plan.What could he say? It was a great time to be a bachelor.

His thrusts got more urgent with the sound of the bed hitting the wall, and he felt the sting of her nails digging into his back. She was getting close, and he knew what would send her spiraling. *Tiffany. That's what her name is, for Christ's sake.* Tiffany put out on the first date last week and was interesting enough to take out again. But after the second date seemed to last forever, he realized that while she may have a pretty good body, her mind left him wanting more.

"Yes, fuck! Oh my God, it feels so damn good." She nearly screamed the words as she held onto him, enjoying the ride. He could feel her tighten around him and buck her hips with more force.

The thrill of the chase never got old. He's a damn good fuck, from what he's heard, and he loved to hear them come apart beneath him.

"That's right, baby. Come on my cock." He thrust harder and faster until the only words she could utter were filled with his name.

"Xander!" She came undone beneath his broad shoulders, grasping onto him with shaky muscles and shock waves of pleasure. It didn't take him long to follow suit, and within a couple of minutes, he collapsed next to her.

Minutes passed, with only the sound of their heavy breathing filling the late-night stillness in the house until he rolled onto his side and made his way back to this world, back to reality.

He's always had the same reaction after sex. The moment it

became clear that his search to find the perfect woman had been met with yet another disappointment.

The need to leave.

This little romp was fun, but he had to get out before she started talking again, and he would have to pretend to be interested. She was nice enough, but there was something missing. There was always something missing if he was being honest with himself.

No matter how great the sex could be, there was always something that just wasn't right. Not the perfect fit. Not the perfect woman for him.

"Oh my God, Xander," she sighed. "That was incredible." She smiled and took in a deep breath. "When can we see each other again?" She had rolled over, mussed hair and weary eyes after an hour of being well-ridden and reached for him just as he sat up and threw his legs over the bed in search of his jeans.

He didn't end up using those condoms, so he didn't really need to clean up. He was starting to regret that decision lately, though. The decision to just pump his load in different women was eventually going to bite him in the ass. *Again.*

He also regretted what happened in the Walmart earlier. With *her*. As he continued to hunt for his clothes, he kept thinking about all the ways he fucked up and how he wished he could redo his encounter with the mystery woman.

This fucking room and my fucking clothes.

In the dark, the room felt annoyingly huge and cluttered when all he wanted was to get the hell out of it.

He tripped over himself while getting tangled up in a bra before he finally spotted his jeans and pulled them on.

"Well, when am I going to see you again? We sure know how to have fun together, don't you think?" She looked up at him with heavy eyes and a sexy smirk at the corner of her mouth. The mental recap of the night played in his head for a brief second.

It was good sex but not the best. It was a boring date, and he had no interest in subjecting himself to more conversation with her. Maybe he could keep it physical and call when he was in a slump.

"We really do, huh? Maybe I can see if my work will ease up these coming weeks. Then we can try and plan another night out." He really couldn't care less if he ever saw Teresa, scratch that, Tiffany again.

"Or in," she added as she sat up and let the covers slide down to her belly.

Boy, she doesn't play around, does she?

"I'm sure we can figure something out." He leaned over the bed, groping her breast while kissing her with enough force to knock her back onto her pillow before he threw on his shirt and grabbed his keys off the nightstand.

With nothing but sex to talk about in the already exhausted relationship, he added, "Text me when you're free this week. I'm already thinking about the next time we can make that pussy come again," before making a hasty exit.

Did he really just say that? He was hoping his pickup lines weren't as cocky as that one. *Good God, I'm turning into John.*

John, one of his best friends, was known for being a cocky asshole as well as a lady killer. He was stooping to new levels if these were the one-liners he was busting out.

The door closed behind him, and he started to feel like an even bigger dick. He knew he should stick around and cuddle. He should probably talk more or at least act more interested in what she would be up to the rest of the night. At least try to act like he wanted more besides fucking, but he couldn't seem to bring himself to care. Another home, another woman and the same outcome. No matter how intense the sex was or wasn't, he always came up short of finding the one.

Women seemed easy to get to the bedroom, but that's about where his interest ended. He was a man with sexual needs, after all, but he always snapped back into this world once he was able to get off.

Then, after that, it was all a blur of different pictures on the walls, different homes to navigate through and a drive back home to his place. Alone.

Living in a small town could be difficult to date, but with tons of tiny towns just a hop, skip, and a jump away, it made his life a little too easy to keep things casual when he needed to.

As he buckled his seat belt and pulled out of the driveway, he looked around the neighborhood and tried to imagine what they did for a living.

What are the people around here like? What was she really like, he wondered. *Thank God this one didn't seem like a whack job.*

He never used to see the signs and signals of the crazy ones. The ones he deemed a seven and above on the crazy scale. Women could be crafty and hide their crazy, but nowadays, he had become a skilled hunter in the art of weeding out the whack jobs. Well, skilled, as in he knew the warning signs before things went too far.

He still needed help when it came to the opposite. Finding the perfect woman. One that he's secretly been dreaming about since his teenage years.

Unbeknownst to his friends, the wild frat boy he was known for wasn't the same person under the surface. All the parties through college, all the women he slept with starting from high school and up until this point in his mid-thirties have all been in a desperate search for "her."

Xander wasn't even sure his immediate family really knew his true nature. The part about wanting to settle down and start a family with a woman that rivaled his hottest fantasies.

Like the woman at Walmart.

Not even trying, but was a stunner. One that's out of his league but only had eyes for him. The idea of it could make his cock hard instantly.

Why was that so hard to believe?

He thought about his buddies from the frat house and what they were doing now. What they drove, where they lived, but most importantly, at least to him, what their family life was like.

He normally got the full rundown on the annual golf trip they always took to some far-off fancy destination just to spend a shit ton on alcohol and catch up on old times. That's when he was able to make a mental note of how his friends were doing.

He could never get the full story just based on the small talk between quick calls and texts for barbecues or poker nights. The real status of his friends and their families came out when they could get away and have a little liquid courage in their system.

His last update on the boys and their families came from the golf trip to St. Simons Island in Georgia last year. Days in the hot, humid sun followed by nights with more drinks and a chef for the home they rented.

The amount of alcohol they were drinking on those trips would make anyone down to spill their souls to each other.

Golf days would always start with questions about his conquests, which always accompanied drinks on the course. Damn, how they love to hear about his dating life. All the men did.

The huge group of guys were sloppy and loud, but they were entertaining. The funny stories always gave the boys a good laugh, but the hotter and dirtier the women were, the more interested they became. He guessed it seemed crazy to some of them, having been out of the dating game for years now, just how easy it was to get laid these days.

Or maybe it was just easy for Xander and John.

The endless women they had taken to bed since the last time they talked or texted and the craziest places they had fucked were always the most interesting topics.

Naturally, not wanting to be outdone by one of the bachelors on the trip, many chimed in with where they have fucked their wives lately and how their conquest was the best. With some being married, many of the stories were followed up by college hookups or their sex lives just after graduating. The time in their lives when condom and liquor shortages were their biggest problems.

But the jaded men always came clean once their alcohol intake took a turn. That was when the truth came out, and the state of their happiness was put on full display.

His inner circle was in bad shape, and it was no wonder they weren't big fans of the marriage game.

Out of the four closest friends he has, two seemed pretty miserable when it came down to their love lives. The two that were happy? One was single, while the other was in a committed relationship that didn't speak the word marriage. So naturally, none of the boys cared to encourage his hunt for the perfect woman.

His friend, Tyler, was a bigwig in the cyber security industry and would travel the country attending conferences, meeting clients and showing them the town. It was a cushy gig, and he got paid mountains just to wine and dine the clientele.

Of course, it all took place while he was cheating on his wife. It could be terribly easy to cheat when the company puts you up in a ritzy hotel and pays you to literally make sure the clients have a night to remember.

Alcohol was always a great middleman, and when it was flowing freely, it wasn't hard to get attention from women.

It was hard to hear about the infidelity, knowing he had a wife and two young kids at home. Xander knew Tyler's wife, and she was a nice woman who didn't deserve any of it. To be honest, he had always thought of Tyler like a brother, but he was an asshole with women.

What was he supposed to say when he bragged about getting pussy? Congrats man? Oh hey, how's your wife doing these days?

It was fucked up, but there was no way of setting him straight. They all lectured him years ago, but the man had no intention to change his ways.

Then there was John, the real estate agent in California. John always had his back no matter what happened, but even Xander couldn't handle John for longer than a couple of days.

More money than God and had an ego to match it. He seemed to have a death wish that Xander couldnt keep up with. The man was always knee deep in women, smoking or drinking. He wondered if Tyler and John were closer to each other than the rest of the gang. He had suspicions, but he was doubtful John was as critical of Tyler's exploits as he was.

John spent his days eating up the commercial real estate market and making millions. While his nights were spent fucking models and parading them around, Xander had a little girl he had to think of. It was a sad, but they had grown apart overs the years for obvious reasons.

Noah, his best friend from elementary, was always quieter about his marriage and family, but Xander knew better than to assume he was happy, especially after how long he'd known him. It wasn't in what Noah said but rather in what he never said.

He would tell the boys that the wife and kids were fine. Melinda was Melinda, and the kids were growing up fast. Nothing bad, but nothing was ever good either. He would always skip right to stories from the ER and ask them how the stock market was doing in their portfolios. Nothing ever seemed to stand out in his life except for his activities and hobbies outside of his family.

Then, finally, there was Mack. The dating scene may have been long gone, but he wasn't in any hurry to marry, probably after listening to the same sad stories they all had. He was in a three-year relationship with a woman who was smart, attractive and at the top of her game in a law firm. They never mentioned they wanted kids and loved to travel often.

Maybe they would never come down from the honeymoon phase, and maybe they would avoid the marriage and kids completely. Who knew?

All he knew was that drunken conversations with his close friends had made him realize two things.

One, they all told him never to get married and to enjoy the life he had. In other words, keep dating casually and fucking every woman he could.

The second thing he realized, shortly after receiving the first bit of knowledge, was that he didn't want their advice. Maybe they meant well because of their own circumstances, but Xander was determined to find her. If he could find a woman like the one he literally ran into, he knew it would be different.

Good Lord. Did I really tell her I planned on using the condoms later?

He didn't know what to say. She was fucking gorgeous. All tan skin and almond eyes. A literal exotic wet dream walking around Walmart. He wasn't certain of anything these days, but he was damn sure he wanted to head back to Walmart right about now.

CHAPTER 3
Mina
Months Later...

"I think I want to write a book."
Mina had been dreading this call, so small chit-chat wasn't needed. *Ugh, why am I so nervous about telling her this?* She had to put it out there at some point, and if she was going to do this, Claire would be her biggest cheerleader. She hoped.

A little breezy weather to distract her, and Sophie by her side had the makings of a great day. Mina was in the middle of making a chalk garden of flowers on the pavement as Sophie made the sun. It was a beautiful spring day in Kings Ranch, and the unpredictable Colorado weather was giving a slight reprieve from the cold. Last week was a blizzard, but this week promised only cool breezes.

Sure, it was spastic, but no one was complaining about that right now. The mountain air and the slight glimmer of warmer weather to come were just what she needed for the extra shot of courage.

"Good day to you, too. Okay, so you want to become a writer?" The intonation of her voice wasn't lost on Mina. Claire seemed none too sure about this idea.

"I'm speaking to the same Mina that dreaded AP English our senior year, right? The same one that called the teacher a Nazi for making us do research papers?"

Brushing the chalk off her hand and admiring the lovely daisy she drew in their makeshift garden, Mina paused to think about high school. It wasn't that long ago, but she realized she wasn't the biggest fan of English at the time. Hell, she didn't even like reading books!

Who the hell was I back then?

"Well, yeah, ok… I do remember not liking that part so much. But you know what, that woman was a Nazi! She was old and a tyrant. I could never just get an A on any damn paper because of her switching between MLA and APA format. I mean, who does that to kids? Pure evil, Claire. Call it what it is."

Mina could practically feel Claire roll her eyes through the phone. The town may have been small, but it wasn't that small. That old Nazi was a nice lady, according to Claire. Tough but nice, and Claire happened to love her. She happened to love all her teachers.

Where Mina lacked, Claire excelled. It was a relief that their talents took them on different career paths, or else Mina would worry she would always be in Claire's shadow.

The one that always had her wits about her and a clear path ahead, and of course she did. Claire was a doctor. Or, as she liked to put it, a physician. "The title of Doctor sounds so stuffy to me," she would always say. But Mina always thought physician sounded snobby.

"You're taking time from teaching to raise Sophie. All I'm saying is, think about it. It's not some easy feat." She did have a good point. Claire always did. But this was something for her.

Something no one would ever understand.

Mina always had ideas. She dreamed of being an artist. Being someone who could paint for a living or write for a living. She had already achieved one career dream. Why couldn't she try for another?

"All right, Mina." Requiring no further debate, Claire seemed on board. "You always have something brewing in your head. So, what are you thinking? What type of novel?"

Smiling as she continued her chalk garden, she let out a nervous sigh. "Well, it's going to be a contemporary romance novel." She let the idea simmer for a minute. It felt personal just sharing this much so far. Like her diary was about to be read in front of her high school class.

She also felt out of her league, given that she wanted to write a romance novel right after she went through a tornado of a divorce, complete with a cheating scandal that rocked Kings Ranch. Probably not the best genre to test out her skills, but a genre she was determined to write, nonetheless.

"Romance novel, huh?" Ever the big sister, Claire was intrigued and attentive. "It sounds right up our alley. What kind of love story did you want to write? The kind that we love reading where there are steamy scenes or the love stories that build up to be sweet and predictable?"

Mina rolled the idea around in her head for a minute. "I'm not sure. I know I love the steamy sex scenes, but the idea of Mom reading it makes me want to hide in a hole. I mean," lowering her voice to a whisper, "How am I supposed to write about the way some woman deep-throats a guy? Would she think I had to be a pro at all those sex acts in order to write about them? Would she think I can deep throat and be impressed, or would she think I'm a closet whore and reconsider her life choices as a mother?"

Claire was laughing so hard she snorted, interrupting Mina's train of thought.

"Oh my God, Mina! You're an adult." The woman was

wheezing now. "If you want to write about sex in a shower, on a beach, or even in the driveway of your own house, you can do it! Congratulations, you're a grown-up."

The statement was a bit empowering, and the thrill of that kind of freedom almost made her giddy.

"Hurry up and let me know what you're thinking! I have to get off here soon." Her sister gasped and the cackled.

"Ha! I'm already cracking smut jokes better than you!"

Mina couldn't help the pride and embarassment from smut jokes directed at her already. "You're really proud of yourself, aren't you?" It was a good one. She'll give her that.

Claire was always in a rush somewhere. Three kids and a husband who traveled for work would do that to a woman. And don't even get Mina started with the work schedule her sister had to maintain. She's a superhero in every sense of the word.

"To answer your question, I don't know," Mina snapped playfully. "I mean, I was just given permission to get as crazy as I want, but I don't even know if I want to!"

The sound coming through the phone shifted, and she could hear the girls giggling in the background. "Hold on, unicorns. Let me grab Soph!" All the little ladies were part of an elite and exclusive club known as the Unicorns.

"Auntie!!!" It never got old hearing all the variations they gave Mina. Auntie Mommy, Mama Mina, the list went on, and she was here for it.

"All right, Unicorn club members, I have a special question for you." Claire was in heaven with this. "Who should the love interest in auntie's new book be?" A long pause ensued, followed by questions asking what a love interest was. After the explanation held them up for a beat, it wasn't long before the real conversation got going.

"Well, I think he should be a Prince," said June, the youngest of the three girls.

"No! There are enough princes that steal someone's heart. Why don't we make him a doctor like Mommy?" Her oldest, Kate, was eight and always the loyal one, but Claire interrupted her reasoning.

"Honey, I think there are plenty of books about doctors winning over ladies as well. What about a pilot?" Claire asked.

"Booooooo," the girls shouted in unison.

"Any other ideas? I don't hear you people throwing out better ones," Claire chided.

"I don't like what daddy does, so whatever you do, don't make that his job." Poor Fiona. She was the middle child at six years old and was probably the closest to her dad. It was the reason she hated his job so much. Kyle worked on the Alaskan oil lines and was gone for weeks at a time. Claire agreed with Fiona before moving on. "Well, Soph, what do you think?"

Mina felt pulled into a million directions as she waited for Sophie to come up with something. It had to be a hard one for her to answer, given that she still didn't really understand why her mommy and daddy weren't together.

"Hmmm," she put her little finger to her lips and looked off toward the mountain. Everyone waited for a minute, not really knowing what to expect.

"Maybe he can be a bookstore owner. Mommy always talks about how much she loves reading." Her sweet girl was always thinking of her mama.

"Great idea, Soph! I think you're onto something." Mina gave Sophie a little squeeze around the shoulders before turning her attention back to the rest of the gang.

"All right, unicorns, do your official handshake over the phone so I can finish up with your mommy." Sophie performed the ritual in front of Mina while she imagined the others doing the same on the other end of the line. Hands to their foreheads in a mock unicorn horn preceded the chorus of neighs that ended the official send-off.

"You know, I think Sophie had the right idea. Maybe you should just write about what you want in a man. I mean, you can dream, right?"

Claire wasn't wrong... She supposed there was no harm in it except for the fact that she may come off as pathetic to people she knew and the fact that she may never get her dream husband. The fear of failure came in tenfold after her failed marriage.

"Hey, you know what? I think I read something like this," Claire went on. "There's some voodoo, yaya power of putting what you want out into the universe and then sitting back and waiting. What if you wrote a list of all the traits you want in a perfect man and then wrote about him in your story? That's the same thing, right? I mean, even if you just put it in writing, maybe it will give you a better sense of what you're after now that you're a free woman."

Mina let out a huff, but she had read about some sort of law of attraction. Putting her will into the universe and then waiting for it to come to her. *Wouldn't that be convenient?*

"Yeah, I think I read that somewhere too." She didn't want to give her sister the idea that she was completely on board with it. To be honest, she thought if her sister knew she already read about it and considered doing it, it would make her look even more pathetic.

Once upon a time, she would have believed in it wholeheartedly. Back when she had a high school sweetheart who said she was his whole world. *What a fool I had been.*

"Mina, don't let me forget to ask you about something for the girl's school later." The change of direction sent Mina spinning in a whole different way.

"Why don't you just ask me now?" She was skeptical about the actual question and the reasons behind it. Was there trouble in paradise for yet another seemingly happy couple? Probably not, and she was grateful for that. Lord knew their family couldn't handle another scandal, even if the whole town would be game for it.

"It's nothing. I think I just need more help. I'm going to talk to Jared and let you know what we come up with. I heard that you might be picking up his kids a couple of times a week to help them out, so we are trying to work out a schedule. Just don't let me forget, okay? All right, I love you! We'll chat soon!"

Finally, her sister admitted she needed some help and some that she wouldn't have to pay an arm and a leg for. She was home with Sophie, so why shouldn't she get to hang out with her little nieces more? It also made perfect sense.

Jared's wife, Beth, was going back to work after raising their four babies, and Mina was going to help with school pickups. Extra time with family and extra time to keep her mind off things. It would prove especially helpful when she had to start splitting time with "him." The one she refuses to refer to by name.

It may not be the most mature notion to never speak of one's ex, but it was better than speaking ill of them, she decided. Even if Evan was a douchebag. *Damnit!*

She would just have to shift her focus for the hundredth time today. The new little cottage was already feeling more like home with all the ideas swirling around her head, and with each day getting warmer, the projects for her could be endless. Besides, this all would work out, she just needed time.

It has to work out.

CHAPTER 4
Alexander

Flights out of Kings Ranch were getting a bit easier to find these days. *Thank the Lord*. With a job that required a bunch of travel, Xander sometimes wondered if he would be able to shake the little mountain town and head for the big city.

Denver wasn't too far from here, and he would still be able to visit his brothers. But, then again, he wasn't entirely sure he would ever ditch this little town for big city life again.

Having grown up in Denver, he was ecstatic to get an entry-level job with a huge beer and wine company that needed a sales manager in the territory that encompassed Kings Ranch, Telluride and just about every other little mountain town through all the passes.

It was a great gig for a kid fresh out of college, and even though he wasn't a green college kid anymore, he still loved this town. He would just have to keep sucking it up with extra layovers or an extra drive to Denver International.

In the thirteen years he had been with Alpine Liquor and Brew, he had worked his way up to being one of the VPs. Not bad for the second to last baby of the family. The competition was just between the brothers anyway. Their baby sister didn't count when it came to busting each other's balls and talking shit.

She was the surprise that came way after and being the only sister, she was pretty much in a different class.

Boarding would start any minute, and he needed to hit the head, but his phone started to vibrate, and he hesitated before hitting the accept button on the home screen.

"Hi, Mom. What's up?" He loved his mom, but she was starting to get more and more interested in his personal life the longer she had to wait on more grandbabies. He knew she meant well, but this bit was getting old.

"Oh, honey! Hi! I was talking to Tyler's mother at lunch today, and she said she heard you were seeing someone new. Is that true? How exciting!"

He could practically feel her jumping up and down on the other end of the phone. *That mother fucker*. Tyler always knew how to piss him off. Run and tell his mommy that he was seeing someone and get a little drama kicked up.

Of course, he was seeing someone. He was seeing a lot of women. But these days, it was called fucking, and Xander didn't have the heart to tell his mother that it pretty much ended there.

"I missed you too, Mom," he chided. "There's not much to tell, Ma. I thought she was a catch, but she was a little too much of a snob for me."

He knew that would get his mother off his back with this fictional girlfriend.

"Well, honey, I'm so glad you figured that out now. Heaven

knows you wouldn't want to get stuck with someone like that! How's work going? Are you seeing your brothers this week? I hope they told you we were heading into town for a couple of days and that Charlie might come, too."

Well, now, that was disappointing. He loved family dinners and missed them terribly when he didn't get to see them regularly. He was starting to feel more and more ashamed that work had been getting in the way of moments like this.

He was especially sad he would miss seeing his baby sister, Charlotte. It was Charlie's last year of college, and they didn't get to see her much now that she was going to Colombia University to get a degree in Architecture. To say they were all proud of her was an understatement.

"Oh, Mom, I'm sorry. I'm flying out today and won't be back until Saturday." Out the whole week, and he wouldn't even get to see the whole family together. *Well, this fucking blows.*

"Mom, I'm going to have to call you back when I land. They're about to board and I still have to go to the restroom." Scottsdale wasn't that long of a flight, and he was sure his mother would be up for hearing all about his week-long trip for work once he got settled at the hotel. She was a night owl, just like Charlie and unlike any of the men in their family. Maybe that was their escape from all the testosterone.

"Okay, sweetie! I love you! Have a safe flight!"

The resort was grand, to say the least, and his hotel points always gave him access to an upgrade with stunning views. He never grew tired of the desert and was happy to be back close to his Alma Mater.

ASU was a wild ride with just enough distance from family for him to spread his wings a little, even if the thought of his college days still made him tired.

After settling in, he checked his watch and debated taking a nap to freshen up before he met up with the new team or hitting the pool. *A wise man once said, sleep's for pussies.* He chucked to himself, "Thanks John, for your worldly advice."

They weren't meeting for a couple of hours, so why not hit the pool to chill like old times under the desert sun? Catch some rays and build a little tan. He couldn't get enough of this weather so he figured he better enjoy it while he had the chance.

The pool was crowded during this time of day, but he found a spot close to a cabana and just out of the way of the kid zone. Being around kids when he didn't have his own present was not his idea of fun.

He sprayed on his sunscreen, donned some shades, and then laid back to see what the spread was. No, he wasn't on the prowl, so to speak, but there was nothing wrong with enjoying the view. He was a man with needs, after all, and he let go of his last Arizona hook-up.

She was a pretty girl with great legs, but she had grown to be too needy, and they didn't have much in common. He wasn't willing to turn it into anything more than sex since she wasn't the one, so it was on to the next one.

He scanned the pool and ordered himself a drink to get the afternoon going. It was on the company's dime, so why not unwind under the Arizona heat with a chilled margarita in hand? Another buzz from his phone, and he couldn't contain his smile.

"Hey sweetie, how are you?" Amelia, his whole world.

"Hey daddy! When do you come home?"

Splitting time was hard enough, but splitting time while traveling for work every week was something else entirely. He missed her so much and hated when work trips didn't coordinate well with his time with her. He was just thankful his ex-girlfriend, Lauren, or his family were always down to take her when he was away.

"Oh man, I have to be in Scottsdale for the whole week, sweetie. But I'll pick you up as soon as I get back to town on

Saturday afternoon. What are you and your mom doing today with your day off?"

Spring break was one of their favorite weeks of the year. Or at least it would be if he was home this week. The weather could be unpredictable in the mountains, but there was always something fun going on in town.

"Not much. We might go to the Spring Parade if Robert gets off work in time."

Robert.

That guy.

Although they got along well enough now, his ex used to be somewhat of a pain. Given the fact that their relationship started nine years ago, as a one-night stand but morphed into a weird roommates-with-benefits situation only to pick back up when she told him she was pregnant with his baby. A baby that was seven months along and making her belly grow by the second.

It was rocky, to say the least, but things finally found a steady pace once Lauren got married and stopped whoring around. Although, he wouldn't have picked Robert for a step-dad. He wouldn't even be in the top fifty choices if it was up to him. The guy was a tool, and he wanted a better option for his baby girl.

"How are Robert and your mom doing?" He always played nice whenever Amelia was involved.

"They're good. He's a captain now, so we got to have a big party for him the other night at the police station. It was pretty cool. Mommy let me have as much cake as I wanted."

Wonderful. Let's give the asshole an even bigger ego.

The rest of the conversation was spent planning out their time together for the next week and trying to coordinate with Lauren about dropping Amelia off for his family's dinner. Her voice never got any less annoying over the years, and he felt like a dick once more as he tried to pay attention to the conversation instead of the tall blonde staring at him from across the pool.

She wasn't his usual type, but she was hot enough and fuck if he was going to pass up a good time when he had been in a week-long drought.

As the blonde started to make her way over to him, he said his goodbyes and hung up the phone just in time for her brash pickup line. One he, shockingly, hadn't heard before.

"Truth or dare."

She's going to be a good time. And why the fuck haven't I used that one before?

As she leaned over and let her cleavage spill out of her black triangle bikini, he let his eyes wander. No need to make her question his interest. *We're all adults here.*

"I think I'll choose dare." She sat down on the lounge chair, placed a hand on his thigh before she grabbed his bicep and inclined her head to his ear to whisper, "I dare you to show me what's underneath those pink trunks."

He took a second to consider his options. He did have to make it to dinner in a couple of hours, but that was in a couple of hours. Then, on the other hand, he knew he was tired of the same routine and should really make an effort to try and get to know her so he wouldn't feel as guilty if it turned out to be just sex. Much like everything with women was turning out to be these days.

The mental gymnastics were tiring when trying to be a gentleman at the same time as wanting to get laid. If he were being honest with himself, yet again, he wouldn't expect his future wife to ask a guy to bed, having just met him, so it was sure to turn out to be just sex.

"How about I buy you a drink first, and then I can see what's underneath that black bikini?"

With a playful grin, she pulled one knee back and slowly let it drape on the other side of the lounger, then propped her hands close to her center, perking her tits up even more.

Apparently, her question wasn't the most seductive thing she would do within the first five minutes of them meeting. She was on full display now, and it almost made him uncomfortable.

There's fucking kids close by, and now I need to hide a boner.

"What's your name?" He asked and looked around to make

sure the kids weren't watching this woman literally spread her legs for him.

"Lindsey. What's yours?" He put out his hand to meet hers.

"My friends call me Xander." The look on her face and the way she slowly pulled her tongue over her bottom lip said it all.

Yeah, I think we could have some fun.

After a couple of margaritas in, he knew he was going to have to get back to his room and start getting ready for the night. So far, he found out that she just broke it off with her boyfriend, likes sushi and has an extensive collection of vintage CDs.

He hadn't really given up any information about himself other than the fact that he loves golf and loved to party in college. He never felt the need to share much when things would be short-lived.

He started to get up and fold his towel, about to tell her that he would have to catch up later for a nightcap, when she reached for him to stop, slowly trailing her hand down to his cock just out of sight from the rest of the unknowing pool guests.

She peered up at him with lips pouting. "So, are you going to show me, or are you going to make me beg?"

The truth or dare question. This woman knew what she was after, and with a recent breakup, he knew it too.

He took all of two seconds of gentlemanly honor to contemplate the situation before roughly grabbing her by the hand and leading her to his suite.

Once they were out of sight of the pool guests, it was a mad dash to his door while she straddled him. With her hands trailing his body, he was standing at attention for any sorry soul that crossed their path. This woman was desperate for him, and she wasn't afraid to let him know.

Before they made it to his hallway, she was literally stroking him and by the time they were at his door, she had already whispered that she was his whore for the night.

"I hope you fuck as dirty as you talk."

They barely swiped his key card before he pulled the string to her top and groped her breasts, their lips locking in a mixture of tongue and teeth. Each racing to get the other naked first.

"I don't have a ton of time, so let's make it worth it." He was half panting and half groaning as he pulled her onto the bed over top of him, giving her better access as she stroked his now free cock. She was completely naked on top as he reached for a condom and kicked what was left of his trunks off of his legs.

She helped him slide it down his length before slowly lowering herself onto him. Making it painfully erotic as they both watched her dissapear inside of him.

"Fuck Xander!" She rocked her hips back and forth as he slowly filled her. She took him in and threw her head back. *The break-up must be fresh if she needed dick this bad.* He appreciated no-nonsense women. As long as the sluts in bed weren't looking for more.

"That's right, baby. Ride my dick and forget about that bastard." She took it slow for a couple of minutes, sliding up and down his length, each time taking more and more of him until he was completely buried inside of her.

Once she adjusted herself, she didn't hold back anymore. The woman was a wildcard. She rode him like she was on a fucking bull and screamed like she was watching from the stands. He was almost certain someone next door would call the front desk with how hard and dirty she wanted it, but he would gladly take the blame. She wanted a good ride, and he was more than happy to deliver.

The headboard smacked against the wall, and the mattress screamed in protest with each thrust. Her moaning in between each filthy word that came from her dirty lips only added to his need.

It wasn't more than ten minutes of riding his dick before she came undone, screaming his name and gripping his shoulders until little crescents riddled his skin. He chuckled to himself as he thought it was nice that she remembered to scream his name, not her ex-boyfriend's. But before she was done rocking her hips in newly released pleasure, he gripped her thighs, picking her up with ease as he brought her over to the floor-length mirror to finish.

The mirror stood tall in the corner of the room, grand enough to offer the room a regal aesthetic but, in his case, also large enough for him to see the whole visual of his dirty work.

He fucked her so hard he wasn't sure if the mirror would fall over. He reasoned with himself that the visual would be worth the hotel charge. He managed to make her come again, standing against the mirror before he let out his own moan and found release. They took a moment. Him standing on shaky legs and both of them breathing heavily after the escapade. It was a whirlwind and he barely managed to get them both back to the bed before he collapsed and grabbed his phone off the nightstand charger. He didn't want to be a dick, but he did hace a job and he was praying he wasn't going to be late for it after the unexpected fun.

"I know, I know," She said breathlessly. "I have to run, too." She waited a few minutes to catch her breath before rolling over and grabbing her bathing suit, clumsily trying to put it back on.

She stumbled around the room searching for her flip-flops, and he, yet again, realized this scene was getting way too old for him. He did notice, however, that she didn't look too old for it herself.

"Maybe after your work thing, I can hit you up again?"

God, she has a lot of energy. But then again, who was he to stop her when she was in need of a rebound?

"Yeah, that sounds like a good time. I'll let you know when I head back in."

With no more than a quick wave over her shoulder, she was out the door, and the room was quiet again, just as it had been mere hours ago before he hit the pool. He took in one last deep breath and rechecked his watch.

"Fuck!"

Fifteen minutes later, he was out the door and making his way down to the lobby, positive he was one of the last to show up for the party bus his work had arranged.

He supposed his work was a lot like Tyler's, after all. They encouraged drinking and getting to know their clients and their colleagues.

He had no guilt, though. He wasn't married, and in the sixteen years at the company, he never mixed business with pleasure. Something he was very proud of and some thing he would need to continue in order to climb the corporate ladder even further. If he wanted to get to the next promotion, he had to keep his dick in his pants.

No complications. No strings with work. Not when he had the CEO position in his sights.

A couple of people were talking by the Greyhound bus, and he recognized the Director he was overseeing for this project.

"Alexander! I'm glad you made it! I'd like you to get to know my team and chat while we all head over to the restaurant since we have a lot to work on this week."

Xander held out his hand as the woman turned around, and he suddenly couldn't feel the ground beneath him. The world was obviously playing some sick joke on his as he watched the woman in front of him hold out her hand.

"I'm Lindsey. Nice to meet you."

Mother fucking shitballs. Of course, I had to fuck an employee.

She introduced herself as if he hadn't just fucked her brains out in his room. *Thank God.* Then he shook her hand and offered respectful pleasantries as his colleague shared her role in the group as well as what it would be in terms of this particular project.

Everything spoken seemed to become background noise as he considered what this could mean for his career should their little escapade get out.

What if she was crazy? What if she claimed I forced her? What if she's done this with other guys I know?

He would need to start asking more questions while on work trips, that was for sure.

As if his whole life weren't just jeopardized, they boarded the bus, and he tried to find a seat near anyone else for the time being. There was a big team he could get well acquainted with before he needed to figure that shit out. Scottsdale was already turning out to be more drama than he could handle.

Fuck my life.

CHAPTER 5
Mina

A couple more months later…

"Wait for me!" It was eight thirty in the morning but still quite chilly. July in the Colorado mountains can bring warm temperatures, but this morning brought nothing except sunshine and a cool breeze.

Spring flew by, and it felt good to be settled into life. The walk was just what they needed. Time together and time outside. This view was everything her soul craved for a little recharge, and now they were heading back to their little cozy home. *Home*.

Each day was spent making this place theirs, and Mina was proud of herself. Sophie skipped alongside Lupe, their trusty chihuahua, and took the lead. Sophie may be her baby, but Lupe was technically her first one. From the moment she laid eyes on the two-pound rescue, she was toast. Now, she watched her trot beside Sophie with her little tongue hanging out. She's always loved her little Lupita.

The bastard tried to take her in the divorce, claiming he was the one who bought her, and should therefore be the one to take her. But in the end, it just took more money to win her dog and for the bastard to give up the fake fight. She knew he only wanted to piss her off. Lord knew that he used to complain about being seen with a chick dog.

The whole memory just pissed her off, along with all the other bullshit it took to get to this point. Ten months ago, she found out about all the other women and the one he stayed with. Eight months ago, they moved to the cottage, and six months since her life as a single mom was made legal.

So many timelines to go by, when really, she just wanted it all to fade away. To just be her and Sophie. Living their lives without drama.

She hated admitting that she ever took him back. Against every fiber of her being, she took him back for Sophie's sake, just to end up leaving him for that very same reason. She realized that sometimes, a person had to learn the hard way that you can't change someone, no matter how good your intentions could be.

He was caught up in his lies while she was fully invested in the family. They didn't want the same things, and it shouldn't have surprised her. They wanted different things. She wanted a family filled with days outside with the kids while he wanted to party and live the single life.

Sometimes in the quiet moments like this one, she wondered if she would ever be a wife again. A mother again. But that idea included men, and right now, men were a whatever subject.

She was doing pretty well on her own, anyway. This, right here, was her life. A little girl with pigtails and a tiny plump dog trotting up to their cozy home.

Besides the little reminders of that sucker punch to her self-esteem, everything was actually going pretty damn great. Her cottage on the end of the street was a fairytale made real, thanks to her parents. The white picket fence with a little gap just wide enough for her walkway up to the door left her with grand plans.

She budgeted what was left of her small savings and mapped out flower beds for each side of the walkway, complete with an arbor to accentuate the entrance.

Her little craftsman bungalow felt like a step into a new era, and with each pass through the picket fence into the grassy yard, she could feel her troubles ease and her shoulders relax.

Her parents weren't kidding when they told her they would help her get settled. That was the understatement of the century. Mina promised to pay rent and utilities and eventually buy the place when she had the money again, but they didn't want to hear anything of the sort. They knew how much money her lawyer had charged her and how many additional charges chipped away at her savings every time douchebag Evan refused to agree to the terms of the divorce. Each email had cost her two hundred and fifty dollars for him to simply say he disagreed and for them to start at ground zero.

"We win!" Sophie held up Lupe in triumph, and Lupe looked like she would give anything for a sliver of sunlight and a long nap. Mina pretended to bow down to them, "I'm not worthy," before she felt her phone vibrate.

"Hold on a sec, Soph." She glanced down, answering immediately. "Hey, mama!" It didn't matter that she was an adult; she would call her that forever. "We just got home from walking a trail. What are you up to?"

She looked over at the ladies and chuckled as Sophie continued their chalk garden, and Lupe sunned herself. She assumed her regular position of laying on her side with her tongue hanging out, as dry as leather. The poor dog may have about three teeth left in total, and Mina wasn't even sure where they were. She would just have to trust the vet on that one.

"That sounds nice. Next time call me, and I'll meet up with you." Her mother's tone gave a little indication of where this phone call was heading, and she wasn't sure she wanted any part of it. "Anyway, did you get a chance to talk to Claire? I heard that she may ask you to pick up the girls every now and then from school. Can you manage? I know that you're going to be helping out Jared once the school year starts. The girls wouldn't be much trouble."

There would be a total of five kids she would be grabbing since two of Jared's were at a different school, and the mother-in-law would watch Claire's youngest.

It was still plenty of children, but she loved her nieces and nephews. She was game for whatever she could help with and game for any new project that didn't involve her love life.

"Yeah, for sure! It will be great, and it will only be for a couple of hours on those days. It should be fun." They talked more about the arrangement and then moved on to her plans for the yard. Her mother had a green thumb and, to Mina's relief, was thrilled to be enlisted for her many projects.

The idle chatter and yard plans could only last for so long, and after about twenty minutes, Mina was hit with it. "So, honey, have you started to think about dating again?" Her mother never let go of hope for Mina to get right back on the horse, so to speak. After all, she had to be there through all of the nights filled with tears and days full of doubts. She just wanted her girl to find love again and get out of her rut.

"Have you been talking to Claire about this?" She knew the answer to that question even though she knew her mother would deny it to the very end.

"No, I just really think that you should start thinking about getting back out there and just having some fun. Honey, you're still so young! You shouldn't write yourself off just because you went through a divorce and have a child."

No one particularly enjoyed hearing how Mina felt about herself. There was a time in her life when she felt like a wanted woman. She knew she was popular, and she knew she was pretty. Being a twin and being remotely attractive would make anyone well-known in a small town, but she liked that it felt special. She felt like she was smart and strong, not just a pretty face.

Once upon a time, she felt like she could conquer the world.

But holy hell, how times had changed. Now, she just felt like a throwaway. Someone who wasn't worth staying for.

He looked the same, had the same body and even had the job that got him out of the house and full of alibis for him to cheat. She, on the other hand, had been the one wondering where he was, only to find out that every last officer in Kings Ranch pretty much knew about the affairs before she did. In her eyes, she was left with a body that grew a baby and baggage no man would want.

"Mama, are you going to tell me about Prince Harry again?" She rolled her eyes and tried to reign in her annoyance. Her mother loved her, after all.

"He's with an American, and I missed my chance. There are no more princes for me." Her mother had actually believed that she could somehow manage to snag the prince. Lord only knew if she went all out and attempted to write the poor man.

"Well, maybe not a prince, but someone is out there, honey. Someone as wonderful as you are."

This conversation was going the same as it always went.

"It's not even been a year, and I think I'm great on my own, mama. In fact, I think I may be done with men for good." Her mother sounded as if she was starting to say something but thought against it.

Thank God.

They chatted for a few more minutes and then wrapped things up. Mina said goodbye and then headed for the front steps. The large expanse of concrete under the bungalow porch served as the best place for the sidewalk chalk garden, and theirs was coming along great.

"What did you add, baby girl?" She stretched her arms out in front of her before yawning and settling into the porch swing. She rocked lazily back and forth as the sound of Sophie's words filled her ears like music.

It was worth every bit of hell he put her through just to have her little Sophie.

The last month of summer meant that the kids were going crazy making every arts and crafts project imaginable while putting glue and glitter on every level surface.

The girls spent a ton of time at Mina's since Kyle was in and out of town and Claire was busy at the hospital most days. The weather was perfect, and life was good. The little unicorn club members had kept her busy, but she was ready to get the girls back in school. Having Soph in preschool would give her a bit of time for housework and writing, so she didn't have to stay up until the wee hours of the morning. The days felt long when sleep was scarce.

"Come on, Lupe, give me some help." She glanced over at her plump sidekick and wondered if she could give her any hints for a leading man that were better than what she had come up with.

"Would you rather date a man with a strong personality or one that's closer to his family?" Sitting crisscross apple sauce, as Sophie called it, she peaked over her writing desk and tried to see if Lupe would wink. Mina had a rule that if a dog winked at you, you ALWAYS winked back. It had to be a code for something.

So, there she was. Sitting and waiting while Lupe continued to stare at her, tongue airing out and resembling beef jerky more and more by the second.

"Ugh, all right, I get it. Both. These leading men should be as unrealistic as possible, am I right? It's an escape, after all. And you know what, Lupe? Should we make him rich or a cowboy or even both?" She wasn't quite sure if she was being totally sarcastic with her attitude at the moment. All she wanted to read about these days was a book about some billionaire who changed his ways for a quirky heroine that put him in his place. Or some big city girl that falls for a small-town cowboy, complete with a six pack and a ranch.

Book boyfriends weren't like the real thing. At least none of them were for her with life thus far. All her talk about book boyfriends made her want to cozy up on the couch with the latest Elsie Silver novel before an idea smacked her on the side of the head so hard it made her swoon.

"I think that should be our next big goal, Lupe. Move this little writing operation into something bigger, like a little bookstore. Maybe one day we can own one on Main Street and just read and write best sellers all day."

A tiny grunt from across the room showed Lupe adjusting on a different pillow on the bed. Moving her tiny body over to a streak of moonlight may as well have been Mina's approval from Lupe and a sign from the powers that be.

"Man, that would be the dream. Soph could walk home from elementary and help me run the store. You would have your own little perch so you could people watch and get your sunbathing in."

She let out a long sigh, "It's been decided. Who needs a man when you can have books?"

All right, back to business. "Leading man material. Right. Okay, Lupe, time to write that list. If we can't conjure up a man for my own life, we can make my heroine win a perfect man in book life."

Clapping her hands and rubbing them together, she started with age. "He needs to be around 35 years old… let's say 36 to be safe. Oh, how we do love an older man." A small huff came from the other side of the room as Lupe adjusted herself, yet again.

"I know it's oddly specific, but hear me out, Lupe. I feel like the heroine, and me," she theatrically placed a hand over her chest, "are done with men our own age. Look at the last one."

Crickets.

"Enough said. Oh! And he's close to his sister! Men who have sisters probably understand women better. It's just a theory, but I'm going to go with it." She waved a finger at her small protégé as if lecturing her. "We haven't figured out what our mystery man will do for work, but he needs to be passionate about his career. Needs to have ambition, Lupe. There's nothing worse than a lazy person who has no drive. I mean, am I right, or am I right?"

She peeked over the laptop before adding, "Except you, Lupe. You have the ambition to be lazy, and I respect that, girlfriend."

She thrummed her fingers on her desk as she thought. *What else….* "Should he have an accent?" She waited. Then waited a moment longer. With no grunt, she took the silence as a no.

"I do love a good accent, but maybe not. I'm not familiar with slang in other countries, and I think a writer should know all that." Looking at the small, yet specific list and back to her cozy bed, she made the call.

"All right, little lady, I've been talking to you for about an hour now, and I think that's a new low for me. Let's call it a night. I think we have a good start so far."

CHAPTER 6
Alexander

"Let's go, Amelia!"School had started this week, which meant soccer Saturdays were back in action.

Amelia bounded off the field, racing toward him while he gathered her water bottle and a snack. She was all smiles and braids, babbling about the girls and how another player was off-side. It was all running like clockwork for a regular soccer day when suddenly something caught his eye. A woman he couldn't tear his eyes away from. Not just any woman. It was *HER*.

"Thanks daddy!" He snapped out of his trance long enough to

acknowledge Amelia, then scanned the other edge of the field once more, desperate to find her. The woman from Walmart. His worst encounter as a single man to date and the only time in his life when a woman couldn't seem to get away from him fast enough.

It only took a second. *Holy fuck*. She was just as gorgeous as he remembered. Xander had been with his fair share of beauties at this point in his life, but she put them all to shame. They didn't hold a candle to her.

Since the day he was born, Xander has always had a type. He was always drawn to exotic women with mocha skin and brown eyes that made you feel like you were on a beach somewhere in Mexico.

Amelia took one last swig before running back onto the field, but he couldn't stop staring. He looked around for a second to make sure he wasn't being obvious as he ogled some mother from across the field, but once the coast was clear, he enjoyed taking her in. Taking his time to admire everything about her.

Her long brown hair and how it casually blew in the breeze made her look like a damn goddess. Her face was a work of art, and he couldn't quite place her. Mexican? Greek? Italian? Who knew, and who the hell cared? She had a petite frame with perky tits, a great ass and legs that turned him on from fifty yards away.

Fuck.

He had better watch it. He would think that being surrounded by children and annoying helicopter parents would be like a cold shower, but somehow this woman was making his cock hard.

In his thirty-six years on this planet, it was safe to say that he never believed in love at first sight until now. Lust, he knew all too well, and he would be damned if every high school and college guy didn't have the same feeling.

But love?

That was a different feeling and statement entirely. But at this moment, he knew it could be real because she was something else entirely.

The rest of the game was fairly uneventful, and he spent the majority of it watching the beauty on the other side of the field. He tried to take note of what she had going on. She had a child… or several. She could be married, given that she talked to another man…or single, because it could be another parent. *Fuck.*

The nature of the event itself made his perception of her single status much more complicated. A dating app would really solve this problem. Swipe right! Swipe right!

"Daddy!" Amelia bounded over with a smile glued across her little face.

"Way to go, honey! You were on fire today." He couldn't help but adore his little lady. She was the best thing that ever happened to him. *And actually*, he thought to himself, *the one person who could help him in this particular situation...*

"Hey, sweetie, do you know those kids over there?" *I'm officially a creepy old man. Using my kid to get a woman.*

Her little face looked around, and she scrunched her nose in confusion. "Which ones Daddy? There's like a bazillion kids around here." *Fair point.*

Xander cursed to himself at the realization that there were literally over a hundred people in attendance today, and they all happened to be smushed into the size of two football fields.

"Touché smarty pants," he said as he bent down to one knee and attempted to point out the group in question. "All right, pip squeak, if you look across the field towards the team that's wearing the yellow jerseys, there is a group standing around a mommy and a little girl that looks about your age."

She tried again, and this time Xander felt a glimmer of hope when her eyes widened like she spotted something familiar.

"Oh! That's Stephanie! She goes to my school!" Finally, the ridiculously long description was getting him somewhere. "I don't know who the other kids are, though."

Or so he thought. One step closer yet still football fields apart. He let out a large breath he had no idea he was holding in.

"You don't know any of the other kids? Like, that little girl being held by the mommy, is that Stephanie's mommy? Or the guy she's talking to, is that her daddy?" *I am so fucking pathetic, but I don't care.*

Amelia looked over her shoulder at the group she didn't have much interest in and waved them off. "Daddy, I have no clue. I think she has a sister, but I don't know how old she is. Oh, and she did tell me that her brothers like to annoy her. Oh! And that her mommy lets her have sleepovers sometimes, but that's about it. We only get to see each other at recess."

So much insignificant information. *I'm being an asshole, but goddamn.*

As Amelia fumbled with trying to peel her orange, Xander could think of a few things he would like to do to that mommy at a sleepover, but now his cock was getting hard again. *Mother Fucker.*

"Here, let me help you with that orange." As if peeling an orange would help him not think of peeling layers of her clothing off…*This is pointless.*

"Well, maybe we should get to know her a little better, don't you think? You have been saying you wanted to have more sleepovers with friends recently." Amelia looked at Xander as if he'd grown two heads.

"When did I say that?"

Well, shit. The kid is smart. "Oh, I just thought I remember you telling me that. Maybe I'm wrong. But it would be fun to have friends over more, don't you think?"

He was grasping at straws, and he knew it, but damn it if he wasn't going to try like hell to talk to that woman as soon as humanly possible. The woman would be around, that's for sure, especially now that he knew one of her kids goes to the same school. But the thought of leaving the park without a name or a smile pointed at him felt painful.

The rest of the teams had already walked off the field, and they were now starting to get in the way of the next round of soccer players trying to warm up for their game. He hated this. He found her again, but he was still miles away from even knowing who the hell she was. He felt like he was on a boat without a paddle, slowly drifting away from the shore.

One more sigh, then they turned their back on the group from across the park and headed to their car. It was safe to say that he glanced back more times than he could count while also pretending to tie his shoes…twice.

"What's up, brother? How are you?" Tyler got up from his spot in the corner booth and wrapped him up in a big bear hug. It had been way too long since he'd caught up with him.

"When you told me you would be passing through the Denver airport too, I thought, man, this is too good to be true!" Although it was a manic-type Monday, the skies were clear, the coffee shop was one of his favorites at the airport, and he got to see one of his best friends before he headed back to Kings Ranch, back to little city life after being away for a week. He was living large on this fine little Monday.

"Yeah, where are you flying out to?" Tyler leaned over and closed out his laptop after writing a quick email.

"Heading to Chicago today. Got to wine and dine some clients up there and will hopefully close a big deal that's been in the works for about a year and a half." Xander took a seat across from him, coffee in hand and some time to kill.

"Damn! Should be a big week for you then, huh?"

Tyler swiped over tired eyes, then added, "No pressure, right?"

It used to ground him when he could see his friends. Bring back old memories and catch up on stupid shit. But these days, it just seemed to bog him down when it came to anything outside of financial shit.

"How's the family doing? How old are the kids now?" Tyler did some mental math, "Four and two! Can you believe it? Kids are growing up so damn fast. Next thing I know, they will be asking me for the keys to the car."

"You got that right," Xander added."It's crazy how fast time flies. Amelia is eight already!"

Tyler blew out a big breath and shook his head in disbelief. "You better watch out, man. Soon, those boys are going to be hanging around her, and we both know how boys can be. We were the worst."

"Fuck. Don't even go there. Little boys look at her now, and I want to kill them. I have to remind myself that they're only eight!"

Tyler laughed, "I don't envy that, man. Lily is two, and I can't think about boys the same after having her. I'm pretty sure, given our wild past, that will never change until she gets married, and I can pass off that stress to the poor bastard." They both chuckle at the thought that they knew was absolutely true.

"Kids aside, how's life? What's Chelsea up to?" Xander knew the last one would sting for him like it always did. He should really be asking, "How's Chelsea holding up knowing you cheat on her all the time? Thinking of leaving? Are you mad she's staying?" But the friend in him always had him asking. He needed to check in on his friends regardless of their choices.

"Eh, Chelsea is Chelsea. She doesn't work, but we have a nanny, so I'm not sure what the hell she does all day." Typical answer. "But work and stocks are great. This deal is pretty huge for me, so I'm hoping I can lock it down and then have some fun in Chicago before I have to go home. I don't want to jinx the deal, but one of their interns last time was a ten and a nice little ride."

The look on Xander's face didn't escape Tyler. He just wagged his eyebrows in response. Xander just blew out a breath of annoyance and shook his head.

"Holy shit. When you said it's a "good ol' boys club," you weren't kidding." Tyler laughed at the reaction while Xander took it in and rubbed his chin. "You're still such a dog, bro." It was the only thing he could manage to say.

"Eh, to each his own, right man?" Tyler said with a grin while raising his coffee cup as if to say cheers.

"What's new with you? Tell me of your conquests so maybe I won't have to step out so much. I can just live through you." He said it with a smile as if he would ever stop his shit.

"Just working and hanging out with Amelia. The usual dating scene. But honestly, man, I'm so over it sometimes. Don't get me wrong, fucking four or five women at a time is awesome. Pussy is great, but sometimes I'm tired of how shallow some of these women are. Like, how the hell are we supposed to go out multiple times if we can't find anything to talk about?"

"It's because you don't need to talk to take her clothes off, man." Tyler sipped his coffee with a confused face as if to say, duh. Xander decided that some things weren't worth arguing.

"So true, so true. I guess I will just have to keep sowing my wild oats." This time, they both raised their cups and toasted to being young, even though they weren't really that young anymore. Mid-to-late thirties is still somewhat young, but when one person in the conversation was married with kids, it didn't seem as cool of a toast to Xander.

"I think I spotted the perfect woman, though." Xander could shoot himself for having admitted that out loud, especially to Tyler. The look Tyler gave him was enough to shut him up from all future conversations concerning his gorgeous mystery woman. "At least from far away." He added the statement as quickly as he could, trying to act casual when his heart rate was spiking more with each second that ticked by. Tyler gave him a sideways glance, complete with eyes squinting with curiosity.

"What the hell are you talking about, man? Do you mean to tell me, THE Alexander McCade has found a perfect woman, and you haven't fucked her yet? How do you even know she's perfect, then?"

Tyler taunted him as if they were now in some type of challenge, and he accepted.

"Give me time," he quipped, "It was at Amelia's soccer game, and she was on the other side of the field." He doesn't need to know about the first failed interaction with her. "Apparently, her daughter, or one of her daughters, has Amelia's lunch break, but that's about as much as I know right now. The woman could be married with six kids, for all I know. But she was hot as fuck, and I intend to get to know her." Xander took a sip of his coffee before adding. "Any way I can."

"Damn, across the field, and you still think she's perfect? Are you sure she isn't the typical Xander fifty-yard fake?"

Xander rolled his eyes. The jackass always loved to gloat or make anyone else in their group seem less than.

"Positive! And I didn't have that many fifty-yard fakes to make it a thing! When alcohol was involved during college, my cock and my vision didn't talk much." They both had a good laugh at the past and all the memories they were conjuring. From grade school to college parties, their days of chasing girls consisted of millions of stories. Some he was proud of, and others he'd rather bury.

But, as Tyler kept on probing, Xander quickly realized he shouldn't have said anything. "So when are you going to see her again?" He knew the real meaning behind that question. Tyler was always a dog, and this case was no different. He wouldn't put it past him to try and sleep with his mystery woman, given the opportunity. They always did have the same taste in women.

"Not sure. Like I said, I don't know anything about her except that at least one of her kids goes to elementary with Amelia. Maybe I'll see her around the school at some point and can ask her out. Or maybe she's married, and I'll never see her again."

He laughed it off in an attempt to make it seem like he didn't care. "We'll have to wait and see, man. I'll keep you posted." *Not a chance in hell.*

"All right, bro. I have to catch this flight, but you have to keep me up to date on this mystery woman. She sounds like she's got you by the balls, and she hasn't even touched them yet."

He stuck his tongue out in a playful jab at Xander before he smacked him on the back and got up from his seat.

"Ha, we'll see about that." Again, with the downplay. He could only try so hard because, if he was being honest, she totally did.

After he packed up his laptop and took a last swig of his coffee, Tyler gave him a hug and a couple of pats on the back as they bid their farewell before he was off to his gate. Leaving Xander alone with his coffee. With the mystery woman firmly sealed in his mind, he realized this was beginning to be a real problem. He needed to figure out who the hell she was.

He made a mental note to do a little digging the minute he had some free time back in town because he needed to get his head on straight and focus on shit outside of this woman. Like Amelia. *Fuck.* Women had never taken his attention from Amelia longer than it would take for him to get off. *Maybe she isn't married, and she loves children. Loves them enough to love Amelia, too. Damnit!*

It was settled. He would figure this out so he could put himself out of misery.

Tyler: Ring Ring

"What the fuck is he talking about?" He found himself mumbling at the text he received. He was about to look around to see if Tyler had forgotten something just as a name flashed across his screen. He was wary about answering it, but there was no point in pretending he was busy. He had been staring into his coffee and pondering his wannabe love life.

"John. What's up, man?"

Instead of being met with a greeting, he just heard laughing on the other end of the phone and knew immediately that he was the joke.

"Dude, she better be hot as fuck for you to be preaching poetic shit about a perfect woman." He was going to kill Tyler.

"Don't be jealous I'm going to fuck her and you won't. California's a long way away, and she's going to be far out of your reach by the time you get to visit." He was going to make damn sure about that one.

My fucking friends' dicks won't come near this woman. But he couldn't help but chuckle to himself with their interest.

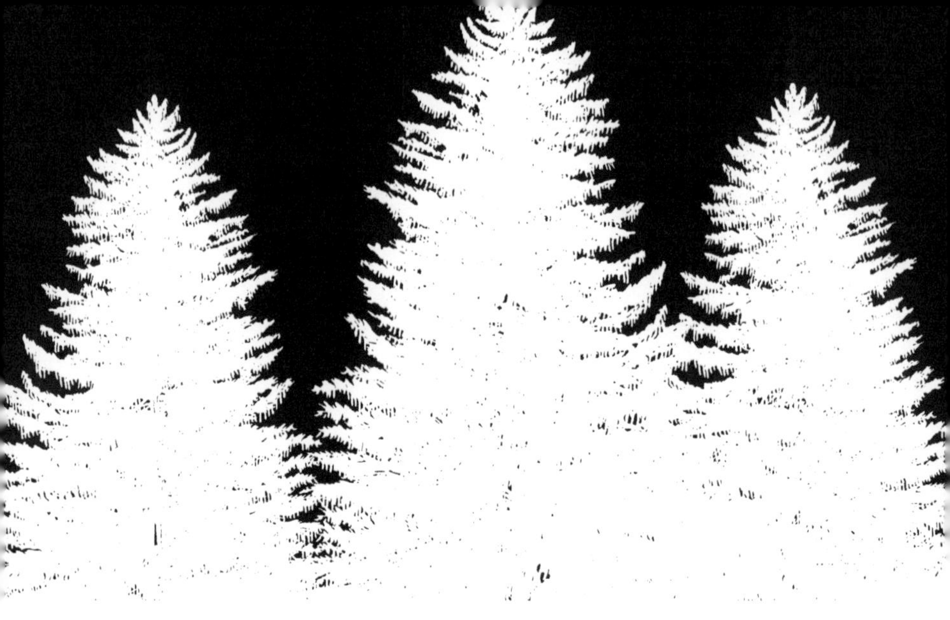

CHAPTER 7
Mina

"Sophie, we gotta go!" She yelled across the little house in an attempt to hurry Sophie up. They were about to be late if she didn't get Sophie to pick out a dang stuffed animal that she felt Fiona would like.

Fi was only a year older than Sophie and in kinder. Naturally, that placed Fiona in the top spot for the coolest kid in the world to Soph.

Stuffy tucked firmly under her arm, she finally made her way down the hall and scrambled into the wagon. "All right, little unicorn! Let's go!" She hustled as she pulled the wagon.
She would not be late on her first day grabbing all the kids. Especially with Fiona being in kinder, she couldn't even think about being late for a little one's first pick-up without mom or dad.

Now that Beth had started her new work schedule, Mina helped with the kids at pickup. Naturally, Beth was the catalyst for Claire, so she finally asked for some help. Sophie was by far the most excited. Having almost all the cousins to herself for a couple of hours a week was her dream come true.

As she approached the school for the first day, she was met with complete chaos. Who knew there were walkers, riders, bus riders and bikers, all of whom had different places to line up to wait for their parents? *Good grief,* she thought, *better get the hang of this chaos now before Sophie starts school next year.*

There was a lot of commotion at the after-school pickup, and with all the different zones and people trying to make it to each spot in a timely manner, it was no wonder her sisters needed help. Working people shouldn't have to work this hard just to pick up their kids. However, she did like the amount of security they forced on the families. *Give and take,* she reasoned.

Her mother's voice crept into her mind now that she was approaching the actual line where the parents had to stand along the fence encasing the kinder playground. All the parents were standing and waiting for the gate to open and for their child's name to be called. Her mother told her that schools could be a perfect place to meet single dads. The school and the soccer field where Stephanie, her brother Jared's little girl, played in a league. The idea of being a stereotypical single mom who trolled single dads grossed her out. Or even married dads. The idea that wives would have to worry about their husbands steering clear of her made her feel cheap or like a slut who was on the prowl.

She had heard, a long time ago, how Evan and his buddies would talk about the single moms they once knew. How they were desperate to fuck and loved having friends with benefits so things wouldn't turn into a relationship and affect their time with their kids. "They were always down to fuck," were his specific words.

How charming.

Well, that would not be her. No sir! Hence the floppy hat, yoga pants with holes and an oversized t-shirt. Her uniform wasn't the only thing in her attempt at not snagging a man. She also kept her head down and only smiled at the women in line.

Things seemed so much more complicated now that she was single. As if she had to wonder what someone's motive was or wondered if other women wondered what her motives were. It was like this giant cat-and- mouse game she really didn't want to be a part of.

At least there weren't any catcalls on the way to school that she had to deal with. The perks of going down the street during school hours towing a child. As the line slowly started to come to life, she let her mind wander. All her fears of being seen a certain way while men didn't have a single thing to worry about while single was frustrating.

Single dads get hotter while single moms get shamed? Fuck that shit. If she were to use one of the stupid lines she had heard from a man, she would be slut shamed forever. But men? The ridiculous number of lines and cat calls seemed to be at their disposal.

Did men actually believe that honking their horn at a woman jogging, who wasn't even facing them, by the way, would make her turn around and beg the guy to stop the car and fuck her?

Every time a horn would honk, or a man would yell something to Mina consisting of, "Hey baby!" or "Damn!" blew her away. It was even comical. She could be the ugliest person with the worst personality on the planet, but that was beside the point, apparently. She reasoned that she would never understand it and would have to let that one go.

Three more spots moved up, and now she was mentally bitching over the ridiculous verbal pickup lines she's had to endure in her life. The kind of asshole remarks that made her cringe or the overly sweet ones that made her feel so bad she had to pretend she had a boyfriend just to be left alone.

They all suck. It's official. I'm going to be single for the rest of my life. Glancing back at the light of her life, rather than continuing to bog herself down with her bleak outlook on men, she gazed at Sophie's profile. Her little button nose and the way her cheeks puffed out had her smiling. She almost missed the man just beyond her little lady. Not just any man. HIM.

She didn't know who he was, but then again, she didn't know any of the other parents. Her kid didn't even go here.

All that mattered was that he was the hottest man she had ever seen, the same man who hand-delivered her the most embarrassing moment in her newly single life.

He was just like she remembered…and dreamed about late at night when she was safely alone and gave into her lust for that damn near perfect man that bumped into her all those months ago. His tall frame was complete with strong, wide shoulders and muscular arms. Arms that weren't the kind her ex had.

She hated the way Evan's neck looked shorter every time she saw him, and he looked like he was holding luggage. The typical meathead that made you question what his dick size was based on rumors of the effects of steroid use that everyone grew up hearing about.

No, these were the kind that were strong naturally. *Dear God.* She wanted to get a better look at him. *Perhaps if Sophie were to throw and retrieve her stuffed animal on the sidewalk just behind them. Then I could look at that face just one more time. Who am I becoming?*

Besides the fact that she was turning into a hussy that was casing the line for dads, if he saw her, he might recognize her, and then she would have to relive her embarrassment. Then again, he seemed pretty distracted on his phone.

She started calling herself just about every name she could think of for being a cheap slut and checking out the father. THE FATHER! She thought he was single before, but what was with the box of condoms if he was married? *Or maybe he's a hot single father? Don't even go there, Mina.*

Single or married, she just looked at him like a piece of meat at the deli that was about to go on sale.

"Who are you here for?" She must have looked frazzled, wearing a dazed resting bitch face. The teacher at the gate had to ask a second time for her to realize she wasn't asking which father she was scouting out, but rather the children she was there to pick up.

"So sorry, I was lost in my own world there for a second." *Smooth, Mina.* After telling the teacher the list of four kids she was there for, they called their names on a megaphone and further woke her up from her little fantasy land. She was now very much aware that she was in the pickup line at school with parents and children all around her.

Just shameful, Mina! You Goddamned little whore. She put on a smile and scolded herself quietly as the kids all ran for her and Sophie. Without looking back, she talked their ears off the entire walk home to Jared's. Never allowing herself or her weak body turn back even once.

After homework was done and the kids had spent what seemed like hours on the trampoline, Claire showed up, and Beth finished up with her work as well. The three women sat in the kitchen around the table, decompressing and filling each other in on their day.

After hearing about some interesting patients at both hospitals, they asked Mina the typical question she was sure her mother had already drilled into them.

"Did you see any cute single dads, Mina?" Beth looked over with a wink and then proceeded to act busy starting dinner. Well, Mina knew she wasn't actually acting busy, but it was a convenient time to rummage through the fridge and keep her head down.

"Normally, I would tell you ladies the same thing I tell Mom. But this time I actually did see someone. A pretty hot someone."

Beth's eyes shot up so fast that she was sure she had said

something more monumental. Or maybe she really has been that convincing that she would never give men another shot.

"Wait, what?" Beth started, but Claire quickly interrupted her.

"Hold on, you actually looked up in the pickup line long enough to notice a hot dad?"

Mina gave an annoyed look and rolled her eyes. "I'll have you know, I wasn't actually trying to notice any hot dads. I was glancing back at Sophie to make sure she was doing good when I happened to spot him behind us. But I will say, he was hot enough to make me lose my train of thought and to consider having Sophie throw a toy so I could get a better look."

They all laughed at the mental image, even if the whole conversation was not Mina's style. She was sure she would never date again and that all men- excluding those already married in her family- were jerks. Not worthy of her time.

She wasn't even sure why she had to open her big fat mouth. How the hell was she supposed to spill the beans about the condom guy?

"I don't know anything about him, so don't even start with the questions. I know he was hot." They sat and waited for more.

"Strong start, Mina. Seriously, you have to give us more than that!" Telling them the truth seemed like a fate worse than death, but if this man lived in town and his kid went to their school, she would be outed at some point.

"He was tall, had dirty blond hair coming out of his baseball cap. Stuck on the phone." She bit her tongue, contemplating her next words carefully. "I know that he shops at Walmart…. because when we went there months ago, I dropped our tampon boxes after he bumped into me."

They continued to stare at her like she had withheld the secrets of the Da Vinci Code.

"He dropped his box of XL condoms, and I had to hand them back to him. It was embarrassing, and I don't want to talk about it anymore."

Claire's mouth dropped to the floor before she let out a howl of laughter. "Oh my God! Mina, we were asking about his looks, but holy shit, this just got a whole lot more entertaining." She could hardly speak. "Why didn't you tell me when that happened? That's hilarious!"

At least Beth had the decency to laugh with her back turned.

"His shoulder felt like hitting a damn wall, and besides the pain, I have never been so embarrassed in my life! The hottest man I have ever seen picked up our tampons, Claire, the super absorbency kind, by the way, and I had to look him in the eye and hand him back his XL condoms. Yeah, that screams good times. I'm shocked I didn't skip over and tell you right then!"

Her sarcasm dripped off every word, and Claire ate it up. She thought she had seen her sister in hysterics before, but she was wrong. Claire wiped tears from the corners of her eyes, barely able to catch her breath. "I would pay to see that whole scene go down."

"I bet you would, Satan. But right now, I just want to forget about it."

Once Beth caught her breath again, she went back to the original problem. "Ok, I have been doing the pickup line all this time, and I want to know who you're talking about." She paused as creases formed on her overly worked forehead. "Although," she adds, "You said he was on the phone and was wearing a hat, so maybe I just haven't noticed him. Some dads have no interest in talking. They want to get their kid and get the hell out of dodge."

"That sounds like this type of father," Mina noted. "He was super distracted, thank God. He didn't notice me staring at him for a minute. But other than his Greek God physique, I really don't know how to describe him. At the moment, he was gorgeous." She grabbed a grape and popped it into her mouth, praying it was the end of their little discussion.

"Oh wait!" Beth blurted out. "Was he wearing a Puka shell necklace? Kind of tall?" She held up her hand to gauge height.

"Seriously, Beth? Puka shell guy?" Mina looked disgusted

with the suggestion.

"Well, I don't know! He's the only father that kind of fits your description of the mystery man."

"Well, no," Mina eyed Beth, "If I had the hots for Puka shell dad, I definitely wouldn't tell you ladies about it. The man needs help. Let go of high school and move on with your life, man."

"Ok, I get it!" She held up her hands in surrender. "I was just about to inform you that, sadly, Puka shell guy is married. I do know that one."

Leaning up against the counter now, Mina crossed her arms over her chest and shrugged. It was like Claire couldn't help herself. She was just handed a gift that kept on giving. "Well, this is tough because your description could be just about every rapist and serial killer that has ever plagued the US, so congrats Mina. Tall, white male, may or may not have dirty blond hair. Wearing a baseball cap. Could be bringing condoms to rape or assault someone." Claire laughed again, but when Mina slumped her shoulders and groaned, she pulled her in for a playful hug.

"I'm just kidding. Maybe next time you go, you will see him again, and maybe, just maybe, one of you will speak to the other."

Mina looked away, trying to downplay her disappointment and the fact that she would most likely never have the guts to talk to the guy. Not that she wanted to. *He could be leading man material for my book, though.*

More small talk rounded out their short time together before the kids had to be wrangled up in order for Beth to finish with dinner and Claire and Mina to leave.

"All right, ladies! I'll see you in a couple of days for my second day of work," Mina joked as they headed out the door and loaded the wagon.

The brisk air of Fall would be on its way soon, and it made Mina sad thinking about the start of winter just on the horizon. Colorado has beautiful seasons, but the thought of snow made her want to curl up in her cottage and hibernate until spring. At least for now, the few blocks they got to walk home from school each day would soon be filled with what small town dreams are made of. The leaves would start to turn colors of gold, orange and burning red while the evergreens gave the perfect backdrop to the mountain views.

Kings Ranch was, in her eyes, the perfect little town. Historic, beautiful and filled with amazing people and events that always kept a single mother busy. Even so, it was times like these when she had to admit she would love to walk those few blocks in this picturesque setting hand in hand with someone. Her sister's father-in-law always told Claire he worried for Mina.

"It's easy to have people to go out and do things with. I worry about the times when everyone goes home, and it's just Mina. She needs someone to sit around a fire and do nothing with. Those are the moments that count." She realized it described life and precious moments perfectly. Moments like this. Quiet walks home.

She was dead set on not wasting moments like the current. Quiet walks home with her daughter. She didn't need anyone else, as much as she sometimes wished it included someone. She had Sophie, and that was enough. It was everything.

She reasoned that she didn't have time to waste on trying to solve the mystery of the pickup line dad. Whether he was married or if he even noticed her. She shouldn't care, but regardless of what she should or shouldn't care about, the image of a certain someone plagued her mind with no end in sight. The image only seemed to play on repeat these days, and it was getting harder and harder to ignore. She was intrigued whether she liked it or not.

That night, it took a while for sleep to find her, but once it did, it was filled with tossing and turning. She woke the next morning with a groggy head and could only remember images of baseball hats and puka shells chasing her.

CHAPTER 8
Alexander

She noticed him. Even though she thought she was being sneaky, he noticed her noticing him. God, it was like he was in high school all over again. All the emotions of young lust and wanting, no, needing to know more about a girl came flooding in and hit him the second he walked up to the line and saw her standing right there.

This was no girl from high school, though. High school girls were never this sexy. Seeing her up close, well closer than across the field, she was every bit as tempting as the first time he saw her. She was stunning. He found it hilarious that she actually thought a big floppy hat and some workout clothes would keep her hidden from all the dads in line. He could only assume it was the reason someone like her would prefer to wear clothes that would make her blend in with this crowd. But there was no blending in for her. It was impossible with a body like that.

Talking on the phone became almost too difficult to manage while being around her, which was not a good thing considering he was talking to the President of the whole damn company about an upcoming project the man wanted him to do personally.

Concentrating on the conversation was next to impossible as he gazed over at the exotic woman gracing the pickup line. He looked around as if trying to find someone down the street as he secretly scanned the line for other dads. He may not know her, but somehow, he felt he had official rights to first dibs.
He wasn't sure if he was the only single dad in the line today, and something about that thought had him feeling pissed off.

Trying to hold his own on the phone while simultaneously being territorial in line was difficult, but it had to be done. He had to make sure he wasn't dealing with a whole truck load of dads who were going to compete for her. Married or not, this woman was going to be getting attention from any man in the vicinity. Even with the damn floppy hat on.

He felt like that ensemble could rival Victoria's Secret lingerie for his woman, and she may as well have been walking down a fucking runway for him. The gymnastics of the phone conversation was awful, but it wasn't all a huge inconvenience. He was able to look distracted while really getting a better look at her.

From his angle, he could tell that she was some sort of athlete. Her thighs touched, and when she barely bent over to scratch her foot, they did that damn thigh gap shit that would make any man weak. He could think of a million things he would love to do to her in that position besides licking her…

He had to get his mind back on track yet again. But God, when she bent over…her curvy ass was on full display as well. *Is it possible to pass out from a perky peach ass?*

Yup, he had his type and good God, she was it and more.

When the line had crept forward, he realized he should probably take inventory of the kid situation or at least see if she had a ring. He wasn't sure how that little piece of jewelry could have escaped his attention when it could so easily put him out of his misery. Although, for her, he would willingly stalk a married woman.

He tried to reason with himself that this woman should be very much off-limits, considering the fact that one of her kids goes to the same school. He didn't date single moms, and he sure as fuck didn't date moms from Amelia's school. Drama and gossip weren't what he was after, and he tried to avoid them like the plague. But this woman did something different to him. She made him want to leave all inhibitions behind and follow her anywhere as long as she had eyes for him.

It was goddamn pathetic, but he was drawn to her no matter the circumstance. He took a moment to scan her hand. The Neanderthal in him had his eyes wandering a little further along her body in complete appreciation before going back to his original plan. *No ring*. She has at least one kid but no ring on a very important finger. One he felt very possessive over at the moment.

For once in his life, he didn't give a shit about how slow the line was. He just took in the glorious view he had as he stood a couple of spots back from his goddess.

The way the breeze moved her hair, the way she talked to her little girl, even the way she scratched her damn foot! She did it again, and now he's thanking God for the mosquito that must have been just as obsessed with her as he was now.

As the duty aide yelled names and they came running, he realized he was sorely mistaken with his original assumptions for a head count on kids. He watched as four kids came bounding up to her.

Holy shit.

The woman picked up four kids from the line. *Four*. Given simple math, he added one more in the wagon to bring the grand total up to five. *Five!*

The idea of instantly having six kids, with the addition of Amelia, should make him run for the hills. With anyone else, it would have. But somehow, he found himself trying to figure out how to calculate how quickly you could put six children to bed so he could do dirty things to their mother.

It takes me about forty-five minutes with Amelia, but if they were to help each other and get through some of it without help, then I could make them all start a bedtime routine at about... Jesus, what am I doing?

Clearly, the lust had messed with his mind if he could be fine with jumping into a Brady Bunch situation with this woman. Watching her in the middle of a small tornado of children should have scared him. He knew that much was true. It gave him hope that his brain was still somewhat functioning because it registered that thought. But he couldn't stop staring. He couldn't help but notice how she hugged them, smiled at them and was genuinely so happy to see each one of them.

She admired their artwork, stopped to tie a shoe, and she scooped some up in a hug while side-hugging another, asking them questions with animation on her face that made her seem like a God damn angel. Watching her was his newfound obsession, but watching her with kids was a whole different ball game.

He needed to know where she went to school, where she grew up, and what her family was like. He wanted to know what waking up on a Christmas morning with her would be like. He just had to know this woman. It felt like he was slowly suffocating wihtout this information.

But it didn't look like that was going to happen today. Once she got the kids, she never looked back. So much for being noticed. He started to ponder if maybe she was married and just didn't wear a ring.

"Daddy!" Amelia came bounding up to him, and he scooped

her up. He put Amelia down, and they walked hand in hand toward the car. The opposite direction of where she was going.

The call had just made him feel like he was on top of his game, only to come crashing back down to earth when she walked away with her little pack of wolves. She'd been able to put him there twice. Feeling like shit because he wanted nothing more than to go with her. Anywhere.

"So let me get this straight. You saw her with one kid, then she picked up four more?" Tyler looked both upset and amazed by Xander's heart or stupidity. "And you still want to pursue her?"

Xander stared blankly at his friend, who was currently trying to lecture him. With no words, he gave another empty expression only to make Tyler puff out exasperation and throw his hands up in defeat.

Tyler and Noah met Xander at a dive bar in downtown Denver for a quick recap of their comings and goings. To say that either of them were even remotely happy for Xander's new love interest would be a bit much.

"Dude, you're fucking crazy."

"Yeah, I agree with Tyler on this one, man. Five kids is a fuck ton of work. You don't even know what she's really like yet, let alone what kind of mother she is. And to have five kids at that! You have a crazy-ish ex you deal with, a dickrod of a stepdad for your little girl and now you want to throw in that many kids?" Noah was normally the one who would cheer him on with women, but with a serious woman like this? He was apparently on his own.

"Oh, and get this, he hasn't even fucked her yet, let alone talked to her!" Tyler had to add. As if Noah would somehow guess that he was able to take her to bed without knowing her name or any details of her life.

Granted, it had happened in the past, but not in this situation. Not this type of woman.

Those types of girls would be grouped into the women classified, in his mind, as "before her." They may never understand this type of classification and this type of woman, but they also didn't know that he had actually talked to her. It just didn't end up going anywhere close to how he envisioned it.

Noah just shook his head in disbelief and took another swig of his beer. They both looked around at the people at the bar and acted as if the world just didn't make sense anymore. Maybe it didn't. Xander had never had to chase women, but this one had him losing his mind.

"Guys, I went on a date the other night with some chick, and I couldn't even take her home." They both raised their eyebrows, asking for more information. "As in, she was the one begging for it, and I shot her down!"

They were tracking now and shook their heads as if he had committed a crime against bachelors everywhere. What he left out of that bit of information was how he jerked off to his mystery woman when he got home and came harder than he ever had in his life. Like gripping the fucking shower wall to steady himself type of hard.

Both friends looked at him in disbelief and silence.

"What does that mean?" Xander asked. Tyler raised his hand to speak first and began the lecture.

"First of all, never turn down a hot woman. Are you fucking crazy? A woman wants your dick, then you give her some good dick. You probably just haven't gotten laid enough, and you think only her pussy will do. Trust me, it won't."

He used to like his friends. Now Tyler was a smug bastard.

"I don't know if that's entirely true," Noah added. Clearly the better friend at the moment.

"But don't stop fucking just because you are seeing, and I

mean it in the literal sense, seeing a woman you don't know from across a pickup line."

Five beers in, and he was wondering if he should switch to something stronger because this shit wasn't helping. His friends weren't helping either. A fleeting thought had him believing he could find new friends in this bar that may agree with him instead of these assholes who want to ruin his dreams and make him feel like a fucking stalker.

"All right, so are you guys telling me this because your marriages are shit, or are you telling me this from past experience?" Xander knew the answer but also knew the answer they would give. He was just about to the pleasantly drunk phase and couldn't give a shit anymore.

"Ouch," Tyler jokingly held one hand over his heart and took another swig of his beer with the other. Figures he would only be able to fake being offended since his marriage really was shit. Or maybe he was finally admitting he was a shit husband.

"Hold on now." Noah was a tad tipsy and was actually offended. "I don't have a shit marriage. Everyone goes through tough times, but we're hanging in there just like everyone else."

He would probably feel bad for calling Noah's marriage shitty, except that the alcohol wasn't letting him. And the fact that he wasn't on board with his mystery woman.

"What we are trying to say." The slight slur now prominent in his friend's speech, "Is we don't want you getting hurt, man. She doesn't even know you exist."

"I'm not saying that." Tyler looked almost pissed now.

Maybe this is jealousy?

"I'm saying that this isn't you. You don't date exclusively. You give us stories about the ultimate bachelor life. You don't do marriage, and you sure as shit don't hold out for one woman."

A hiccup came from the other side of the table, Xander turned at Noah, waiting for him to say something that would make him look like more of a decent human being than the asshole comment Tyler just threw out.

"That too. I just don't know if this marriage life is what you want. You have it all right now. I don't think you're ready for the reality of a wife and kids. It's not what you think and probably not what you want."

Well, now he knew what they really thought of him. He never knew that their shitty marriages had given them a perception of him being this shallow. He took a long swig of beer, trying to rein in his thoughts.

"Just because I've never been in love doesn't mean I wouldn't welcome it. Maybe you guys are right. Maybe it's not what I'm expecting, but maybe it is. Maybe life with her would be nothing like what you guys are saying. I just want a date. I want to get to know her." Xander could feel his pulse coming back down from the spike his anger took on. The rest of the noise from the bar came back to life in his ears, and he spoke his peace. Whether they believed him or not.

"Get a damn date, then maybe you will stop overthinking everything with this one fucking woman." That was possibly the nicest thing Xander was going to get out of Tyler tonight.

CHAPTER 9
Mina

"You want to be fuck buddies?" She blurted the words out in shock, then turned the screen around so Claire could read them herself.

"Who even is that guy?" A question Mina asked herself last night as well. Good to know that Claire didn't know the guy either.

"I looked at his profile, and apparently, we went to high school together. Who the hell does he think he is?" Mina was still pissed. Sure, the revelation that someone other than her ex wanted to have sex with her still, even after having a baby and being about ten years out of high school, made her feel pretty good. Like she wasn't written off by society, but then she was pissed because the guy wasn't remotely attractive.

She could feel her inner monologue roll her eyes at herself. *And just who do you think you are, Miss Priss?* She quickly added, "Like, maybe I'm not a ten, but he's disgusting and apparently has no morals." *There. I'm not an arrogant bitch.*

"Okay, first of all, WE are a ten." Mina bowed her head, both acknowledging and apologizing for momentarily forgetting she was an identical twin.

"Fair point. If I look like you, which my reflection in the mirror this morning says I do, then we are indeed a ten. Proceed."

"Second of all, that's how all men are, Mina. It's not that he's lacking morals. It's that you're hot, and he wants to bone. So, he's taking his shot. A far, far away shot," Claire said lazily, "with a deflated ball in a court halfway down the block. In a rainstorm filled with lightning and everything else you can imagine to get the picture."

Mina was starting to feel better. Claire always knew how to rationalize and make light of things. "With Shaq standing in front of him and with two broken legs," Mina added.

"And wind gusts at hurricane speeds," Claire snorted.

"And arthritis in his wrist."

"Yet through all this, he still stupidly took the shot," Claire finished. "Now block him so all those beautiful images can be put out into the universe. But leave that computer out. We need to get you set up on one of those dating sites so you can actually hang out with men other than our brother and father."

Mina gave a horrified face. "I don't do dating online, Claire. It seems so weird and impersonal. Talk about giving someone the creeps; those men would be doing what that asshole just did. Reaching out for an interest in what I look like or what they can get from me."

"That's a very unfair thing to say since plenty of people get married after meeting online," Claire chastised. "And what other choice do you have? You don't go out besides to children's sports games or to school pickup. We have limited options here, girlfriend, so you tell me a better one if you don't like this one." She eyed her warily while scrolling through a website.

Claire had busted out some sass, so she knew she meant

business. The names and faces were all strangers, and she felt so slimy trying to check them out.

"Is this what you want? Do you want me to troll a website and see if any men pique my interest? Without even looking into their profiles, I can tell you right now that their pictures are speaking volumes over here."

"Oh, stop it and move over!" Claire was interested now. Sliding onto the barstool, practically sitting in her lap, Claire took over. "Let's see if anyone loves to read or travel or anything." Claire scrolled to a man with his shirt off and clicked on it.

"Oh yes, Claire," Mina drawled. "This one looks very smart and into reading." Mina hung onto the words, accentuating how ridiculous this all seemed as Claire stuck her tongue out.

"Let's just give his profile a little look-see, and then we can pass judgment."

Mina spoke up and loudly read the profile the man had, not so eloquently, typed up. "I like working out and having fun. Am looking for someone who is into living life to the fullest and going along with me for the ride called life."

They slowly turned their heads to each other and, in unison, "Right, okay, moving on." Mina hopped up and headed for the front windows in her living room.

"What are you doing?" Claire asked as she saw Mina start to pull the cords on the blinds, scrambling to the next as if she couldn't make it to the window fast enough. "It's the middle of the day, Mina."

"And that's why I'm closing them, Claire." Mina had a bite to her words that wasn't lost on Claire. "I will never be able to live with myself if a self-respecting adult happened to wander by the window and saw us looking at those men. And think of all the small children in this neighborhood, Claire! They would be subjected to the horrors of adult dating."

With a roll of her eyes, Claire resumed her search and faced the screen unamused.

"Old and alone!" Claire yelled from over the screen.

Reminding Mina what her future could be should she keep up with her antics. But the idea of trying to meet men through a tiny little box that constantly reminded her that she wasn't tech-savvy was a bit more terrifying than she wanted to admit.

Is this how it's always going to be? Checking out men at Walmart or trying to sift through the least creepy-looking pictures online only to get up and close the blinds? Yeah, I think I'm out.

"I think I'm done, Claire." The heaviness in her voice was heard loud and clear as her sister's head popped up over the laptop screen and zeroed in on Mina.

With a long sigh, Claire closed the laptop and pushed it to the side of the counter, then made her way over to the armchair by the window. She must have known this would happen because the woman already knew her speech.

"It's ok. We will look maybe when there's been a bit more time. I know it isn't easy hearing about all the stupid shit he does and all the places he's been. The man is a top-notch asshole."

That was the understatement of the century. The man wasn't just parading around his new love interest, he straight up flaunted his conquests and haunted her dreams. The affair wasn't the only traumatic thing that man had done to her, and she held onto some memories harder than others, unfortunately. Sometimes, she could still feel his hands on her and how powerless she felt as he groped her and held her down. The vile things he said in her ear and the way she couldn't break free of his grip. She was his, and there was nothing she could do to change that. Whatever little control she thought she clung onto in her life shattered the day "it" happened.

Her parents raised her to believe in herself and believe she was beautiful and strong, but he ruined it. He single-handedly ruined her. The secrets she held onto from that awful day always came back to haunt her. She not only lost a battle of strength, but she also lost a battle of worth. Everything changed, and even though she carried on, it was with a whole new perspective. Like a child who was told Santa wasn't real. Her perception of the world would always look a little different now.

Finding out he stayed with the other woman was a whole other set of problems. From people around town calling her to her friends reminding her that she would be around Sophie, she just didn't want to hear any of it. She didn't care to know, but she could never get too far without someone or something proving to her just how little she meant to the man who promised her forever.

He was a magician. He somehow made her the talk of the town while making her feel like nothing. This whole exercise in dating was more than she could bear. She wasn't ready for it. And she was starting to think she never would be."I don't mean for right now. Claire, I think I'm done with men."

Claire reared back and held her at arm's length. "What do you mean? You're only 28, Mina. You have a lifetime to find someone who will love you the right way." Walking over to the counter and grabbing the laptop for extra effect, she began shaking it. "These guys are not your only options! Don't freak out just because our first time with a dating site was terrible. We have to keep trying!"

Mina tried to be strong, but her shoulders slumped, and she felt so defeated. *We*. She appreciated that Claire honestly felt like this whole process was a "we" thing. But at the end of the day, she was the only one waiting for her daughter to come home. Or staying up all night because she heard a noise outside and she wanted to protect Sophie. She was learning how to trust herself to be alone, and at the moment, she wasn't sure she wanted the added stress of having to learn how to trust anyone else.

She had plenty of men in her life, and they were all brothers and a father who were great to her and her girl. She didn't think she had the energy for any men outside the ones she already believed in.

"I don't want to." The burning in her eyes threatened to breach while she tried to keep her emotions in check. "I'm done with the cheesy pickup lines and the horns blindly honking as I run in the opposite direction. I'm done wondering if the next man in my life will do the same thing. He didn't just walk out on me. Every time he was gone, he left Sophie, too. Even if he won't ever admit it, he had his fun and partied like a bachelor before he came back to play daddy. I don't want to deal with another asshole Claire. I really think I'm just done."

"I get that you're still hurting from being betrayed. But you can't let him win. It took you a long time to get it back. I saw you work on it every day. You had to fight just to get a fraction of that spunk and make your way back to us. Don't let him win because you're afraid."

The words hung in the air and stung her all at once. She knew she was right, she just didn't like how Claire worded it. That fear was just one more thing he held over her. She let out a long sigh and conceded.

"I want to sometimes." She inhaled deeply, trying to gather herself for the admission she was about to lay out. "I want to be a family again and not be just a twosome that tags along. I see everyone paired up and the dads on dad duty while the moms get to talk or vice versa. But I notice how Kyle or Jared are always picking up where Sophie's dad should be. It sucks, Claire. And I'm not dead. I know I want sex again, and I want to feel wanted. I want to cuddle with someone and watch movies together when Sophie goes to sleep. I want to buy sexy lingerie and have a wild night in with someone that I actually want to wake up to. But most of all, I want to trust someone again."

She lost her battle with the tears and she hated herself for it. In barely a whisper, she admitted what she hated most. "I'm just scared, Claire. How do I trust someone again? How do I know that the next guy won't make me feel like I'm nothing?"

Claire grabbed and looked straight into her eyes. "We never know, Mina. That's the terrifying thing about love. We have to take the leap and hope that it's everything we've been praying for. We have to have a little faith."

She could see her sister through the blur of tears and the hiccups from crying.

"Faith and some tissues. Apparently, we can ugly cry with the best of them, and I'll tell you what, I'm here for it. It's not our worst look."

Mina laughed and wiped away as much as she could without completely soaking her shirt. After a few more sniffles and swipes, she felt like she could speak without the waterworks starting up again.

"I just need time. Maybe more time will help me not be so scared."

Claire gave a little half smile, but she may as well have waved a victory flag. "Maybe a bit more time is all you need," she said as she hugged her sister once more. "Time and more run-ins with the hot dad from the pickup line."

As Fall continued to show its beautiful colors in the Rockies, Mina reveled in small-town life. There was a festival coming up with a community Friendsgiving, and then the Holiday season would turn Kings Ranch into a literal snow globe. Main Street already had string lights up year-round to illuminate the quaint village setting, and given any holiday, the shop owners and locals decorated as if their town were the set of Hallmark movies, staged and ready for action.

There were hay bales and pumpkins leading up to every shop and every step, welcoming any and all into their cozy spaces. The staircases welcomed any patron with a perch to watch passersby, complete with a colorful array of leaves on the ground. She loved it here, plain and simple.

Yet, even with the holiday spirit in full swing, Halloween proved uneventful as the mystery man, aka hot dad, thankyou

Claire, only showed up briefly a couple of times after she had already picked up the kids. Always on the phone and always preoccupied.

She thought she caught glimpses of him eying her, but she, too, was always busy with the kids to really pay attention. She didn't want a distraction anyway. She didn't need a distraction. He was serving his purpose quite wonderfully anyway as a perfect leading man in her fictional life. Every time she needed a little bit of reminding, he would show up and be the beautiful muse of a man she needed.

His job was ever-changing in the story, but she figured she could nail that one down when she either finally talked with him or finished the book.

She had thought the holidays, with so much hustle and bustle, would serve as a great distraction for when Sophie was gone. But the truth was, it only seemed to get harder. It was getting harder and harder to accept the terms the judge set for them all that time ago. Like she should have fallen into a routine or pattern by now, but she just felt lonely when her daughter left.

Today was one of those days for Mina. It was the type of day where she wasn't needed as an aunt and Sophie wasn't home to be her partner in crime. The annoying prattle of do-gooders and their advice came into her mind, but she was tired of hearing it. People kept on telling her to enjoy these days and just relax. What she wanted to tell them was, how do you relax when you never wanted your child to leave in the first place? How would they feel if a stranger decided on how much time they were allowed to see the child they birthed? It didn't make any sense to her, but she didn't have a choice.

After she collected herself from the living room floor, she did the only thing that helped her calm her nerves. She worked out. After a half hour of intense cardio, she was a bit less anxious and ready to take on the day. Or at least ready to take on a shower.

Another noticeable trait recently on days when Sophie wasn't home, was that she did her hair and actually put on regular clothes. The kind of clothes you need a real bra for and pants that have buttons. It helped her feel a bit in control of things. She may not have been able to control the situation and the fact that Sophie had to leave, but she could sure as hell control her clothes and her hair.

She checked herself in the mirror, added her usual minimal makeup, then she was ready to hit the road. Her first order of business was to pick up some much-needed groceries for the house and for the festival. She was going to bring her famous pumpkin pie and some freshly baked rolls.

If love had a language, then hers would be food. Well, food and books. Food was her way of showing love and keeping traditions alive. Sharing a meal was personal to her, and she was positive that was why she hated casual dating.

She hit the market on Main Street and reveled in how it was having a moment. The flowers and pumpkins stacked along the entrance added to the charm, and the small, even rows of goods rather than full-scale aisles made the experience feel less claustrophobic. If the definition of charming had a picture, it would be the local market.

She entered the store with her mantra in mind. *Eyes down, don't look at men and don't act interested.* Not that any men around town did the shopping. She was so determined not to be a stereotype that she was almost letting it get in the way of her being friendly. She would need to work on that, but she didn't want a distraction, and she sure as hell didn't want to be a stereotype. So, therefore, eyes down.

Slowly, over the past year, while her mom and sister schemed to help her start dating again and while she simultaneously dragged her feet, she jokingly referred to herself as the old maid town mascot of sorts. Although, she was pretty sure you had to be a world-renowned cook or mother to like a billion children to reach the status where everyone knew your name.

That was a problem for sure, and she often wondered how she would reach this mythical status. Maybe she could aim to be besties with someone who held that title, and she could be the Thelma to her Louise. *But that's me and Claire...*

She picked up the vanilla extract and decided that that plan wouldn't work. She could start baking as a vendor if she needs to pass the time. Maybe a baking club or a knitting club. *Or a book club! Now I'm on to something.* She reasoned that she would need to tell Claire about that last little idea later.

A little loop around an aisle led her towards the deli section, where she contemplated what she would need just as someone very familiar and yet mysterious came into view. *Holy hell, of course, hot dad would shop here!*

Mina did a quick self-assessment and adjustment of her shirt, then realized what she was doing. *Am I primping?*

"Pontius Pilate!" She tugged her shirt and looked down to act busy. As she was just about to start grabbing fruit nonchalantely, she heard that same mesmorizing voice.

"Excuse me?" To her mortification, her words were not under her breath like she had planned, and he now partially covered his phone and asked, "Did you just say Pontius Pilate?"

Maybe their first encounter wasn't the most embarrassing moment of her life. She cursed worse than a college football coach in a losing game during the fourth quarter, but in public and around Sophie, she threw in any word that would come to mind. Anything was up for grabs when trying to cover for her foul mouth.

Today of all days, she had to summon Pontius Pilate? Not even a "Cheese and Rice?" That one, she could at least feign ignorance and then ask which aisle. But no, she had to choose this one off the top of her head.

"Yes." She stammered like a fool. "I..." She was flailing. She envisioned a fish flopping on a dock and imagined even he would be doing better than she was. "I was thinking about taking a class in Christianity, and something jogged my memory and out popped Pontius Pilate." She smiled and tried to play it cool. She was now a bad liar, and she was most likely going to hell.

"Right. Was it the fruit that did that?" She could hear the humor in his voice, holding up a finger while he told the person on the other end of the line he would have to call them back. "Do you remember me?" *Oh God.*

"I want to apologize about our first meeting." Her shock must have been burned on her face with rosy cheeks that gave her away. "It wasn't my finest pickup line, I assure you." He was all smiles with a devil may care attitude to match. *Is he joking about pickup lines? Like ones including condoms after he held the tampon boxes?* Maybe here was a God if she didn't have to be the only one embarrassed by their first little tete-a- tete.

The hot dad and XL condom connoisseur was talking and apologizing to her. How would she be able to form rational statements now? Luckily, she didn't have to just yet.

"My daughter must go to school with your kids." Kids. That was an interesting word choice. *He must mean Jared and Claire's kids.* But who was she to correct him? She was, after all, not looking for anything in her life except more inspiration for her story.

"Ahh, yes. I may have seen you at the elementary school." *I may have stared at you a time or two, or twenty, but who's asking?*

Moving his hands to his pockets and adjusting his stance, he almost looked nervous, but that couldn't be possible. This guy was always glued to his phone and constantly sounded like he was telling people what to do. He seemed to be the executive sort of guy. *Now that would be an interesting job for my leading man.*

"How old are they?" Her thoughts were interrupted by the actual scene playing out right in front of her. *Why is it hot that he's asking about the kids?* He looked even more attractive than he did five seconds ago.

With his hand scratching the back of his neck and his eyes staring straight at her, she could swear she caught him watching her mouth rather than her eyes. She must be imagining more than a scene for her book.

"Goodness, let's see. There's Max, that's twelve. Steph, that's eight-" he let out a groan, apologizing as he looked concerned at the small screen in his hand.

"I have to take this work call. I swear it should only take a minute. I'm so sorry." He put his phone to his ear and stepped a couple of feet away, starting to talk angrily to someone on the other end.

It dawned on Mina that he looked sincere. He actually looked sorry about the interruption. Like he was actually interested in learning about the kid's ages. She had to brush off the thought. That whole sincere bit may work for others, but she just couldn't take a gamble right now. No matter how much of a hot dad he was. She just needed to play it cool and get her head on straight or back to her work and her story.

Yes, the story is where I can dream. This...whatever it is with hot dad is dangerous territory for me.

If the book was where she could dream, then dream is what she would do. *The electricity between them would be physical, and they would feel the literal sparks between their touch. A quick glance and husky breaths would lead to them making out in the grocery store bathroom. Scandalous!*

Something she would never do in real life but wished she had the guts for every now and then. To be so adventurous. She looked up, trying to locate a bathroom. *Just for writing purposes. Nothing more.* It wasn't as if she hadn't imagined doing that with hot dad before. *Maybe.*

Giving her head another shake, she got back to the storyline. *Their kisses would turn frantic, and their hands would be feeling all over while trying to rip off what clothing they had on. A quick look in the mirror, while her back was to him, would have their eyes meet just before he bent her over and...*

"I'm so sorry! I have to figure this out. There's been a problem with one of the projects, and I have to handle it personally." He took a minute to make sure he slowed down and looked her in the eyes before telling her, "I'm really glad I got to talk to you today. Even for just a minute."

Taken aback, she didn't know what to say. Suddenly, it felt like her tongue had swollen, and she froze. The only thing she could muster up was a nod and a smile.

He smiled back, apologized one more time and then yelled over his shoulder on his way out the door, "I'll look for you in line!"

Just like that, she was simultaneously ripped out of her steamy sex scene that was about to go down and also from her conversation with the hot dad. She still didn't know his name, and somehow, she felt hot in the middle of the local grocery store with a certain itch that couldn't be scratched.

"Knights of Columbus, make it stop!" Without looking at who she could have possibly offended that time, she huffed and headed for self-checkout. She had done enough talking and shopping for one day.

CHAPTER 10
Alexander

It had to be the fucking President of the company asking him to fix a problem. At this rate, he was never going to figure out her name.

A few calls later, he was in his car and headed to Denver to catch a flight out of town so he could unwind this massive fuck up his colleague created. This was the kind of shit he had to put up with when working for a great company that still had some roots firmly planted in the good ol' boy culture.

It was a mixture of extremely smart, capable people sprinkled with some that were utterly incompetent. One of the directors who reports to him tends to lean on Xander to make his life a living hell. And by lean, he meant that he literally had to ask for help with almost everything. This was a man who was supposed to be just as well-versed in the company as any of the other directors, yet the man was incorrigible. He was also a man who had a late father who was best friends with the President's father. Therefore, favors were called in, and he was now just under Xander in terms of rank, yet still needed help at every turn.

It didn't matter that Xander worked his way up from the bottom and knew the ins and outs of the company. This mother fucker would cost him his next promotion if he had to focus on making him meet basic standards rather than working on his own flourishing side of the business. He would rather be a team player than let the whole ship sink, but this was getting ridiculous.

He tried to calm his mind and his anger by taking deep breaths and taking in the scenery. *Breath in…breath out*. The breathing didn't work so much as the scenery did. *This never gets old.* The views surrounding Kings Ranch were unmatched, and even though he was driving away from the idyllic little town and may not make it back in time for Thanksgiving, he couldn't deny the feeling of pride that came with living there. The swell of complete assurance he got from just leaving this little bit of the world behind, knowing he gets to call it his home.

It made the stress and anger slowly slide away, and he felt his shoulders easing up. Christmas would be here before he knew it, and he would be working less during the slow season. He put his phone on the console and dialed a familiar number. The same one he dials every time he drives to or from Denver. After two rings, she picked up.

"Honey!" The same reaction, whether it had been a day or a month.

"Hey Mom, how are you?" He couldn't hide the smile in his voice. Talking to his parents always filled his tank.

"Oh sweetie, we are great! It's a beautiful day, and the weather is fantastic! How are you? Where are you off to so close to Thanksgiving?" She knew him all too well.

"Ha! How did you know I'm traveling for work?"

"Oh honey, you're a slave to your habits." The woman was always right. She was also the only person capable of squeezing countless terms of endearment into a conversation without making him feel uncomfortable. His father had married a literal angel.

"Now, more importantly. I can tell there is something in your voice you need to tend to."

How the hell was this woman so in tune with her children? This was why things always felt better when he talked to them. "Aww, ma, you always know me so well," he lovingly joked. "Carl screwed things up again, and now I have to head to Pennsylvania and try to fix it." He could hear the uncharacteristic grumble from her end of the phone.

"Do you think you'll be able to make it to Thanksgiving, dear? The family would miss you so much if you had to skip again." They were his lifeline. The idea of missing another get-together, let alone a holiday, sounded miserable already, but not getting to see the nieces and nephews playing with Amelia would be heartbreaking. His work kept him from her enough as it was, but keeping her from her cousins wasn't something he liked to think of.

"I'm actually not sure. I hope like hell I can, but things may be worse than he's letting on. I have to figure it all out once I get there." He couldn't lie to her. On the off chance that he would make it back home in time, he would rather it be a happy surprise rather than the outcome he's afraid may happen. The idea of fixing all of Carl's fuck ups in under three days with this scale of a project sounded impossible, but he refused to give up on the glimmer of hope he was harboring.

"Well, don't worry about us, honey. We know you want to be there, but sometimes work has other plans. We will talk with Lauren and arrange a time for Amelia to see everyone."

He could always count on his mother for support. She never judged him for his ambitions, she just made sure she put it out there in the universe that she was still interested in more grand-babies.

"Is there anything else you want to talk about, honey? You sound different."

Again, with the sixth sense over there. He contemplated not saying anything and just seeing where this whole thing went. But there was something about this one that had him all twisted up. It wasn't just the insane amount of lust building up or the nonstop, heart-pounding hormones he couldn't control even being in the same damn line as her. It was just different. Nothing was the same, and for the first time in his life, he found himself saying, "Mom, I think I found her."

I sound more psychotic than the boys gave me credit for.

"You think you found who, dear?"

The poor woman was being blindsided by his confessions of somewhat stalking a woman from afar. He took a deep breath and tried to put his thoughts in order.

"Mom, I think there is a woman I want to ask out. Like on a date. And would you believe it Ma, I'm actually super nervous. I feel like a damn high school kid trying to get the homecoming queen's phone number." He laughed and knew his mother was smiling on the other end. Driving and spilling his guts to his mother never felt so juvenile and good at the same time. He could hardly pay attention to the road.

"Oh honey!" He could just see her, hands clasped over her mouth and jumping up and down while praising Jesus that her baby boy may have found his forever after all. "What's her name? Where does she live? What does she do? Oh, sweetheart, I can't tell you how excited I am for you!"

Now to the embarrassing part. The part that made him seem like a stalker. *I'm pretty sure I really am a stalker at this point but just don't want to admit it to myself.* Or perhaps he didn't want to admit to himself that he sounded like the world's most desperate man. Either way, his mom would have to understand.

"Here's the thing, I've never actually talked to her long enough to get her name, or any other information for that matter." Well, actually, he got to know that she either enjoys throwing out biblical terminology or she is actually enrolling in a religion course. He wondered how old she was and if she had any degree or if this would be the first one.

"I finally got to talk to her today for just a minute, and then my boss called about Carl messing things up." *Fucking Carl.* "So, the mystery woman may be completely unattainable, but I think I'm going to ask her out anyway. Like you guys always say, nothing ventured, nothing gained."

There, he got it out, and now she knew the woman may not even be available. Or maybe he just wanted to say it in case the mystery woman snubbed him and his ambitions. He was a catch, right? *At least my mommy thinks so,* he mocked.

He was so in over his head with this one that he had stooped to the point of gushing to his mother. *The brothers would kick my ass for being so pussy whipped. But, I think you have to be getting pussy to be pussy whipped... What the fuck am I then?* The more criticizing he did, the more ridiculous he felt.

"Oh honey, yes, we do always say that!" The woman couldn't stop saying "Oh" as if she was squeezing a baby's cheeks or scanning Instagram for every cute puppy video online. She was honestly that genuine in her excitement, and he loved her even more for it.

"Can I call you back later when you land? I just have to tell your Aunts! They're going to be over the moon for you!"

He wanted to tell her not to call in case it all went south, but he couldn't deflate her mood. Her kids were her world, and the prospect of more grandbabies was just too much for her to hold back.

"Okay ma, just promise me you'll keep it to those ladies and those ladies alone? I'm already getting crap from Tyler and Noah. The last thing I need from my brothers right now is a lecture about how crazy I sound about a stranger." He hoped to God he would be able to hunt this woman down and get her name before the news made it to his brothers. He knew she could keep a secret, but with his sister and sister-in-law, that was a different story. He realized how pathetic this was sounding, but it wasn't going to stop him from trying.

"Oh honey, your secret is safe with me!" He could see her doing a little wave in the air as if saying, scouts honor. "But you know they would be so excited for you."

"Yes, I know."

"But only if you felt comfortable enough to tell them, sweetie. They want nothing more than to see you happy." Again, he knew this was true. But he also knew men.

Hell, he would be laughing his ass off if he had a younger brother drooling over a woman he hadn't even talked to yet. Saying ridiculous things like, "I think I found her" or "I'm nervous to ask her to dinner." He knew damn well he would be giving him shit about being a pussy for not asking her out yet. He was no fool to this game, and he couldn't really be mad at any of them for playing.

"Maybe sometime soon," he thought out loud. "But for now, please don't say anything to Brent or Theo. And for sure, don't tell Dad! He would definitely tell them, and they would all have a field day."

She made her promises, then they said their goodbyes. God, he loved that woman. Maybe that was why he always had such a hard time lowering his expectations. His dad and middle brother married amazing women. They never settled, and it showed in every aspect of their lives.

He knew how interwoven those women were because his one and only sister-in-law was like the big sister to his little sister. He knew whoever he married had some pretty big shoes to fill when stepping into his family.

Theo was a whole other story, and with him being the oldest of the three boys and not a single long-term relationship to his name, Xander was pretty sure his mother wrote off the idea of grandbabies from him. Either way, both men could only bring home the best at this point. They both respected the hell out of the women in their lives and loved them dearly, so their opinions and approval mattered.

With Lauren, he had to bring her around simply because he knocked her up. He didn't really have a choice in the matter, and that ended with chaos and a fuck ton of cleanup in his life. She was crazy, just like the rest of them, but she was carrying his baby, and he had to respect the fact that his family needed to like her.

It took a while for them to catch on that he wasn't a new father who was overwhelmed but rather a new father dealing with a woman who was insane while caring for his baby.

He smiled to himself at just another memory of his family being amazing and staying the neutral party when she was giving him hell. They always showed love and respect, but he knew they understood his pain. With the others, it just seemed to get crazier.

He thought about the time when a different girlfriend of his stormed out of Noah's New Year's Eve party at around eleven at night, and it brought on a wave of nausea. She was over him for being too involved with his friends that night instead of babysitting her when she didn't feel the need to interact with anyone at the party. It ended with every partygoer looking for her in the winter snow and skipping out on the countdown.

How did he always end up with psychos?

Or another time when he was dating a woman for a year, and she found an early birthday gift he got for her but was convinced he was cheating on her. She ended up breaking into his place and leaving a note that suggested she would hunt him down if she ever found out there was another woman involved. The whole breaking and entering thing, mixed with threats and being stalked by her throughout the town, was enough to file a restraining order for Amelia's sake.

Was it any wonder that he gave up and accepted the life of a bachelor after those women? He wanted to find 'the one,' but every red flag that popped up along the way made it painfully clear it wouldn't be easy. Other than Amelia, the only good thing to come of all his past disasters was knowing how to spot the red flags a mile away.

Maybe that's why he felt like this time was different. None of the warning sirens were going off in his head when he watched her or when he talked with her. Hell, he knew he should be getting them with the number of kids she had, but he just wasn't. It would be a lot to handle, but she would be worth it. He was sure of it.

Maybe his search had finally ended. If it was her and she was everything he had been dreaming she could be, he wouldn't just bring her around his friends and family. He would parade her all over Colorado, showing her off.

If he could lock down a woman like her, he would never go anywhere else alone. He would brag to his friends, knowing she was his, and they would all be jealous as hell because they settled. Maybe they didn't take their time, or maybe that was just what marriage was like for them, but he was positive his marriage would be different. He had been waiting it out this long and keeping his standards high. Maybe, just maybe, it paid off after all.

CHAPTER 11
Mina

"Happy Thanksgiving!"
Her mom and sister greeted Sophie and Mina at the door as they quickly hurried inside to get out of the Colorado weather. A light snow had blanketed the ground in Kings Ranch overnight, which made the day that much more magical.

"I have the pie and a sweet potato casserole for you all." She juggled the two as they made their way into the foyer. Her sister's house was a McMansion.

It was just over the river on the other side of town, but it may as well be on the proverbial other side of the tracks. A gorgeous mountain retreat with an expansive porch and views for days.

Hugs and kisses were given with happy greetings as they tucked their coats away into the closet and settled into the warmth. "Oh, my favorite!" Her mother gushed as she smelled the desserts and led the way into the main living area, where the rest of the crew was already laughing and nibbling on appetizers.

As they came into the main area and the rest of their family caught sight of them, a bunch of cheers from the crowd rang out, and the little girls squealed at the sight of the last unicorn member. Her family never failed to bring a smile to her face. Always so warm and welcoming.

Sophie ran over to the ladies and picked up a game piece while the women settled back into their last-minute preparations for the big feast. Her house was something out of a HGTV makeover dream. The foyer opened up to a large open area with vaulted ceilings and wall-to-wall windows along the back of the living room, revealing a panoramic view of the town.

With the men watching the game, the children playing, and the women cooking in the kitchen, everyone was doing their own thing but in the same long great room. It was such a homey vibe. Her home may be a miniature version of this, but the feeling was the same. It was comfort.

The gathering was just what she needed. The food was incredible and the company was even better. She hopped on a bar stool and picked at the spinach artichoke dip just as Beth leaned in, looking like a child in trouble as she looked out over Mina's shoulder to check her surroundings.

"So I found out about the hot dad in the pickup line." She wiggled her eyebrows, as Mina tried to downplay her emotions.

Finishing her bite, she dabbed her mouth with her napkin before asking, "What do you mean found out? Like other people know about the hot dad?"

Beth giggled and continued stirring the homemade Mac n' cheese. "Well, apparently, everyone knows about the hot dad! I just didn't really know since my days done line up with his much. But I asked about a dad that picks up a little girl, and then all of a sudden, all the mothers started gushing."She nodded and raised her eyebrows at Mina like they were the last to know this bit of juicy gossip. "They spilled on all the details without me needing to ask anymore!"

Mina had mixed emotions with all the news just dumped on

her. On one hand, she was dying to know all about the hot dad. He had to leave her so abruptly the other day, and she wanted the scoop. But on the other hand, and it should be no surprise to her, he was seriously already known as 'the hot dad' at the school. So, what chance would she have with him now? *I don't even want a chance with him!* She had to remind herself that he was great eye candy, but men couldn't be trusted.

Claire looked at her with scrutiny written all over her face. "Oh, come on, Mina! We're all dying to know, so don't act like you're the one person who doesn't care."

Damn her sister for always being right. "All right, spill it. But I am NOT going to ask hot dad out, people. Let's get that out of the way right now. Just because I want to know the scoop doesn't mean I need to take action. I'm just curious. That's all."

They're like hound dogs trailing a scent, I swear.

All three of the women gave a little smile of victory. It irritated and embarrassed Mina more than she would like to admit.

"And must we all call him hot dad forever? Does he have a name?" Claire loved a good nickname. Take her own, for example. She dubbed herself Claire Bear and poked fun at Mina for always being the smaller twin. Meenie Weenie was slung at her only during the most inconvenient times.

"Of course, we need to call him hot dad. What else would we call him? Even when we figure out his name, it will always be hot dad."

Well, that settled her argument. She waved her hand, implying for her to spit it out.

"Alright," Beth began. "So, he has one daughter named Amelia and an ex that switches off days with him. He's there way less, so that's why I haven't seen him. I guess your day of helping us lands on his days to pick her up. Sometimes, there's a grandma who picks her up too, but no one knows if it's her mother or his. Apparently, they were never married, but no one knows much more than that other than the mom is married to a police officer now. He sometimes comes with her to pick her up."

Claire interrupts, "I feel like we know more about a grandma and a baby mama rather than the hot dad."

"Same." Mina and her mother added.

"Come on, Beth, what else did those mothers dish out? There has to be something juicy behind their story, or what about his love life? What about his job?"

It was hard to choose a favorite person at the moment. Beth was dishing it out, and Claire was begging for more so she didn't have to. She could kiss her sisters for being so nosy.

"Calm down! I was getting to that. All right, where was I," Pretending to lose track and look irritated, "Oh right. He isn't married, and he has never dated anyone from the elementary school. Apparently, other moms have tried. Even teachers have tried. But no one has been successful when it comes to hot dad. He always says that he doesn't have time between work and his time with Amelia."

As if on cue, the other three women let out an "Awwww," in unison. *Damn hot dad for being so sexy! Why are good dads extra hot?*

"All right," Mina started, "Hot dad is even hotter because he's a devoted father, but he's also not interested in dating. So, we can all put that to rest now."

She hoped that would be the end of it. They didn't need to know she ogles him from afar. She wasn't ready to get back in the saddle, so there wasn't any point in keeping this going. She needed them to stop with all of this just as much as she needed it to stop with herself. The lure of hot dad was getting to be too much. She had to watch it.

"Oh, I don't think that's all there is," Claire smirked and looked over at Mina with mischief written on her face.

What does she have up her sleeve?

"Why?" Mina spit out, now irritated that her sister knew more than she did. "Does hot dad have a twin brother, and you're worried there's going to be some type of twisted love triangle?"

"Ha!" Beth shot out. Her mom started laughing as well. "Wouldn't that just be the icing on the cake? A couple of hot single dad twins with only one twin left."

More mocking. Fabulous.

"All right, then what? What do you know that you can't help but torture us with."

Suspicion now twisted Claire's features. "Why didn't you tell us that you spoke with a mystery man at the grocery store the other day?" Mina's cheeks flushed, and she was sure she hadn't hidden the emotions well. *Guilty.* "So, are you cheating on hot dad now? Who is the mystery man you were talking to, lady?"

Beth and Claire couldn't get enough. It was as if they ditched their regular soap operas and grabbed the popcorn to sit front row and center of her love life drama. The joke was on them, she didn't have a love life.

"What? Were you talking to another man? Are you seeing someone we don't know about?" You would think it was Christmas come early for her mother. The excitement that her daughter spoke to the opposite sex and there was a sliver of hope for more grandchildren had sent her mother spinning.

"Oh my goodness, I just chatted with hot dad for a second. It was embarrassing, to be honest. I let a 'Pontius Pilate' slip, and he excused himself from a phone call just to ask me if I actually said it! I was mortified, yet again."

"Again? What am I missing?" Her mother was confused, but she had no plan on helping her out with that. *Sorry mom.*

"A lot! Just go with it!" Beth added but didn't say more. It was a small relief.

"Good grief, I forgot you still do that," Beth said.

"How did you recover?" Claire interjected. "Mom, try to keep up."

"What the hell did I miss?" She almost felt bad for her mother, but she wasn't going down that path again. Condom conversations wouldn't be revisited with her mother.

"I made up some story about wanting to take a religion course or something. He seemed to believe it." Mina waved it off in hopes they would just let it drop. She picked at the appetizers and looked around.

"Annnnddd then what? That could not have been it. Did you get his name? Does he know who you are? Did you run out of the store? Give us something, Mina!" Claire was dying.

They really were just as interested, if not more so, in her dating life, or lack thereof, than she was.

"That was pretty much it! I didn't even get his name. He was asking me about my children, and when I was telling him the names and ages, he got a work call, and he had to excuse himself. That was it."

They all just sat there, their mouths gaping. "You didn't correct him that only one kid was yours?" The venom in her voice was lethal. Mina tried to counter with confidence.

"I don't need to correct him. He doesn't date, and I'm not interested." As if on cue, Beth backed slightly away from the counter as Mina and Claire stared off.

"Holy Hell, Mina! You had an additional four kids with you, and you didn't think to correct the guy so he wouldn't run for the hills? What the hell is wrong with you? Do you ever want to date again, I mean, seriously?" Claire was physically irritated with her sister as she aggressively cleaned the countertop.

"Again, why do I need to correct someone when I don't plan on dating him anyway? It's never going to happen. He isn't even interested, and he doesn't do the dating thing, remember?" Mina also wasn't ready to be let down again. She couldn't say it, but it was in the room like a big elephant, and everyone felt it.

"Yeah, but that was with other women. It doesn't mean he's not interested in you! We have to fix this." Beth seemed legitimately concerned with the situation. She seemed to be mentally calculating who she could talk to in order to spread the word that would somehow make it back to hot dad. The fact that she grabbed her phone and narrowed her eyes was proof. She was in the zone.

"Honey, we just care." Her mother eyed Claire and then paused as if she wanted to say more. She wanted her married off again and not feeling like a third wheel in the dating scene. She also really wanted more grand babies if she came right down to it, but wanting to see her daughter happy came just before that.

"I know, Mom," she sympathized. "If it makes you ladies feel any better, he made sure to turn back and tell me that he would look for me in the line." She knew that would be her golden ticket out of this guilt trip.

In unison, yet again, all the other ladies cheered. *Annnndddd they're all happy again. Easy enough.*

"Well, thank goodness there's more time for us to fix this. I texted Brittany, Ashley and Hannah about spreading some word about my young, single sister-in-law who picks up the kids for me." A click of a send button and a wink of an eye. It was all it took to make Beth feel happy again. "That should help us move things along. Those women know how to gossip, and they sure as hell can talk loud in line. Someone is bound to hear something."

"Bound to hear what?" Kyle walked over from the couch for some appetizers and overheard some of the conversation. Just enough to get the ladies going again.

After the mortifying retelling and her brother Jared also joining in on the conversation, Mina was now sure that the men in her family thought she was a loser of sorts. At least not a desperate one, though. It was clear that the other women were a driving force in her dating life, so she was going to hang on to that little bit of dignity as long as she could.

Everyone had a good laugh at her expense, and she even joined in. Who wouldn't laugh at themselves if they claimed four extra children and let a biblical name slip in front of a hot single man?

"So, what's the deal, Mina? Are you afraid?" Jared, her sweet older brother, was always her guardian. He was always the brother who acted like he didn't care when the boys flirted but was the first to tell her about the guys he heard were no good. He was always there in the background, watching and moderating. No matter what.

"I just don't do the dating thing very well. The introvert in me screams when thinking about going on a date with a stranger and having to sit and talk for hours. I think I'll pass."

"As in pass on life?" Jared let out a chuckle. "You're gonna have to get out there again at some point, Meenie Weenie."

She rolled her eyes. "You too with the shitty nickname? Don't use that one just to please Claire. We both know you swap out M with whatever bullshit name Claire uses when you want to piss me off."

He stuck his tongue out in an act of playful defiance. They both knew it was to goad her.

"Well, I still think you need to join one of those cross-fit gyms where you have to work out with a small group, and it would force you to meet people." Kyle also always rooted for her and wanted her to find more friends outside the family. "Or what about those singles activities that are planned, and you just show up? I bet that would be fun, and they would probably do it somewhere bigger, like in Denver, so there's more to do and more people each time."

Everyone had an opinion. All good ones, she had to admit, but she just didn't want anyone concerning themselves with her love life. Because there wasn't one and probably wouldn't be one for a while. She could ogle the hot dad and make up steamy stories about him for the foreseeable future.

"Yeah, maybe." After a bit, the men grew tired of having to be around so many feelings and went back to their game. She was almost out of the woods.

In a low voice, almost inaudible, Beth asked about the only other hot topic. "So how is Evan treating you these days?"

Eye rolls immediately followed. They already knew the answer. Her ex was a bastard. Or perhaps a coward. His self-absorbed ego drove his vanity, and nothing else really fit in. His head always took up too much space in any room. The woman he cheated with the last time was still around, and now they were engaged. But the worst was how he allowed her to treat Mina, as if she was merely the help.

"Oh, you know, the same. They act like I'm an awful parent, and then his girlfriend, nay, fiancé, acts like I'm not even there when I try to speak to her. It makes for awkward conversation, let me tell you."

Mina always tried to lighten the mood, but the ladies hated how he treated her. "Last time they found out about us sleeping over here at Claire's, they decided to yell at me and hold onto my car door, so I had to sit there and take it."

Her mom looked to be in physical pain listening to the story. But unfortunately, it was a common occurrence. They were always harassing Mina, and when they weren't, they were telling Sophie things that weren't true.

"So, I guess I have to become a videographer by trade now since they only stop when I turn the camera on them." Mina tried to laugh it off, but she knew this was all a bit much to deal with. Her ex was certifiable, but to the rest of the police force, he was just another one of the boys.

"I just find this super ironic," Beth added. "He's the one that goes out and parties all the time with that woman. They're the ones hitting the bar scene and telling people they each sleep around. Why the Hell does he yell crazy things at you when he's the one doing it?"

It was a puzzling scenario once it was laid out like that. He was the one parading around town with multiple women and his own fiancé by his side, but he would accuse Mina of being the terrible parent who slept around.

"I think he knows he's the fuck up, but he doesn't want to feel any of it. So, he just puts it all on Mina." Claire felt strongly about that one.

"I think it's a mixture of that and him being jealous that Mina doesn't need anyone to keep on going. He jumped into bed with that woman and can't go anywhere without her. On the two rare occasions he was alone when Mina picked up Sophie, he was nicer to Mina. It's like the new one is jealous, so he has to play a part." Beth added.

"Pretty sure he's just an asshole. He just wants back in Mina's pants when his slut isn't around." Claire said it like it was a fact.

"Either way, I just try and make it through each exchange with my head down so we don't get into anything. I don't need the drama."

She didn't want anything close to it. "And that, right there, is why I don't need another man in my life."

CHAPTER 12
Alexander

As the sun streamed into the hotel window, Xander felt like he had been hit over the head with a hammer and gutted like a fish. His eye sockets even hurt, and barely opening the one eye that didn't feel glued shut felt like a chore. He remembered last night vaguely, but he knew there was enough alcohol to accommodate a Navy vessel, let alone him and his two friends.

Why can't I ever say no to them? He knew that his body wasn't the same as it was in college. And hell, even in college, he still had bad hangovers. The second he and the boys got together and started doing shots, he would always get back into the rhythm, and he always had to keep up. The fraternity days can't be erased, and old habits die hard.

He turned over and was shocked to find a blonde passed out beside him. A blonde he recognized from another escapade who was very much naked. *Lindsay.*

Dragging his hand down the length of his face, he swore he would beat himself for this colossal fuck up if he hadn't already felt like he had been hit by a truck.

He tried to be quiet as he racked his brain for details of the night. *How the hell did this happen?* Had he fucked her again? He actually fucked her four or five more times before he left town the last time, but that was before. He never intended for them to see each other again, and he sure as shit never intended to make this a thing.

Hell, is that what she thought this was? A thing?

Like he's going to invite her back to his house and his town now that she may live close by? He wasn't supposed to fuck anyone anymore. He was sure of it, and now this cluster fuck happened.

He couldn't help the groan that escaped his lips, pressing his eyeballs in hard. Trying to erase any images of the night that may seep out if he wasn't careful.

"It's fine, you know." Her breathy voice startled him out of his misery. He looked over as she was starting to stretch with a big smile plastered to her face. Her long legs were on full display as well as her tits, void of any sheets to cover them.

"You look like you're contemplating running out of here." She propped herself up on her elbow, making him shift uncomfortably. "Don't worry. I know you're in love with some other woman."

His head whipped back as if he'd been slapped, and she just smiled like a Cheshire cat. "How do you know that?"

She let it stew for a minute as she picked the sheets up so she could cover herself. He felt himself start to relax a bit once her nakedness was out of sight.

"Because your friends gave you shit about it all night."

His head flopped back onto the bed, relief hitting him instantly. He had never been more grateful for his friends and their annoying banter, but it still didn't save him from the fact that he strayed. He was certain he would call it that since they hardly spoke more than a sentence to each other, but to him, he was off the market.

"Calm down. We didn't have sex." For the second time in under five minutes, the woman had given him whiplash of the neck.

"What? You're naked and in my bed. What do you mean we didn't have sex?"

She laughed at him as she got up and searched for her clothes. "Check your bottom half. I got you down to boxers so you would be comfortable. I sleep naked. I'm sorry to make you uncomfortable, but we were both trashed, and I needed a place to crash. You offered me your room, and when you insisted on the floor, I insisted nothing would happen."

There is a God, and he's helping me keep my drunk dick in my pants. "So we really didn't…" He trailed off, not wanting to finish the sentence, waving a hand between them so she got the message.

Half-dressed and looking a bit worse for wear herself, she finished the statement for him. "No! We. Did. Not. Fuck. I would have loved to, but you were gushing like a little schoolgirl about some exotic woman with gorgeous eyes and a great ass. It was actually adorable." She paused and looked a little sad, pursing her lips at the memory of him spilling his guts to her last night. "Kind of made me jealous. But I don't mess around with men that are involved, and you couldn't shut up about how involved you wanted to be with her. So, it was just a sloppy night of drunk people bunking up."

He could feel the relief wash over him. He wouldn't be cheating on the woman he had barely spoken with, but for some reason, none of it would have felt right.

"Thank God," he breathed out, lying still on the bed, trying to gather enough strength to sit upright. "No offense," he added. "I just…well. You obviously heard about her and why it would be a major fuck up for me if I ruined my chance."

At this point, she had found her keys and was ready to head out. "Yeah, yeah," she almost cooed. "I heard alllll about how amazing she is." She smiled and headed toward the door. "She would be a fool not to fall for you and your big dick."

He could hear her laugh as she opened the door.

"But if she is a fool, you have my number." It was the last thing he heard before the door clicked shut.

An hour and a half later, he found himself cursing the downtown parking options while running late to meet his friends for breakfast. "Xander!" The guys didn't look nearly as rough as he did, which pissed him the hell off. *How were they always better at handling alcohol?*

"There he is, good ol' lightweight McCade!" Noah and Tyler chuckled and patted him on the back as he slid into the booth.

"Shut the fuck up. How the hell do you two look so good? We drank ourselves into oblivion last night." Rubbing his temples and reaching for the coffee pot left at the table, he wasn't even being dramatic about it. He had forgotten what they were celebrating, but whatever it was, he knew it wasn't worth getting knocked on his ass for.

"When you close a huge ass deal, you are meant to drink yourself stupid! This might make me part owner now." Tyler raised his mug of coffee to cheers the boys. "But we can all say the deal closing took the back seat when you went about breaking your celibacy with the hot blonde last night."

Xander nearly choked on his coffee as the others eyed him

shamelessly.

"Even my little ride was put to shame with that one." Tyler had to seal his asshole status. *Mother fuckers always gossiping like girls.*

"How the fuck do you two know about Lindsay?" *Of course, they don't know what really went down. Why would they?* They must have just seen them walk to his room together.

"Oh, Lindsay is her name, eh?" Noah was teasing him now, too. They both loved torturing Xander and his apparent fall from grace. They were the ones against him wanting to give up that lifestyle, after all. Figures it would be when he was out with them that he had to run into her, falling down drunk, no less.

"Yes, her name is Lindsay and don't even start with that shit. Nothing is going on with her." Noah and Tyler look at him, amused.

"Anymore," Xander added.

"Ahhhh, we knew it man," Tyler almost yelled. The man had no filter and apparently now had zero volume control. The night may not have made him look shitty, but he was definitely talking louder than normal. "She was hanging all over you last night when we were leaving the last bar. She said she would take you back to your room."

Noah elbowed Tyler in the arm. "Who are we to stop such a kind and thoughtful woman?"

This was hilarious to them. The idea of him losing his willpower and sleeping around again seemed to make their outlook on life much brighter.

"I meant what I said. Nothing is going on anymore. We didn't hook up. We were both drunk out of our minds, and she needed a place to crash. We just went to bed."

The expressions they gave him would make someone close by think he had just smacked a puppy.

"Why the hell wouldn't you guys hook up? You're a bachelor! This is your lifestyle, and it's a fucking good one at that!" Tyler was clearly regretting his choice of choosing marriage.

"So you seriously didn't fuck her?" Noah looked at him as if he was almost sorry. "We knew you were going on about that other woman, but we didn't think you would pass up an easy lay. Gotta hand it to you, man. That's impressive." Noah was always better at smoothing things out.

To the guys, he would always be the one sowing his wild oats. Him and John, always the eternal bachelors. But he was over it all. It was such a strange feeling to be captivated by a woman he knew nothing about, and yet she had him. He couldn't stop thinking of her.

She had surfaced out of seemingly nowhere and messed him all up. It was probably less than twenty words she had spoken to him, and yet he would kill someone just to get another twenty. He couldn't even imagine what life would be like if she had more of a firm hold on him, but he was dying to find out.

He was out of his mind to be anything for this woman. He never had to work hard with women but for this woman? He had become obsessed and was willing to hunt her down. *What the fuck?*

The next day felt like a breath of fresh air. It was as if he had a new lease on life, and he was ready to hit the ground running. He was home, he had Amelia, and he would possibly see the mystery woman at the pickup line. The exotic goddess that had him walking around half hard every damn day could be there, and he couldn't think of anything else besides catching a glimpse.

The last time was such a cluster fuck between the call and the need to leave town and fix Carl's mess. He needed to get her name and get this woman on a date. For his sanity, though, simply a name would be monumental. He kept thinking of the worst-case scenario for his fate with his mystery woman. *Husband. Boyfriend.* The thought of it ending before it started was like a punch to his gut. *Lesbian.* Now, that line of thinking made him readjust himself. That was a whole different ballgame, even if he couldn't compete with the wrong equipment.

He needed to focus again. In an effort to not be disappointed in the event that she turned him down or they barely spoke, a name would be the holy grail of achievements.

He was up before the alarm clock, per usual, and was drinking his coffee by five am. The mountains were dark, and he loved the still of the morning. He loved being awake before the rest of the world started stirring. It was his quiet time to think, recharge and map out his goals for the day. Having already laid out the most important goal for him to achieve, he started to line up his work schedule and think about dinner plans before he heard little footsteps come down the stairs adjacent to the kitchen.

With a blanket over her shoulder and quick steps across the kitchen floor, she hopped up on his lap and cuddled into his arms. "Hey, sweetie. How did you sleep?" He kissed the top of her head and watched the sleepy expressions animate her face.

"Good." He plopped her down on the barstool next to his and got up to start some breakfast.

"How about we have some pancakes this morning?" A special treat he normally saved for weekends.

"Yes, please!" She bounced on her stool and started to hum a song while she tried to calm her wild morning hair. "I think this may be the best Monday ever." It was the little things that kept him so wrapped up in their town and his family. Only his girl could brighten the morning just at the prospect of pancakes. Being gone was hard on him, but moments tucked away like this were his saving grace and what kept him going. The kitchen felt warmer and cozier than it had in a long time.

After half the day was gone, he was trying to time the pickup just right so he could catch a glimpse of the mystery woman.

Some days she wasn't there, and since he wasn't there every day either, it was a crap shoot.

He pulled into the parking lot early and sat in his car like most of the other parents, waiting for the gate to open. No sense in standing along the gate when the temperatures were barely hitting the forties these days. He scanned the line that was starting to form but couldn't see her.

There were other dads, which made him internally grumble, along with some familiar mom faces from around town. The gate would open soon, and she was still a no-show. *Mother fucker.*

He didn't realize how disappointed he would be if he didn't see her today. He had seen her in his dreams every night since the moment he spotted her months ago, but he was dying to talk to her again.

A couple more minutes passed and to his utter dissapointment, the gate opened and his time was up. He let out a sigh and heaved himself out of his car. As he put the collar up on his coat and shuffled up the path to the next spot in line, he couldn't help but feel the pang of anger and disappointment that had built up.

It was cold out, and he was a grumpy bastard now. The day had gone to shit in a matter of minutes. To make things worse, something hard ran into his leg from behind him. He was about to rip the asshole's head off when he looked down to notice a handle that snagged his thigh. Her wagon handle.

"I'm so sorry! I lost my footing and the wagon kind of slid forward!" She looked so freaked out from hitting someone or the fact that he looked like a growly mother fucker.

In an instant, he tried to change his expression to ease her nerves. It took everything to reign in his excitement that she was here, and absolutely adorable how worried she seemed about a little bump.

"No problem. Are you ok? How's the little one doing back there with the collision?" She laughed at the description, and they both looked back at Sophie. Bundled in what looked like two jackets and a couple of blankets, not even an actual collision would have probably fazed her at this point. She could double as a marshmallow.

"I think she's good," she assured him. "But how is your leg? I hope I didn't get you too hard?"

Well, that's the understatement of the century. If she only knew.

"I'm good. You barely got me." He didn't want her to clam up again, so he blurted out the first thing he could think. "Is that a feather boa she's wearing?"

The woman was so fucking gorgeous, and all he could think about was how good her legs looked in winter leggings under a lazy looking jacket. The fabric clung to her ass, which made his pants tighter in all the wrong areas for the moment.

When his comment made her little girl smile, he was snapped back to reality. He seriously needed his mind out of the gutter. *A boner in front of her kid. Yeah, that'll really impress her.*

She laughed and corrected him. "Well, it's actually a feather boa purse strap to a very fancy Cinderella bag." He held up his hands in apology and then bowed to the little girl.

"Please forgive my mistake, Miss…?" He was looking from the little girl to the woman in hopes of getting someone's name. He was desperate, and at this point, he could give two shits about which one gave up their identity first.

She cleared her throat. "Oh, of course! This is Miss Sophie Reed." The little girl held out her hand to him in what he thought was the most adult-like thing he had ever seen a child that young do. "Nice to meet you, Mr."

"Wow, did you teach her to shake hands with such authority?" He was legitimately impressed. "Well, it's an important skill, so I thought, why not now?" She smiled shyly, nervously. He was positive he had never seen anything so beautiful in his entire life.

She was a stunner when she was doing her thing, but laughing? Smiling? It was a whole new type of turn-on for him.

"I now have the name of the princess, may I have the name of the queen in charge?" She blushed, he was most likely making a complete fool of himself with this way of asking, but he didn't give a shit. He would gladly do the moonwalk in front of the entire line if that meant she would fork over the tiny bit of information he was desperate for.

"Oh right," she laughed. "I'm Mina." She looked back at her daughter, pausing before she added, "Washington."

A different last name? There may be a God, after all. He held out his hand as his face split into the widest grin he could contain. He was sure he looked like a goddamn animated cartoon character with the level of excitement he was trying to hide just knowing she had a different last name.

"Alexander McCade. Xander, to my friends. It's nice to finally, officially meet you." As they shook hands, he took note of his large, rough hand having totally eclipsed her small, dainty limb. He already felt love at first sight with the woman, but whatever dark magic she held over him also gave their contact a literal force of energy. A tangible electricity he felt the moment they touched. Was it the cold air? The fact that he finally touched this woman? *Mina.*

Whatever energy she conjured up was something he wanted to feel and taste every damn day. Not to mention the fact that it would likely carry over to another particular area of their lives. Whatever it was, he wanted more.

"Amelia's dad!" Of course, he had to be called for the gate right when they started talking. He moved up and retrieved his daughter in a big bear hug. It was literally the only moment in his life that he was sad she was talkative. He glanced up to give an apologetic smile to Mina. But Amelia was showing him a project and talking his ear off.

The lady at the gate named all of her kids, and they came bounding over, all dressed up in winter gear. Reality hit him, and it was fucking freezing out here. No wonder the kids all tried to shuffle the parents to their cars quickly.

He looked over again and deflated. She was swarmed with

kids trying to hug her or get her attention with details from their day. He had missed his chance to get this woman alone, even if he got her name. He waved over at her, and she smiled with a wave as she walked away with her wagon and a million kids in tow. With that many kids and the way his heart was free-falling, he should be afraid. He should be very afraid.

CHAPTER 13
Mina

It was a spark, as corny as that sounded. The second he touched her hand, she felt it. Something more than just the static in the winter air. It was a type of magnetic pull she hadn't ever felt before. Not to mention, just the sight of his sea-green eyes against his sun-kissed skin had made her temporarily tongue-tied.

It literally felt like her tongue swelled three times its size whenever he was near her, and she became a babbling idiot spouting off biblical terms and nodding like a dumbass. Trying to speak to the gorgeous businessman seemed impossible while trying to figure out how to smush her tongue to one side. All from simply staring into his eyes.

He was like the sun, cheerful and bright. But if she wasn't careful, she was pretty sure he could be just as dangerous if she kept on looking at him. She never remembered faces, but his eyes could pierce straight down to her soul, and she knew, right then and there, she was in trouble.

It was a crime for men to be that handsome. The way his plaid jacket clung to his shoulders and biceps made him look like a lumberjack from Hollywood rather than some business guy stuck up in an office somewhere. The man wore jeans like they were made for his body, while his boots peeking out the bottom were a tad too clean and didn't quite match his brusque exterior. Like she had thought, a businessman with a sexy lumberjack vibe. His five o'clock shadow was begging to be touched, and she felt her fingers twitch when she looked at him. As if her own fucking digits were daring her to brush the side of his face and touch the roguishly handsome man.

She was positive her ovaries and fingers were in cahoots
She shook her head and kept on going with the gang of kids all around her. "Onward toward the house," she playfully said.
She didn't need this, she reminded herself. This would be too much work. Someone to have to trust, someone to have to care for, and this particular someone was feeling more and more like someone she would fall in love with. Fall hard in love with.

She would just have to ignore her ovaries and her fingers with their insubordinate behavior. She didn't want to give in to lust no matter how charming the man seemed to be. She just couldn't risk that kind of heartache again, because she knew in her heart of hearts that this time it would be worse.

Everything Evan had done to her and all the reasons she never wanted to be put in that position again came flooding back in like annoying heartburn. A position of being vulnerable. She stayed loyal even when she was well aware that they weren't the same people anymore. Hell, they weren't even on the same field or playing the same game.

Evan had gotten more and more bitter about the choices he made with his life and starting a family so young. He had started to go out when Sophie was a baby and wanted to start partying more and more. The signs were everywhere about what he was up to, but Sophie was the little piece of string tying them together. He turned into a reckless philanderer while she played house on her own. Pretending everything was alright when the whole world didn't feel right, much less their home life.

Then everything spiraled before her eyes. The cruelty in his words, the abuse she came to encounter and finally, the affairs that came to light. She knew some of the people around town looked down on her for not staying longer and trying to make it work for her little girl, but Mina didn't see it like that. She knew that if she stayed any longer, she was at risk of losing herself. She wanted to leave him to make sure Sophie would always know her worth, so in the end, she left so she could remember hers, too.

She was damn grateful her brother lived across the street from the school on days like this. Days when the chilly weather didn't exactly beckon all the children for a long walk and days when she needed a distraction or a quick getaway. She needed to get away from that man and anything that would pivot her thoughts like he did. She didn't want the heartburn and the fear that kept her up at night anymore. She wasn't ready for it.

The gorgeous eyes that set her mind spinning were out of sight right now, and she needed to make them stay that way. He wasn't for her.

He could turn out to be just like him.

She opened the door and shuffled all the kids inside as she left her heart and the winter air outside.

The time flew by, and it was nice just to be in the moment, listening to all the little chatter from the kids. Eavesdropping on the different ages was hilarious as she listened to the Christmas gifts they were going to ask from Santa, the things they heard about elves and even their plans to try and catch a reindeer.

All of it was music to her ears. Christmas time was always Mina's favorite. Who doesn't love all the Christmas feels?

Especially in a town like Kings Ranch. The whole place made the shift for Christmas the day after everyone stuffed themselves with Turkey and homemade pies. It was in full swing, and with the gloomy mood that hung over Christmas last year, she was ready for a re-do. She and Sophie planned on going home and turning their little house into the North Pole. This year was their year, and she wasn't going to let anything stop them.

Before long, Beth and Claire migrated in and set up shop in the kitchen, ready and sounding off on their usual line of questions. She was a constant headline in their eyes.

"It went fine," she started. "Better than fine, I guess." She couldn't stop smiling while talking about the encounter, and she fucking hated herself for it. Her hormones were betraying her, as well as her ovaries that had dreamt of having his babies. *Calm down bitches!*

"I accidentally bumped into his leg as we were walking up to a spot in line, and when he turned around, he looked like he was ready to kill me."

The women looked horrified. This was not what they had in mind, and she kind of liked keeping them hanging there.

"Holy shit! Were you right? Is he really an asshole?" She wished it was that easy. But it was quite the opposite.

Her lips betrayed her as she thinned them into the best version of a straight line as possible, but it was no use. Her cheeks and mouth curved up no matter how hard she tried while thinking about the encounter. The one she shouldn't care about and was terrified over, but felt nonetheless. The energy between them was literally charged.

"No, actually. He seemed sweet."

A collective sigh could be heard when the women took in what she was saying.

"He was more than sweet, really. He was fucking adorable and seemed like a great father, God damnit." Claire threw her hands up and started to tear into Mina.

"What more could you want, Mina? He seems like a ridiculous catch!" This is the part that no one else would understand. Hell, she didn't really understand it herself. She may have been able to move on from the mess, but she couldn't seem to fathom how to trust someone again. She still couldn't wrap her head around giving her heart away. Not to mention Sophie's little heart.

They just didn't understand that she wasn't disagreeing with them. Of course, it's what she would want in a man. How could she want anything more? But she just didn't know if she could do it.

"I just don't know about all this, you guys. I told you I was done with men, and I really think I meant it." She tried to make them see things from her perspective. "How would I go about a new life like nothing happened? How do I believe it when someone says they're going out with the guys or just going to the gym?" She had no words left to try and make them see it. The feeling in her heart felt like a brick wall had been erected and had no plans of coming down. She was a closed book when she used to be a wild child with empty pages to fill in. A hugger that turned recluse.

Claire came over to the side of the island she was at and gave her a little nudge. "Hey, you know we will be here for you, don't you?"

Mina looked up, trying not to acknowledge the stinging in her eyes.

"We wouldn't let you do it alone. This guy, whoever he is, is going to have to go through all of us." Beth looked over and gave her a little smile, telling her she was all in, too. She would never know what she had done in a past life to deserve these wonderful people.

"Thank you." She always hated being the center of attention, and with the amount of crying, talking and healing she had to do publicly with her family, she should be used to it by now, but she wasn't. "I mean it," she said quietly. "Thank you for always making me feel better. Less like the whole male population are a bunch of scumbags."

She smiled at them, then quickly added, "Your husbands excluded, of course." They snickered and then tried to draw Mina back to the very thing she kept trying to avoid.

"So how exactly did this man seem like a wonderful dad in the short time you were in line with him?" Beth leaned over, a pose she had grown accustomed to lately. Mina cleared her throat and tried to talk without wanting to gush all over again. She absolutely despised women who could gush and cry at the drop of a hat, and now she was one of them. Like a literal bleeding heart and it made her sick.

"Like I said, he just seemed sweet. He had commented on Sophia's little feather boa purse strap and joked about how the tiny bump for her was a collision. He asked her name and then asked for mine. It was just…I don't know." Again, with the lack of vocabulary lately. "Really sweet."

"Well, I don't think I've ever heard you call a man sweet before," Claire eyed her. "I feel like this must be a good sign, right?"

Mina tried to hide the smile forming on her lips again. She squinted her eyes, trying to look serious, but she couldn't fool anyone. "Yeah, I would say it's a good sign. I swear to God and St. Jude himself that when he shook my hand," she paused to make sure they were both looking at her so she could lower her voice. "I swear I felt something like a goddamn spark went off between us. How insane is that?" She wasn't sure why she thought she sounded so corny, but she was afraid of all of the words that had started coming out of her mouth and the thoughts that had been generating in her head since this guy showed up.

Everyone was quiet for a beat, and she looked back and forth between them. "Do these things actually happen? Like, is God warning me to stay away, or are movies serious when people have sparks between them?"

Claire chuckled at her sister, reveling in the way she was gushing while Mina moved on to trying to make the encounter sound somewhat scientific.

"I mean, the second our hands touched, I felt it. Maybe spark is the wrong word. A charge is the only thing that describes it, but it wasn't completely physical…" She was drowning here and she knew it. "But it was physical?" She gave up on the idea, having realized how ridiculous she sounded. She had never felt a pull like that before, and it was quite possibly the most bookish thing she had ever experienced.

However, the whole idea made her feel silly now. She shook her head as if trying to snap herself back to making sense of things. "I don't know, just forget I said anything. It was probably just the cold air.".

Beth smiled as she busied herself, and Claire got up and started gathering her stuff to leave. "I know what you're talking about." She grabbed a jacket and wrapped it on her forearm as she reached for some gloves strewn over a chair. She smiled genuinely before looking back into her sister's eyes.

"The kind of pull where time almost stands still and makes you feel like you can't talk or can't think straight because some-one has taken your breath away?" The smile she plastered on her face slowly fell as her sister went on. She was sure she was the only one who could make her feel this seen in a moment like this. "It's that gut feeling that makes you scared because you hardly know someone, but at the same time, it feels like they've been woven into your life from the start and every fiber of your being knows it makes sense."

Claire continued to grab items as Mina slowly nodded her head. Of course, she would know her inside and out. This wom-an was literally her other half, understanding her every thought. She said it so eloquently that all she could do was keep on nod-ding like a fool.

She smiled back and then gave her a wink. "Well then, it looks like you found a reason to try again, after all."

The short walk home didn't seem so cold after her little side conversation with Claire. Like being heard made her feel hopeful even when she wasn't sure what to do with it. At least for the moment, it helped her with all the Christmas feels.

She and Sophie talked about all the decorating they wanted to do that evening and all the things Sophie was wishing for this year. "First, we need to make the sugar cookie houses, mommy. Then after we decorate the tree, we can decorate the houses." Sophie loved decorating sugar cookie houses. She was never a fan of gingerbread, but then again, neither was Mina, so it worked out perfectly.

Skipping down the street toward their little cottage, her daughter looked positively ecstatic to start the holiday season, and Mina was right there with her. Only this Christmas, she wanted something a little different. Though, even if she found said thing, she wouldn't allow herself to enjoy it. "That" was off-limits.

"Mommy, when will we have a daddy for this house?"

What in the fuck just happened here? She wasn't sure if the ladies were talking a bit too loudly or if Soph was getting old enough to notice her house looked different than most. "What do you mean, honey?" She tried to act casual, but to say she was shocked by the blunt trauma from that shot out of left field would be an understatement.

"I mean, at daddy's house, I have a mommy and a daddy. At your house, I only have a mommy. When will you find a daddy for this house?"

Apparently, she had been noticing. "I don't know, sweetie. I like things the way they are." She wasn't exactly lying about that, even if she had a wandering eye and some steamy fantasies. "I love it being just you and me. And besides, whoever I have as your other daddy would have to be pretty amazing. I wouldn't bring just anyone around, you know? This next daddy will need to be pretty perfect. So, I think I'm going to take my time looking."

That should keep her at bay for a little while. Just because the truth had fifty shades of daydreams of getting fucked by Hot Dad, it didn't mean it wasn't the truth. She really did need to take her time. Only the best would do for her little lady. And she was starting to think Claire was on to something by keeping his nickname. It kept Xander at arm's length. *Hot dad, I mean hot dad.*

Sophie seemed to roll the idea around a bit. "I think that's a good idea." She seemed to understand this line of reasoning. "But what about that nice daddy we met in line? He seemed like a super nice daddy and even called me a princess. He called you a queen, Mommy!"

Clearly, Sophie belonged in the family. *A bunch of matchmakers, these ones.* She had to admit, the girl had good taste. She wanted to tell her daughter as much, but she didn't want them both getting their hopes up only to be let down. Again.

"I think you have a fair point, sweetie. Maybe we will see him again, and we will get to know him better." She needed to take things slow. Even if her hormones wanted to jump him every time he came close. She couldn't fall so fast and hard. She could end up getting hurt and drag Sophie down with her.

A week later, she was sitting on the counter in her kitchen and trying to type anything that would come to mind as she talked with her sister. "We don't need him."

"Right! Okay. Now, who's him and why don't we need him?" Claire was always ready for battle.

"I mean, it's been a week since we've seen him at the pickup line, and the guy was a no-show for Sophie. Therefore, we don't need him." She was ranting at this point, but she didn't care. It had been playing like a record each time he didn't show up. "The idea of waiting around and wondering where he's been or who he's been with. We don't need him!"

Claire started laughing at her, LAUGHING! "Oh, okay," she started sarcastically. "You don't need him because this week has been brutal without him, and you don't want to get attached to the guy you've become obsessed with?"

Now she's mocking me? What fresh hell is this?

"Oh, so now you're mocking me and my passing interest who, might I add, you wanted me to date! And now I'm the crazy obsessed one since I said I don't need him?"

"I'm sorry! I'm not saying you're obsessed. You still need to give him a chance."

"Those were your words, Claire. Obsessed."

"Pontius Pilate Mina," She let the words slide off her tongue. "Give me a break."

The phone line was quiet, but she was pretty sure she could hear silent wheezing on the other end.

"Well, now you're just being cruel."

Claire burst into a fit of laughter with her last jab, and she wasn't amused by it. Not one bit. Well, maybe a little.

"Damn you! Even when I'm pissed, you can make me laugh. I'm fucking up my story over here, and all I can think of is why hasn't he been around at the pickup line."

The phone line finally grew quiet as Claire's laughter died down enough for her to speak again.

"What the hell is wrong with me, Claire? I don't want to like the guy. Life would be easier without him. I just want to live my little life and not go through all that shit again." She was being honest. No matter how hard she wanted to jump his bones.

"You're human, Mina. No one wants to hurt again, but we were made to love and be loved. Especially you! You are the wildest, sweetest, kindest person I know. And after going through all that shit, you are the strongest and bravest."

Her breathing was getting back into her normal range as Mina reasoned with her words.

"And that kind of personality needs to be loved. It would be a shame to let all that go through life without someone else to go along for the ride." Damn, she loved her sister.

"Kyle is so lucky to have you." She meant it, too.

"He knows," she said before they both started laughing again.

"I'll be the brains, and you be humility, okay? Now, get back to work on your book. Gorgeous Alexander will be at the pickup line one of these days, and then we will see where this whole thing takes you both."

CHAPTER 14
Alexander

It was snowing, and he was worried he would miss her. He had no idea the ins and outs of her schedule. He just hoped he would hit the lottery today and see her.

Last week he missed her because of more fuck ups from Carl's shitty-ass work ethic. First, it was messing up his time with his daughter, and now it was messing with his time with his woman. Well, she wasn't his woman, but he sure as hell was planning on making her his. He was done fixing shit for Carl. He was all for "the good of the team," but it had gone on for far too long. He had to draw the line in the sand at some point, and there it was.

He was wrapping things up at work and needed to hustle so he could make it to the line early. He still didn't even know if she was single. A different last name said a whole hell of a lot, but it could also mean she was just remarried. That could explain the army of children. Either way, he was going to make more small talk today and find out. He hoped.

He sat in the crammed lot and watched as the other parents did the same, recounting his shitty driving on the way over. He was daydreaming about her again. Something he found himself doing all the time, even at the most inappropriate of moments. He was thinking about trailing fingers up her body and feeling the sensitive skin on the inside of her thighs right before he almost slammed into the back of another car.

The other guy looked fucking pissed, but he didn't give a shit. Hell, he was looking for a fight with all of the extra built-up tension he was holding onto these days. It seemed that his new found habit of jerking off into yesterday's t-shirts wasn't getting enough of his lust-induced anger out.

She always walked here, so he figured she must live close by. He needed to stay alert until it got closer to line up so he could time his walk up perfectly. No taking chances when there were a billion kids that could intervene and other dads that loved to linger around.

He felt the minutes go by in cinematic fashion as if the loud ticks of an old grandfather clock were ticking away, aggravating him further. Some parents even started to get out of their cars and quickly shuffled into a line on the fence while duty aides made their way to the crosswalk.

Another shitty day in paradise.

He shouldn't have been surprised with how quickly his day turned to shit, considering how far gone he was for this woman. He was like a man-child throwing a temper tantrum because his favorite toy was picked up by a friend. He may as well have been stomping his feet on the ground with how ridiculous he felt. *I need to find a fucking hobby.* As he tugged on his door handle and placed a grumpy foot on the asphalt, he noticed a woman with the same build getting out of a car that was parked at a house across the street from the school.

How could he not notice her, really? There were only a handful of women in the world with her body; he was sure of it. He had memorized every bit of hers that had been available to his eyes, from her dark brown hair down to her small feet, always bundled up in boots. Finding new little bits of her that were uncovered was a new pastime of his. Second nature, really.

He couldn't wait for the day when he could peel off her clothes piece by piece and really get to know every square inch with his mouth and his hands. *Fuck, if she's not single, I'm officially a certified stalker.*

With a hand on his truck door and his eyes on the prize, he was, quite literally, on the prowl. He tried to time his walk to be in pace with hers as she jogged over, hoping like hell he would be able to walk up to the same place in line when she did. He couldn't be too quick in case someone walked in between them, which wouldn't allow for conversation. All would be for nothing, so he tried to act like he dropped something on the ground. Then he had something in his boot and had to adjust it, then tie it... again.

At that point, he looked like he was just shuffling, and it was obvious he was trying to stalk someone at a glacial pace. *The world's worst-ever spy, over here.*

By the time he had gradually made it to the line, he was still too fast for her as she dodged school traffic and waited for the duty aide to allow her to cross. If it wasn't for the fact that she was heading right towards him and had to pass by to get to the end of the line, he would have missed his chance.

He didn't care if all the other parents behind him hated him for the rest of the year. He saw his only opening, and he was sure as hell going to take it.

"Oh hey, Mina! I saved you a spot in line." He had surprised her as he gestured with his hand for her to squeeze in right in front of him. When she looked up, she was surprised to see him.

She gave a little smile and looked around before asking, "Are you sure?" When she leaned in, he didn't care if she was going to tell him off or whisper something else. He was immediately wrapped up in her scent. The smell of vanilla invaded his senses, and he forgot what he even asked her. He could only think about how he wanted to eat her up in more ways than one. "Are you sure they won't kill you?" He was only about ninety percent sure she was teasing.

These parents seemed to be hard-core with line rules. Either way, he would go down for this. "I think I'll take my chances," he teased before he touched her lower back with feather-light pressure, guiding her next to him to her new place in line.

His hands ached to grab and squeeze just a bit lower. *Eyes back up, dirtbag. You're at your kid's school.* He was positive that everyone in the damn pickup line was staring at them for his brazen display of hitting on the hot mom.

"You're solo today. No little Sophie?" Did it sound stalker-ish that he remembered her little girl's name when she only told him once? Maybe someone else would play it cooler, but he would have memorized their social security numbers at this point.

"Not today, unfortunately. She had to go with her dad," she trailed off like she wasn't sure what to say. "My ex," she corrected. "So, it's just me." Just one more question before he was out of the woods.

"So, if your little girl is with her dad…" he gestured toward the line they were in. She looked over to where he was motioning and smiled.

"Oh, they aren't mine. I pick up my nieces and nephew to help my brother and sister. Both them and their spouses work a bunch and need some help on certain days. Since I'm home right now with Soph, I help out when they need me."

Somewhere, in some other life, I must have done something just shy of a miracle to deserve this opportunity.

"What about you? Does your wife work?" She was so stiff and awkward all of a sudden. Her eyes kept glancing to the floor as if she found her shoes more interesting than his face. Like she was embarrassed to ask or possibly be talking to a married man. "I only see you sometimes, so I figured your wife must grab your little one when you can't."

"Oh, my ex picks her up on days I'm working or can't make it. No wife for me. Not even with my ex."

There it was. Officially out there that they were both single. Although, he was hoping the last part didn't make it seem like he never wanted a wife. *Am I overthinking this?* He most likely was, but it was out there anyway because he didn't want her to think he had ever settled. Then again, maybe she was insulted? *Holy fuck, this is getting difficult, and we haven't even been on a date.*

Thankfully, there wasn't room for any silence to grow as the line moved forward fairly quickly.

"That's a lot of little girls you're in charge of. Does your nephew ever feel left out?" Maybe he sounded pushy, but he wasn't good at small talk, and the idea of being the only boy surrounded by that many girls sounded scary. He was looking for advice from a kid now, it seemed.

"He fits right in with them, and they learn so much of the rough and tumble side of being a boy from him. Honestly, I'm pretty surprised the little ladies haven't used any unicorn horns as prison shanks in some of their fights."

"Did you just say prison shank?" He couldn't contain the bark of laughter or the volume of his outburst. He had never heard a woman utter the words prison shank before, let alone when talking about kid's toys. He found her fucking hilarious. He couldn't care less about the current looks they were getting from the other people in line.

Her cheeks turned the cutest shade of pink, and her hand flew over her mouth in disbelief she let that word pass her lips to an otherwise stranger. But it didn't take long before she started laughing, too.

Her nerves visibly melted off as he struggled to catch his breath. She bit her tongue between her teeth in a wicked grin that lit up her whole face. She was trouble. A good kind of trouble.

"Amelia's dad!" *Fuck. Did the line move faster these days?* He felt like a damn hourglass was set up, and the last few specs of sand were slipping away in front of him. He knew the drill for what her pick-up was like now, and he had no intention of missing another chance.

Amelia ran over to him, immediately filling him in on her day, until she saw what was playing out in front of her. She grew quiet, eyeing them with speculation written all over her face. The cluster of kids Mina picked up were all making their way over, and she was about to say something before he interrupted her.

"Maybe I should get your number so we can get the kids together for a play date. I think your niece is the same age as my Amelia." *Did I really just ask for a play date through her niece? Who does this shit?*

She looked a bit embarrassed, clearly never having been hit on at the school pickup line before. He was a rake, as his sister-in-law would call him, *fucking Bridgerton.* But he couldn't give a shit at this point. He would lose it if he had to go another day, not knowing if he stood a chance with her.

After what seemed like the longest thirty seconds of his life, she looked like she was about to say no. He could tell she was rolling the idea around in her head as she glanced around nervously. They were somewhat holding up the line with this un-conventional play date invitation. It was like a traffic jam on an escalator. Mina stood stalk still while someone bumped her from behind. The play went on repeat until he gently grabbed her by the elbow and led her and the army of children to the side.

He was sure the glares had turned to curious stares, well on his way to becoming the gossip of the week, but he didn't care. This was his shot and he had to take it.

"Yeah, of course. We should definitely get the girls together." She seemed to just want to get the hell out of Dodge and away from all the prying eyes, but he would take it. After she gave him her number, they said quick goodbyes and headed in their respective directions with the kids in tow.

When was the last time he had to ask for a woman's number? He couldn't remember. Maybe that was his sign that all the crazy ones are the type to ask men for their numbers instead of vice versa. When he thought about it for a second, Lauren had asked a waitress for his name after he left a restaurant and hunted him down on Facebook. Then there was Kara, who asked his friend for his number and asked him out. *I'll be damned, I'm onto something.*

Then there were Nicki and Rose, who asked him out while at bars downtown. It was official, he would need to write that one down in case he had a son one day. *Always pursue the ones you want, and stay away from the rest.*

He watched her walk away like she was on the set of a movie and the scene called for a slow-motion clip. The snowflakes fell like feathers to the ground as she held gloves with a little girl and skipped across the crosswalk. She chatted with the crossing guard and tossed her hair to the side as she looked back to make sure all the children were following her like a mother goose and her goslings.

Her nose was slightly red from the cold, her head was under a beanie, and despite the layers of warmth trying to hide her, she was the most beautiful sight he had ever seen. He wished he could be the one to help her out of that big coat. The one to rip her beanie off and toss it onto the mud room floor while the kids unloaded their bags and boots. She was the kind of pipe dream guys in high school dreamt about, but now he was the one wishing on every last damn star for it to turn into something.

There was no point in wasting time now that he had her number. If he wanted her, he was going to have to chase her. He took one more glance to make a mental note of the sight of her in those leggings and boots with her beanie on. He could think about that later in the shower… wearing nothing else.

But right now, he had to figure out how to approach this. Should he ask her out? Should he pretend to want a play date and then ask her out before it ever happens? Being honest with himself, he would like play dates for his daughter, but everyone would know they would be complete bullshit. He wanted her number, and he got it. It was time to cut the crap and make his move.

After he got Amelia home and set her up with crafts to keep her busy, he tried to find the courage to text her. What the fuck would he say? *Thanks for being the star of my spank bank? Oh, how about I've thought about you naked about every other minute since I spotted you this past summer? Just your local stalker.* All the tension from thinking about her was getting him worked up in other ways, and now he had two problems he had to deal with. He used to control his barbaric habits and only fuck women rather than jerk off. It had never been an issue because the longest stretch he ever had was two weeks before getting laid again. But she was a whole new level of lust. He couldn't go more than half a day without needing to rub one out. And God, that was always the highlight of his day since he had seen her. Never had anyone made him cum so fucking hard when they hadn't even touched yet.

"What are you thinking of?" The question jolted him back to the present and back to the reality that his little girl was sitting across from him.

"What do you mean, honey?" He tried to play it cool, but he was just dreaming about sex across the table from his daughter. Seeing the confusion on her face gave him the immediate rush of standing under a cold shower.

"You look super confused." He could keep Mina to himself, but he really didn't want to. He needed advice, and he wasn't ashamed if it had to come from his eight-year-old daughter. She may be a girl now but one day she would have the brain of a woman. That had to count for something when asking for advice.

"Well, to be honest. I am a bit stumped." He dove right in and spared no details of his pathetic love for a woman he didn't even know. From where he first saw her to how today was the first time he had the opportunity to get her number. He was shameless for this woman, and he wanted his daughter on his team, rooting him on. He hoped like hell she wouldn't laugh at him, and to his surprise, she was excited for him.

"We have a lot of work cut out for us, Dad." He wasn't sure if he should be offended or proud that she knew Mina was out of his league. "But I think we can do it!" Either way, he decided he was grateful he had a girl on his team, helping him navigate the female mind and grateful his daughter was happy for him to find someone to love.

His little girl was chatting up a storm and mapping it all out while he looked on with pride. The stars seemed to line up, and maybe luck was on his side. *All right, game time.*

CHAPTER 15
Mina

Unknown: It was really nice talking to you again today. Can't wait to get the girls together.

Mina: Same! It was great talking to you

It had only been an hour since grabbing the kids, and he had texted her. It had to be a good sign, and she was smiling despite herself. Yet, as soon as her smile spread over her lips, she felt her stomach sink.

It wasn't lost on her that the police patrol car was driving quite slowly past the line when she was talking to Xander. She really needed to figure out how to make Evan stop following her. It was stalking and harassment, and she was growing tired of it more and more by the day. But for the time being, everyone was home, and the older ones were pretty much babysitting the little ones. She was free to act like a lovesick teenager before her sisters came home to collect their children.

She realized she was staring at her phone, willing it to ping. The same person who didn't want to fall in love or date because she was done with matters of the opposite sex was now waiting on a text from a relative stranger. Just the other day she believed all men were cheaters, or liars. Someone who would let you down, or someone who wanted to push you down in every meaning of the word.

Except Xander didn't seem like he would fit into any one of those categories. He seemed pretty fucking dreamy. She wanted to focus all her time and attention on Sophie while she had to deal with her ex. She wasn't looking for anything. She had a full life, or so she kept telling herself. But she couldn't deny that her hand was itching to hold his, and she wanted to see him walk through the door and talk to her about Sophie's feather boa purse again.

Was she being crazy? She had too much baggage to want to bring in someone else, but she didn't care right now. Carefree Mina didn't care about any of it, so maybe he wouldn't, either?

Hot Dad: While we try and figure out
schedules, I think we should go out first.
Maybe I can take you to dinner next week?

Yes, she had the audacity to use Claire's nickname for him. She would take the eye roll from God. That would have to take a back seat to what just came across her screen. What she had been hoping and praying for, at least in private. He was a Greek God, and she was just her.

What are his intentions? Why does he want to date a single mother who was someone else's trash?

She had to remind herself to stop thinking of herself in that way. Evan did that, and she wasn't going to stand for it anymore.

Not if she could help it. She had to break out of her comfort zone, if only to stop believing she wasn't worthy of men.

Mina: That would be nice. What did you have in mind?

Hot Dad: Not sure. What type of food do you like? There is a lot that goes into planning a date, especially when one wants to impress the woman thoroughly.

She couldn't help but giggle. *Impress me thoroughly.* Somehow he made choosing a restaurant sound sexual. Maybe he was just as smitten as she was.

Next week was going to seem like a lifetime away, but it was probably for the best. She needed to do some major self-care in the meantime. She gave herself a once over and thought about shaving her legs and putting some more effort into her nails. She would also need to pluck her eyebrows and maybe buy a new wardrobe. Her leggings and oversized sweatshirts were looking a bit rough these days. She was pretty positive that every single one of them had a hole in the upper inner thigh area. *My thighs love each other, what can I say?* She also figured that it was someone else's fault if they looked there, but that was the old and slightly grumpy version of her. She needed to look like she cared. She was also getting some freezing breezes passing through some sensitive areas, and given the time of year, it wasn't pleasant.

Mina: Hmm I love food in general. We live in a pretty magical place, so I don't think you will have trouble impressing.

Hot Dad: Can I text you later? I have
to get some work done, but I
would love to talk more.

Mina: Of course! Can't wait.

She really couldn't. She didn't want to admit how much she looked forward to talking to this man. To Alexander.

He was gorgeous and nice. Seemed to have a good sense of humor and seemed like a great dad. *How had this man managed to stay single all this time?* Maybe that was the wrong question to ask herself. Down the rabbit hole she went, and she was spiraling pretty quickly. What if he just wanted to use her for something? She had no idea what that would be, but she would need to figure it out.

"Mommy!" Steph yelled as Beth walked through the door, having gotten home early. Of course, she would need to talk to someone else about it.

They would have their doubts about his intentions, too, wouldn't they? How could a man that perfect have a child, be understanding, look like he stepped out of an issue of GQ and still not have a woman? He must be a pyscho. Or the devil. Or possibly a sexual deviant... that's not helping. That was it. She cracked the code, and now it was depressing.

"Hey, lady." She tried to sound normal, but Beth could see right through her. She was a terrible liar. Not a bad thing, but just not so great when one was trying to mask her emotions.

"What's wrong with you?" Beth's question was enough to make her spill the beans, but Steph beat her to it.

"Mom, auntie Mina was getting a guy's number in the middle of the pickup line. Everyone was watching them. It was kinda weird." Beth's jaw nearly dropped to the floor and her eyes grew three times their size. Steph, on the other hand, just stood there, smiling and glancing back and forth between her aunt and mom.

"What? I didn't ask for anyone's number! He asked for

mine!" She knew she probably sounded childish, but she had to clear the air. The last thing she wanted was for them to think their auntie was some little floozy prancing around school pickup lines looking for a single dad. It was the exact reason she would always wear her crappy old clothes and look down when she went everywhere. That and she just wore her crappy clothes most days because she liked them, but that was honestly beside the point. She didn't ask for it.

"So, he asked for your number? What did he say?" Beth was all ears. *Of course she is. She's a whore for gossip, too.*

"Well, we were about to leave when he said that he wanted to get the girls together for a play date." Beth thought about it for a second before scrunching her forehead.

"Which girls? You don't even have Sophie today."

"I know. He asked for my number for a play date with Steph, Kate and Amelia, who is his little girl." To her delight, this one made Beth laugh out loud and give a little snort she couldn't hold in.

"He wanted to go out with you so bad that he asked for a play date." She paused. "With a kid that's not even yours?" She kept on laughing, and it didn't take long for Mina to join in. It was pretty ridiculous when she thought about it. The man had some balls to ask her out, on a play date with someone else's kid. Holding up the school pickup, no less.

"What's so funny?" Claire had snuck in without them hearing.

"The dreamy and smooth Alexander asked Mina out." Beth's cheeks were bright with laughter.

"I think I'm missing something here. Do we hate him all of a sudden? Why is this a joke?" Claire was so confused.

Beth gathered herself. "A play date with our girls." She gestured between the two women. "So apparently, we will be going on the date and not Mina!" Beth kept up her little amusement while Mina lost hers.

"Ha Ha. Very funny. Just a second ago, you were saying he wanted to date me so bad that he asked your kid to a playdate.

Now I'm the loser on the sidelines. This is going great." Mina gave Claire a look with SOS written all over it.

"So, tell me how he asked you out, sis." Claire pulled her scarf off and sat down at the now infamous barstools for her weekly dose of gossip. Coffees in hand, Claire was ready to hear the scoop. It was the lifeblood between the twins. Between the late nights of Mina staying up because her crazy ex terrified her or Claire working all night at the hospital, they needed it like they needed water.

A long holiday season was in store for her, and she felt for her sister. The idea of a play date actually seemed like a good idea. Lord knew the woman could use a break. Mina explained the meandering course of her proposed date before filling them in on her most recent cop car sighting. The level of exhaustion she felt could rival her sisters as her anxiety took hold of her worries about the stalking and the ulterior motive that could be behind the date.

"All right, so what do you think it is?" She took a deep breath and prepared herself for the worst. "Could he be after my money or a pedophile after Soph?" It was as if she had turned into a comedian. They both laughed with such intensity that it almost scared her. *Again, with the ugly laugh. These two.*

"What is with you both? It's flattering, but there must be a reason he's after me and Sophie. He's gorgeous, and I guess I'm cute, but I'm not on that level of cuteness. So, what is it? I'm serious, guys, I need your help, and I'm not in the mood to have my ego stroked or to be messed with. I'm kind of over this all, and I don't want to be jerked around."

"Oh honey," Beth started. "How is it that you are that blind? Do you not know?" She took a minute to collect herself from her lasting giggles.

"You're a ten. Like a total catch. You've got it all." Other than wanting to hug her sister-in-law, she was embarrassed because she just didn't believe this bullshit, and she didn't want them to sugarcoat anything. She needed to hear the hard parts now, so she didn't get too caught up in all this.

"Look, I don't need you guys to try and make me feel good just so I can get out of the house and go on a date. I want to hear all the shitty stuff now, because then I won't get my heart trampled on by Mr. Dreamy. I know I don't have much money, but I have all the savings from the divorce, and maybe he knows about it. Maybe to a doctor, it's not much, but it's the savings that will support me and Sophie."

Claire nodded, noting her jab. "I understand where you're coming from with the money thing. But we aren't laughing at the size of your account. Just the idea that he would want you for your money. The guy clearly likes you, Mina, and it has nothing to do with money."

They gave her intent stares, willing her to understand, but she wasn't having it.

"You've heard about those scam artists on TV. They try to make women feel wanted only to steal their money. Or what if he is some sick pedophile or murderer, and he's after his next victim?" She was serious, which made them break down all over again. "You guys are so mean! God damnit, where is a pillow I can throw at your two!" The laughs just morphed into ugly snorts and wheezing as Steph and Kate taddled on their auntie Mina for cussing.

"Oh my God, Mina! Will you knock it off!" Claire was laughing, but she was annoyed with her sister and it was obvious. "You're a damn ten with perfect tits and a bubble butt that screams for men to touch it. Why on earth do you think you are some decrepit old maid with a train full of baggage?"

Maybe they were right, but she couldn't help it. She had another man's baby, and then he left her for a younger woman. The whore was able to keep her body intact and steal her husband and daughter. Who wouldn't feel like they had a ton of baggage with all that mess? She wasn't competing with her so she shouldn't care, but damn her, she did.

"Aren't men weirded out about sleeping with a woman who's

had a baby? Like a baby that he wasn't part of making?" She thought it was a legitimate question, while the other women gave her a mean side eye.

These fuckers.

"Mina, your vagina isn't scary. He would totally still fuck you." Claire seemed to miss the point here.

"Okay, I never said my vagina was scary. Jesus, Claire. I was just saying, what if he's grossed out that I birthed another man's baby?"

"Let me tell you something about men," Claire started. "They don't give a fuck." She made sure to enunciate each word to drive home the whole point she was after. "Mina honestly, your vagina isn't scary, and you are totally hot and fuckable. I know a shit ton of single men at the hospital that want you, but I'm not a monster and would never push men on you. But in short, you have a hot body, and you're a catch. So stop overthinking this. Men want ya, sis. So own it."

"First of all, thank you. Second, why do you keep saying my vagina isn't scary? I never said it was!"

Just then, the door to the garage shut, and Jared walked in. "Why are you talking about Mina's vag, and why the hell is it scary?" He looked so confused and disgusted at the same time.

"See! You need to stop saying that! I get what you're saying, so thank you. Let's talk about this later." Mina raised her eyebrows and then looked in Jared's direction so they would follow her eyes and catch a hint.

"Oh my God," Beth groaned. "We are all adults. Just because he's your brother doesn't mean he shouldn't know what's going on, and he obviously knows you're fuckable. He had to fend off the football team for you two. I think he gets it."

He looked concerned and confused at the same time. "What did I miss? But if it's seriously about Mina's vag, I'm out." Beth had a point. He already knew guys had interest. It just didn't seem like he would care when speaking of his little sister's dating life. Although, this was Jared she was thinking of. He was the kindest brother anyone could ask for, and after the hell she went through, he had become especially protective over Mina.

"Mystery man held up the line to get Mina's number. But the best part was that Cassanova asked for a play date with our daughter since she's the same age as his."

"And mine!" Claire chimed in. "Let's not forget that Kate could be in this plot." Claire continued to find this hilarious. Meanwhile, Mina was worried this was just for the chase, and he would want back to his bachelor lifestyle after he got what he wanted. Back to what was most likely a parade of women, corporate calls and endless fancy trips for work. She could overthink the shit out of this, but now her brother was intruding on her thoughts with some thoughts of his own.

"Okay, hold on. Who the hell are we talking about? The guy that talked about the scarf thing"

"Feather boa purse strap," they all said in unison.

"Alright, alright. Holy shit, you three! So he asked for your number? But used our kids in order to get it?" Jared chuckled. "Smart man. That's one way of getting a single mom's number without scaring her off."

Beth shot him a look of annoyance as she held up her hands in frustration, needing to know what this all meant. As if he had some sort of code figured out because he was a guy.

"What? It's not like I know what the man is thinking. But he better be prepared to go through me and Kyle. I'm not going to have some asshole getting close to my sister again."

That's the spirit. He used to be the one to trust so easily, but now he knew better. She loved him so much.

"Well, on that happy note, I better get going. I have some texting to do, and I need to find out if Mr. Alexander McCade is a psychopath." Humor can mask a lot, and for now, it continued to mask her fears. Asshole, psycho, pedophile… All legitimate possibilities in her mind, but she didn't have time for that right now. She wanted to be a normal person and maybe just get excited for a hot minute before she put her walls back up and possibly turned frosty toward the man. She also needed to get home and work on her book. The steamy part of her book, to be exact, and there was a hot dad she had in mind for the starring role.

The house always felt so empty without Sophie, but she was trying, really trying to make her time alone seem less lonely these days.

She would play music loud, make delicious food that made the house smell like a hug and take the time to work out or work on her book. Although nothing compared to the pitter patter of little feet and the constant attention her daughter required of her, somehow, the loneliness eased when she thought about Alexander.

His booming laughter today was something she had only read about. *How can a laugh tell you so many things about a person?* He seemed so genuine, kind and fully present with her every word. So interested in her that it felt surreal. Somehow, in the few times she had heard it, his laugh felt like home. Like hers, actually.

She walked over to the window to check on the wildlife outside and to get out of her own head. The deer had left her yard and the sun had already set. It was a chilly night in Kings Ranch at a mere eighteen degrees with the temperature still dropping. The low was supposed to hit thirteen.

As cold as it was outside, her cottage felt like a cozy corner of the world, especially once the fire was going and her tree was lit up. It really was the most wonderful time of the year. With Lupe in her cozy sweater, she cuddled up next to her on the couch and draped them in a fleece blanket.

There was no sense in wasting a perfect night of snuggling just because she didn't have a man to do it with. Lupe snored as if she agreed. *Always my loyal sidekick.*

The book was slowly coming along, and she was knee-deep in a sex scene between the two main characters. Having never written a book before, let alone a spicy one, she discovered that those kinds of scenes called for more than she imagined.

An intensity that rivaled watching the act play out on a screen. She had to be descriptive with their hands, their breathing and how it drove them close…to many things. She was no more than an hour in before she found herself all worked up with nowhere to go. *What is it called when you're crabby from going so long without sex?* She had been hangry many times. *Am I sangry? Is that a thing?*

Writing this book may have been a bad choice if she was always going to end up this angsty when she needed to get her work done. Maybe she should look into writing self-help books on how not to murder your ex-husband. She was a pro at that one. Or perhaps she should get into knitting. Anything, at this point, would help as long as she could just stop feeling so hot and bothered. How long had it been since she'd had sex? A year?

She tried to do some mental gymnastics of the timeline. She hadn't slept with Evan in over a year, she was positive on that one. So there it was. At least a year.

She had a make-out session with a hot guy who worked with Kyle, but she thanked her lucky stars she pushed him off of her before it went further. Sex would be great, but not with a playboy who only wanted a booty call. *Fuck. Maybe I should have been sluttier back in the day.*

She had only had sex with her ex-husband, and now she regretted having literally no experience otherwise. Does that make her even more of a loser? She was divorced with a child and had only slept with one person. *Screams worldly.*

Once again, she had been thrown into a harsh memory of Evan relaying the disgusting notion that men preyed on single moms. *They're a bunch of smart assholes.*

She hated to admit it was a smart move on their part because that was exactly the boat she was sitting in right now. She had no time and interest in dividing her attention between her daughter and wanting a sex life. *Sex is meant to be built up. Meant to be scandalously delicious with every kiss and touch leading up to hands all over and being consumed with moaning and….* There she went again. It was pointless, and she knew it.

Letting out a huff, she put the laptop to the side and grabbed for the remote. *I should turn into a slutty single mom.* She may not seriously consider it, but if she did, at least she would never be sexually frustrated. She would also have no dignity, but hey, she wasn't judging herself.

She was on her own and literally not even left to her own devices because she didn't own a vibrator. She needed a Rom/Com or a holiday read. Just something happy and stupidly fake so she could forget the fact that she needed sex to survive.

She flipped through Netflix and decided on her favorite classic holiday movie. *It's a Wonderful Life*. Nothing like George Bailey running through a small town screaming Merry Christmas to get her out of her slump. That and the fact that an angel narrated the movie, so she was forced to get her mind out of the gutter.

The ping on her phone rang out into her tiny living room and sounded like a little bell from the movie. She looked down at the screen, expecting more questions from Claire, when his name popped up instead, and she gasped. How did she forget he told her he would text? She gave a little squeal, followed immediately by an eye roll.

Squealing. Really? How old am I?

But she couldn't help it. It was him. He said he had some work to do and that he would text back, but with how random she saw him and how inconsistent their conversations were, she kind of didn't believe him. But here he was, texting her and suddenly, she couldn't care less about the movie and her hopes of celibacy.

The devil on her shoulder was back, and she wanted to get fucked by the hot dad.

CHAPTER 16
Alexander

Teresa had been her usual self, and he felt like a gigantic asshole for going out to break it off with her. Apparently, she was under the impression that they were possibly going somewhere in their relationship. He wasn't sure how she could think such a thing when she regularly called just for sex. He was already kicking himself that he forgot about the date they had planned, but it was perfect to tie things up with a neat little bow.

He had no intention of staying out long. Now that he actually had Mina's number and confirmed she was single, he had planned to tell her over the phone, but when he made the call, she told him she would be early for their dinner.

The one he fucking forgot.

Either way, it was the perfect opportunity to cut ties with Teresa, so he tried to make it quick and told her as soon as they ordered drinks. In fact, he tried to get away with just appetizers, but the damn woman wanted a meal as if it were the last supper. Like eating together after a breakup was a totally normal thing to do.

The dinner had been painful. He kept wondering how he had fucked this woman multiple times when she was so dense. She even asked if he wanted to go back to her place for some break-up sex. He wanted to shake her shoulders and tell her not to let men treat her like he had because she was clearly alright with being used solely for sex.

As she rambled on through dinner, he mentally berated himself at the thought of other men treating his sister the same way he had been going through women his whole life.

For the first time ever, he was putting all other women to the side and putting all his eggs in one basket. Betting on one thing. He barely got her number, but he felt all in. To say things had moved fast with Mina was an understatement. He was a changed man from the moment he locked eyes on his target, and this date was confirmation of everything he had been feeling since that day in Walmart all those months ago.

Mina was different.

After the date, he couldn't help from speeding into the driveway and nearly slipping on the ice as he hastily made his way up the garage steps and into his house. The little mud room didn't know what hit it when he threw his boots off and flung his jacket in the general direction. He would deal with cleanup later. He didn't know if his coat was a snowy mess mixed with his boots, but he didn't care.

He grabbed a log, made a roaring fire and then sat back on the couch and went to work texting Mina. The night had been long enough having to put up with the cold weather and uninteresting company. Mina was what he wanted, and once he had gotten home, the anticipation of texting her had almost killed him. With only the crackling of the firewood humming in the background, he got to work.

Xander: Are you still up?

Ha! That's comical. It's barely eight-thirty. The date had felt like hours.

Mina: Yup! How was work?

God, he felt like such a dick. He had to remind himself that it was all in the name of breaking it off with that woman. No attachments. He could have easily slept with this one, too and wouldn't have had to feel guilty or even tell her. But he would have because he knew there was something more. Something there that could be incredible if he just doesn't fuck this up.

Xander: Eh, work was work. How was your day?

Mina: Uneventful. Speaking of … what is it that you do? You always seem stuck to your phone.

Xander: Yeah, feels like I'm chained to the damn thing. I work for Alpine Liquor and Brew. Have you heard of them?

He debated telling her his salary, his pension status and how much he had in his 401K. To say he wanted her to stay for the money wouldn't be accurate, but he was willing to entice her with everything he had. *Bring on the shallow and corrupt methods to trap her*. Sure he was only half kidding, but he would pull any card to get a winning hand. He wanted her to know she could be taken care of, as sexist as it sounded. He was proud of the fact that he found someone he not only wanted to take care of but also had the means to do it.

Mina: Yup! Sounds exciting. Your parties must be ragers

Xander: Used to be. Then I had a kid and Amelia insists on carding at the door 🙄

As the conversation went on, he realized how easy it was with Mina. Like he had known her his entire life. Or better yet, like he was dying to know someone like her his entire life.

She was smart, with a master's degree in teaching. She was funny and could recite one-liners better than any comedian, and she could even talk football like his college buddies. Having been around it her whole life with her dad and uncles coaching the sport, she was probably more familiar with the game than he was. She was like one of the guys but sexy, hilarious and down to earth. To top it off, she had eyes for him. The idea was making him lose his mind.

With the fire roaring, he sat there on the couch all night, not caring about the time or about work in the morning. The world could wait. He just wanted this moment with her.

As the week inched on, their conversations got riskier and more distracting. Work and any semblance of life outside of it, took a hit, but things with “text Mina” were going great.

The constant texts throughout his day were what kept him going. If little hints about her life were his daily doses of medicine, the innuendos and her spicy sense of humor were his drug.

They texted throughout each day constantly about everything and anything in their lives. It got down right dirty at times and he was losing his mind to try and stay focused on anything outside of Mina.

Once he found out that she had only slept with her ex-husband, it was game over for him. All the things that no other man had done to her crossed his mind daily. Daily, as in every other minute of every hour throughout the day. She hadn’t asked him how many women he had been with…yet. But she had to have known how notorious bachelors could be. He was hoping she would understand.

He had about twenty years of fucking under his belt, and although he wasn’t ashamed, he didn’t exactly want to divulge that information either. She would have to understand that those were the “others” and that she was “the one.”

He was pretty positive that he couldn’t explain the workings of a man’s mind without her wanting to punch him in the throat. How could he explain that pussy was sometimes just pussy, and a man could find even the tiniest detail of a woman attractive to get hard and fuck?

He knew society wasn’t fair to women. Hell, he took a Women’s Studies class in college, thinking he could skate by and hit on girls. All he ended up doing was feeling like shit and hating himself by the end of it. He didn’t want to be the one to tell her that sex could often mean nothing more than wanting to get laid. He had a sister, and he had nightmares of men like him trying to talk to her while she was away at college.

Women wouldn’t understand, and if they did, he was positive those weren’t the ones you could bring home to meet your mother. Fuck the double standard bullshit, it was the truth. The things that go through a guy’s mind would shock most women. He was positive that the things that went through his mind would make her run for the hills. She would be disgusted with him and men in general. He sounded like a pig to himself. It was just how men were built.

Xander: How long did you make
your ex wait?

Was it obvious that he couldn't stop thinking of getting her naked? Sure, he could imagine a million different ways her body could turn him on with clothes, but the idea of having her naked in his own bed made him go to the dirtiest places and made his hands ache with the need to touch her. Or grip his cock so he could release the same built-up tension that plagued him daily now that she had come into his life. It was only getting harder to wait until next week for their date. He already had to jack off twice a day to keep his sanity. This woman would be the end of him.

Mina: Three months…I was a senior
in HS

He let out a pained groan. Although he was sure he would die if he had to wait that long, he was relieved. He loved knowing she didn't rush into it. Even if that meant he would have to resort to fucking his hand three times a day. He was a patient man, and sure as hell, he was going to find out soon just how patient he was capable of being. Until he heard the words come from her own mouth that she wanted him, he was going to keep it locked down. God, he wanted her to say it. *Maybe in that beautiful mouth and those plump lips…*

Xander: What are you up to on
Saturday morning?

His thumbs typed it before he processed the question. He had to figure out a date asap, and waiting until next week would literally kill him. He needed to take this woman to breakfast, lunch or dinner. Anything as long as she was there.

Mina: Nothing after 8am. You?
Nice change of topic btw. Did I
scare the virginal boy in you?

Xander: Wanna move our date up?

He was supposed to be in Denver for Tyler's annual holiday party, but he couldn't give a shit about his friends right now. He had no plans on taking her to bed, but that didn't mean he couldn't just stare at her from across a booth.

He felt like a barbarian. He could sate his lust by just staring at her like some mindless fool from the opposite side of a booth. *Lord, help me*.

Xander: I also need to go to
church with your last
confession.

Xander: I'll pray for your
sins 😉

The three little dots showed up on the screen, and he had never wanted them to be replaced with words so fast in his life. Sure, the date was planned for four days away, but he couldn't wait any longer. He wanted her, plain and simple. A day sounded better than four, and he was willing to move mountains for this woman, let alone a holiday party.

Mina : I'm listening and thanking
you for your prayers.

Mina : Should I even ask how long you waited last time?

Xander: Breakfast at 8:30?

Xander: And don't bother, I don't remember her name.

Xander: You should probably start praying for my sins too.

Mina : 8:30 it is

Mina : And noted. Getting on my knees right now

Xander: ☠️

CHAPTER 17
Mina

The date was set and she instantly had to remind herself she was still young. Not some haggard woman who's kept herself in a cave since she became single, though it wasn't like she was really going out of her way to change up her leggings and oversized sweatshirt routine either.

Did she even own jeans anymore? Saturday may be the day when she had to rejoin society and wear adult clothes, real clothes. Clothes that didn't double as loungewear when she really didn't feel like peeling them off after a long cuddle session with Lupe.

I'm not an old maid. I'm just a twenty-eight-year-old divorced single mother. That line of thinking didn't exactly stir confidence and she went right back into trying to think of what would make her feel a bit more herself. Maybe a fresh haircut? *It has been about a year...* Yup, she definitely needed to pluck her eyebrows and shave her legs, even though it was winter and no one would be touching her legs…among other things.

The man was a walking sex symbol, so she needed to feel confident. Looking in the mirror, she settled on a plan to make it all happen.

"Why does Jared have a stick up his ass?" This was not the conversation she was planning on having the morning of her date. Fifteen minutes before Xander was supposed to pick her up, to be more precise.

"He thinks this guy sounds a bit much. With the fake playdate and then switching it to a date but then moving it up, I think he's just worried about you. I told him to calm the fuck down, but apparently, you might be his favorite sister. He has some protective shit he's going through hardcore right now. Let's give the guy a break." Claire was trying to calm Mina down after she got a text from her brother saying he wasn't sure the date would be a good idea. She knew he was just worried for her, but it was just a date.

Why on earth is he getting so worked up over a date?

"Besides ignoring Jared, Mom and I think that maybe you should look for any red flags about this guy. Single, at his age, and with a great job, it makes us wonder. Not that you aren't wonderful on your own!" She was backtracking, and Mina hated how everyone was so hot and cold about her dating. One minute they were all forcing her to get out more, and the second someone asked her out, they wanted her to go back into hiding.

"We just want to make sure you don't end up with a crazy narcissist." She trailed off. "Again."

"Okay, you people act like I can spot this shit on the first date. What am I supposed to do? And how do you know he has a great job?" She tried to calm her nerves as she changed her outfit for the sixth time in the span of four minutes.

Xander was scheduled to be there any minute, yet there she was, half dressed and questioning every life choice she had made to get her here. Minutes from going on a date with a man she admits to have fallen for against her aversion to men, and now she had to try and calm her family's nerves along with her own.

"You all wanted me to go out! Now you want me to stay in? And seriously, are you guys stalking him online? I barely told you the position he told me about." *I could use some tequila right about now.*

"Nothing much, we just looked online, and to say the guy makes great money is an understatement." Well, that was just great. Now her family was stalking the guy and looking into his salary. "Ignore Jared. Maybe just ask him casually if he's on any medications as you order your breakfast."

Mina rubbed her temples. "You want me to casually ask him if he is on any medications? Are you insane? I'm shocked you didn't dig that one up on your own! Do you want me to finish the job and ask for his tax returns as well?"

"I didn't say you have to ask him outright!" Convenient that she found herself hilarious in this moment. "Me and mom were just saying that maybe you can weave it into the conversation. Like, oh my God you're so hot, it must take work to keep up this body. Do you have a gym membership or perhaps, a regular appointment with a psychiatrist?" She waffled her words. Struggling to keep a coherent strategy. "You know, subterfuge. Or maybe offer him water before his meal and mention it's in case he needs to take his meds. Tell him men in his age group should take vitamins or something."

Her whole life seemed to be a joke to her sister at this point. She was about to scold or cuss her out for the terrible advice just as she heard a knock at the door. She may have had a slight headache, but she sure as hell loved how hilarious and ridiculous her family was.

"All right, fairy godmother from hell. I think that's him at the door. I'll do my best to ask about any major mental issues in his family as well as if he has herpes of the ass. Does that work you and mom?"

Claire snorted as she gave her goodbyes, and Mina squeezed on her pants in time to open the door, catching him with his hand in the air, ready to knock again.

"Hi!" *Good grief, he's good looking. How did I forget this?*

"Come on in. I'm just finishing up getting ready." He was doing it again, his whole GQ meets lumberjack vibe. He smiled and gave her a warm hug, greeting her with a good morning that made her insides swoon.

She was sure she could feel herself melt as she held the door open just enough for him to pass through. Somehow her door frame seemed too tiny for those broad shoulders, and she had the strongest urge to reach out and slide her hand across them as he walked past.

She showed him the couch, allowing him to lead the way so she could eye him without judgment.

"I'll just be a minute!" Then, she headed back to her room for a last minute once over. "Feel free to walk around and get comfortable."

She could hear his shoes make the hardwoods creek as he walked about. She felt inadequate now knowing his financial status, but she couldn't change her clothes without him noticing and she couldn't change anything else either. She glanced in the mirror, surprised that she actually liked what she saw. She was wearing a light eye shadow that brought out her brown eyes, and her mascara had her lashes looking long and full. Although her jeans were tight, her cream-colored cropped sweater had a button-down front and was tucked in to give her the look she was going for, complete with boots. *Suck it up, buttercup. These jeans make your ass look great. Let's just hope they don't rip.*

With no more pep talks left to give, she headed back down the hallway and caught the sex symbol as he eyed her gallery wall in private.

"See anyone you know?" She caught him as he leaned over

to take a closer look at a picture of her entire family. All her siblings, their children complete with her parents in the middle. The family they created surrounded them on their favorite bench on their property. It was her most treasured picture.

"I do, actually. I think I've seen your sister-in-law a couple of times in the pickup line. And, of course, the little lady and yourself." As he straightened himself, he smiled and walked over toward Mina before he paused, looking nervous. "Thanks for changing plans and coming out with me this morning. I didn't think I could make it to next week."

She loved his honesty and the fact that he couldn't wait because if she were honest with herself, she couldn't either. "Of course! I didn't have plans, you did. So, thank you for changing them for me. Next week would have seemed like a lifetime away."

They both laughed nervously, unsure where to go next in their conversation just as Lupe came out of the bedroom and started bounding over to Xander as if she'd known him her whole life. *Well, well, well.*

"She's adorable. It's a she, right?" They seemed like two peas in a pod as he knelt down to scoop up Lupe. The dog had literally never acted like this with a stranger before, and it baffled and intrigued Mina to no end.

"Yeah, this is Lupe. My trusty sidekick when Sophie's gone." *She used to be an annoying guard dog.* This man seemed to have charmed her as well.

"Well, it's nice to meet you too, Lupe." As he placed her plump dog back on the ground, he somehow managed to get hotter with that simple act. Men made her weak when they were animal lovers and good fathers. Her uterus was signing over its rights to him as she stood there. She may have believed that she was done having babies, but not where this man was concerned. She was ready to have ten of his babies if he wanted her to.

"Shall we?" He gently placed his hand on the small of her back as he motioned for her to lead the way out the front door.

Was it just her, or did his hand on her lower back do things to him too? It was a gentlemanly move, but it was the sexiest thing anyone had ever done to her.

She walked for the door as she internally scolded herself. She should definitely have gone on some test run dates and then built herself up to this. She needed to go through the JV guys before expecting to keep up with this gorgeous man because he had varsity written all over his beautiful face.

CHAPTER 18
Alexander

He was thanking God the roads were clear because making it down the main drag to the restaurant seemed difficult with her in his truck. Driving seemed difficult, period.

She was adorable when she grabbed her beanie out of her bag and pulled it over her hair. His history with women would have led him to believe that she wouldn't dare do such a thing. The women before her would primp and add lipstick on car rides, they would never touch finished makeup or hair.

But she did, and it was sexy as hell.

She looked great in hats, but then again, he was coming to find that she looked great in anything. A burlap sack could probably rival her painted-on jeans. Jeans that were so distracting that the crease of her ass would forever be burned into his mind. When his eyes had wandered up, it just led to more trouble. He wanted to unbutton her sweater each time he looked over at her.

Their conversation on the weather didn't help either. He could barely keep his eyes on the road when he could make out her hard nipples beneath her sweater. He wanted her in less clothing, but he was also thanking the Lord her tits would be on display for many months to come with all the snow they got in Kings Ranch. *Good Lord man, just fucking drive.*

He had made reservations at an idyllic café on the main drag, nestled between a bar and an old bookshop. He had done a little more digging and found out she had a beautiful cottage in town, with the help of her parents but he was sure she didn't have much else to her name. Not that money was even on her radar, though.

He had come to find out that her parents raised her to rely on herself, making sure she was educated and held multiple degrees. But degrees and feminism aside, his father raised him and his brothers to relish hard work and the idea of providing for a wife and family. It was the manliest thing he could think of, even if it sounded sexist. He wanted to be the one providing for her and her daughter. He wanted to be the one, period.

It also led him to question how much her ex had bothered to help her out. The asshole seemed to be opposed to providing anything other than scraps of money from what he could gather so far. It was a small town, but without having time to reach out to his sister-in-law, he couldn't get any gossip. Besides, he didn't want to reach out to them unless today went well. He had a good feeling, but with his friends already busting his balls about how blue they were over Mina, he had decided to wait.

When they made their way to the little café transformed from an old mining town saloon, he held the door open for her and glanced around the street at the local traffic. There were some tourists enjoying the stunning views of the mountain town while others were bundled up and heading to ski over in Telluride He loved it here, and now he may have a whole new reason for loving this town.

"You coming in, or did I scare you off already?" He didn't realize he took a moment too long to get inside until her beautiful voice broke his train of thought. She looked radiant standing there in her beanie, it somehow made her eyes even sexier, and he couldn't remember a time in his life when he had ever seen almond-shaped eyes this demanding of attention. This intoxicating.

"Just breathing in some clean mountain air. Trust me, I don't think it's possible to scare me off." He made his way inside the crowded café and thanked every lucky star that the hostess let Mina lead the way so he could stare at her ass more.

Settling into their table by the front windows, she left her beanie on but placed her purse on the floor and her phone on the table.

"I can move it if you don't like it on the table." He must have eyed it without realizing it. "I know it's not polite, but I always have it close by when Sophie's with her dad." She looked like she was thinking hard about what to say next. "Her dad isn't the most attentive man. It just makes me nervous when she leaves." She worried her lower lip before adding. "It helps if I'm by it."

Why would he say no to that? He was fascinated by anything that came out of that beautiful mouth, but any man who could leave this woman was in need of a mental check. He wanted to know what kind of dipshit he would have to be dealing with because he had every intention of dealing with him. He understood what it was like being nervous when your child left, but he also thought it might be more intense for mothers. He figured it came with creating them for nine months while the men just sat back and watched the miracle unfold. He needed to know what made this woman tick, but that also meant knowing what the hell that man did to her.

"Tell me about this ex of yours. What's the story there, if you don't mind me asking." She smiled and tilted her head to the side as if not sure how or where to start. "If you don't like talking about him, I understand. We don't have to." He didn't want to pry even though he really wanted to know everything.

"What do you want to know? I'm an open book." She gave him a smile, reassuring him she was just fine.

"Well, I guess, for starters, how did things end and why?" He knew this would say a lot about her past. How he was with her, how she handled herself, and maybe a little peek into their marriage.

Another deep breath and a sip of her drink gave a clue that he should buckle his fucking seat belt.

"You asked for it." *This should be good.* "It wasn't a quick ending, but more like a long and steady fuse that burned until everything blew up in my face. We had moved into a new home to be closer to the station." She paused, most likely realizing he knew nothing about the man. "Sorry, he's a police officer, I should have started there." When he nodded, she continued. "But even with Sophie and the new home, he didn't seem happy, and he was getting worse."

Concern flooded his system, not liking the way that came out. "What do you mean worse?" Barely a minute into the explanation and he was already feeling his heart rate spike.

"He just got mean and then meaner and stayed out late and then later. He wouldn't even come home sometimes, and even though I knew something was wrong, I didn't want to face it. I really just didn't want to believe that people had affairs or snuck around. Like it was all bad luck for other people, but not me and my family."

Although she kept her tone light and upbeat, the message she was giving was anything but. Things were making more sense, and he was starting to see the bigger picture in her divorce mess. Her shy demeanor. The reason she never looked up in line or why she didn't seem to talk to people outside her own family.

After another moment and another sip, she came right out with what he knew was coming. “Finally, after about a year of him putting me through hell, I knew I was just denying what was really going on and what I didn’t want to have to deal with. So, I looked at the phone records, and everything was right there in front of me.”

He gave her a nod, silently telling her he understood her pain. He didn’t, really, but anyone who could do that to someone they loved deserved to get the shit kicked out of them. He was more than happy to step into that role if he ever had the chance.

“He tried to deny it, and the woman even tried to reach out to me and tell me they were just friends, but I was the last to know what was going on and to say it was humiliating would be an understatement. The whole department knew, and even worse, some of the guys reached out and apologized that they hadn’t told me before when they knew he was cheating on me way back while I was pregnant with Sophie.”

The shock of hearing how long the cheating went on for made his stomach drop and had him choking on his water. “Did you just.. say back when you were pregnant?” He mumbled in between coughs.

She winced at the sight of his revelation. “Are you okay? Too much? Kinda heavy for a breakfast date.” She laughed and looked down at the menu.

Heavy wasn’t the type of word he would use to describe the kind of rage that was flowing through his veins. It wasn’t that he couldn’t handle it. It was the feeling of him wanting to go murder the son of a bitch. It took all his energy to unclench his fist and ease his shoulders back down from their spike in tension He wanted this man to pay for what he did, but right now, he was at breakfast. That would have to wait.

“No, not at all. I want to know everything. I want to know you.” She gave him that million-dollar smile and kept going. “If you insist,” she said sarcastically. “No water this time,” she joked. She cleared her throat and started up again. “I ended up taking him back because of how often Sophie would ask for him and how much he begged me to forgive him. Guilt, I learned, is a powerful thing. But it didn't take long to realize that he just wanted us both. He went back to her and tried to have Sophie and me too. When I found out the second time, or hundredth, depending on how much cheating he had done at that point, I left him for good."

The way she looked down at her hands but immediately straightened her shoulders gave her away. She had been hurt but was still here. Still moving forward.

"How did Sophie take it when you left?" He wanted to care about the question that rolled off his tongue. It was the polite thing to ask. But he couldn't stop thinking about how that prick put her in that position. He left her with few choices if she respected herself.

"I felt bad that she would ask about him, and she would wonder what happened, but I didn't want her growing up thinking she could allow men to treat her that way." She paused before adding, "I just feel like we can tell our children everything, but they watch us more than they listen. Waiting for us to do the things we talk about constantly and they just sit back observing all the little moments when we think they aren't looking."

The confidence in her voice was tangible. "I want her to respect herself and know that she's worth more. So, I had to be worth more. So, I left him."

He loved her boldness to fight for herself. "It takes a strong woman to walk away from a marriage. Good for you, Mina." Strong didn't describe how he really thought of her. She left her cheating husband and has been doing a hell of a job raising her little girl. "So where does this leave you guys now with all of this?"

She bobbed her head from side to side and scrunched her nose as if trying to figure out how to approach the question. "It's going, that's for sure."

He eyed her curiously. "Going how…"

They both laughed at the leisurely pace it was starting out at. "It's going as in things have slowed down with the harassment."

What the fuck? "Harassment? Hold on," He tried to stay calm. He really did. But the word harassment was creating images in his head of what he would do to the man if he saw him. "What has he been doing? Maybe he needs to know what harassment looks like from someone his own size."

She laughed nervously and waved her hands about.

"Sorry." He tried to remind himself not to look like a giant Neanderthal. "Go on. I'm sorry for interrupting." His visions of torturing the bastard would have to wait to come to fruition. For the time, a napkin under the table would have to do.

"No, I'm sorry. That sounded bad. I mean…It is… bad." She didn't sound convincing as she tried to spit out the words. "But I have it under control." She looked as if she was trying to convince herself as much as she wanted to convince him. "Sort of. He just took things too far once."

Her nerves had picked up, and it was evident with how fast she blew through the story. "His dad threatened to tell the department and have him arrested. After that, he never came back to the house again."

It was a lot for him to process. *Threaten arrest? What could he have done that would make his own father threaten him with an arrest?* He was going to find out, but if she wasn't going to offer more right now, he would have to wait until she was ready. *This motherfucker's a piece of shit.*

"They still enjoy stalking me online, or causing scenes, but I've learned to hold my own with them. Kind of proud of myself, actually."

He was stunned and had a hard time putting words together. The woman of his dreams just told him she was physically harassed in some way, was currently being verbally abused intermittently and stalked online, yet she seemed like she was just happy to be there.

"They still do all that shit to you, and you're okay with it?

How do you handle it without flipping out all the time?" He was genuinely interested. He could use some pointers on how to deal with his ex when things go back to being less than favorable with her. She looked calm, like what she just told him was no big deal, like everyone had to go through that kind of shit. *Oh yeah, sure.*

"I guess I'm just glad I'm out of it, you know? I have an amazing family that took care of Sophie and me. They supported us when other women aren't so lucky in these types of situations. Not everyone has that. It may not be the image of how I expected things to go, but I'll take any time with Sophie I can get."

"Have you folks decided yet?" The waitress interrupted. Had he decided? He wasn't sure what the waitress was asking about, but he knew he was sure as hell about her. He would choose her every second of every day if she allowed him that grace.

As she playfully ran through the menu and talked to the waitress about the Benedict styles, he found himself staring and couldn't rip his attention away from her. How could he ever listen to another woman talk after being mesmerized by just one conversation? He thought he knew it before, but he was falling harder and harder. He couldn't care less what he would eat for breakfast as long as she ate with him.

She laughed with the waitress and smiled as they chatted about something. Her eyes wrinkled around the edges, and her nose crinkled as she giggled, sending him into a haze. She was a firework on the fourth of July, and he couldn't stop watching.

Without breaking his gaze, he ordered whatever Benedict she chose and sent the waitress on her way. Selfishly, he wanted her all to himself.

CHAPTER 19
Mina

While he casually said, "I'll have whatever she's having," she revisited how she got to this point. Got to this date.

From the beanie now making her head an omelet of sweat to her word vomit he was able to rope out of her so effortlessly, she was in it deep. She had only been texting him since the start of the week, and yet, she just divulged some deep shit without batting an eye.

Not to mention all the sexy texting they had done. The man was a smooth talker, and she was a nervous chatty Cathy. The combination was screaming disaster. *I'm definitely not ready for varsity dates yet.* But to his credit, the man didn't seem scared. Just like before, he just kept asking questions and kept acting, no, not acting. He was literally interested in her and her life. He seemed eager to kick Evan's ass.

That alone made her happy in a wicked way, but besides that, she loved that he wanted to be on her side. That someone other than her family wanted to be on her team. It sounded dreamy, and even though she had been letting herself indulge in the fantasy of falling for Xander, she was still afraid.

Her sisters and mom were hell-bent on the idea of her riding off into the sunset with a gorgeous single father, and now she found herself on a date with THE most gorgeous single father in town. One who happened to be right at the pickup line where she grabbed her nieces and nephews. One who had all eyes on him but only had eyes for her. *Those damn sea- green eyes.*

Why did Christian Grey come to their school pickup line? Her imposter syndrome was hitting her like a ton of bricks. *I get divorced, my parents buy me a cottage, and on top of that, I have a walking sex symbol plopped into my lap for breakfast. Fuck my life, right?*

Other single moms were struggling to make ends meet, and here she was, sitting across from Xander, licking his lips after the coffee he sipped. *Licking his fucking lips*.

The smallest, most mundane thing was putting her over the edge and daydreaming about him licking others things. *More dirty thoughts, awesome Mina.* She didn't go through enough to earn a handsome man like this without a catch. She just couldn't figure out what the catch was.

Those wickedly gorgeous eyes bore into her like he could hear every private thought, and she kept finding it hard to breathe. It was nerve-wracking being face-to-face with someone she had been texting all week. Again, not just texting, but sexy texting. *Was that sexting?* She didn't know, but either way, the gorgeous mountain man slash business executive was sitting right in front of her in all of his Greek God-chiseled splendor.

How could she talk to him about her ex or her family when just last night he asked her "if she prefers it in her or on her?" Damnit, he was smooth and had the dirtiest mouth she had ever heard. His filthy words were sinful, but she would willingly go to confession every damn day if it kept him talking.

"What's the deal with your ex?" She needed an ice bath to

counter the thoughts that jumped from her mind mere seconds ago. "You know my story now. So, what happened to make you go your separate ways?"

He didn't seem nervous about it at all. *Gorgeous bastard.* In fact, he seemed eager to divulge everything to her. Like he wanted to hand over all his private thoughts and secrets as if he were handing over a business card.

"Well, I wasn't married to her, so things were a bit easier to break it off." He adjusted his coffee mug to the exact place of his liking then moved his napkin to his lap in a very eloquently correct manner. He seemed to be in his element being put on the spot. *How often did this guy date?*

"But she just wasn't the one. I knew she wasn't before she moved in with me, but her roommates had a disagreement, and they left her with nowhere to go. We had been on a couple of dates."

He rubbed his face and scratched the stubble of his beard as if he was embarrassed about this turn in his explanation, and somehow that action seemed endearing. The whole look on his face seemed innocent, despite his admission. "A couple of one-night stands would be more accurate regarding our time together."

She didn't expect to feel so nauseous when hearing about his past relationship. He was human and a damn good looking one at that. He was probably out fucking the world, but she couldn't seem to stop the pang of jealousy. She didn't realize his past would bring up all these greedy feelings.

The only saving grace was his voice. Maybe she could get through hearing about his past escapades if she just focused on his voice. It was mesmerizing. She could feel the rise and fall of her chest easing with each new sentence he laid out in front of her. It had a calming effect while she got lost in his intonation and the way his voice seemed to engross her. Both low and smooth, with a faint gravelly texture attached to words when he spoke quietly or reached the end of a thought. It was sexy. She remembered now why she thought his voice was sexy in

Walmart. She wasn't entirely ashamed she zoned out on it for a hot second.

"After playing house for a bit, I was on a work trip when she told me she was pregnant, and I needed to get back to town."

Talk about a slap to the face to get her back to reality. She knew this was where the story was headed, but it still stung a bit. She was juvenile about her seemingly growing jealousy but she couldn't bring herself to care.

"That must have been a big shock." It was one thing to want to get pregnant, but it was a whole different kind of terrifying experience when life was going to come into this world and you didn't have a thing to say about it.

"Yeah, it was a shock, to say the least, but the worst part was that she kept it from me while I was traveling. She had worn oversized sweatshirts while I was home, and we didn't sleep together often, so it was easy to keep her secret. When I found out, she was already seven months along."

Now it was Mina's turn to pick her jaw up off the floor. *Seven months and she kept it a secret. Holy fuck.* She tried to mask her emotions, but this one was just too much.

"Oh my God! What did you do?"

He chuckled under his breath at the memory and scrubbed his chin once more. The simple act was sexy as hell. After a moment and a quick bite of his lip, he rested his back against the chair and his elbow on the armrest. "The only thing I could do. I stood by her, and we had the baby together."

Regardless of her persistent fears, she knew he was a good man. This just showed her where his morals were. He tried even though she wasn't the one. He tried even though she lied to him and kept it a secret. He tried, period.

"After a couple of years of hell, I found out she was talking to another guy, and I was off the hook from having to make it work. I took a promotion back in Denver, and I got the hell out of town. I was thankful I had a way out."

She found it hilarious all of a sudden that the man she happened to go on her first date with happened to have a past riddled with Jerry Springer drama just like she did. His understanding would come in handy, that was for sure.

"So, I would visit Amelia every other week, and then when the year was over, and my job could relocate again, I came back." This man was full of surprises.

"When you came back, what were things like with your ex?" She was eager to know if she would need to sleep with a knife under her pillow with the way this one was being painted.

"She had a couple of different men she had gone through, and then one stuck. She's married to a police officer, ironically." He winked at her. "And now they seem to be happy. She's calmed down a lot these last couple of years. They're happy, so I'm happy."

The wink...Lord give me the strength.

She understood what that felt like, possibly what every sane person felt like when they had a crazy ex to deal with. She just wanted Evan to be happy with that woman or any other woman, but he never seemed to be. There always seemed to be trouble in paradise. The paradise he created for himself. She couldn't understand it.

Her mom and sisters swore it was because he wasn't over her and didn't want her to move on. They said that as long as he created drama and caused chaos, he had her attention. It was true, but it sounded pathetic. Then again, any man who cheated on his wife and baby was pathetic in her eyes.

"Wow, that's a lot to handle." She wasn't kidding, either. They both had their fair share of wacky stories, and it seemed like God did have a sense of humor to get them together in this quaint little eatery to learn all about each other. Both their exes sounded crazy with their own individual flavor of it. Mina's was an abusive steroid-loving cop, while he dealt with a bitch that loved riding the crazy train, among other things. It seemed like a comedy.

"It is, but it seems like you've had more to deal with." She could argue that, but what was the point? They had both been through hell with exes, and she knew it. “I feel like I’ve learned a lot about women from my past.” He smiled, and she knew that could be meant in more than one way. “Do you feel the same?

This was some heavy shit for a first date. He stared her down with an intense look that replaced the warm eyes she had seen mere minutes ago. A look that was just as intimate and complex as his question. Was he implying that she didn’t know what she wanted in a man…or in bed? Whether she wanted to settle down because of her past or didn’t intend to do so because of that same past?

After a couple of moments, he looked hungry for an answer, and she was desperate to give him the one he was hoping for. She wasn’t quite sure what he was expecting, though. She had just learned how to live as, well, herself. Someone who didn’t need a man to make her feel whole. All eyes were on her, it felt like the buzzer at a basketball game was about to go off.

“I’ve always known what I want in a man. My ex was just really good at pretending.” Maybe she didn’t know enough about relationships in general, but she wasn’t wrong. She knew what she wanted in a man. She’d always known it. She was just naïve for a little while about the intentions of others. But life had a way of hardening those naïve intentions and showing you the bare truth.

“At least for a little bit, anyway. He was a chameleon that couldn’t hide forever.” She met his gaze and hoped like hell she looked confident.

“Chameleon. I like that.” He took a moment to smile and make her feel at ease with all of this. The intense stare had morphed into a look of piqued interest. It wasn’t every day someone described their ex as a chameleon, she was guessing. “Tell me more. How was he a chameleon with you? What did he think he had to be to get the Mina Washington,” he said with that devilish grin.

He had to know it made all women weak. It made her uneasy, but at the same time, she loved it.

“Well,” she started. “I love to do things with my hands, whether it's yard work, home projects or art. My ex-husband told me he loved all that. But the second I was out of the picture, I learned from friends that he was relieved because he hated home projects and having to do everything from scratch instead of just paying to get it done. I thought it was just strange. People don't have to have the same interests, but why lie about it?"

He nodded in agreement. Then continued to smile. And smile some more until she got the hint and relented.

"Being humble is another huge thing for me. I can't stand cocky jerks, and he put up a strong front until it crumbled, and his real personality came out. Same with another jerk I had a moment of weakness with." He popped an eyebrow as she quickly added, "Nothing super steamy to write home about, but I figured out his intentions quickly. I had to learn the hard way that being competent and confident is very similar to being cocky and arrogant if the men were good at manipulating. It just so happened, that those two were."

Again, with the nods of agreement. As if he was cataloging all her answers and storing them away. "They made you believe in a confident leader but turned out to be cocky jerks. It's a very fine line, isn't it?"

She laughed despite herself. It could seem to be condescending, but he was reassuring. Like he understood her and sympathized somehow. He seemed to have some of the same types of experiences, which only put her further at ease.

The whole conversation turned into something she hadn't expected. All the nerves and then watching him shake his head or offer sincere support in those eyes made her feel like she had known him her whole life. It was shocking. Who was this man, and how did he manage to muscle his way into her heart without even checking in to see if it was okay with any of her plans?

To her horror and his extreme pleasure, she kept on going. From mirror selfies to tinted zit cream and cover-up, she added more examples of their vanity, and by the end of it, they were both rolling. She was pretty sure they were the most despicable examples of men she would ever encounter, and her judgment was not to be trusted.

"So you were into arrogant, meathead pretty boys." He could barely get it out over his coffee.

"If I had bacon to throw, I would." Raising her eyebrows to show her seriousness for the situation, he held his hands up in surrender.

"That's heavy, right there. No one, and I mean no one, should waste bacon." They were all smiles trying to catch their breath. She couldn't remember the last time she had laughed that hard with anyone outside of her immediate family. It was a big fat blank spot in her life, and somehow, this man had filled it on day one.

"That comment alone means we were made for each other." She covered her shock with a laugh that they both kept up due to the bacon comment, but she really had to control herself. Did she really just say that? What was happening? This morning was a complete roller coaster of emotions. Between the smoke show he put on every time she saw him and the need to ask him those meddling questions about his mental health, she was sure he was going to be her downfall. She just knew it.

"So," *there's no easy way of asking this*. "Do you have any deep dark secrets that I'm missing?" *Please don't hate me.* She plastered a fake seductively teasing smile on her face. "Any psychos in the family I should be aware of? Besides your crazy exes, of course." *Those bitches do sound crazy, so I'm not wrong there.* She didn't want to go on. But yes, she went on. "Any meds or illegal drugs you need to confess to now?"

He stared at her with the biggest grin on his face. *Okay, you don't hate me yet. That's a good sign.* "I'm just thinking of our future kids should this progress even further. You know. It's always about the children." *My God, will I just shut the fuck up?*

She arched a brow and steepled her hands beneath her chin to rest herself on the table and look him square in the eyes. Cool and confident. Sexy and yet mysterious. At least, that's what she was going for. *Like you didn't just ask him about any ax murderers in his family because you want to have his babies. Oh yeah, Cool, Cool.*

He threw his head back and howled so loud she was sure everyone in the café was staring at them now. It was such a good laugh she almost forgot what had set this little frenzy off. *Is he laughing with me or at me right now?*

Either way, she was just happy she didn't have a drink in her face or was left without a ride home. She would also have to figure out ways to make the man laugh more. Anything was worth hearing that sound.

"For the children," he repeated as he was trying to catch his breath. "Of course, of course. We have to make sure we would be compatible in every way for the children."

Damnit, the way he said *every* as if he somehow had the swagger of a Latin Salsa dancer made her knees weak. That one word sounded so sexy with his voice. *The man should do audio books for the smut I read. It would be a lucrative opportunity for him, for sure.* She was positive this man had enough experience in his bachelorhood that he wouldn't have any issues in the bedroom. *There go my ovaries again. We all agree we want him, ladies, calm the fuck down.*

He looked at her as if he knew exactly what was racing through her mind, and thankfully, he interrupted those dirty thoughts to put her out of her own misery.

"I don't take any medications and none of that runs in the family. We just have to watch our backs because of some crazy exes, but we should be good."

She couldn't help herself, "Are we talking rabbit on the stove crazy or slashing tires type stuff?"

His forehead creased, and he looked a little suspicious.

"Aren't those the same type of crazy?"

Good grief, this man. She shook her head as if he should be following her train of thought. "No way. I feel like slashing tires is just a step above throwing eggs. I mean, when you go to animal sacrifice, that's a whole new ballgame."

The look on his face didn't exactly show much of the cards he held. Was he on the same page? Did she just put herself out there like a psycho?

"I mean, who didn't get a little love crazy in high school, right?" *Good cover, Mina.* Maybe he would chalk that up to being young and reckless. Although it really had been since almost high school since those days of pranks and mischief were over.

Thankfully he did seem to track this conversation and added, "You don't even want to know what guys do in high school. Their dirty minds work overtime." And just like that, it was back to her ovaries and their overwhelming awareness that she needed to have all of this man's babies.

Her legs had never clenched so tight, and now a familiar tension was building low in her belly. All he had to do was say dirty minds, and this was where she ended up. Nerves taught with tension and on the brink of...something.

God had a sense of humor. One vibration of a misplaced phone and she could come undone right in the middle of the little Americano café in front of Xander. She was going to have to be strong because all the coiled nerves would soon drive her to make bad choices.

CHAPTER 20
Alexander

This woman had bewitched him, and he had no intention of breaking the spell. *Feed me to the lions.*

Watching her talk and eat seemed like the creepiest thing in the world, but he couldn't stop himself. Everything about her was sexy, down to the way her hands moved from her napkin on her lap to her silverware on the place setting. *Could hands be sexy? Were hands ever sexy before her?*

It was like he came out of a fog he had been stuck in his whole life. She was the real deal. The version of sexy that he held in his head before her seemed silly when looking at the woman across from him. She didn't just look sexy. The damn word was made for her.

The dainty way she sipped her coffee. Her posture made him think of her as a student and how she had told him she was a good girl in high school. *Her posture?*

How he was able to think of gripping her hair in his hand while he fucked her from behind just from her posture was beyond him, but it happened. He wanted to make the good girl across the table do every dirty thing he could think of.

The couple times they had bumped knees under the table sent his mind spinning with the idea that her thighs were tense. Who the fuck was this woman, and why did it take so long to find her? A couple of weeks ago, he was banging five different women, for fucks sake, and now he was doing his best to listen to her talk about her crazy ex while he gruffly swept his hands through his hair to help him stay on track.

Why was I the one to mention high school boys and their dirty fucking minds when she was talking about crazy pranks on exes? He was hoping that she figured he meant that they did disgusting pranks, but it was an honest slip of the tongue based on the dirty things he wanted to do to her.

He already felt like a college kid waking up every morning trying to figure out ways to get in her pants, but now, after being this close, he was going to go back to high school status and relearn how to walk around concealing a constant boner.

Climbing the corporate ladder was never going to be easy once he had Amelia, but now, with her as a constant distraction to both his heads? It was going to be damn near impossible.

"How was it?" The waitress looked down at them with a sly smile as both plates sat relatively untouched after two hours of talking. "Looks like you were both famished," she teased. Mina bit her bottom lip and looked up through long lashes as she giggled at the waitress. *God, those lips.* One look at her with that expression, and he was instantly repositioning himself to give himself some space.

"Yeah, it seems we had better things to do." He could think of a few things right now. "But the little we had was amazing," he added thoughtfully. "We just need the check." *And a new sense of self-control, but who's asking?*

He had to kiss this woman and fast. It was all he could think of as he watched her help clear the plates at the table and while he sat alone when she excused herself to use the restroom.

He was fidgeting. He doesn't fidget. He was a man who found the hunt of getting women to bed a thrill and was never nervous. He's fucked more women than his friends combined. He'd been climbing the corporate ladder with ease and loved to negotiate business deals like it was a game of chess. This version, though? He didn't know who the hell he was around her.

He knew she was different the moment he laid eyes on her, and he knew he was ready for a change in his life, but he had no idea everything else in his life would fall to the wayside just for a fucking kiss or a goddamn smile. This woman was a drug, and he was the addict dying to chase a high.

"Ready?" That smile again. He felt like the fucking king of the world for making that appear.

"For anything. Let's do it."

His brain was now a waste of a muscle, his body would have to function on it's own, he decided. He placed his hand on her lower back, and she took it in stride, leading the way for them. He was a legs-over-ass guy, but this ass? He wanted to watch it swivel with each step all day long. As the bell to the café door chirped and they stepped onto the pavement outside, the cold blast of air should have hit him hard, but she had him running hot.

He took her hand with confidence before they walked the short distance to the truck. At some point along the short distance to the passenger door, she intertwined their fingers as if she had done it a million times before. Fitting together like the last few pieces of a puzzle clicking into place. It made him feel like his life made sense now.

He was midway to grabbing the door when he decided to take his shot. Instead of the handle, he grabbed her other hand, making her pivot until she was looking up into his eyes. Even their height difference was a turn-on. He towered over her while her petite frame fell into his shadow.

That knowing smile she gave him signaled his green light, and without another word, he leaned down and placed a light kiss on her tempting lips.

He languidly perused her lips, as their kiss took a leisurely walk toward this new territory. Each inhale felt like he was breathing her in, while each exhale felt as if she was doing the same to him. It was intoxicating. It was erotic as hell, and it was only a kiss.

He wasn't ashamed to make out in the middle of Main Street on a busy Saturday morning. He had to taste her, and once he did, he couldn't get enough. He tilted her head to the side as he palmed the back of her neck and drew her in even closer. Their mouths opened for their tongues to explore further and deepen the connection. Even if it ended with this one date and one kiss, he would be happy knowing he had literally kissed the woman of his dreams. Who else got to experience that kind of thrill in their lifetime? Up until this point, he had never realized the gravity of it.

In contrast to how it started, their first kiss ended with a slight nip on her lower lip and an inhale of her surprise. She slowly opened her eyes and looked up. She looked like pure sin. Her eyes far off and heavy and her voice gravely with the kiss that had clearly rocked her just as much as it did him.

"That was amazing." She sounded as if sex should naturally be the next thing they do in this very second. He couldn't even imagine how other places would taste if her lips tasted this sweet. She was all-consuming, demanding of his attention in every aspect.

He didn't want any of it to end, but he needed to tie up a

loose end before he went out with her again. A certain loose end that involved giving one of his regulars back her stuff. He had no intention of keeping another woman's shit in his house ever again.

"What are you doing for dinner?" Maybe she was seeing someone else too? Would she have told him? He did forget about Tina until he saw her stuff. Should he even ask or tell her? Would it scare her away if she knew he had her stuff, even if he forgot about it? *Jesus, Xander.*

"Nothing. Just me, Lupe and a good movie." That sounded just as tempting as Super Bowl tickets to him. To be fair, dog-sitting for this woman would trump Super Bowl tickets at this point. He just had to be in her orbit in any way he could.

"How about I pick you up at five sharp for some dinner and putt-putt? Amelia thought we might want to go there for our first date but I told her maybe for our second." He teased as he pulled her back in for one more kiss. "I wish I could take you to lunch, but I have to button up some work, and then I should be good for dinner." Yes, that was a lie. The second one he had to tell her in order to break it off with one of his past regulars, but it was worth it. He would come clean to her tonight just to ease his conscience.

"Five sounds fantastic. Can I pay for dinner or golf?"
This was just too much. She was adorable. He was all for foward-thinking, but he didn't even make his regulars, who only wanted sex, pay. She would never pay for anything. Ever.

"Not a chance. In fact, what is going on with your phone." He laughed as the words came out of his mouth. The phone that had been on the table during breakfast was an eyesore to say the least. The thing had literal cracks splintering the screen and he was sure she has sliced her finger on more than one occasion trying to unlock it.

"Ha! Yeah, I guess it is getting old. But it still works, and that's good with me. I just have to watch out for random cuts to my ear." She was laughing, but the entire situation horrified him.

This woman. *His* woman. She should not have to worry about cut-up fingers and ears, for Christ's sake. That would not do.

"Good grief, woman," was all he could muster. "What are we gonna do with you?" With that, he decided he had more errands to run before five. "Let's get you back so I can knock out some work and make some reservations."

They hopped in the cab and the rest of the ride home went as if it had been played on repeat for fifty years. They held hands and she leaned into his shoulder while his other hand draped over the steering wheel.

Once they got to her house, he opened the door of the truck while he guided her into his arms. Their third kiss spoke of more to come later. More things that he was dying to do and parts he was aching to touch. She playfully ended the kiss with a nip to his lower lip that time and he groaned in anticipation for all the things they've yet to do. It was pure torture watching her walk back up through her yard to the little Craftsman.

Her rounded ass and those damn legs that took each stride up the walkway and away from him. He never wanted to bite an ass so bad in his life, he settled for his fist instead.

Once back in the truck with his hard cock tucked inconspicuously into his jeans, he groaned. "Fuck, this is hard." It was all he could say before backing out of the driveway and heading to his house across town. He had shit to do.

By the time he made his way back to her side of town, he officially felt like a scoundrel. *Do people even use that these days? Maybe just asshole.*

Tina was home and he had to hand over her stuff in a box like they were college roommates that broke up. It was fucking embarrassing.

She wanted to know if he wanted to come in and have breakup sex. *What is it with women and breakup sex?* But he told her the truth. Maybe it was harsh, but he was off limits, and he was damn proud. Now he just had to make Mina off-limits to all other men.

He was positive she wasn't the type to date multiple men seeing as how he was the second relationship she'd had in literal years, but he couldn't even fathom her going out with men like his buddies Tyler or John. The kind that put on a strong suburban vibe only to step out on women with the first sign of attention they got from a hot little number.

No, that wouldn't do. She was his, and he had to figure out how to make her see that. He also wasn't sure when he had gotten so goddamn possessive. This sense of primal territorial shit was new to him, and he needed to calm down or risk scaring her off.

He pulled up and noticed there was a slight buildup of snow on the driveway. No doubt she was on her own, trying to keep up with the Colorado winter. He would have to fix that right away. She shouldn't have to do shit with the snow, a man should be doing it for her. *Christ.* There he went again, acting like a Neanderthal. He had been taking the Lord's name in vain quite a bit lately. His mother would definitely not approve, and somehow, in this situation, he found it hilarious.

When he rang the doorbell, it took her all of one minute for the door to swing open as she stood on the threshold. As if she had been waiting all day for him. He loved it so much he felt himself grinning like a fool... again.

"You look beautiful." Of course, she did. Her hair was down again and tucked into that beanie. Her winter wardrobe wasn't anything that should have made him think of sex, but honestly, this woman could wear a UofA sweatshirt with tube socks and he would need to jerk off. The fucking Wildcats were sneaking into his fantasies now. He was a mindless meathead.

Dinner went off without a hitch, complete with more talk

about their mutual love for all things travel and culture. It was as if they were both old souls that reconnected. Like two lines that had run adjacent to one another and finally intersected.

"Oh, I almost forgot." He opened up the back driver-side door and grabbed a small bag. While he was away dealing with "errands" he set up the dinner to coincide with her gift. "I got you this." She looked tentative as she shuffled the tissue paper to one side and reached into the bag. He wasn't sure what he was thinking now that he had time to mull it over. It was their first day together, and now he was pretty certain the gift would freak her out. Maybe he should have let her go with him. Maybe he should have waited. Either way, he saw a problem, and he fixed it. It was done now, so he would have to ride this out and hope he made it to date number three.

She brought the small box up to her chest, and although he was slightly distracted now, he held his breath and waited.

"A phone?" She looked up at him, utter shock splashed across her face. "You seriously got me a phone?" Her chin finally closed from its initial surprise, and a strangled smile started to peak the corners of her lips.

Was she insulted? Relieved? Freaked out? The woman could mask many emotions behind a smile.

"Your phone was giving you little cuts, and even if most of that was said as a joke, I just thought you shouldn't have to deal with that. You needed a new one, so I got you the newest they had." He was oozing nerves, and he was sure she could feel it. The nerd in him rambled on and on about the different features this model had and why he thought it was important that she had said features. It was a bold move, but she was worth it. He wanted her to see that.

"We're right by Vicks, and they can transfer all your info over. He already told me when I called." She just stood there and turned the box over in her hands.

"Seriously? This is the nicest thing. I just can't accept it. It's too much." The words came out as a meek reply, barely audible with all the foot traffic a Saturday night had. He knew she would say that. He knew she wasn't the kind of woman to take freebies unless he forced them on her. Hence, the phone that was already resting in her gloved hands.

"I knew you would say that, but I insist. I'm a single guy with one kid, and I'm lucky enough to have a job that pays me too much, so I can spend it on people I want. And I want to spend it on you. Consider it an early Christmas gift." He winked at her before gesturing her "this way" with a hand.

When she walked out of Vick's an hour later, it was with a new phone case, new Airpods and, without her knowing it, a new laptop on preorder so she could write her novels on something with better storage and the capacity for updates. He couldn't have her trying to chase her passions on an outdated piece of tech. *I'm a nerd. Sue me.*

She kept thanking him over and over and insisting it was too much. But it wasn't. She didn't understand the kind of hold she already had over him. Nothing would ever be too much for her. He was a poor fool in over his head with no intention of coming back, and if she wanted him to hand over the keys to his house and car, he would do it for her in a heartbeat. All she had to do was ask. To him, she hung the moon and stars, and for that, he would give her anything she wanted.

CHAPTER 21
Mina

A new phone. Who the hell was this guy? *He must have money. Scratch that.* She knew he had money thanks to her mother and sister. She was sure the poor man had probably been run through multiple databases by now, while his social media accounts were definitely combed clean.

Although she couldn't wait to hear their reactions, how would she explain these kinds of gifts? They were her biggest champions concerning her love life, and they preached that she should be treated like a queen, but even if he had all the money in the world, it wouldn't change the fact that a phone and accessories were a ridiculously kind gift.

She was a teacher before staying at home, living off the divorce money to stay with Sophie. She knew how much all this cost, and it was hard for her to accept that he bought her a phone on a whim because of some deep-seated need to take care of her. Then he insisted on AirPods and a phone case. It was too much, and yet he wouldn't take no for an answer. He went on to say that he would prefer to have her on his phone bill so she wouldn't have to worry about paying one more bill, but he allowed her some grace when she put her foot down. It was, after all, only their first day together.

Our second date? Do dates have to be separated by days or just outings?

It was all insane to her. His whole knight and shining armor bit was intense and overwhelming, and yet she was embarrassed by how much she loved it. She was supposed to be capable and independent, but here she was, accepting extravagant gifts in the name of what? It couldn't be love because that would be too soon. Lust? Maybe that was where his head was at, but the act of giving her something this grand and bold was sexy as hell. It made all her feminist feelings go straight out the window. It was the sucker punch to her gut she never expected to love so much, and it made her resent herself a bit more for falling for this man and his ways.

By the time putt-putt was over, it was still fairly early, and she was hoping she wasn't the only one who didn't want the night to end. The lights on Main Street were woven back and forth across the street to make an illuminated tunnel, and a bite of cold, crisp air still hung in the car for a good while this time of year. She had to rub her arms and legs as they scrambled into the truck and tried to defrost themselves and the vehicle itself. The radio switched on as the truck started to heat up, and Michael Bublé's "A Cold December Night," filled the small space, making the evening more enchanted.

She felt herself melt into the seat as warmth seeped into her fingers and toes, slowly working its way to her core as her heart filled up on the lyrics she had never listened to before. Words had never been more fitting as the melody played in the background. She wasn't sure of anything that would last like people did in the movies, but she was positive that she was his for the taking as they drove down the main drag and looked out at the little landscape riddled with holiday charm.

"Do you want to go to a movie?" The tiny town filled with boutique stores and a main market wasn't the type to feature a theater. That would mean they needed to drive to the bigger town over, which would still only have two showings at best, and they would most likely not be able to make either one.

"Have you checked showings?" His body visibly deflated with her question, and she shamelessly felt relief that she wasn't alone in wanting to stay out longer.

"Have you ever seen *It's a Wonderful Life*?" He sat up a little straighter, whipping his head around like a dog on the trail of a treat.

"I haven't. What are you thinking?" It was a boost to her ego that the man didn't need much convincing.

"It's my favorite holiday movie. I watch it almost every night during Christmas time." *Do I sound like a spinster?* "We could watch it at my house if you want." She wasn't quite sure why she thought to be nervous about asking him over. He was the one who wanted to spend more time together, and it took all of half a second for him to give a "heck yeah" and head down Main Street with a new purpose.

Life seemed too good to be true, so she was going to ride this fairy tale as long as she could. Hell, she would ride something else, too, if her hormones wouldn't calm down. But they sure as hell had to calm down because they were minutes away from her house, which meant she was minutes away from being alone with Xander on a couch, near a bed, with no one else in sight. Or within earshot, for that matter. *Be strong. You can NOT fuck him on the first day.*

She reasoned with herself that this was the third date since they went out to breakfast as the first, then went to dinner and putt-putt for the second, and now a movie would technically be the third date. *How far do women go on the third date? Would*

I fuck him on the third date? She decided it was best just to let that one simmer. No need to answer such questions when she was afraid of the answers she'd give.

When they pulled up to her house, she sighed at the idea of coming home together. She was in deep, and these little happenings weren't giving her much to work against it. Her goddamn heart kept swooning at the sight of this man and his little gifts while his mind-blowing kisses weren't helping the situation.

She grabbed his coat as he admired all the pictures on her gallery wall yet again.

"You look so much like your sister it's crazy." He had been told they were twins, but sometimes people couldn't wrap their heads around it.

"Just wait until you meet her at one of these infamous playdates. She's a trip." If this gorgeous man ever did meet her, she couldn't wait to see what Claire had in store for him. "You would like her. I always say she's the better twin, so I'm sorry if I disappoint." She wasn't kidding. She always felt that way about Claire. She wasn't just a trip, she was a whole damn vacation and honeymoon rolled into one. It was her Claire, her person.

He looked from the picture to her before really gazing at her. Like he was looking into her soul, if that was even possible. With all the baby Jesus, Mary and Joseph comments she had been making lately, she could get behind that idea.

"Not possible." He slowly rolled up his sleeves and moved on to the next picture, simultaneously moving on to the next topic, clearly dismissing her ridiculous notion. "So where are we watching this holiday movie? I can't wait to see what you watch every night."

His voice did that thing again. The thing where he could make a regular statement turn into a lusty sexual invitation somehow. Her stomach immediately erupted with butterflies and she was positive her heart was in a freefall simply watching the way his forearms looked as he finished rolling up his sleeves.

She immediately decided it was a piece of real estate that was severely underrated and didn't get the attention it deserved. The man was clearly a lumberjack in a past life and the way his sleeves rolled up to just below his elbows seemed inappropriate to stare at. Women have boobs, but what do men have? At the moment, it was forearms.

Some type of tattoo was inked across one of them, making it all the more risqué. The little home seemed too small, and she needed some air to regain composure. This man was something else.

"Well, I only have one TV in the house, so we will make a cozy camp in the living room and watch on the couch if that's okay with you?" *I'm going to lie next to this man for the next two hours.* The idea made that familiar coiling sensation come to life in the most delicious way possible.

"I'm going to make us some popcorn if you want to grab some blankets from the hall closet and make us some sort of nest on the couch."

"Nest, huh?" He chuckled to himself as he made his way to the blankets, and she realized how odd that sounded.

"Sorry, Sophie likes to play animals. I'm pretty sure we could rescue every wolf, turtle, donkey, bird or horse if they needed saving." She threw her hands up in mock confidence, her tone sarcastic. "I have been a mother to them all."

He threw his head back, laughing again. The sight made her heart swoon yet again. She loved the visual of Xander relaxed and carefree. "Ahh yes. I remember those days. Amelia loved playing dinosaurs. I had to be a T-Rex a lot." *Good God, that's adorable*.

She decided she needed to convert to some religion where they believe in multiple Gods. *Is that poly somthing? I should have paid more attention in history.* She deemed it necessary so she could pray to more of them for help. One wouldn't cut it with this man. He was going to be the end of her sanity. *To think I told Claire I didn't need him...*

"All right, I'll get us set up with a nest, and you grab the popcorn." He tossed the words over his shoulder as he lugged the billowy pile of blankets from the closet and started crafting their space. She was scared to death with how much this evening made her feel. It felt homey, cozy even. Like everything fit into place after a lifetime of what-ifs. She wanted to lean into this magic and ride off into the sunset with this man who appeared out of left field, but she knew better than to believe in the make-believe. Life wasn't a fairy tale. She needed her game face on and top stop swooning all the damn time.

She wasn't the little girl who believed in Prince Charming anymore, and she didn't want to fill her head with the notion that her white knight had so easily waltzed into her life. Love wasn't so simple, and she wasn't naïve to how terrified she became each time her heart ached for his attention. She was caught between desperately chasing a fairytale and shaking her own shoulders to wake the hell up.

After mulling her fate over her air popper, she slapped a smile on her face and rode into battle with the popcorn in hand. The battle of her heart that is.

He didn't seem to have any qualms over their state of affairs as he looked starry-eyed and more enamored with her by the second. He made quick work of her wills as they settled into a comfortable position on the couch, only to change it up after mere minutes of watching. He couldn't hear that well, and she wouldn't be complaining, even if it was a fake excuse to get closer.

They settled into a good old-fashioned spooning session, and she felt all of sixteen again, complete with raging hormones the second she felt a particular bulge just behind her ass. She was sure he tried to hide it, but it was there, and it was driving her wild. How was she supposed to ignore the intoxicating mix of his breath on her neck, his arms around her and the warmth of his body behind her?

"What's your favorite part about this movie?" He whispered

into her ear, leaving a wake of gooseflesh down her neck and sending chills down her spine.

"Hmmm." She knew what it was. She had seen this movie a million times. She was just taking the scenic route to the answer so he could stay right there by her ear and huddle in close. "The end. When George realizes how great his life really was, Clarence writes him a note. You'll have to see. It makes me cry every time."

She wasn't sure why she was almost whispering, mimicking his volume. There was no one else home, but it oddly seemed right. Like it all seemed to be building up to something. The quiet movie in the background, the low lights of the tree illuminating the room, and the chill in the air gave more to the moment, and that song kept playing on repeat in her mind.

He leaned further, brushing his lips over her ear. "I don't think I'm going to make it that long."

It took her a moment to register what he intended to do with that statement, but his mouth was on hers before she took in her next breath. She immediately got lost in his hard lines and wandering hands. The scratch of his short beard, just before his lips pressed deeper, was the first polarity of sensations that drove her mind wild. It was a constant symphony of slight nips of pain followed by gentle touches, a combination she had never experienced before and immediately knew she could never get enough of.

The bite on her lower lip gave way to him using his tongue to coax and twist her own. It sent their breath into ragged gasps and their bodies into a frazzled mess of limbs. His hands cupped her jaw, stealing kisses before they made their way to her throat, holding it possessively while he devoured her and made quick work of her willpower.

With each moan she let out, his hands traveled further down her body, groping and grabbing with trained authority. Like he had been schooled in how to drive her wild, and she was just along for the ride. It was maddening.

He peppered her collarbone with kisses as his hands pawed and pinched her breasts. Teasing her to insanity before he reached around and palmed her ass. He took his time to make sure he reached every angle and elicited shivers in every wake. She moaned with each pass made on her inner thighs, and he groaned in appreciation like a starved man. As if he needed her as much as the air he breathed.

She couldn't help tugging his hair and biceps, gripping them like she couldn't get close enough. He was already on top of her, but her body begged for more. Needed more. She noticed her eager movements made him bolder as he grabbed harder, trying to ravage her body. He made her feel like a rag doll as he gripped her legs and threw her body underneath him completely. Legs straddled him, and knees were up, giving him access to all of her and allowing her to feel his hard length on every sensitive nerve. She hadn't truly dated since high school, but she was positive none of the high school boys could throw her around like this. Not back then and not now.

It was carnal.

It was raw.

It was sexy as hell.

The second she brought her hips to meet his, he threw his head back and groaned louder with pleasure, and she was relieved she wasn't the only one overcome with the headiness of it all.

He started to push back on her thrusts while he went back to groping her breasts and teasing her until each was painfully taut.

Between gasping and slipping her tongue in his mouth, she breathed out, "We should go to my bed." *We should definitely not go to my bed.*

Her brain was losing the battle of self-control as he nodded and bit her lip in agreement. "But you can't fuck me," she spoke breathlessly, painfully as he paused.

Both of them panted and shuttered at the sudden break in their assault. She looked up at Xander with his disheveled hair and swollen lips. His erection painfully rubbed at her core, and she was living the pleasure and pain contrast that he enlightened her with.

It had to be the hottest thing she had ever seen, but she didn't want to give in to her lust. She wanted more and from the look on his face, she was sure he had never encountered this type of request. He looked thoughtful as he blinked back glossy, lust-filled eyes. As if the haze of sex was fading in and out, and he was trying his hardest to gather every last brain cell and listen to the words leaving those same lips he had been devouring just moments prior.

"We just can't. We need to wait." She wasn't so sure she believed what she, herself, was requesting. Looking up at Xander, she looked at his sexy lips and the ragged breaths leaving them. She wanted to throw caution to the wind and be reckless. Live on the edge and walk on the wild side, but the good girl in her won out the second he nodded, speaking only the few words necessary.

"We can't." He was out of breath and shaking visibly as he sent a hand through his already tousled hair. "Fuck. Right. We can't fuck."

He picked her up in the same breath and continued to place kisses along her neck and collarbone. As he walked down the hall and fumbled against doors and walls, their laughter just added to the heat of the moment. The stumbling only created more of a frenzy, and she didn't want this moment of pure sensation to ever end. Tongues met teeth while his hands gripped her ass and held her body to his chest from inside her jeans, teasing the sensitive skin skimming her panties.

With full confidence in her not slipping out of his grasp, she worked miracles and undid his belt and the button to his jeans. She slid the zipper down while he kneaded her and made her gasp the second he slid his rough fingers into her wetness.

The moans that were filling the hall were coupled with the metal of his belt hitting the hardwood and his pants shuffling along the ground. She was lost in the moment and feeling everything his hands were delivering, making her more eager than ever.

She felt reckless. The giggles mixed with tongues and clashing hands gave her a sense of freedom. Like this moment was only for them, and they were allowed to be young and give in to their teenage whims.

Her head hit the pillow, and only then was she able to surmise that they had made it to her bedroom. Taking off his shirt and what was left of his pants, he then went for her clothes like a man possessed.

"God, I can't wait to get you naked." Her whimpers between each breath and each stolen kiss fueled the fog of the moment. Like the heavy haze of lust they had been drowning in since they'd started talking had all led to this. All the stolen glances, all the fantasies and every painful moment that went into the waiting was for this moment.

As he stood at the foot of the bed, naked save for the boxers straining from his length, she got onto her knees to meet him at the edge. He lifted her sweater over her head and pulled her into him, meeting her mouth with a merciless kiss. With one hand holding her in place biting at her hip, he expertly used the other to unhook her bra. He was intoxicating, like she could drown from such pleasure. She reached down and stroked him through his boxers, gripping him and appreciating at his size.

She had read a thousand different books on heroines being so young and naïve, wondering if it would fit, and here she was, wondering the same. His size, his rough hands and his strength in each grasp only drove her to need more. The evidence of his lust was on his boxers, and it had her licking her lips and pissed at the thought of the greedy fabric beating her to the little bit of desire she craved on her tongue. *Who the hell is he turning me into?*

She bit her lip and moaned at a thought that had never crossed her mind before.

"Fuck, you're perfect." He cupped her breast before placing

his knee on the bed and pushing her shoulders back. As she fell back onto the pillow once more, she watched him rake over her body with his eyes.

He took her in as he made his way to the last piece of clothing she was willing to part with. It was intoxicating being wanted by someone so badly. He gripped the waistband of her jeans and peeled her out of them, leaving her in her ruined panties, on full display for his prying eyes.

Without breaking eye contact, he leaned down and kissed her core as if his tongue could penetrate the thin fabric. She couldn't grapple with the contradictions of this man. The sweet and sensitive side he seemed to have as a father and then this side of him that screamed master of sin.

He sucked on the fabric and moaned in appreciation. "I've never tasted pussy this good, Mina. You're fucking delicious and dripping for me."

This was relatively new territory for her. Her ex was too rushed for her to enjoy oral sex. He seemed to want what he wanted, and she was there to help him with that. The other wiseguy was a sloppy and clumsy drunk that never made it past her mouth. But this man? Fuck. This man, with his face between her thighs, was all devilish charm and complete sexual authority. He was in charge, but with that power, he wanted to make her come apart as if she was the only one meant to experience it all. It was fascinating to her, and she could officially confirm book boyfriends weren't a bunch of bullshit as she had previously believed.

It all felt heady and a bit unnerving, being splayed out to him as he said those words, so eager to taste her.

"Are you embarrassed?" He continued his onslaught of dirty kisses just over her panties, her wetness soaking through onto his tongue, making his words more accurate by the second as she bit her lip nervously. This man did things to her that she never even thought of doing with anyone before.

"How can you be embarrassed? I can taste that sweet pussy

through your panties, and I'm starving for it." Her cheeks flushed, but she never wanted anything more in her life than this moment with him right here, right now.

Her legs fell open a little wider in appreciation, and he continued with manhandling her. Teasing her and making her squirm. He settled himself further down the bed and slowly draped each leg over his shoulder. Kissing and kneading her thighs while making it back down to her center.

The marks on her legs would be visible in the morning as each nip and rash from his stubble sent tantalizing prickles of pain and pleasure to her core. He drove her close, keeping eye contact with her as he placed gentle kisses on her legs and the backs of her knees before he took a second to lick her center again through the thin material. He made a show of how little that piece of privacy was doing to hold him back.

With the index finger of one hand hooking her panties to the side, he gripped her ass and dove in. His tongue claimed her like a ravenous man. He took his time with his onslaught, slowly letting his tongue work its way through her and sucking intermittently. Mina screamed out in pleasure. No one had ever made her feel this good.

She grabbed his hair and pulled him closer, riding his face as much as he was sucking and using his tongue on her sensitive flesh. She didn't know who she was at that moment, but he made her feel wicked. "Fuck, Xander! Oh my God, don't stop." He took his tongue out and replaced the aching emptiness with his thumb. Giving her body attention in every way it craved. With his thumb piercing her, relentlessly gliding in and out, he brought his mouth to her core and sucked, sending her to the brink.

Legs trembling, she grabbed her own breasts and pinched herself, loving the brief pain it brought. She was scandalized and worshipped. Loved and feasted on. It was hypnotic.

He pressed her legs further apart, baring her all to him before hooking his thumb deeper inside her, finding that spot that sent her falling over the edge in ecstasy.

"Fuck, Xander!" She practically screamed as her legs tightened around his shoulders, and her fingers threaded his hair. Pulling at his strands as he stroked and sucked to draw out her orgasm as long as possible.

Her ears were ringing, and her throat felt raw with her erratic breaths finally coming back down from her high. She could hear him literally groan as he lapped up her cum. Reveling her taste before peppering her with gentle kisses. *Mother fucking fuck. This man is trouble.*

CHAPTER 22
Alexander

He should regret leaving marks on her flawless skin. He should feel bad he more than likely corrupted this good girl at heart, but he didn't and he wanted to keep going.

Her silky legs, her ass, even her stomach was sexy. This woman was a permanent installment in his dreams as of late, but somehow, the dream version of her sliding up and down his cock seemed PG compared to the real deal. Her pussy tasted better than anything he had ever put his lips to, and even after he just got a mouth full of her, he was still salivating for more.

He wiped his thumb across his lower lip, savoring the last bit of moisture off and making a show of sucking her off his finger. Every last drop of her cum was his, and he wanted her to know it.

He gently pulled her legs from behind his shoulders and tucked them back onto the bed. She was all loose limbs and weak after her orgasm, making him a proud bastard for claiming that win as he pulled her in close and clutched her to his chest.

She turned and found his mouth again, sure to taste herself on his lips. He held their kiss as his hands groped and kneaded anything in their path. He wasn't sure any part of the night could be more erotic until she found his thumb skimming her chin and brought it to her lips, wrapping her tongue around it before she started sucking.

With eyes on him the entire time, it was as if she were showing him just how far she was willing to give her thanks.

"Yeah, suck it, baby. Show me how bad you want to suck my cock." The tease sent him spiraling. She looked so damn good with her cheeks hollowed out. He couldn't even imagine the sight of her lips around his dick.

It was her turn to shift their position, and he found himself under her with an achingly hard cock and a wet pussy rubbing him to insanity on the outside of his boxers. Her fingers gripped his hair before she turned her kisses from his mouth to trail along his torso.

She found the hidden tattoo on his chest especially pleasing as he noticed she took extra time to outline the border with her tongue and grind against his cock harder while sucking on the bare skin. He was convinced she was a siren sent to kill him. *No good girl should be this bad.*

After what seemed like a lifetime of torturous pleasure, her mouth made its way to his hips, and he thrust into her eager hands as she pulled his last article of clothing down. Gripping the base of his cock and stroking him, she looked up while slowly taking him in her mouth. Inch by aching inch.

"Fuck…" It was all he could say. All other rational words seemed to have vanished from his mind once her lips wrapped around his dick. He held her hair back so he could watch her innocent gaze turn sinful as she took him in.

How she was able to make him see stars with those pouty lips was beyond his reasoning, and the way she licked the side of his shaft and played with his head made his eyes roll back. He was a dirty bastard that had his share of memorable fucks, but this woman was everything he never imagined. She teased his head with short bobs before taking him to the back of her throat and making a mess of his cock.

He had never been so proud to have a woman suck him off. This woman was his dream, and watching her mouth do scandalous things felt otherworldly. It was his turn to grip the sheets as he tried to contain his composure, but it was no use when she increased her pace and sucked him harder. He met each bob with a thrust of his hips and gripped her hair to fuck her mouth. He wasn't sure if she could handle the rough turn it was taking, but she kept humming in pleasure, making him mindless and out of control.

This sexy and shy woman was taking everything he had to give and making him fall apart.

"Baby, if you keep going like that, I'm going to come soon." He practically growled the words as she sucked harder, making a mess and hollowing her cheeks further. He gripped her hair at the base of her neck, positive he was leaving marks on her. "You want to swallow my fucking load, sweetheart? Or do you want me to paint your face with it?" *I'm going to Hell.*

He knew she probably hadn't done either before, but he couldn't help it. He possessed few thoughts at this point, but ruining her made him want to pull out of her before he did something that would make her run. She wasn't very experienced, and he had to remember that before he ruined his chances with her for good.

With one more thrust to the back of her throat, he was pulling out of her mouth before he felt her grip his hips with need as her nails dug into his skin. As if on cue, she flattened her tongue and drove him wild as she stroked the sensitive skin, covering even more territory.

His growls turned louder, and his thrusts more violent. He gave her one last warning, giving her a chance to change her mind before she moaned in pleasure, shocking the hell out of him as she pulled back, leaving her mouth open and tongue on display for him to finish.

Apparently, she wanted the best of both worlds, and the thought and visual were all it took to shoot hot ropes of himself all over her tongue and chin. He groaned and shivered with the force of his orgasm as she pumped his cock, making sure to get every last drop out of him.

Through heavy eyes, he could barely make out the images of her as she swallowed everything he gave her and tidied up the rest with the sweater that was tossed aside earlier.

“I’ve never done it like that before,” she said below dark lashes and a shy smile. “And it was a lot more fun than I expected.”

He wasn’t sure what to expect from a woman who had only been with one other guy, but this wasn’t it. Somehow, he wasn’t sure about her past sexual exploits anymore, but he was going to revel in the fact that she knew exactly what she was doing with him, and her skills could possibly send him to an early grave.

He had never had a blow job that mind-blowing in his entire life, not even from sluts he banged in college. Maybe it was the fact that she blew his last brain cells, but all he seemed to care about was calling his asshole friends and telling them the perfect woman did, indeed, exist because he fucking found her.

He pulled her into his arms and kissed her dirty mouth despite knowing where it had just been. “Good Lord, woman.” It was the only thing he could say. He didn’t know what he did to deserve any of what she had to give him, but he didn’t want to linger on the idea. He would gladly just accept this as long as she was willing.

He looked over at the clock, cringing when he saw it was one thirty in the morning. “Damn, I think I have to go before we continue to ruin the no-sex rule tonight.”

With a giggle and a nod, she rolled onto her stomach to watch him get dressed. She was like an exotic pinup model. He was still in shock this day had actually happened, but more importantly, he needed to make sure it would keep on happening. Make *them* keep on happening.

“I like it this way.” He knew she understood he was talking about the “no fucking” rule she put on them for the foreseeable future. “I already know it’s real, but I want to make sure that you know it when I spread those pretty thighs with my dick instead of my tongue.”

Her smile looked a bit curious. “And you’re so sure already?” She asked as she hopped out of bed and pulled an oversized t-shirt over her bare frame.

He knew he sounded crazy, but he meant every word. He knew she was the one. Every woman in his long, long line of dating had proven she was above and beyond the rest—more than he ever dreamed of.

“I am. I’m done looking.” He meant it with everything he could swear to.

“No, you’re not. How do you even know? This was our first day together.” She had a shy laugh and shook her head playfully, swiping her sultry hair out of her eyes. But he was. She was it for him, and looking at her like this, he had never felt so sure of anything in his life.

As they made it to the front door, he had to spill the beans on the other women he had been seeing. Every single person he knew had dated multiple people, but the fact that she wasn’t just any single person made him want to let her know the truth. All of it. She was sure to have trust issues, given her past and how protective her family was. He needed her to trust him, and she needed to know that she was the only one.

"Hey, I just wanted to let you know that earlier today, I wasn't just working." He was more nervous than he expected. "It was a little white lie, so I could tell you the truth now."

She looked up at him in the doorway. The lights from her living room illuminated her from behind, and she looked ethereal. She just stood there, all tousled hair and a baggy oversized shirt that left little to the imagination given the washed-out color. Waiting to hear the news, she had a curious look now claiming her face.

"All right. So, I was seeing a couple of women before you and one left some of her stuff at my house. I had to drop it off and tell her it was officially over." He held his breath and tried to gauge her reaction. With any other woman it would have seemed completely normal to date multiple women. With her? It was probably not something she was used to. She just got divorced from a lying cheater, for Christ's sake.

"Okay…" She paused and seemed to put her guard back up as she crossed her arms over her chest. "So you don't have any other women on the side, right? Like, not anymore?" She stood up straighter and mussed her hair to the other side of her part. He wanted to devour her in a kiss for looking so confident and sexy when he knew she was probably freefalling into her nerves. "I'm sorry. It's probably normal, but I won't date anyone if they feel the need to test the waters elsewhere."

He had never been so turned on by such a proud statement. His girl was spicy. He loved her spirit.

"I won't put myself in another position to be fooled around with, so I understand if we need to end this." She was a vision even when she was clearly upset. She must have thought he was screwing around with her, and yet all he could concentrate on was how her tense posture just pushed her tits up even higher through the thin fabric, revealing her hard peaks underneath. *Concentrate.*

"No other women. I wanted to tell you that I'm not seeing anyone, and I told the others I'm off the market for good. I just wanted to let you know so you knew where I stood with our relationship."

She seemed to calm down. To his disappointment, the Neanderthal in him was sad when her hands relaxed, and he lost sight of her nipples. *I'm a fucking pig.*

"I wanted to let you know just in case you were seeing someone else on the side."

It dawned on her that he wasn't the only one who could be dating other people. She shook her head and smiled as she leaned into the doorframe further, trying to beat the cold air. "There's no one else. Just you."

He felt like one hell of a lucky bastard. "I meant what I said earlier, I'm done looking."

He reached down and scooped her into a warm hug as she threaded her hands behind his neck. They intertwined as if they had done this motion a million times before. He kissed her again, deeply. A goodnight kiss that meant so much more now that they cleared the air. A promise of sorts.

When she leaned back and looked up at him, she smiled like an unruly, stubborn child. "You still don't know that." He kissed her again, grabbing her bare ass under her oversized shirt and making her squeal.

"I just do. I've been looking for a long time. To be honest, you probably won't know for a while, and that's okay. I have no problem trying to prove it to you."

He paused and sank back into another deep kiss, gliding his fingers past her ass. Teasing them both again. Only when they needed more air and he realized the chill was going to be too much for her did he release her.

He gave one last kiss on the forehead before heading back to his truck. Before hopping in, he looked at the woman of his dreams standing in the door frame, soft light cascading around.

"In fact, I think I'll have a great time proving it to you."

CHAPTER 23
Mina

Mina: You still up?

Claire: Are you being tortured or held captive by hot dad?

Mina: No, just wanted to fill you in

Claire: Did you BANG hot dad?

Mina: No! I have morals

Claire: Boooo

Mina: But other things…

Claire: You're such a whore

Mina: Go suck a dick

Claire: Maybe I will. Nighty night

Mina: Who's the whore now…

The banging on the door should have been the most annoying noise to wake up to, but Lupe proudly took that honor with her obnoxious, offkey howling.

Mina scrambled through the house, tripping on toys she could swear were not out just the night before. However, her legs seemed more wobbly than normal this morning. Her sister's muffled voice came into earshot and she hurried to get her out of the cold.

Unlocking the door and letting Lupe loose on her visitor, Claire stood on her porch looking put together and fucking adorable in her Lululemon leggings and winter coat, holding out a bag of what looked to Mina like burritos.

"Yay! He's not afraid of your vagina! Congratulations." It was obvious that her sister got more sleep than her. Claire pushed past Mina and made her way to the kitchen.

"Good morning, angel of death. What brings you to my door at," She leaned back to look at the kitchen clock. "Seven thirty? On a Sunday? Damnit, Claire. What the hell?"

Claire took in the annoyance and smiled. "Well, Kyle is on kid duty because he promised to make the little ladies his famous pancakes. So, I decided to come here and bring some burritos." She held the burrito out, a full arm's length from her own body,

"It's early, but I come in peace."

Mina eyed it warily and added, "We need coffee, too. Maybe I'll dish out some deets of Hot Dad's bod if you make some coffee."

With her hands raised up, Claire agreed. "Fair enough. Let's get some food and caffeine. Then I can interrogate you. The family has spoken, and we need details."

Mina sat at the kitchen table and unwrapped her burrito. She wasn't sure if a burrito ever looked as good as the clump of egg and bacon spilling out of the tortilla. *I wouldn't be so damn hungry if I actually ate yesterday.* Too bad her stomach wasn't keen on the idea of being relaxed around Xander. She was in a constant state of nausea around the man.

"When did you all talk? You people are ridiculous," she mumbled over a mouth full of burrito. Claire waved her off, but she started to get lost in the burrito and the sound of the coffee machine starting up. She demolished the thing in record time. Sustenance toppling manners this morning. She was starved, sleep deprived and completely confused about how desperate she was for this man.

"You look angry and confused." Claire snapped. "Care to indulge me a little? Your resting bitch face is extra intense this morning."

Mina blew out a big breath and tried to wipe the grogginess from her eyes. She pushed her palms into her eye sockets until she had herself seeing stars. "Do you have coffee? That might help me." She was going to play this up as long as she could. Claire was dying for info and she was dying for a coffee. Claire passed her the first K-cup-filled mug and grabbed the creamer from the fridge.

"All right, you have the first one. Now spill the beans, lady." With coffee in hand and that safe and warm feeling washing over her, Mina started to spill. She felt giddy, then like a dirty whore telling her sister about the rest of it.

The whole thing made her head spin. From the way he

scanned her pictures on the wall with what looked like reverence to the way he put his hand on her throat in possession. It was definitely an all-consuming night.

Having his eyes on her felt like she was the most important woman in the world, and she honestly never had that before. It was the stuff her girly teenage dreams were made of, and she never felt so enraptured.

She just also happened to feel so very overwhelmed. So entangled. It was like a hallmark movie mixed with her favorite smut book. It was everything. By the time she was done dishing everything, Claire looked at her with a cheeky little grin. The same one she'd made her whole life. She may be minutes older, but Claire always acted like the wise older sister who had her shit together while Mina was the wild child at heart trying to rein in her emotions.

"Why are you looking at me like that?" *Like you know what I'm thinking and it makes me feel stupid because I don't know what I'm supposed to be thinking.*

Her grin cracked into a mega-watt smile. "You like him, but you're freaked out." Her face was a contradiction, and yet she knew exactly what Claire was feeling because she felt it every damn time she was around that gorgeous man.

"Well yeah, I'm freaked out! Who wouldn't be freaked out? The man said he was done looking, and it was our first date, Claire!" Claire smiled into her coffee, and Mina felt absurd for even admitting any of this.

"I swore men off just a couple of months ago, or did you forget that?" Her confession was cut short by a loud snort. The noise startled Mina as she looked over at her sister, shoulders shaking and trying to hide her fit of laughter in her mug.

"Are you laughing at me? I mean it! I've never been happier in my life simply after I stopped worrying about men and started building the life I wanted with just me and Sophie. Now? What the hell am I supposed to do? He professed the end of his search, for fucks sake, Claire! How am I supposed to let another man ruin me and Sophie?"

"I'm not laughing at you! I just think it's pretty funny that you swore all men off at twenty-eight, only to be hit on the first time you go out in public, at a school pickup line, no less." She knew her sister was right. She made some grand declaration only to eat her own words weeks later. It was embarrassing and amazing at the same time. This shit didn't just happen to people, but apparently it happened to her.

She just didn't know how to handle the turn of events without the fear of losing herself to another man. A man who could walk away.

"I'm not saying you need to let all your guard down, but you have to live, Mina." She took a minute to set her coffee down, and she knew Claire meant business. "You left that asshole to show Sophie that no one would ever have the right to treat her that way. But if you never allow yourself to date a good man, the kind that you're dating right now? You're just showing her that the fear won. Show her that you are worth being treated like a queen. That she deserves to be treated like one, too."

Fear.

What all of it had come down to. She was afraid of getting back out there only to be broken again. She didn't want it for herself, but she especially didn't want it for Sophie. How could she teach her daughter that she was worthy of being treated with respect if she didn't allow herself to get into a loving relationship?

"Sophie will learn everything she needs to know if you would just give yourself the permission to feel all the things you wish for her." Mina went back to sipping her coffee with the lull in the conversation, and the two women settled into a relative silence.

The birds chirping outside acted as medication for her soul. The quiet of a mountain town could be soothing to anyone, but for an introvert, it could be a saving grace. It grounded her thoughts, and she started to feel sad that her perspective of the world around her was always being met with suspicion. She shouldn't always be fearful. She knew she never used to be.

"And by the way, that declaration of his undying devotion to you,"

Mina looked up, not ever realizing she had let her head drop to stare off into her coffee.

"Maybe it was your first day together, but wasn't it your third date? Like, breakfast, dinner and putt-putt and then a movie makes three?"

"You're just trying to make me feel less slutty about me coming on his face."

Claire smiled. "Did it work?"

"I don't know, Claire." She threw her head back in frustration as if the ceiling would hold the answers she was searching for. "It took Kyle like a year to propose, and you want me to be calm because it was technically date three when he said he was done looking?" She wanted to cover herself in a blanket and hibernate all winter with Sophie…and trips to Xander's bed. *Damnit, I'm a slut.* She groaned as she wrapped her entire body around her mug of coffee. She decided it was her moral support this morning.

"First of all, we were a lot younger. Things are different when people are older and have their shit together. Both of you have degrees, careers and children, for fuck's sake. And be real, Mina. You are crazy about this guy, and he's even crazier about you! You became some porn star slut for him last night, and now it's like you don't want it to happen because it's all so perfect."

"It is all so perfect. It's TOO perfect." She clamored. The volume not helping her head. "He seems too wonderful, and I haven't suffered enough to deserve someone like that. Things like this don't just happen, Claire! It's like a damn Hallmark movie. It isn't real life. He's going to turn out to be married or be a serial killer or something."

Claire rolled her eyes, not liking the pushback. She was over this. "Why do you feel like you are meant to suffer? It's not your fault that your family loves you and doesn't want you to be homeless."

She knew Claire hated the way Mina always felt like she wasn't worthy of getting nice things. Hating that Mina felt like her husband cheating was her cross to bear for the rest of her life.

"Why do you feel the need to suffer just because you had an asshole ex-husband that cheated on you? You suffered enough, Mina. No one should go through what you went through, and yet here you are. Thriving and feeling guilty about it."

With her coffee done, Claire put her mug in the sink and circled back to Mina, grabbing both her hands in hers. "What happened to my wild and crazy younger sister?"

"It's six minutes, Claire." She huffed out.

"Six minutes is six minutes. It's who we are and how we're built. I'm always the responsible one, and you know it. You're the wild child that somehow makes it all work."

They both just sat there in silence once more. Staring at their hands and taking a minute just to be. Claire seemed like she was at her wits end, and Mina just didn't know how to say that she felt beneath this man. Why was this man interested in her?

"I'm not the doctor, Claire. I don't have any money." Claire winced at her words. "I'm not the pristine single woman he's used to dating. I'm someone's throwaway, so why would he want me?" Mina was about to take another sip when Claire spoke up again.

"You failed to mention that he snagged a gorgeous woman with a body like a teenager and a brain that could keep any man on his toes. Throw in her little sidekick and her awesome family, because yes, we are awesome, and you are the whole package, babe. I don't care if divorcee comes with your name when he talks about you with his friends or if he mentions that you were cheated on."

Thank God for Claire and her loyalty.

"Fuck everyone and their perceptions. Let it be a Hallmark movie because I can't wait to see where this goes."

A knock at the door startled both of them, almost causing

Mina to spill her much loved coffee.

"Dear God, if that's hot dad wanting to get some action this early, I'm going to be both pissed and jealous."

Mina waved her off as she headed for the door, although she wasn't sure what she would do with Claire if it was Xander. She may have a problem opening her heart, but it seemed her legs were working just fine these days.

She opened the door to find a man she didn't recognize. "Can I help you?" Now, this was something she was sure she'd seen on 60 Minutes. Why hadn't she locked the security door after Claire? She was hoping Claire would casually walk by, knife in hand, cool as a cucumber. *Easy killer*.

"Hello, Mina Washington?" The man looked like a normal enough guy. What if she said no? Would he still try to kill her?

"Yes…" Before she had a moment to ask him what he needed, a paper was shoved into her hands, and he turned on his heels before calling out, "You've been served."

Standing in the doorway with a blank expression wasn't exactly the definition of being unfazed by all the shit that seemed never ending with her ex. Claire was right behind her before she registered her presence. No physical knife in hand, but she shot daggers at the man's retreating form.

"Well, there you go. I bet Hallmark movies don't have people serve papers right after the best night of their life."

Touché Claire.

CHAPTER 24
Alexander

"You told her what?" Xander wasn't surprised with his reaction. He was expecting it, actually. He knew that whenever he finally found the one and wanted to settle down, certain friends would never be on board with him leaving his bachelor days behind. He knew that this particular friend would have the hardest time with it. Tyler whisper shouted in their now usual corner spot in the airport café.

"What the hell were you thinking telling her all that?" Xander found his disgust amusing. Tyler looked as if he was literally seething at the idea that Xander would throw away endless amounts of casual sex for a lifetime with one woman. *Typical Tyler.*

"I told her that because I was serious. Why else?" Tyler took a minute to gather himself and then let out a guffaw as he threw up his hands, gesturing defeat. He shook his head and took another drink of his coffee.

"I don't know what the fuck you were thinking, but I'm going to have fun watching it all blow up." He wasn't sure if he was jealous, joking or genuinely just being an asshole.

"Well, thanks for the support, man. Knew I could always count on you." Xander had taken enough of his shit over the years and hid enough of his secrets. He tried to play it cool, but he was losing his patience at lightning speed as his "friend" sat across from him, making lude comments about his girl.
He knew how his buddies could be. They were the first there if something bad happened but the first to bust your balls if you were happy. They were a bunch of jackass dicks, in his opinion, but they were his.

"I just don't get you, man. You have everything you could want. You seem to think marriage is going to be easy and that everything will be great sex and all that. You don't know what it's like." Tyler sat back with one arm draped on the back of the booth as he gripped his coffee with the other hand. All dressed up in his fancy, over- priced suits, and his hair gelled up to perfection. He loved the guy, but he was such a douchebag sometimes. Right now, he looked like a smug prick Xander wanted to punch in the face.

"I think you fail to remember that I had a relationship with a crazy person. I didn't even want any part of it except for Amelia. I stuck around for that!" He paused and ran his fingers through his hair in frustration. *Fuck him if he thought all that was easy.* "I know it won't be easy, but just because you aren't happy with your shitty marriage doesn't mean you know everything."

He knew he had hit a nerve, but he didn't give a shit. Tyler struck first, and he was tired of his friend being a prick.

"Fuck. Why are you hell-bent on living through me when you have an entire life waiting for you at home?"

The silence between them was deafening, while the tension was almost physical. He had never said it outright before, but it was time someone told him to stop being a fucking asshole to his wife and kids. "Listen to me. You have a wife that loves you and kids that look up to you. What are you doing when you screw around? Are you waiting for her to catch you?"

Tyler looked away, lips pursed. He looked lethal as he clenched his fist on the table. The noise from the airport and busy café filled in the silence, and they just sat there waiting for the other to speak first or not at all. Xander was past the point of worrying about how many lines he was crossing with this conversation. He was tired of acting like it was fine to be an asshole or that he was one just like him. If Tyler could walk all over his private life, then he would be damned to sit by any longer without standing up for himself.

"Look," Xander started but was cut off.

"Don't." Tyler looked down into his cup of coffee and swirled it around as he paused. "Don't try and act like you're so perfect and you know better than everyone else."

He looked hurt, and Xander couldn't, for the life of him, figure out why. He was always the one bragging and making it clear about his infidelities, and now he wanted Xander to feel bad like he had an excuse for his behavior? *Fuck that.*

"No, you fucking stop," Xander countered. "Don't act like I'm the asshole here. I'm making you aware because I should have done it a long time ago as one of your best friends. Man, I know the back story, so don't act like I don't."

All the guys from their inner circle did. He knew that there was someone he couldn't let go of. The one that he dated for a couple of years and loved but treated like shit. Then, one day, she had enough and left him. Once she was gone, he finally realized what people meant when they said, "the one that got away."

He still acted like the idiot college kid who wanted to party and fuck anything that moved, but he never got over her. He found out after college that she married some wealthy dude and rode off into the sunset on their private jet, never looking back. Tyler had been chasing an image ever since. Xander was pretty sure it was a way for him to prove himself or to try to get her back. Either way, it was his insecure way to feel like a man. He got his man card punched every time he got attention from other women but neglected the family he had at home. Sure, it was a sad story, but it was all Tyler's fault. He had to face the truth and stop running around on her or get the balls to leave.

The loudspeaker announced that his flight would be boarding soon, and Xander knew he had probably fucked up his friendship for good. It was worth it, but it still didn't take the sting away. They hadn't ever crossed this kind of line. Not seriously, anyway.

"I've got to run, and I know what you're saying." Tyler didn't look him in the eye, and Xander wasn't sure he was even able to. He wasn't sure how many heart-to-hearts the man put up with concerning his family. "But my wife and kids are none of your fucking business."

Well, shit. This is how it's going to be.

"So just worry about yourself, and we'll be fine." He got up and shuffled his papers and laptop into his briefcase before checking to be sure he didn't leave anything else on the table.

"It's almost Christmas, man. Enjoy your piece of ass while you can. Once you fuck her and realize she's just like the rest of them, let me know so we can go out. I'll buy you a drink."

Xander didn't hide the disappointment on his face as his lips set into a firm line. He had hurt his friend's pride, and now he was on the warpath, apparently. The man was an absolute dick.

"Yeah, sounds good. Have a good holiday with your family." He wasn't going to give in to the tantrum. Tyler would come around. He always did. But then again, that was when Xander always needed a wingman, and he was always willing to assist. He wondered what would be left of their friendship once his personal life finally became what he had always dreamt of. Mina was Tyler's type, after all, and it would drive him insane to know that Xander had found her and he was happy.

Xander sat there and watched Tyler put his bag over his shoulder and turn on his heel to leave. Without a word, he walked off towards his gate as Xander gazed on, wishing he could beat the shit out of him. He even looked like a prick walking with his cell phone in hand, a loud booming voice on display so each passerby would know his every business call or lunch date he set up. The expensive suit and trench coat, complete with designer leather shoes, gave him a certain aesthetic that always seemed to mirror the husband to the one who got away.

The buzz from his pocket saved him from his miserable thoughts on the future of his friendship. He gathered his coffee and bag as he smiled and accepted the call from his mom.

"Hey ma, what's up?" The sweetest woman on earth. "Oh, hi honey!" He may be a grown man, but he never got tired of how his mother let the word honey linger in the air as if she were wrapping him in a hug with every greeting.

"Dad and I are on our way down, and we were wondering if we could grab Amelia from Lauren a bit early?" It was supposed to be his day with her, but he had yet another last-minute fuck up he had to fix today. *Thank you, Carl.*

He planned on catching the last flight out and being back by late night or early morning. Days before Christmas were important with his family and even more important with Amelia.

"That would be great mom, thanks! You guys know where the key is, so you can make yourselves at home and then grab her afterschool."

"Oh thanks, sweetie, but we will pick her up and get settled in at Brent and Carly's. We thought we could spend the night over there, and you could meet us all once you get back from your trip."

They normally spent Christmas hopping between the brother's houses, or really just his if it was his year to have Amelia for Christmas, but this year, he didn't have her. It was going to be hard enough waking up to an empty house, but Amelia wasn't even going to be in Kings Ranch.

Lauren's dipshit husband was having them visit his family this year in Wisconsin. He was going to be alone in the house and would have to wait until she got back to celebrate with her. But on the flip side, he had Mina to keep him busy, and he was positive she would be flipping out right about now with the declaration he made.

Should he have a fucking therapist with the type of shit he's been spewing lately? He didn't know, but every bit of it was true, so he could give a fuck. In fact, the image of her freaking out made him smile. *Does that make me a sick bastard?*

"I forgot you're staying over there this time. Thanks for grabbing her. I'm glad you guys will be there with Amelia in case I don't get back in time to send her off." He almost growled at the phone even though he was speaking to the savior in all this. He just hated having to give up time with his little girl, and he sure as shit hated that Lauren and the asshole were taking her away for Christmas.

He was positive his family was aware of how sappy he was, but it still felt like a little secret to him. He loved Christmas time and especially Christmas time in Kings Ranch. Family together, nowhere to go, and nothing to do but chill by the fire and watch the kids go nuts with their gifts from Santa. It was a dream come true. Quite literally, for all of them.

But this year would be the first time that Amelia wouldn't just be down the street or down the hall. His mother interrupted his mopey thoughts.

"Everything is going to be just fine, honey. It will be a great Christmas. For everyone." The woman was a hopeless optimist, and he had never been more grateful.

They said their goodbyes as the noise of the crowded airport slowly worked its way back into reality. The shuffle of bags, the chatter of people, and the beeps and loudspeakers that went off constantly all brought him back to the moment.

He was completely surrounded, and yet he was terribly alone. He had never hated work trips per se. He just hated being away from Amelia. But at the moment, he hated it. He had no desire to climb a corporate ladder, no desire to fix any of the shit that Carl had done, and he had no desire to take credit for fixing said problem.

He just wanted to drive back to Kings Ranch and crawl into bed with Mina. Smell the crook of her neck and breathe in her intoxicating scent that made his head spin.

He couldn't stop himself from wondering if she was with Sophie or if she was alone. If she was awake already and making breakfast or if she was able to sleep in today. He never really cared about that type of stuff with anyone else, and yet he was terribly interested in the little things that filled Mina's day.

He wanted to see her in his t-shirts and nothing else after a long day at work or walk around the house in his socks to keep her feet warm. The sight of a growing belly and knowing it was his baby inside her was a jolt straight to his dick, and he knew he was in over his head. He had it so bad he didn't know what else to think of except for her.

This was the magic his parents had. The kind of shit he thought was fake. The kind of woman he had been blindly searching for since as far back as he could remember. She was the one, and he knew it deep down to his soul.

Without skipping a beat, he slid up on the home screen of his phone and typed out a text.

Xander: Busy on Christmas Eve?
We could go shopping together and
maybe hit up my family's party if
you aren't busy.

Fuck, I sound pathetic. Was pathetic the right word? Forward, maybe. That was the word. The exact opposite of how he was just thinking he needed to act around her. But he couldn't stop himself. Couldn't stop his fingers from swiping across the screen and hitting every letter that made it all come to life.

He never seemed to have trouble in the past, but then again, that was just getting women to bed. This whole, woo the woman of your dreams bit was a new one for him. *They were the practice, and she is the God damned grand prize.*

Xander: I can't stop thinking
about the other night.

He needed to stop himself before he actually did hit that pathetic mark. Forward was one thing. Pathetic would be too much for him to handle.

He put the phone down on the café table and stared at it. His hands felt the itch to type out more, but he held back. He needed to let her breathe a little. He didn't want to scare her since he was pretty sure she was just barely getting out of her shell that the asshole put her in.

Chuckling to himself like a madman, he thought about the only two cops he knew of. *Two assholes to deal with, and they both happen to be cops. I can't make this shit up.*

He wasn't oblivious to the reputation that came with that line of work, but he had always hoped it was just generalizations and didn't hold much truth to it. He knew better now. He was on the fence about ever reaching out for help with that whole part of public service. He was coming to find out that a lot more assbags worked in the police force than he cared to admit.

Xander: We should get out of
town together. Just us two.

Pathetic had won out. Each text got progressively creepier or more romantic, depending on the type of woman she was.

Fuck it.

He picked up his bag and grabbed his coffee. He needed to move. He needed to think. He just needed her. That was it.

CHAPTER 25
Mina

"What the hell am I supposed to say?" Mina was freaking out about the possibility of meeting his whole family and of going on a vacation. A vacation away from Sophie. This was uncharted territory, and she wasn't exactly the most adventurous person these days.

"Well, what do you want to say?" Claire had a flat tone on the other end of the phone, clearly amused, and it pissed her off.

"I don't know! Of course, I want to meet them. But I don't want to be away from all of you on Christmas Eve, especially when I don't even have Sophie until late. Like right before bed. And of course, I want to go away with him, but what if something were to happen to me and I was killed. I would leave Sophie without a mother, and it would ruin her life." Mina was panting now.

She knew she sounded crazy. But the truth was somewhere in

there. Between the impending doomsday worry, she was afraid to leave her little girl. She was also afraid to be in over her head, but she wasn't kidding herself anymore. She already was.

"Okay. I'm going to pretend you didn't just go all psycho on me, and we're going to walk this one back."

She took a minute to let Mina breathe and also to make sure it was safe to proceed. "You like the guy." It was a statement because there was no questioning it at this point. No denying it.

"Yes, I really like him. But how-"

"We will work on the rest in a second. So, you like him a bunch. Let's start there. Maybe it's fast, and maybe you're afraid because of all the feelings right now. But if you like him, why not go?" Mina let it hang in the air for a bit.

"Honestly, the dinner may start too late anyway. You may not have to worry because it could clash with when you pick up Sophie."

Throughout her life, Claire was the practical one. This kind of moment spoke volumes to that. "Yeah, you're probably right about that." Her blood pressure was dropping and she had Claire to thank for the averted panic attack.

"Now, why wouldn't you go on a vacation with him? You totally should, by the way." So much for the missed panic attack. Claire was always the braver one. She traveled with Kyle and left the kids with his or their parents. But Claire got her kids full-time while Mina was stuck with a half-time type of life. The idea of travel was a whole new thing for her. She wanted to go away with this hot, sexy single dad, but she also didn't want to have panic attacks every time she thought about Sophie.

"I want to go." She didn't know what to say, and yet she knew exactly what to say. "I'm just afraid. I think that I'm going to get lost in lust and fall in love with him even more. What if he's an asshole just like the last one and then I took time away from my daughter just to be selfish and waste it with a jerk?"

She knew she sounded insane with the amount of times her

heart had taken solid leaps of faith, only to hide away behind new walls that were constructed when reality hit. She was a damn yoyo.

"What if he isn't? Why are we back at this again, Mina? What if he's exactly what he seems, which is wonderful from what you've told us."

Mina knew Claire hid her insecurities because this man seemed like everything she had ever wanted for her sister.

"Evan texted me again." Claire pivoted, giving Mina her full attention.

"That's why you're really freaking out." What seemed evident to her entire family still seemed far-fetched to Mina. He was a master at manipulating and a piece of shit in her family's eyes. "What did he want? Just to bitch again, or did he actually say anything about the papers he served you with." The venom in her voice was palpable.

They still hadn't talked about how he wanted to get more time with Sophie. It didn't even make sense with his work schedule, but the asshole wanted more time. The only person it hurt was his own daughter, but Mina knew that wasn't his concern. It was always about what he wanted and when he wanted it.

"Kind of. He said that he had seen me out, quote-unquote, whoring it up with some guy while he was caring for our daughter and being the best father he knows." She dropped the air quotes to make him sound extra douchey.

"Good God, that totally sounds like that asshole. He talks about himself in the third person and makes himself seem like God's gift to the world."

He was always talking about himself like he was the most amazing father he had ever heard of. All the while, he was cheating on his wife and rarely home to see his little girl.

"What are you going to do? Are you going to tell Xander? Have you still been seeing his car?" Claire pressed before going another route. "Look, why don't you hang with Xander, do some shopping, and then head back home so you can pick up Sophie with plenty of time to get things done? Worry about the legal shit another day. Like any day after Christmas. Court can be put off if we figure out what the asshole wants from you."

She still had a couple of days until Christmas Eve, and her sister was right. She shouldn't be wasting her holiday time worrying about more stunts her ex tried to pull, considering he already ruined her last Christmas.

"Yeah, I think that's a good idea. I'll text him and tell him so we can plan." She took a second before offering up the real answer to what was troubling Claire. "And yeah. I keep seeing the cop cars around the neighborhood or following us at pickup. I think I saw someone the other day when I was walking Lupe."

He had been physical once, and the one time was enough to strike fear into her for good. The security cameras around her home, the alarm system and the wrought iron door were all in place to make her feel safe, but they just served as constant reminders of what he had done. She couldn't shake the feeling that Evan had something terrible up his sleeve.

With all the drama he put her through during and after the divorce, she wasn't sure she would be able to handle it while trying to start a new relationship—one with someone who seemed perfect.

"I could make this real easy for everyone and call this whole thing off. End it before I'm in too deep and Sophie is too invested. Evan's a psycho, and what if he brings Xander into his shit?" She had a legitimate stance. Last summer was brutal, and she couldn't bear to look at people around town for months because of the damage he did. The looks on their faces when she was at community events. Evan had found out about her one slip-up, the insignificant make-out session, and turned her into the town whore. He spread rumors like wildfire about her personal life, and it took a long time to settle everything down.

The way other police officers would stare at her on the sidewalk made her feel like a prostitute. It was humiliating, and she wasn't sure she could take any more. What if Evan tried to bring Xander down simply because he was tied to her now?

"Don't even start with that!" Claire wasn't about to let that asshole dictate life after she was finally free of him. "You can't control him, and Xander is a grown ass man. Just tell him the truth, Mina. All of it."

She let it swirl around in her head for a bit before she allowed herself to speak. She made it sound so damn easy. The truth? She had already told him the bulk of the shit he pulled. The abuse, the threats and the bullying. She just failed to tell him to what extent and the details.

Thinking back on all of their history together, Evan had put her through the ringer. She always just felt lucky that she got out before things got worse. But now, she had to figure out how to tell Xander what was still happening and see if he was even willing to deal with all of it. She would have to come clean with what Evan was capable of, what he put her through.

"All right. I'll tell him. I'll see if this is all too much for him to deal with." She was positive it pained Claire to hear the tone of her voice, but she knew she was doing the right thing. She had dealt with crazy for a long time and still had to deal with it. The man deserved to know what he was getting into.

She had never hated Evan more. The constant muted threats, the verbal bashings and now the prospect of a ruined relationship. She hated that one man could do so much damage to her life even when he was meant to be out of the picture.

Maybe her family was right. Maybe Evan was trying to stay in her life by torturing her. She couldn't understand the point of it when he wanted out in the first place. She had to remain under his thumb for whatever reason. It was maddening, and she was just so tired.

They had said their goodbyes, and with the final click of the tone, she felt utterly disconnected. To her family, to Xander, and to life. She didn't understand the point of his abuse, which made the idea of explaining it to Xander that much harder. If Xander did plan on sticking around, then he had to start understanding the man who was at the center of her turmoil. She just had to find the words and find them soon. Christmastime would end soon, and then the work would start. She would have to face her ex in court. Things were bound to get a lot more interesting.

CHAPTER 26
Alexander

"I'll see you guys later tonight!" He headed out the door and put his phone in his back pocket as he stepped down the porch stairs and across the frozen tundra that was his brother's front lawn.

Winters in Colorado could be brutal, but the sun was shining today and he had a shopping date with Mina. She already gave him hell about being a last-minute shopper and he loved every minute of the lashing. *When did I become such a masochist?*

It didn't take a rocket scientist to see that he loved any side of Mina he could get. The sweet, shy Mina drove him mad trying to get her out of her shell, while the spicier version made his palms itch with a need to spank her or fill her smart mouth with something other than colorful words. *Good God.*

The chemistry they had was explosive and he was aching to find out just how far that reached in the bedroom. But she wanted to make sure it was real, and he was more than happy to prove it.

Today was meant as a shopping day, to lure her out and about with him. But he had other intentions. He couldn't wait to see Mina's face when she opened her gifts. To say he went over the top was an understatement considering the laptop that was still on the way, but he wanted to give her the world. Maybe one day soon she would allow him to take her on a trip, but for now, he would settle for showering her with gifts.

He took one last look at the back seat of the cab to make sure they were all there before shifting into reverse. *Time to go get my girl.*

As he pulled up to her house, he noticed a car parked in the front of Mina's cottage and felt his blood pressure rise. He had to give himself a pep talk about a million times already concerning her ex. He thought about when and where a meeting could occur and how to handle himself like a gentleman for Mina's sake, but somehow, he knew all the pep talks in the world wouldn't prepare him if that meeting happened to be today. *Lord help me not kill the mother fucker.*

In all the times they talked each night, she still hadn't elaborated on what he did to her or how bad the bullying was. She brushed it off or would change the subject, but he knew better than to think it was nothing. This woman was a soldier headed to the front lines every damn time she was forced to be in his presence, and he commended her for her attitude. He just wasn't sure he could have the same composure that she had.

He knocked on the door and was greeted by Mina…but not. A mirror image of the woman he loved, but the smile on her face was different than usual, and there was something slightly off about how she stood in the doorway.

"Good morning, you must be Xander."

Confusion filled his mind as if he had dreamt of their entire short-lived relationship until it hit him. "You must be Claire, Mina's twin."

Her smile widened as if hinting he had done a good job telling the difference. *This is going to be interesting.* "Come on in. Meenie Weenie." She sing songs. "Xander's here." Claire moved to the side as she held out her hand to shake his. She seemed cool and confident, but he could tell she was there to give him a good once over for the rest of the family.

He now wondered how many times they were able to trick people. They looked more identical than he could have ever imagined, and besides their mirror images, he was now dying to know about her nickname.

Mina wandered into the room with some boxes in hand and placed them on the kitchen island before walking over. She tried to hide her nervous smile as she bit her lower lip and held out her arms. He wrapped her into a hug and then nestled the crook of her neck as he took in her intoxicating scent that always drove him wild.

He had figured she would be nervous in front of her sister, but after the initial stiffness, she melted in his arms before looking up and finding his lips. "We're almost done. Just need a few minutes, if that's okay?"

He waved them off before adding, "Take all the time you need." They set about finishing up whatever they were doing, and he took advantage of their distraction to become a fly on the wall—watching the twins with fascination. He was positive every guy in town had done it at some point with these two, given their looks and their personalities, but it was his turn now.

Their hair was the same length and the same exact shade of dark brown with slivers of gold that gleamed when the sun peeked in through the windows. They shared the same exotic almond eyes and the same mannerisms. Watching them was entertaining. This could be trouble, and he would have to take inventory of any tiny difference so he wouldn't confuse them in the future.

Mina described her family as protective, and he could see the real reason behind this visit even if Mina didn't. He was just shocked her brother and father weren't in a closet ready to pounce.

Mina smiled at their stacks of gifts and what they had accomplished. "I'm just going to grab my coat from the room! I'll be right back." As she shuffled out of the room, Claire gathered more things but turned her attention to Xander.

"She's told me a lot about you. It's great to meet you." Xander felt bold. Or nervous, he wasn't sure, but he was going to go with bold. "I'm curious to know more about this nickname. If she's Meenie Weenie, what's yours?"

She seemed feline in her actions as she closed a closet door and perched herself on the arm of the large chair across from him. "I'm Claire Bear. I have to tell you, I'm glad I had to run some errands this morning and got the chance to catch a glimpse of the hot dad everyone's talking about at the kid's school." She smiled, and he knew she would be a wild card. A tough one to crack.

"Uh haha." he cleared his throat and tried to think of what to say to that. *Thank you? Oh, that's not me? How the hell did she get Meenie Weenie, and you got Bear attached to your name?* "I think that's a different dad. But I'll take any compliment I can get these days. How did she end up with that name?" *And where the hell is she?*

He had never been nervous in the presence of a woman until this very moment. Her assessment of him was going to be the deciding factor for their future, of this, he had no doubt.

"I'm glad we have a minute to talk before Mina gets finished up." *And here it comes*. He wasn't in the mood to get threatened, but he was willing to take whatever her family threw at him. A brick to the forehead, punch to the gut, or in this case, twin mastermind. He just really wanted to know about the damn nickname, though.

"She's been through a lot." He nodded his head in agreement. He understood this already. She told him a bunch, left out some, and he was still surprised by her positive attitude. "So I want to make sure you won't be putting her through anymore." She looked over at him with a stern look, and he had to admire the woman. She just wanted to keep her sister safe, emotionally and apparently physically.

"You don't have anything to worry about," he started. "In fact, I think my heart may be the one at greater risk."

She looked over to her sister approaching, then looked down and nodded in agreement. Quietly, as if entirely to herself, she mumbled, "I'm afraid you may be right about that one."

"Ready! Sorry I kept you waiting. Hopefully, Claire wasn't a total beast during the rest of the introductions."

He looked over at Mina and couldn't help but grin like a fool. He should be hounded and poked and prodded. He should be put through the wringer or expected to go through several forms of interrogation tactics in order to spend time with her. He would expect nothing less from her family. Staring at her as she stood in front of him, looking divine in the literal sense, he would do anything to be in her life.

"She was amazing. I can't wait to meet the rest of them someday." She gave her sister the side eye and helped Claire gather her things. Apparently, she's done running errands and is walking out with them. It was oddly convenient. "But what's with the nickname?" He really was worried about the source of its creation now that it had been avoided each time, he questioned Claire.

Mina opened her mouth to speak but was cut off.

"I think she had a small fetish with wieners as a child." They both turned their heads to stare at Claire as Xander's mouth dropped open, and Mina's eyes grew three sizes.

"Like the dick kind of wieners. Not the hotdogs." Claire couldn't get through the word hotdog before she was cracking up.

"It was because I was the smaller twin, asshole." Mina turned a shade of pink he hadn't seen on her before. "God, you suck. Just ignore her, Xander."

This was just too good. He decided he loved her sister.

"I think everything is in your bag, and I have all my stuff, so we should be all set for Operation Santa."

Xander held the door open and carted out multiple bags to Claire's car as the ladies chatted about what time Sophie was getting picked up and their plans for tomorrow morning. It felt like they had all done this a thousand times before. Like they were a well oiled machine gearing up for Christmas like it was old news. He loved it.

About an hour later, they pulled up to a quaint little store on the main drag of Telluride. Tourists bustled about, shops were decked out in holiday magic, and the street itself was lined with garland and string lights.

"Hey, I got you a couple of things for Christmas, and I was figuring we wouldn't have much time later between family and getting stuff done."

His mother was huge on gift giving when he was growing up. She spent hours sifting through stores for the perfect shirt for his sister, the perfect card or the perfect tie for their father. Gifts had to hold meaning, and with the gifts in the back seat, he hoped she was able to feel the meaning behind his.

"Want to open them now?" He was a grown ass man sucked back in time to elementary school, asking girls out on papers with a yes and no box for them. Feeling every bit like a child, he just wished she would check the yes box and put him out of his misery.

"You got me something…else? As in more than the surprise

phone and AirPods?" She looked over at him with wide eyes, eyebrows sending wrinkles across her forehead.

It didn't take long to open all the gifts, and once she was finished, she seemed good and overwhelmed. "I can't believe you went to all this trouble. My gift for you is nothing compared to all of this." The look in her eyes went from pure gratitude to embarrassment.

Well, shit. I thought I was killing it.

He hated that he caused her embarrassment, even if he had a damn good time watching her open all of it.

"You don't need to be spending your money on me, Mina. I have everything I've ever wanted. One is on vacation right now, and the other is sitting across the center console." She lifted her head up to meet him with an all too familiar gaze. The smirk that told him she wasn't so sure she believed him. But he would gladly take the rest of his life to prove it. She stared a bit too long with those big almond-shaped eyes, and he may have been thinking of her eyes looking up at him from a bit of a different position. *God, I need help.*

"Open the last one." It was all he could say, and he hoped to hell it didn't sound as gravely to her as it did to him when it left his lips.

Walking through the town with a Lululemon bag must have felt odd for her, he imagined. Seeing her open it and look at the logo with no clue what it was could have possibly been the best thing he'd ever seen. The look on her face was pure embarrassment, but the fact that she didn't know the brand? It had him wanting to buy her more. He had only dealt with high maintenance women in the past, and she was a breath of fresh air.

Where the hell did this woman come from, and how had he

missed her in this small town?

She went from grateful to nearly fainting at the sight of the price tags, and he vowed never to make that stupid mistake again. If she thought Lululemon was a top-tier brand, then she may faint from some of the birthday gifts he was starting to plan.

As he looked over at her, hand placed firmly in his, she looked overwhelmed but happy. She had that traffic-stopping smile again on her face, and he felt like life couldn't get any better. He found himself internally beating his chest when she directed those sweet smiles at him. He wanted to be the last man she ever looked at like that. Fuck that. He was a greedy bastard and wanted to be the only person alive that she looked at like that. End of story.

They made their way to a couple of stores and hit a place that could exchange her size of clothing before they meandered their way over to the bakery, grabbing some coffee and pastries before finding a cozy spot in the corner.

The sun spilled into the big bay windows, only adding to the warmth from the corner fireplace. *Coffee in hand and a croissant to split with a beautiful woman, what more could a man need?*

"So, what have you been up to while I was out of town? You don't have Sophie until what time tonight?" He knew all the things, but he loved hearing her voice and loved getting lost in conversation. He watched with delight as her mouth moved with each syllable and her hands wrapped around her mug. She could talk about the life cycle of a butterfly, and somehow it would be sexy.

It was his attention to her mannerisms that sent a trigger through him. Something was off. Their whole morning was going so well and relaxed, but maybe he hadn't noticed she wasn't acting like herself because he was so caught up in giving her the gifts.

He sat across from her and saw the signs he had missed

before. He just knew she was leaving something out. She normally hums random melodies, but this morning, he missed the light songs in the background. *How did I not hear it?* She seemed on guard, tense even. It could be all the new gifts and her nerves, or it could be something else.

The hustle and bustle of the bakery was distracting enough as every patron came through the French doors, dousing them in a fresh batch of cold winter air. But it was more than a distraction from the chimes on the door or the people all around. It was between them. Did he do something wrong? Maybe she was just trying to act nice, but really, she hated all the gifts? He was now backtracking all of his smug pride. He went from nerves to elation, then on to guilt, and now confusion. *This love thing is a real mother fucker.*

"What else is going on? Something seems off." With those quesitons, she looked at him and tried to feign ignorance. "Are you alright?" He watched her closely and noticed how she tucked her hair behind her ears and took an extra sip of coffee before she looked up at him. He didn't miss how her eyes wandered off before making their way to meet his.

Is this where things end? Is she going to let me down gently but feels embarrassed since I just got her all those gifts?

This wasn't going according to plan, and now he felt like a damn fool. As he looked at her with fresh eyes, he noticed she wasn't sitting up as tall as she normally did. Her smile failed to meet her eyes. She tried to deny it again and chalk it up to being tired, but he wasn't having it. *Well, this is going to shit.*

"What's up? You can tell me." He prodded. She tried to shake it off with a brief scrunch of the nose and a wave of the hand.

"It's nothing really. Just some drama with the ex, but what else is new." He knew that was the norm between them, but he also knew that this guy was an all-star asshole, complete with badge bunnies to boost his ego—the worst kind of person in power. *Probably bragged about his mediocre conquests and his average size dick, too*. Men like him shouldn't be allowed to be police officers. It brings a whole new level of danger to the ball game.

"Well, we aren't in any rush. Tell me what's going on." He didn't want to push or make her feel obligated, but he was struggling to hold it together where that man was concerned. All the hell he put her through was about to end. *No more. Not when she's my woman.*

The chest pounding started back up, and he took deep breaths to keep his Neanderthal at bay. Who knew that finding 'the one' would turn him into a territorial beast?

"It shouldn't be a big deal, but Evan served me with custody papers. He wants more time with Sophie even though I already go around his work schedule." It's as if she took a weight off her shoulders, but her face didn't look like that was all she was worried about. He could see the tears in her eyes that she was trying like hell to keep at bay.

"All right, so we can get a lawyer and figure this out." It was a no-brainer for him. He had to deal with a crazy ex who wanted to make a battle out of custody. He had the money, so he fixed that bullshit. As far as he was concerned, he would give this woman his lung if she needed it, so money was nothing. He would just pay for a lawyer. "What else is bothering you?" She furrowed her brow and practically inhaled coffee.

"It's not that simple. You don't know him." Of course, he didn't know him like she did, but it didn't matter. He knew how to deal with that class of douchebag. Maybe he was a simple man, but this seemed like a problem that had a solution.

"What's there to know? You need a lawyer, and we won't stand for any of his bullshit." He sounded crass, but he was done with letting this guy walk all over her. He did it to intimidate her, and he wouldn't stand for it anymore. He already made Mina work their custody agreement solely around his fucking work schedule. Now the asshole wanted to uproot her life and Sophie's because he was having a tantrum? *No fucking way.*

He also wasn't going to let him intimidate her with this mundane bullshit he was attempting. He just needed to call his lawyer and figure it out. But not today. It was Christmas Eve, and this was not how he planned on spending it, let alone how he planned for her to spend it.

"It's Christmas Eve. Let's not worry about your ex. Just know that I meant what I said when I told you I was done looking. I'm all in, and I have money to cover a lawyer for you."

He had never in his life made a declaration of love and so often. But here he was, putting himself out there like a damn fool only to be questioned about the legitimacy of it all. He wished he just knew how to make her see it.

He reached over the table and placed his hand over hers. It seemed like a lesson in polar opposites when he watched his hand engulf her tiny one. Her skin was dark, and his light tanned. She was petite, while he was tall and broad. He was even eight years older, but here they were, and he couldn't imagine a more perfect fit.

He gave her hand an extra squeeze before he held eye contact. "Don't stress about it today, okay?" Her eyes wandered around the café once more, clearly trying to avoid him as she gathered herself, then finally made their way back to him as she nodded her head in agreement.

"Okay. We just have to talk seriously about him and about what this…" she gestures between them, "all means."

He gave her a tight smile, not liking the idea that she still seemed to not trust the genuine comments, but he would take what he could get right now.

"Good. We will sit down whenever you want." He picked up her hand that was intertwined with his and kissed the back. "Just not today."

CHAPTER 27
Mina

It had been a couple weeks since Christmas, and she had been keeping this secret long enough. She knew he could sense that something was off, and the poor man had even asked a couple of times how he could help or if she wanted to meet with his lawyer in the coming weeks. But she didn't want to take advantage of his kindness. She didn't want to take anything, period. It just felt wrong when he was giving so much, and all she could return was her time and the rest of her heart that wasn't permanently scarred from the last man she trusted.

How do people blend families? How do people deal with exes? It all seemed like too much work, and she was sure he would grow tired of the prospect and move on. She couldn't imagine that many people in this world would be okay with a crazy ex, even if he had one himself. She had Sophie to think of and she wasn't willing to send her little heart into a frenzy again.

It was the same conversation she had with herself every day this past week. The same self-talk that made Xander out to be more of the man from her past than the man she knew could be her future.

Her fears had been driving her to keep looking for an excuse for things to go wrong, and with each new thought, she was making more and more. *Xander won't want to deal with this once he realizes it doesn't just go away. He'll get tired of you just like Evan did. Evan called you boring, and maybe Xander will think so too.*

Weeks of the same questions asking if she was okay and weeks of her lying. She was well aware that he could see through her, but she just couldn't bring herself to start the conversation. She knew that once she did, it could actually end. She just hadn't been ready for that. She knew he would probably say something chivalrous and insist on going through anything together, but she wasn't going to fool herself into believing that he wouldn't eventually get fed up with the constant nonsense. The bachelor life was sure to become tempting after a while.

The coffee shop they had ventured to that morning was the same one every local popped in to grab their daily dose of caffeine and gossip. In the past, she had avoided it like the plague when she was the topic of the smut circulating through town.

Looking around at the little space, she wondered how such a quaint little establishment had helped fuel some of her worst days. The looks and double takes when she would walk on the street, the way people would ask questions that were none of their business, it was all funneling back into the forefront of her mind, and she didn't want any part of it again. Especially not if Xander would be dragged through the mud with her this time.

"Are you going to tell me why you've been so lost these last few weeks?"

The question caught her off guard and yet she was expecting it. She forced a smile but she hated herself for having to go down this road. Hated the doubt and hated her ex for possibly taking her away from this wonderful man.

"You've been super patient while I've been going through some stuff, so thank you for being so kind." She inhaled a deep breath, steeling herself.

"But," he slowly added. He was no fool. He knew there was a catch and he may be caught in the crossfire.

"But, I have to be completely honest about everything that Evan has done and continues to do." Her back was ramrod straight, anticipating the need to build up her exterior, face the worst. He, on the other hand, nodded and spoke his assurances that it's all he had ever wanted. So genuine and sure. *Damn him for being so perfect.*

"It's just that he said one of his friends saw me out on a date and now he's threatening to say things now." The worry on her face pinched at her eyes. She knew he hated that her ex held this much power over her. "He has a habit of lying and making things up about me. I'm worried he's going to say something about you too."

When she finally let him in on her anxiety, she felt a wave of relief only to be swallowed whole by the fear of disappointing this man. She didn't want him going through life held captive by the asshole as she had been for so long. The thoughts were putting a sour swirl in her stomach as she looked at the worry on his face.

"I can handle whatever they want to throw out. I just want to make sure that you're okay in all of this." Of course he was sweet about it. He was sweet about everything. A perfect gentleman. Life around them had ceased to register for her once they started the conversation. The sweet little coffee shop was now part of the battlefield and she had already dodged enough bullets in the past, she didn't want to be caught in the crossfire again. Yet, here she was. She thought small towns were meant to be the quiet and peaceful life, but she was sorely mistaken. Given drama, they can be hell on Earth.

"I'm not sure we should keep this going if he's going to rope you into his web." She didn't even want to look up at him and see what was written on his face, so she chose to keep her eyes on their hands, now wrapped together at the center of the table. A gesture he had done at some point without her realizing how much she needed his touch to sooth her.

"He's sick Xander. Like, seriously messed up. I'm afraid he's going to try and ruin your career or something if he finds out who I'm seeing. He's hacked into my alarm system once and set things off just to scare me. It's just a lot and I don't want you to have to go through this too. I just dont know if we should keep this up if it might bring you down, too."

Xander reared back at the statement as she withdrew her hands and placed them in her lap. She kept avoiding his gaze and willed the tears to stop their determined descent. She would rather make her nails bleed in this coffee shop before she would cry a river but they may come regardless.

"What do you mean we shouldn't keep this up? Do you want to stop seeing me, or is this about being afraid of that asshole?"

The burning behind her eyes grew more intense. Even with her best efforts, a single tear slid down her face, and the façade was broken. This wasn't going how she planned, although she didn't plan on trying to break it off. It just seemed like the inevitable at this point with Evan pulling more stunts.

"No, of course I don't want to stop seeing you." She paused and took a moment to think about how to say the mess that was in her mind. "I've never met anyone like you, I can't help but gravitate toward you in everything I end up doing at every moment of the day. My phone, my thoughts. Every part about my life right now is pulled toward you." She paused and took a deep breath. Trying to center herself and find the right words.

"I'm just worried, is all. This is so fast. It's all new, and these feelings are so intense." She threw her head in her hands and dabbed her eyes. *I was never supposed to fall in love. He wouldn't understand, and how could he?*

He didn't go through what she went through with Evan. She

meant what she said. He was sick. Twisted in every sense of the word. His newest threat of court wasn't about seeing Sophie more, it was about controlling Mina. She was just put into an impossible situation because it was her word over a cops. Who would believe her, especially when all his little cronies were out keeping tabs on her?

"It's a small town, and word gets around. I don't want your credibility to be lost." She didn't want to end things with Xander, but she refused to drag him under. None of this was part of her plan. She was never meant to meet someone. Someone this wonderful.

She couldn't help but think of the difference between what she felt for Xander and what she had experienced with Evan. A marriage that grew apart, and loyalty, rather than love held her to him. This type of love was all consuming. It was fast and overwhelming, and every raw emotion she never wanted to experience but dreamed of having. But who was she kidding? Every time she would think about possibly giving men another shot, she always circled back to the realization that they would end up leaving too. He would get bored of her or of life more settled, and then he would move on. He said he wanted to fight with her, but what if that got old? She wasn't sure she would ever be strong enough to face that kind of rejection from Xander.

She picked herself up before, but if Xander bailed, she would be broken forever because whether she wanted to fall in love or not, she had. They hadn't even slept together yet, but here she was, heart in pieces for a man she had known for a little over a month. The man she wanted to believe in and fight for and love. She never imagined something this strong, and she wasn't sure she was ready for any of it.

A tug on her hand made her peak at him through her fingers. "You know, I never expected to fall in love this fast either."

Her eyes widened, and her cheeks grow hot. She wasn't sure which part of her ramblings were out loud, but either way, she knew she was caught.

"Sweet baby Jesus why can't I get a grip on my mouth?" Her head hit the table with a thud, and Xander broke into a deep belly laugh. The sound made her look up and rest her head on her palm. God, she loved his laugh. It made her feel alive. Like she could take on the world. Like *they* could take on the world.

"I think I like Pontius Pilate more. But baby Jesus has a nice ring to it, so I think it may be a close second." She rolled her eyes and tried to hold back her smile but failed miserably. How could he make her laugh when she was trying to break it off to save him from the slaughter, so to speak?

"Don't smile so much, people around us are going to think you actually like me." He looked at her with those sea green eyes, and she felt like she could drift away in them. "What's a small town without some real drama? Us liking each other seems too easy. We need a little bit of spice."

How did she find this man?

Or better yet, how did he find her? And why did he want her? "You can have anyone you want. I mean, I've heard about how you're in demand at the pickup line. My sisters cyber-stalked you, so we know you make great money. I have nothing but baggage and little to my name. So why me?"

The man had the audacity to bark out a laugh at the idea. He wiped his eyes and tried to stifle the wave of laughter by grabbing his coffee. "Don't you get it, gorgeous?" He shook his head as if he couldn't understand. "You're what I want. You're what I've been looking for." He's said all this before, and yet she didn't believe him.

"I've been looking for you my whole life. I don't mind a little extra drama and a little convincing." He wagged his eyebrows as he looked over at patrons eyeing them, then smiled.

"Gotta keep these townies on their toes." She shook her head in disbelief of her charmer. Maybe it was time to stop asking questions and time to take the leap of faith. With him, he could ease her tension with his words and make her feel safe. Safer than she had ever felt before. He made her feel like what she usually dealt with was about to change, and somehow, she believed him.

He changed the topic, speaking of a birthday for a friend's kid he wanted them to attend together and about needing her sisters number for some advice on a date idea he had. It got her head spinning again but for all the right reasons.

Just like he did with every aspect of her life, he just fixed her problem, wanted to fix her fears and kept on planning their future. He gave her a wink and leaned in close. "As long as they don't go all *Fatal Attraction* on us, I think we'll be just fine."

CHAPTER 28
Alexander

John: Trip to Costa Rica? Play around with some senoritas?

Fuck. He always used to travel with John, but right now, all he could think of was getting Mina away so they could have time together. He was dreading the fact that John would be the biggest dick about him being in a relationship solely because of the travel partner he stood to lose.

Xander: Sorry. Trying to plan a trip with Mina…Maybe Tyler?

John: Turning into a bore

After dropping Mina off, he had to run some errands and call this twin of hers. He also had to figure out a vacation for them to get away for a bit. Scheduling around Sophie would be tricky, but he was in the same boat. He needed Claire to help him figure it all out. Dating with children wasn't easy, but hopefully, with some good planning and some luck, she would be the last woman he ever dated. *Is it too early to get a ring?*

He would have to table that one while he figured out how to ask her and when she would be comfortable. She said it again that morning and it made him wonder what he could do to convince her. Hell, it was starting to piss him off that she had no faith in him or in them together. It was fast, he understood that. But it was real. Even though it scared her, it was reassuring that she felt the pull just as strongly.

In the beginning, he wanted to make sure it was love and not just lust. He would never want to rush her, and he has always had the bad habit of thinking with the wrong head. It had gotten him into tons of fun over the years but also into a ton of drama. He had a little lady to prove it.

But now things felt different for him. Like the universe shifted and it wasn't just lust with Mina. It was the strongest type of sexual attraction he had ever felt. He'd never had to wait this long for a woman, and although he knew he would wait forever if he had to, fucking Mina was now a thought that flitted through his mind about every other second.

Learning to hide the evidence of what she did to him every fucking second was getting to be mind-numbing. Every time she was close to him, he had to adjust himself inconspicuously. He's had a hard-on pretty much since the day he first laid eyes on her, and no amount of fantasizing or jacking off could control it.

He sure as shit was having a hard time being a gentleman and the blue balls he was getting could be medically damaging.

As he drove home after hitting the local market, he had the daunting task of talking with her sister. They looked damn near identical, except for Mina seemed to wear her heart on her sleeve while her sister was more predatory with her emotions. Like she had always taken the older twin role with complete authority. He just had a couple of questions he had to get to the bottom of, and he knew she would be the one person who would fill him in. He hoped.

The dial tone echoed in the truck, and although tempted, he didn't hang up like the pussy he was telling himself not to be. He needed to talk, damnit. Waiting for an answer felt like an eternity. Maybe she wouldn't answer, but that would leave too many unknowns. That wouldn't work.

Three rings later, his finger hovered over the End Call button just before he heard a click. "Hello?" A pause draped the cab of the truck, and he suddenly didn't know what to ask or say. "Xander?" *Well, shit.*

"Hey, Claire! There you are. Sorry, my phone is being weird in my truck." *More like I'm being a little bitch, but who's keeping tabs.*

"My sister said you might be calling me." A little chuckle echoed in the truck and he hated the confidence slipping away from him. *Get it together. You want her to be your sister-in-law.*

"She also gave me your number to make sure I didn't confuse you with a telemarketer." Her voice held onto the amusement, and he was pretty sure she knew what was up. *Devious woman.*

"Perfect. So, I have a couple of questions about Mina that I hope you can help me with." Would he always be this nervous around her sister? Or was it purely because he wanted to lock her down and was afraid he couldn't do it alone? No matter the real reason behind the nerves, he was finding it hard to speak.

"Shoot!" She replied cheerfully. Clearly, she loved Xander being in the hot seat.

"So I was wondering if you could confirm Sophie's schedule so I can plan a getaway for the two of us. I know her time with Soph is the most important thing, and I agree. I just need help working around it." He could practically hear her smiling from the other end of the line.

"Oh my God, yes! I would love to figure that out for you! Text me the dates you're thinking of, and I'll get you the dates for Sophie's schedule." She sounded more excited than he thought Mina would be. "I'm seriously so excited for you guys. Now, just be warned, Mina will probably be nervous or try to have an excuse."

He knew that was coming. He was still trying to figure out how to counteract it.

"She never leaves anywhere without Sophie, so this is going to be a doozy." *Well, shit.* It was intense, even for him. "But I think you're just the man to change all that." The statement piqued his interest, and a smile gnawed at his lips.

"Oh really? And why is that?" Now, the tables had turned, and she was in the hot seat, although he was guessing she liked this limelight.

"Because I think you're the one and she's afraid to admit it." The silence was deafening. "No pressure." She added with a laugh. *God damnit. That's a fuck ton of pressure.* It's one thing to try and prove you're the one, but when someone else thinks you're the only reason it could all get screwed up? That's when shit gets real.

"Oh yeah, no pressure, huh?"

She laughed at his comment, the same laugh she shared with Mina. He could get used to this after all. She was a wild card in some ways, and he was beginning to think Mina was too.

"Is there anything else you want to know about my sister? Favorite candy? Favorite hiking trail? Perhaps her ring size?" There she went again with the wickedness. *She's toying with me because it's easy.*

"One more question." He didn't want to completely give

away his plans but fuck it. He was head over heels, and he had no intention of keeping that a secret. "And yes, to the last one. She's the one. I know she told you that I've been telling her I'm done looking. I want you to know that I'm serious when I say it. I've partied a lot, dated a lot and slept with a lot of women-"

"Tempt me more with these awesome stories so I can throw my sister at you." The sarcasm was loud and clear.

"What I was about to say, was that it was all in search of her. She's everything I've ever wanted and then some. So, if I'm missing something," he lingered on the word so she could catch the weight of the meaning behind it. "Anything at all pertaining to her past or her ex, please help me by filling in any gaps." He waited, giving her a moment. "If you can."

The car filled with silence again. Maybe she wasn't getting the meaning behind his second half of the confession, or maybe Claire would guard her sister rather than help his cause. He was praying she was willing to help.

A heavy sigh came from her end, and she seemed to stop whatever she was doing because it felt as if something had shifted, and she now gave him her full attention. Or rather, she allowed him into her space a bit more to demand his full attention.

"My brother called my husband the other day. He wanted to know who the hell this dad was and what he thought about him." *Well, this isn't going where I thought it would.* "If there is anything you should know about our family, other than the fact that we're fucking awesome." She chuckled at her own humor and he was grateful she lightened the mood. "It's that we love each other fiercely, and you happen to be chasing after our most protected member."

He let out a huff and couldn't help but prepare for what sounded like his impending doom.

She followed up with a quick, "But honestly, we mean well." He let it roll around for a minute before he got up the courage to ask the question he'd been dying to get an answer from.

"What did he do to her, Claire?" He had made it home a couple of minutes ago but couldn't switch the car off and couldn't switch his phone over. He just sat in the driveway, sinking deeper into his seat and deeper in thought.

He knew he might not be ready for the real truth behind her fears and her reluctance to a relationship, but he knew he needed to try. The rumble of the engine was the only noise between them and the silence seemed to stretch out longer than he could bear.

"He broke her."

Three words. Three words were all it took to change his whole perspective. He felt the chill of the outside air creep in, but he was pretty sure he was chilled to the bone from something else entirely.

He broke her.

He broke her.

As if repeating the words would help him conceptualize it all. He knew she was strong. He knew she had been through some rough shit. But hearing those three words come out of Claire's mouth felt like he'd been gutted.

He broke her.

The knife to the stomach wasn't enough as Claire went on, twisting it with each new addition.

"He wore her down until she felt like she was nothing. And then, once the affair came out, he started spreading lies to try and cover his own wrongdoings. Mix that with the verbal abuse and the time he physically abused her." Her voice trailed off, and he didn't know what the hell do to with himself.

"When she's comfortable, I'll let her tell you the specifics, but long story short, it changed her. At least for a little while." The woman of his dreams and the one he's been searching for sounds like a God damned warrior at this point. He dealt with crazy, but he never dealt with it like she had to.

"After she left and before the divorce was final, he was out partying and ignoring his own daughter. I remember Mina seeming numb to life in general outside of Sophie. She told me she felt like she was garbage that he decided to throw away one day. It nearly killed me to hear those words come out of her, Xander. And to top it all off, she stopped singing." He could hear the tears in her voice. "It sounds so dumb, but she stopped singing for a long time." Her voice broke, and she sniffled away the tears.

"I'm sure you know what that means by now. He pushed her down and made sure she didn't feel worthy of getting back up. And for a little while, he took her from all of us."

Singing.

Something so small, but he had been around her long enough now to know that she was always humming something under her breath when she moved around her home or as she searched for something on the shelf at a store. It was her. She was the melody of his life now and to know that the soundtrack could be shut off would be devastating.

"She's my other half and the wild child baby of the family, but he left her as a shell, and she's been clawing her way back to life ever since."

They both just sat there with their grief, overcome by what someone they love had to go through. As if the skies above were weeping with Claire, the soft flurry had returned to accompany the day and their frame of mind.

"Fuck, Claire. How the hell am I supposed to handle that?" He was serious. He wanted her more than he wanted anyone or anything in his entire life, but he was terrified. While he was out sleeping around, she was fighting her way back to herself, and he felt like if he wasn't careful, he could break her.

"Long story short, my husband told our brother that it didn't really matter what any of us thought of you, Xander." Slack jawed and wide eyed, he was surprised to hear the words.

"My husband pointed it out to all of us that we haven't seen her this happy in a really long time. Maybe ever. It won't be easy, but honestly, we're all rooting for you in our own ways. The one and only other guy she went on a single date with, ended in a disaster because Evan found out and spread more rumors throughout town about her being a whore. She's worried he's going to spread gossip about you, and it could affect your reputation. Being a teacher before she stayed home with Sophie, she thought she would never be able to teach again, and now-"

"She's worried he could jeopardize the career I've worked my ass off for." He supplied.

"Exactly." The pieces of the puzzle were starting to fit, and things were getting a bit less foggy. It made more sense than he thought. She wasn't just worried for herself; she was worried for him, and she had good reason to be. The asshole loved drama, and he loved to fuck with people's lives.

"This is all a game to him, isn't it?" He could never stoop so low, but he understood what the guy was after. He couldn't wrap his head around how he let her go in the first place.

"I think it's all a way to keep him in her life somehow. Even bad press is good press if it keeps him in the headlines for her, you know?"

He hated the mother fucker so much that it made it nearly impossible to think straight. But regardless of what Claire was saying, all Evan had was chaos and cruelty. He needed to show her what real love looked like because she only knew the kind from an immature dick.

"He won't be in the headlines for long. Mark my words."

CHAPTER 29
Mina

She was relieved to see Xander after this morning's confession. Saying something is one thing, but following through was a whole different story. He meant what he said, and he showed up just like he said he would. Looking so damn good it was sinful, on top of it all.

Once he hit the doorframe, the wait was over, as he grabbed her by the hips pulling her close and claiming her mouth. The kind of kiss that didn't just serve as a greeting.

No.

This kiss said so much more than that, and she loved how he had a way of using his body to show his love. She couldn't help but wonder how good he would be if a kiss could make her senseless, especially since his tongue had shattered her to pieces. The thought gave her goosebumps and sent a flicker of warmth down her body. That was something they haven't done yet and the tension was palpable. She felt like a different person around him. Always dying for more but not wanting to say it outright. She understood that he wanted her to be sure and that what she felt was love and not lust, but wouldn't it be good enough for him to feel it or that she said it in her ramblings? That was enough of an admission for her, at least.

With hands still, firmly on her hips, he moved her backward without breaking their kiss, into the living room and away from prying eyes. She loved this side of Xander.

His hands roamed over her backside before he gripped the underside of her thighs and helped her wrap her legs around his waist. She interlocked her ankles behind his back while he moved one hand to the nape of her neck, putting more pressure on her mouth. Whether it was from the admission this morning or his love for her in general, something brought out the dominating side of Xander, and she was a slave to it, barely holding her ragged breaths between each jarring kiss.

She was shameless for him. But before things moved further along, he slowly eased her down, slowing his kiss and easing her back to the present. He grabbed her face in his hands and moved his lips with a renewed sense of control. She wanted to cry from the distance it put between their stolen moment and what had almost happened. But it would have to wait, yet again because he seemed to have things to say and more to share.

He let his nose linger on hers, standing there for what seemed like years as their foreheads met in the middle. His hands had moved to wrap themselves around the base of her chin and up behind her ears. It felt purely intimate despite being fully clothed.

"I have a surprise for you." She hadn't been expecting any more gifts, but honestly, he was all about spoiling her rotten. More gifts would be the last thing to shock her at the moment. She broke free of his hands and tried to get a hold of her senses.

"What could you possibly have for me now?" She demanded playfully. He reached into his overnight bag and pulled out an envelope. It was plain and gave nothing away. He handed it to her and then stood back and leaned against the island. Oozing sex and bawdiness. The sight made her pinch herself internally. *The headlines could read, bookworm nerd lands the town sex symbol.*

She stared at the paper in her hands and grappled with the weight of it, trying to guess the surprise. She could leave this man hanging all day just to keep all of his attention on her. That damn devilish grin was almost too beautiful to bear. She was sure many women lost their dignity in the face of that smile. She was one of them.

As she reached in, she noticed the paper had a heavier and waxy feel to it. A perforated line was another clue and as she pulled the tickets out, she gasped in shock. "You didn't!" His smile widened at the sight of her excitement. She held onto the ticket with one hand while she used the other to cover her mouth, mumbling as she read aloud to confirm she wasn't losing her mind.

"We're going to Charleston? As in Charleston, South Carolina?" She couldn't contain an errant squeal as she closed the small space between them and leapt into his arms again. She wrapped her legs around his waist and smothered his face with choppy kisses. He chuckled at her assault and met her with his own, hands roaming from her neck to her rear and everything in between. *This is what bliss is.*

She was consumed and overwhelmed and all of it felt so right. This time it was her turn to hold his face in her hands as she lost herself to her happiness. She couldn't control her excitement and fear, but it was a blur, and she was going to let herself bask in all of it.

"How on earth did you plan this?" She asked in between kisses as her hands roamed his hair and shoulders. She was grateful the man was built like a lumberjack because his large frame made this position impossibly easy to make out in.

"I listen." She could feel the smile as she kissed his lips. "And I called Claire."

She giggled in between each kiss. She loved him so damn much it hurt. This man who listened to her, called her sister to plan trips and showered her with support as well as gifts.

They let their hands continue to pursue and their mouths more exploring as Xander walked them into her bedroom. She was grateful for her tiny home as she quickly felt the soft fabric at her back and the dip in the mattress on either side of her. She had been straddling him just moments before he adjusted them and took his position on top.

He broke their kiss, looking at her as he sat back on his heels. "Your love of architecture." He brushed gentle kisses along her neck that sent aches of pleasure in their wake before he paused again. "Your love of history." He unhooked her bra and slid her shirt up, exposing her to him just before he leaned over, sucking and nipping. It wasn't lost on her that he was going through the reasons why he chose Charleston, but the man could tell her he was taking her to Yuma and could make it sound poetic.

The assault on her body was almost too much. He let out a sigh and looked up at her face before breathily whispering, "Your love of beauty and excitement." Then his mouth was on her. She gasped, arching her back off the mattress. *God, he's good.*

Using one hand to cup her breast to his mouth, he used the other to slowly work its way up to her throat, squeezing gently. It was deliberate and steady. Forceful but gentle while he set his mouth to work. The moment was suspended in time as he took ownership of her body with his hands and mouth. Drawing out her need and reveling in the pleasure of her noises as he went. Once he was finished with the relentless sucking and teasing, he trailed kisses down the center of her stomach, heading straight to her core.

"One day, my baby is going to be growing right here." He said as his tongue licked and sucked her skin. It was erotic, and she wasn't sure she would be able to speak outside of moans. He grazed his fingers on the edge of the fabric and her lower stomach before pulling her joggers off.

The skills he learned as a trained frat boy were going to good use, and she was now the biggest cheerleader of his college days.

When his kisses met the sensitive skin on the inside of her thighs, he looked up at her with a roguish charm only he could possess, "Your love for ghosts and graveyards and everything that's sinister and dark." He palmed her core as she whined from his procrastination.

"We're still on reasons? I can't think anymore." He let out a low chuckle before his tongue slid into her, and the humor shifted to appreciating moans. Her head slammed back into the pillow before she had time to breathe again. He licked and sucked, relentlessly so. Like he wanted nothing more than to devour her, and it set her body on fire. He squeezed her hips as she rode his face harder, loving the feel of his stubble against her soft skin.

"God, it feels so fucking good." Her words spilled out of her mouth in between moans, moving her hips faster with each swipe of his tongue.

"Let me make that pretty little pussy come." *Holy Fuck, his words...* As her hips thrust forward and met his tongue, she felt his grip tighten around her, nipping into her flesh. His tongue flattened, painfully pleasing the apex of her nerves and keeping pace with his relentless rhythm. It was waves of pleasure pulling her closer and closer until he broke off, pausing to look up at her from between her thighs. The small break from his mouth left her feeling empty only to be filled by his words alone.

"I love you, Mina."

The words slid so easily from his mouth and finally, for once, she let herself revel in the meaning. Like taking wine at a long and lazy dinner. She was consumed, moved and manhandled all at once. She could feel his fingers, digging into her skin on her hips with a biting force while his other digits moved in circles. She was sure she didn't even have the ability to open her eyes at this point.

"I want all of you, Mina. I want this. Every. Fucking. Night." His words were a punishment, taking his tongue away from her needy body, while his fingers were the reward as she started drowning in the motion of them as they continued working into her. He kept up their pace and he returned his tongue to her body with a reckless abandon that had her over the edge and screaming his name.

"Xander! Fuck, I'm coming!" Her ragged breath hitched. She screamed the only words she knew. "Fuck!" The blood pumping in her ears and the moans coming out of her mouth blocked out everything else in the world. Coming apart beneath him was all she felt and all she knew. He was intoxicating. She knew this. But this level of sex and lust filled her head with emotions that were so much more potent than anything she had ever felt.

After a few moments of living in the blissful high, she started to come back down, and her breathing started to even out. He kept kissing her gently and possessively as he licked up every last drop of her lust and dotted her thighs with nips.

She hadn't realized the aggressive hold she had on his hair until she regained feeling in her fingers and eased them out of his scalp. "Oh my God, Xander." As she spoke, she could feel his breath on her sensitive flesh, and she shivered with the ghost of his lips being so close.

"You taste so fucking good." He kissed and licked her as if he was worried one single bit of her would go to waste. She had never experienced a man lust for her cum, but that was what he was doing. He had devoured and thoroughly enjoyed her before he ripped his shirt off and tugged his jeans down, leaving him in strained boxers.

She already knew he was well endowed, but as he pulled the waistband past his hips, his dick sprung free, and she felt herself wondering if she would be able to walk the next morning.
He stroked his length as he used one knee to spread her thighs wider.

Coming back to positioning himself upright, nestled right

against her core. He held himself close, letting his head brush up against her opening, pausing there and driving her wild.

"You ready?" The poor man seemed like he could hardly hold himself up, let alone hold himself back. When she nodded and lifted her hips to meet his thrust, he groaned. Taking a moment before he reached down for a condom. She watched as he tore the foil packet open before she placed her hand on his, stopping him from finishing the task.

"You don't need to. I'm on the pill." The heat in his stare was so intense she thought he would keel over on the spot.

"You sure?" She kept her eyes on his as she arched her back and helped him line up to her entrance.

"Positive. I'm yours, Xander. I want to feel everything." He smiled and shook his head.

"God, woman. You can't talk like that and expect me to last long." He wasted no time as he pushed into her. Stretching her and filling her with a sting that was proof of his size. His body tensed up as she let out a strangled moan and they waited for her body to adjust to his size.

"Holy Fuck." It was official. His orgasms had made her stupid, but she was fine with the lack of vocabulary as long as he kept them coming.

"You take my cock so good." He leaned down and kissed her as he slowly continued to fill her up to the hilt. Moving in and out, taking his time to worship her body as she adapted to his. Hard muscles suffocating in ways she never knew she needed or wanted. His hands worked her breasts until they found her throat, giving a firm hold to keep him balanced as he pushed into her over and over. All of his filthy words had her reeling. Between what he did with his mouth and what was coming out of it, it felt so dirty, and she loved every second of it.

The duality of his actions, of his words, of him. He could be sweet and gentle but could make her feel like an exotic exploit that he refused to share with anyone else. It was a dynamic she never wanted to change. He made her feel dirty when he put his hands around her neck or when he made her kiss the arousal from his lips, then made her feel like the most prized possession in the world. It was dangerous but Mina knew that she was already gone. Long gone.

His slow and steady thrusts quickened, and their kiss went from teasing to ravenous. The way his tongue dominated her mouth and his body kept moving with an unrelenting pace was almost too much for her. He was all consuming and right now she was letting him devour her again. Her hands clawed at his back with each thrust, and the sound of skin slapping skin mixed with moans echoing throughout the room. She had never been fucked like this in her life, and it was everything she had dreamt sex could be.

"I don't know how long I can last with your tight cunt around my cock." His words were jarring but she craved everything that came from his mouth. He had a wicked tongue that he knew exactly what to do with. The thrusts came harder, and he gripped her shoulders to hold her in place, almost pinning her down.

"Come again for me, baby." She was mindless with passion. As she bent her knees more and opened herself up to him further, he let out a low growl, clearly on the edge. He pushed harder and harder. She was sure she wouldn't be able to walk straight for a couple of days but watching him this wild was worth it.

It was only a few thrusts later that she exploded into another orgasm, finding her second release just before he came to shouting her name. The culmination was everything. It was earth shattering in a way she had never experienced. Like they were made for each other and this moment.

He gripped her to his body as if she was his life boat. Holding on for dear life before he slowed his thrusts, gripping the headboard with his other out of need. As if he would be blown over from the shear force of his climax. They moved in unison as their breathing came back to them. His aftershocks sending little tremors through his body that spilled over to hers. She held onto him, until he kissed her over and over again. Soft and gentle as he let her enjoy the lasting effects on her way back down. She had never been relished after the deed was done. Even after gripping her neck, he showered her with more kisses. After talking so crude, he massaged her body. He was hypnotic.

"Are you okay?" He asked as he sat back on his knees, admiring his handy work now visibly escaping her. It was carnal as he groaned and pulled her to his chest before slumping onto his back with her at his side.

"God, the sight of you with my cum dripping out." He bit his fist before kissing her deeply, again. The scruff of his beard stung her cheek, but she welcomed it.

"I'm sorry if I was rough. You felt so fucking good. It was hard to control myself." She could hear the smile in his voice as he went back to kissing and holding her. Making her feel adored. Sleep clouded her vision as she lay in his arms and let the rest of the world fade away.

This was her happy place. He was her happy place, and they stayed there, overlapping with her on his chest and his arms wrapped around her body. The idle movements of his fingers circling her shoulder calmed her and sent her into an ease she hadn't expected. Like his presence alone was her safety net.

Falling asleep had become hard to do with her nightmares creeping in every time she closed her eyes. But being enveloped in his arms was different. It was peaceful, and it was home. She let herself drift in and out of consciousness as the rhythmic sound of their breathing and the gentle rise and fall of his chest lulled her into comfort. Surrounded by him and a million possibilities for their future, she was pulled under just as she heard the hushed whisper,

"Marry me, Mina."

CHAPTER 30
Alexander

It left his lips before he realized what he had said, but he had never been more sure of a single thing in his entire life.

Thinking back on last night, he was trying to wrap his head around how she would have taken it if she were awake. *Was she awake and she was just too afraid to say anything?* Hell, he wanted to say it on their first date, and in a roundabout way, he did. He was sure she was the one and he didn't see any sense in waiting. But he understood that she had more obstacles than he did.

In order to make it to the altar with him, she needed to face those issues and feel comfortable with her ex.The way she described the man, he was a power-hungry prick who held far too much control of this town.

On the one hand, you would think someone on the police force would have to reign in their kind of crazy. But on the other, he held a position that gave him that power almost absolute. Who would take anyone else's word over that of a cop? This was quickly turning into a sticky situation, but he just needed a plan. He was acutely aware of the kind of destruction Evan left everywhere he went. The level of manipulation he had to have in order to keep his life and the pawns he held in this town in order was astounding. The man had skills, but only the kind Xander had no interest in possessing.

First things first, he needed to tell Amelia his plan. His daughter was already in love with love in general, but also in love with the instant family she would have. He never kept his daughter in the dark about Mina and each day, his favorite cheerleader asked about the progress he had made. She was due back from her mother's in another day, so he had time to get some things lined up and figure out what to say.

Lauren may be better, and her husband might seem like a nice enough meathead, but he wasn't going to go out on a limb and pretend that his side of things was going to go perfectly smooth, either. When he lets them in on the fact that he has met and fallen in love in a shockingly fast time, he is almost positive she will have something snarky to say. Lauren will pitch a fit just to be pissed rather than say anything out of any real sense of mothering.

As he decided he needed a solid plan for both the exes, he saw lights flicker behind him from his rearview mirror. He put on his blinker and checked his right side before pulling over, then checked his dash to make sure he hadn't been speeding. *This better not be her ex*. He hadn't been doing anything except running into town to grab some groceries. Now he wasn't so sure he would be able to take the high road today if this turned out to be her ex.

Putting all other ideas aside, he checked his glove box and gathered his shit before the officer could make it to his window. He could only make out the uniform as they came around the driver-side door in the middle of the little town square. If any of his brothers had to run into town for something, he would be in for it.

Once, a long time ago, every cop was well aware of the McCade boys. Each one was more infamous than the last. But times were different now and they had each outgrown childish pranks and teenage partying. This wasn't something he was used to anymore.

He rolled down the window as the officer came into view and he looked for a badge or a name tag of sorts. *They must have one, right?* Yet this officer didn't, and its absence made him uneasy, making the devil on his shoulder perk up at the prospect of foul play. A feeling he hadn't felt since college... and since Mina came into his life.

"Do you know why I pulled you over, sir?" The man wore the typical aviator sunglasses that every typecast cop wore, and given a donut, he would complete the look. He pushed the glasses up the bridge of his nose as he looked at Xander. His posture was threatening with his hands crossed over his chest and stance wide. For such a minor traffic stop this was sure turning into a show. Xander still didn't know why the hell the cop pulled him over in the first place. The guy was dripping with douchebag vibes, but who was he to judge? Apparently, he was the one who fucked up and broke the law.

"Honestly, I'm not really sure. I don't think I was speeding." Xander took off his sunglasses to try and get a better look at the man outside his window. But he was a shield behind the mirrored frames and uniform. A hunk of muscle that kept on with the stereotype, but no distinguishing features to speak of. Medium-height white male. He wondered if it was her ex and this would be how they faced off the first time. The man was sick but this would hit a new level. He was snapped out of his head when the cop spoke up again.

"The license showed that your documents are past due. Can you get them out for me, please? Then I'm going to need you to step out of the vehicle."

Step out of the vehicle? What the fuck is this guy on?

"I assure you my registration is up to date." *I didn't do anything, asshole.* "And is it really necessary to have me get out of the vehicle when I have the papers right here?" He tried to hand the cop his paperwork through his window as the cop stepped back and gestured with his hand to come out of his truck. *Fucking prick.*

Judging by the asshole vibes coming in loud and clear, he was either her ex or one of his friends. This was all just too damn frustrating to be real.

He stepped out of his truck and handed the nameless cop his paperwork. The officer took hold of his papers, still icy to Xander and still acting as if he had robbed a bank.

"Thank you, sir. If you could please stand over here and place your hands on the bed of the truck where I can see them."

Is this guy for real? "Is this seriously necessary for a potential expired registration?" The hint of anger wasn't hidden from his voice anymore. He wasn't sure if that was a good idea or not, but he stopped caring. "I told you my tags are up to date and I haven't done anything wrong. This seems a little extreme."

The cop didn't like the disdain in his voice as he repeated himself. "Hands on the bed of the truck where I can see them, sir. I have reason to believe you have a concealed weapon on you. I need to make sure this stop is as safe as possible while I check your paperwork in my vehicle."

The man was infuriating, but Xander was stuck between a rock and a hard place. He bit down, grinding his teeth together to steal his anger before replying.

"My gun is under the driver-side seat if you want to check it. I assure you that the paperwork on that is also current and legal."

The cop did little to acknowledge what Xander said as he went back to his cruiser and started typing away on his screen. Xander was left in the middle of another bustling day in downtown Kings Ranch as onlookers and passersby went about their business. *Yeah, this isn't embarrassing at all.*

"Alexander McCade. Getting into trouble this afternoon?" He looked up at the sidewalk in front of him to notice an older woman he knew all too well.

"Hello Mrs. Jensen. How are you?" It had to be one of his mother's oldest friends. This situation may have been funny about fifteen years ago but not now. He was a father for fucks sake and this woman was absolutely sure he was loving his bachelor life when he really wasn't. *Of all of my mother's friends, it had to be her.*

"I was pulled over for having nonexpired registration apparently." The look on her face didn't make him feel better as she clearly didn't believe his situation, tutting her disapproval. She never trusted the McCade boys. Maybe it had something to do with his middle brother fucking her daughter in their hot tub one night and getting caught. But that was neither here nor there and that was a lifetime ago. The old hag never forgave any of them for the trouble his brother's dick got them into. *Fucking Brent.*

"Mrs. Jensen, how are you?" The cop came back from his vehicle and handed Xander the papers as he thoroughly kissed ass.

"Oh, fine dear. And how is your little one?" *So now they are best friends?* He reasoned that it made sense given the kind of shit day it was turning out to be.

"She's getting bigger by the day. I told her she needs to stop growing so I won't have to scare off all the boys that are going to be coming around." The sound of his voice was like nails on a chalkboard as he faked his way through the exchange. He was probably just like Evan and fucked around on his wife while she was none the wiser.

Mrs. Jensen said her goodbyes and left the men on the street as Xander came to the conclusion that he must be in a twilight zone.

"Papers came back clean, man. Sorry, I had to take up some of your day." Xander took him in and wasn't sure what to say. He didn't have to wait too long before the dickhead started back up.

"Where were you heading on this fine day in Kings Ranch?"

Fine day? "The jeweler, actually. Going in to look at rings and then to the grocery store." He wasn't entirely sure when he decided to check out Rings, but knowing it could get back to her ex was making his skin itch with gratification. The prick wanted her back and he was going to make damn sure Evan was painfully aware that she was off the market.

"Jeweler, huh? Someone in your life about to become a bit more special?"

It was officially the strangest day he has had in quite some time, and that was saying something. He reached for the handle of his truck door as he talked to the cop over his shoulder.

"Yeah, that's the plan, boss." He was done with this cop and done with this conversation, so all polite talk went out the window. He didn't mind cutting it all a bit short. He lifted his leg into the truck and was about to close the door to the shit show he just went through when he could hear the cop walk back to his as well.

He shut the door in time for the cop to pull out onto the street before he rolled down his window by Xander's truck, clearly waiting for Xander to do the same. As he rolled down his window, the officer gave him a toothy smile before waving to him.

"Make sure you tell Mina we all said hi. Take it easy, Alexander." Without another word, the cruiser pulled into traffic and crept further down the street.

CHAPTER 31
Mina

Everything felt like it was coming to a head and getting there in a fucking hurry. She heard, from a friend of a friend that knows the asshole, that he intimidated Xander through a friend.
God, it's all confusing to keep track of.

A routine traffic stop based on bullshit and then a little message just to make it clear that they were both being watched now. None of it made sense, but she knew Evan's twisted mind didn't work like that of hers or Xander's.

He was a narcissist.

A manipulator.

A psychopath. He didn't operate like the rest of the world. He actually believed he controlled it. He never liked that she was the one that left him, and she had always been terrified at how far he would go.

"What do you think he's going to do?" Mina couldn't stand

that it had been a little over a week and Xander hadn't said anything about the incident. She was positive Xander didn't want her to worry, but his discretion made her wonder what else she was unaware of at this point.

"What do you mean what's he going to do? Has he done anything yet? Has he told you about it?" Claire seemed annoyed with how worried she was, while Mina was annoyed at Claire's lack of emotion.

"You know he hasn't told me anything." She scolded.

"Then why are you stressing about this? Xander is a big boy, and he can take care of himself. In fact, I'm fucking over the moon Evan is stupid enough to pull shit on someone who will call him on it. You have always felt trapped by the fear of him taking Sophie from you, but Xander? I can't wait to see what he comes back with."

She knew she was right…to a certain degree.

"Your telenovela just got way better." Claire wasn't helping. Her anxiety was always kept at bay through the years, but it was currently on the verge of making her throat close up. *Breathe in, breathe out.*

"Speaking of the big boy, you haven't told me how the darker side of Hot Dad has been, lately."

Was Claire seriously jumping from Evan spiraling out of sanity to Xander in bed?

"All good in your real-life dark romance world?" Her mind went back to a week ago after they slept together for the first time. What he said when he thought she was sleeping…

"How you can bounce between such different men and different scenarios is beyond me. It's a skill." Claire cackled on the other end of the line as Mina kept going. "But you will be happy to know that his cock is still huge, and now I know he is quite good at using it." Claire had always rubbed it in Mina's face how her husband was in the bedroom, now it was Mina's turn to brag. "But Claire," she almost didn't know how to say it without being somewhat shy. "He knows how to do more things than I even knew were possible."

"What the fuck! Okay, now you need to spill it." They went about gossiping and exchanging stories. Mina spilled on Xander and his many talents while Claire offered her congratulations and any new juicy topics in her marriage.

"There's something else too." She was vague and she knew it would kill Claire.

"Good grief, if the man has made you enjoy getting fucked in the ass, then I'm really going to lose my shit. I think I would have to admit defeat and take back everything I've ever said about not wanting it."

Mina almost spit out her water as she coughed and choked, her eyes stinging. Claire had a way with words. "Oh my God!" She coughed. "I'll let you know how to take it in the ass when I'm sure he will teach me that too." With Xander in the picture, it was a whole new world, apparently.

"I was going to tell you about something a bit more serious than anal, so gather yourself." She could hear Claire take a couple of mock deep breathes and then report back, "Okay, I'm ready. Shoot." Mina opened her mouth before Claire chimed in again.

"But if you tell me that you could deep throat without gagging then I'm going to tell you right now, I don't even know who you are anymore. There I said, you may continue." Another rumble of laughter left her before she was able to speak up.

"What I was going to say, before you so rudely interrupted with your super intelligent and mature comments, was that after he thoroughly fucked my brains out, I started to drift off to sleep. And he didn't think I heard it, but he asked me to marry him. I think."

There was a long pause, and she wasn't sure what to say. She knew she was freaking herself out so it would make sense if it freaked her sister out too.

"Okay. First of all, how do you think someone asks you to marry them? And second, how fucking adorable is he? You two are so dang cute! I'm seriously jealous of the little love story you guys have." She paused.

"You know, without the whole stalker ex and bullshit harassment...and his crazy exes, and the court stuff... But besides that, its adorable."

Well, that took care of her fears. Claire was thinking along the same lines she was. It was all adorable and terrifying and so fucking cute. She kept telling herself that Hallmark love stories didn't exist but she was currently living in one and she wasn't sure about what to do with it.

"Right? What the hell is all this Claire? Is this guy for real or is he playing me because I don't think I've ever heard of a nonfictional guy being this romantic. I don't know what the fuck to do." It seemed easy enough, but she had learned that in life, when things seemed too good to be true, they usually were. It seemed blaringly obvious to Mina that he fit into that category.

"Yeah Mina, I think you're right." She grew quiet as she realized her sister would be thinking the same thing. She was most likely bringing her back down to reality and away from these crazy fantasies.

"I think he's after your money." Claire mocked her.

"Sometimes I hate you." She deadpanned.

"Wait a minute, you said you now know. Was that the first time you guys had sex?"

That was the statement that shocked her sister the most? Out of everything else she had told her, she hung on to that little bit? "Yes, Claire. I didn't want to jump into bed, and he wanted me to make sure it was real. After he gave me the plane tickets and told me all his plans, he kissed me…"

How could she describe the kiss? Possessive? Overwhelming? However corny it would come out, it still wouldn't do justice to what it felt like in the moment. It felt like it was the only thing she ever needed for the rest of her life.

"He kissed me like I've never been kissed before and then

we didn't stop." She sighed.

"I didn't think you guys waited that long. I just really thought you didn't want me thinking you were whoring it up with the hot dad." *I should have been whoring it up.*

"Thank you for that sweet sentiment, but after he literally made love to me and fucked my brains out, he kissed me all over and treated me like I was some precious stone needing to be thanked and cherished and rubbed and cuddled. I don't know how the fuck to describe it, but it was…it just was."

She could hear Claire practically vibrating with her energy across the phone line. "And then he asked you?"

"Kind of. It wasn't a question so much as a statement I probably wasn't meant to hear. He stroked my shoulder lightly, planted a kiss on top of my head and then said, "Marry Me, Mina."

She couldn't deny that it was the most romantic thing she had ever heard of in her entire life. The man was drop-dead gorgeous, and he was all about her.

"Aww! Mina! Holy fuck, that is the cutest thing I've ever heard!" She gushed before adding, "Don't tell Kyle I said that!"

CHAPTER 32
Alexander

"What's up, cocker?"
Oh, the terms of endearment he and his brothers use. A thing that will never grow old. Between cocker, broski, or any vulgar term they could finagle into a greeting, they would never stop trying to out 'burn' the other.

"How are you, old man?" His middle brother hated being called old. Maybe it was his ever-shiny balding head or the fact that he flat-out refuses to believe the hair won't come back. Either way, Brent fucking hated it, which meant Xander and his oldest brother, Theo, loved it.

"Fuck you, man. I was calling to tell you congratulations. I heard that you may or may not have been looking for a ring for Mina." Good grief, his mother. It wasn't really a secret. He just wanted to be the one to tell his brothers. It was a big deal, and after all the searching, he just wanted to be the one to do it. "But now I feel like the fuck you part will suffice."

"Ouch. You wound me, brother."

"How come I had to hear this shit from Mom? The woman is pushing seventy, and you felt you should trust this kind of excitement with only her?" He rolled his eyes but loved it. "The woman is having a heart attack at the idea of her baby boy giving her another grandchild. You better be serious about this one. Fuck knows you've looked long enough."

The hint of humor in his voice wasn't lost on Xander, and he could practically hear the air quotes around the word looked. He knew what he meant by that comment, but his brother was the same back in the day. All of them were, to be honest. The McCade boys were a force to be reckoned with, and the whole town knew of their reputation.

"Shut the fuck up. Yes, I'm serious, and yes, I'm done looking. I've never looked at rings before, so that, right there, should tell you that the search is finally over. She's the one." He felt it deep down in his bones, and it felt so damn good to let his brother in on the revelation. "Besides, Mom has Charlie in case me and Theo don't give her any more little rugrats."

"I'm happy for you! I can't wait for her to join the gang. I'm sure Carley and Mom will love her. Theo is a lost cause, so whoever he brings around will just have to suck it up."

They laughed at his joke even if it did seem like his mom really had given up on his oldest brother. At forty-three and living life as a bachelor still, she may have been onto something.

"So when do we get to meet her? When are you going to ask her? Does Amelia know about any of this yet?" There were so many questions and so many things he didn't know how to answer yet.

"Amelia knows everything. She's probably been more of the mastermind than I've been at trying to get this woman locked down. She's going to go with me when I make the final arrangement for the ring and stuff. As for when you all get to meet her, I was thinking sometime soon. Now that the holidays are over and things have calmed down, let's try and get together for dinner. Maybe in the next couple of weeks."

He wasn't sure when she would feel comfortable meeting all of them, and he purposely left out the last part because, well, he really didn't know when she would be comfortable with him proposing. The shit with her ex was making her nervous about the whole situation. They would have been married by the end of the first date if it was up to him, but he was pretty sure her ex would have arrested him on some type of bogus charge for that too.

"Are you going to tell me when you plan on popping the question or will I have to hear about that from mom, too?"

He couldn't keep the humor from his voice. "Man, you will be the first to know right after the big show. I promise you that." His brother grumbled, but he didn't care. "But you know what? I could use some brotherly advice on a different topic if you have any to spare. The asshole ex she has is a cop here in town, and even though we haven't told anyone we're seeing each other, I already got pulled over last week for some bogus traffic violation. When he let me go, the cop told me to tell Mina hi from them. I don't know who 'them' is, but it pissed me the hell off."

It more than pissed him off, he wanted to kill someone, and he was pretty sure that was just the start of the bullshit he was going to go through.

"Seriously? A fucking cop pulled you over and then told you to tell Mina hi?" he guffawed loud enough for the sound to reverberate inside his truck. "Fuck. That can't be good."

"Yeah, thanks for the wise words. Got any other shit advice you want to bestow on me?"

Brent chuckled at the sarcastic comment his little brother

slung at him.

"You know what? I don't need to hear you make fun of the fucked-up situation I'm in." He decided he should possibly call Theo about this.

"I'm sorry, I'm sorry." He wheezed. "I know this sucks. The dude sounds like an absolute psycho. It's just so fucking ironic that you dated such crazy women, and now the woman of your dreams has a fucking whack job of an ex. You seriously just can't catch a break, brother."

That, he was sure of.

"Yeah, yeah. I know. But seriously. Did you ever have to deal with a girl's crazy ex?" His brother hadn't had experience with many crazy women, but he sure as fuck had been in many fights in his younger years. There was bound to be a run-in with a crazy person he had dealt with.

"I don't know, bro. I just feel like he and his buds are being super immature and will cut their shit off after that stunt. They're cops. How much worse could it get?"

He has a point. How much worse could they get? It only took two days to find out.

"Another shot!" Tyler yelled across the bar towards the overrun bartender in a skimpy white tank top. He probably wanted to fuck her once she got off shift, but Xander already spoke his peace, so he left it alone.

The boys all came down to Kings Ranch to do their annual Superbowl watch party at Xander's house. Back in the day, he could keep up with them, but now he just didn't have any interest to. He wanted to be at Mina's drinking coffee rather than at the bar drinking bourbon with his boys.

"Fuck that shit, if we do more shots, then I'm going to need an IV bag and won't be able to watch the damn game tomorrow." He threw it out there as a joke, but he knew he was already going to end up with his head in the toilet tonight and most of tomorrow. He didn't know what those assholes did to hold their liquor like college kids, but he sure as hell missed the boat on it.

"Don't be a pussy. One more shot before we get some food." This whole bar-hopping bit had gotten old. He could be balls deep in Mina if he could just get away. "All right asshole, tell us about your girl. You said she was "the one" so what the hell is going on with all that?" Leave it to John to make Mina part of the conversation as he ogles a brunette across the room. How had he never noticed his best friends were such assholes with women?

"Things are great, man. Starting to think I should be over there instead of here with you dirtbags. Dude, we're over here at this table." John flipped him off before taking a long swig of bourbon.

"Yeah, tell us how Mina is these days. Any second thoughts on wanting to get married?" He couldn't tell if Tyler had finally come around to the idea of marriage but he didn't care. In reality, Xander was his source of entertainment outside of his work/travel schedule. The man would really have to be a better husband if Xander were to become one soon.

"Actually," he held up his hand and flipped off the boys with his ring finger. The collective shock in their group was almost tangible as they registered his intentions.

The shouts that ensued added to Xander's high, and now their drunken mess of a watch party would be lucky to make it to game day. In celebration of their shock at the news, Xander yelled out, "Another round of shots! Here's to getting locked down!"

Whether or not they agreed with the situation, his friends finally didn't disappoint as they hollered and pounded their fists on the table. The rest of the bar joined in, regardless of the fact that they had no idea what the hell they were yelling about.

Then again, they probably did, considering their sloppiness and loss of volume control at this point. Xander knew he was going downhill fast. He was now positive he should have remembered not to skip lunch on account of being busy because now he was really feeling it.

"Fuck man, it's been like two months, and you're positive?" They already knew the answer, but he was sure Tyler had to point it out for good measure. He probably would have done the same thing, though he wouldn't have been as much of a dick about it.

"I'm sure as fuck, man." His words were now working their way out of his mouth onto slightly slurred lips and he was pretty sure he had reached that level of intoxication where he was making an ass of himself. Call it nerves from having had to think about defending his decisions from his friends or anger driven by Mina's ex, but he wasn't handling his alcohol well.

"I'm sure. And I'll tell you what. Her asshole ex-husband won't be able to say shit to me when she's mine. And neither will his little snitch bitch buddies."

Confusion crossed every face as his friends took in his words. Xander had failed to fill them in on all the current events in his life but he was letting them have it now.

"Then those little ass-kissing mother fuckers can go to hell." Confused or not, they were all hammered and laughing at Xander's inability to make coherent sentences. They just slugged more shots and patted him on the back, not knowing the trouble Xander had walked himself right into.

"Excuse me, can you step away from the table and talk to us over here, sir?"

After some spilled bourbon and choked laughs, they turned around to find an officer with a shit-eating grin on his face. A different face than the last encounter but the face of trouble, nonetheless.

All the hooting and hollering rang out, his friends still oblivious to the snake that was coiling right in front of Xander. But this time he felt bold. Maybe it was the alcohol or maybe he just wanted to set a precedent, but he wasn't going to stand for them singling him out because he was dating Mina.

Before his brain caught up to his common sense, he hurled words at the officer. "Fuck you. I not going anywhere." Maybe it was more of the alcohol after all, either way, he was just grateful he hurled words and not his fist.

He couldn't remember the last time he was an asshole to a cop. All his buddies held up their hands, the only "white flag" they could wave in a bar. This wasn't what he had in mind for a laid-back weekend with the boys.

Tyler put a hand on the cops chest as well as one on Xander's while Noah's head whipped around in disbelief of the situation. Shouts of "Hey, Hey!" and "Calm down" rang out amongst them all but they still didn't know why Xander was going off on the cops.

"Xander, don't be an ass. Just talk to them." Noah didn't want any trouble and he was about done with them all for the night. He was always the one to bail them out of shit because he was always the one smart enough to know when enough was enough.

"Fuck that. I don't need to listen to these assholes. They're the ones that stopped me on that bogus charge just so they could tell Mina hi from her ex-asshole. You pricks can go be meter bitches for all I care, but I'm not interested in talking."

Tyler took things up a notch as he swiveled his feet and got in the cops face, spitting mad and cussing obscenities at the cop. He may be a dickwod of a husband, but he was a good friend.

His best efforts were valiant in Xander's eyes, but they were of little use as the cop took his hand and twisted it around his back, effectively man handling him as he pushed his body up against the hightop.

"What the fuck? You're a real piece of shit, you know that?" He breathed against the table. The cop didn't seem amused anymore and was eager to tell them all.

"If you sit down with your other friends and keep your hands to yourself, I won't have to haul your ass in." Tyler looked like a hurricane about to make an impact but he kept his cool. With his lips tucked into a tight line and his face beet red, he nodded his defeat. The cop did as he promised and let Tyler go. With Xander still being a drunken loudmouth, the cop reached around and punched Xander across the face before grabbing him behind the back and putting cuffs on him.

The assault set off another shock wave as all the guys jumped back onto their feet in frustration. "What the hell is wrong with you?" Noah was furious but also wasn't sure what he could get away with since his friend already got cuffed and his other had just been let go.

"Public intoxication, disturbing the peace and threatening a cop. Does anyone else have anything to say or am I booking just him?" The whole bar looked on as if waiting for the next bell to ring and the next braul to break out.

The men had entertained the bar for long enough, but now they all stood in silence, knowing the officer had won this round. There wasn't anything they could do that wouldn't make things worse right now. "Jaysus fucking Christ," John mumbled to himself. His accent coming in strong with the alcohol. "We'll get you out as soon as we can, Xander. Just hang in there."

With a smug smile, the cop pushed Xander along the bar toward the entrance, talking into his ear the whole stretch. "Yeah, just hang in there Xander. I'm sure you'll get your phone call real soon."

These pricks just keep on coming out of the woodwork.

CHAPTER 33
Mina

"Xander is where?" The panic in Mina's voice must have been apparent to Evan, though his tone seemed annoyed by the fact.

"I just wanted to call and tell you that Alexander McCade, he says he's seeing you or something, is in jail right now. I wanted to call as a courtesy."

Like hell he wanted to call as a courtesy. She was about 99.9 percent sure that he was the sole reason he was in jail in the first place. Rubbing her temples was the only thing Mina could get a grip on. The only thing tangible at this point with her life spiraling out of control.

"Evan, did you do something?" The whole situation was bullshit, just like the first incident. "I'm serious. First, the traffic stop and now he's in jail. I need you to be honest for once in your life." Mina knew it was going to be a hard pass for him, but maybe if she begged enough, she would be able to get the truth out of him. What she ever saw in the man was beyond her. He had changed so much from when they were together, and yet, he was exactly as he had always been, apparently. A chameleon.

"Like I said, Mina. I called to be nice." He lingered on the last word as if mulling it over. "Mina, are you sure about this guy? Like, do you even know who he really is?"

There it was. What she had been waiting for. He hated to see her happy, as if he took pride in making her life miserable. Like she wasn't allowed the pleasure of having a normal life. She couldn't understand why he was always the one to create drama when he was the one to cheat. Why it would be him, she would have to answer to for the rest of her life. She just wanted a nice, quiet life with her daughter, but Evan seemed hell-bent on wedging himself in whenever he saw fit.

"We can still go back to how things were when we were together, and I can protect you, you know? I can look out for you and Sophie. You don't need another man in your life, and what's happened between us doesn't have to be permanent."

She reared her head back from the phone as if she'd been slapped. *This is what he was after?* He didn't find enough pleasure in making her life a living hell by cheating and exposing the villain behind the veil. No, he had to make sure to keep on twisting the knife.

She had known that her family believed he wanted her back even through all the cheating nonsense, but she chalked it up to them just wanting her to feel wanted. She couldn't believe they were actually right about it. They were right for so long, just as she had been wrong about him for so long.

"This is what all the bullshit is about? You want us back together?" Her tense voice was barely audible through the phone line, but she wasn't sure if she could keep her anger and frustration at bay.

"I'm just putting something out there for you and Sophie, that's all."

Of course, leave it to the insecure asshole to say something without really saying anything.

"You realize you're engaged to one of the women you cheated on me with, right? A woman you would sneak off to fuck while me and Sophie were at home wondering what you were doing and wondering when you would come home. If you would come home at all." Seething never felt so good. "A woman you paraded around town before people even knew we had separated."

She was sure his buddies on the other end of the line in Lockup could hear, but her voice couldn't be lowered, and she wouldn't be tamed. Not by him anymore.

"Just to be clear, the woman among many women you insisted on fucking behind my back while I was pregnant or taking care of our kid?"

"Mina, I'm just saying-"

"I know what you're saying. I'm telling you I'm not interested. I will never be interested. You're an asshole that just won't quit, and I wish you would just leave me alone."

She hung up the phone and then started dialing around to try and figure out how to get Xander out of jail.

It took until 3:46 in the morning for the text to come in from his oldest brother, letting her know that he was finally able to grab Xander and had taken him home. *Crisis averted. For now.*

She wasn't sure how much more of this crap she could take. And who was she kidding, thinking the crisis was averted? He went to jail because her ex was a con man with hurt feelings. Evan had reached a new level of crazy, and now he wanted her back on top of everything. She wasn't sure if she could handle any more men in her life, but now, she wasn't sure that the men already there would be able to hash it out on their own.

"It's a fucking dick-measuring contest, Claire. I don't know if I want anything to do with any of this." She didn't really believe that did she? She hadn't believed in love like the kind she had found with Xander, but the consequences of said love were getting to be a heavy burden to carry.

"Of course, it's a dick-measuring contest, Mina! They have dicks, and they both want you. They're both trying to bang their chests and do some stupid mating dance to lure you their way. Evan's just a dumb fuck that doesn't realize he doesn't have a chance in hell." Claire continued to be unfazed by each situation as they came.

Xander had gotten out with no charges and still hadn't called Mina to cry about it. He was a man worth fighting for in her eyes, but she wasn't sure how far Evan would take this or how much more he could use his badge to drive a wedge between her and Xander.

Every day had been more exhausting than the last, and yet every day with Xander had her feeling higher and higher.
She was pretty sure she shouldn't be shocked by anything Evan did at this point, but she didn't expect to hear that one.

"If you are actually considering taking that dipshit back, then I will have to kill you. I'll use my bare hands and I'll do it in the name of freeing your soul."

The statement jarred Mina enough to bring her back to the present and out of her own thoughts. "What? Ew, gross, Claire. I'm pretty sure I just threw up in my mouth. Thanks a lot."

Claire rolled her eyes before swiping another cookie from the baking sheet. They hadn't needed to move any to the counter to cool yet because they were binging their feelings.

Claire had brought the ladies over for a tea party and a support session while Kyle was off with his buddies for Super Bowl Sunday. Something Xander was supposed to be doing as well, but now she was pretty sure they were all recovering somewhere.

"I'm pretty sure I will either be able to write novels after you finally settle down or I'll weigh an extra hundred pounds from stress eating. You should really get your shit together Mina, this concerns us all."

"I'm glad that you are really taking my feelings into account with all this. I'll try and get my life a bit tidier," she drawled sarcastically. "So sorry about this mess." She kept on before slowly grabbing a cookie from the counter as well. "Now, if you'll excuse me, I'm going to ponder my life choices while I take down about seven more of these."

She walked over to the table and made herself cozy on her perch for the afternoon. A chair with a vantage point of the little ladies and the living room. Their blanket spread and their teapots full, the Superbowl tea party was in full swing. It was possibly the best Super Bowl Sunday she has ever had minus her personal life being in the middle of a shit storm.

"I don't know if any of this will work out Claire." She hated the way she sounded so serious all the time now. Love had made her carefree and reckless only to make her feel stupid the second things hit a dose of reality. She had to consider Sophie's feelings, not just those of her own heart. On top of that, she had to face the fact that it had only been two months. Two months! This man wanted to marry her on day one and was running his mouth in a bar that he wanted to get a ring already. She wasn't sure she could handle this type of love now that she had a little girl. The kind of love she had literally prayed for as a teenager made her terrified as an adult.

She had always wanted a timeless love story where the main character would throw caution to the wind and ride off into the sunset, consequences be damned. But now that she had it, it all seemed so painfully juvenile. Like she was too old to fall for someone so fast and she sure as hell was too old to act like she didn't have responsibilities. Even if this type of love made her feel worshiped in a way she had never experienced before. Xander was madly in love with her, pulling out all the stops trying to prove that he was worthy of being her husband. Then there she was, worrying that she couldn't handle that type of love. She felt like a Goddamn idiot.

"I know that look." Claire threatened. "You're on a deep dive and I feel like you need to come up for air." As she leaned over the table, she winked at Mina and grabbed another cookie. Mina wasn't sure when she had joined her or when the damn cookies had been placed in the middle of them, but she didn't care. "You know, you don't have to carry the weight of the world on your shoulders, Mina. God won't strike you down for being happy."

She tried to look away, shielding herself away before the flood gates broke open again. God, she hated how often she cried over men.

"I feel like you need to hear this." *Cue the waterworks*. "But it's ok if you want to be happy. You don't have to feel guilty just because you're a single mom and some gorgeous guy wants to take care of you."

The thought hung in the space between them. It was what she felt guilty for constantly. All the other mothers out there barely made it by while she had family and then happened upon a happily ever after. It didn't seem right.

Is this what survivor's guilt feels like?

She could only guess it must be because she survived the verbal lashings and the humiliation, but she couldn't grasp the fact that she found a happily ever after despite it all.

"Is it Claire? Why did this all happen to me? Why did I get so lucky that this all seems to be falling into place? He's drop-dead gorgeous, has a career he's passionate about, loves his family, loves his kid-who, by the way, loves our kids, and to top it all off, he wants me. He seems to be head over heels in love with me, though we've barely started dating. How is any of this okay?"

She was officially the broken record, but saying it all out loud again had her believing she was pretty sure she had some sort of survivor's guilt after all.

"Honey, your ex-husband had an affair with a slut, a lot of sluts, then asked her to marry him so that same woman who harassed you could help raise your child. Then, for fun, he just put your current boyfriend in jail and is plotting against you. I'm not sure why you still feel like this is all a walk in the park. This is a fresh hell, and somehow, you're skipping right through it like little Ms. Sunshine!"

Mina couldn't help the smile her sister forced out of her.

"Even if he didn't break you down, you would still deserve the world. The fact that you made it back to yourself after all the crap and continue to deal with him while still acting like a badass is something to behold." Claire always knew how to get to her. "Stop feeling guilty just because a man is finally treating you the way you deserve."

She wasn't sure why she insisted on this feeling. Like the whole world could be filled with love stories, but the last chapter of hers was written off a while ago. She wasn't being fair to herself, and she knew it. She knew her story couldn't be over yet. She just needed a bridge to the next chapter.

Looking down on their joined hands, she noticed the difference in their lifestyles with ease. The manicured nails, the beautiful clothes she wore outside her usual scrubs, and even her hair that was cut and colored to perfection. Mina's own nails were cracked and chipped, in need of a little TLC from her personal salon in her bathroom. The clothes she hunted down on sale or at the local Thrift shop could be masked as upscale, but to the trained eye, she would never pass. She couldn't even dream of getting her hair dyed when she had to cut her own hair to stay on budget.

All of those little things didn't mean much, but Mina knew she tried hard to keep it all together. It wasn't as easy as she let on while her ex harassed her about everything from who she talked to down to how she styled Sophie's hair. She put on her brave face every day, but she was so tired of it. She was tired of being so damn serious all the time. She's been one foot out the door with this man simply because she felt like she hadn't suffered enough. But as she stood across from Claire, she finally wanted to give it all. She wanted to try to be "all in."

She wanted to know what it would feel like to love someone without any inhibitions. The worry and the stress with her ex would always be there, so why couldn't she have this? *Xander had said it before, right? That they would get through all of it together.*

"Maybe I don't deserve this, Claire." Before Claire was able to protest, Mina looked her sister in the eyes and smiled. "But maybe I do." Her smile cracked wide open, almost deviously so. It spread wide with the satisfaction and contentedness of knowing that she didn't need to feel that guilt anymore. It was a peaceful feeling, and Mina could only imagine what it would be like to let it grow.

"Good." Claire mirrored her sister. They were identical in every way, down to their grins and passing hands as they reached for more cookies. "I was worried I would have to give you a sucker punch to the ovary to make you listen, but I'm glad you came to the conclusion yourself."

Mina almost spit out a chunk of cookie but managed to choke it down with some water. "Always so eloquent with words."

"How did it feel to tell him off?" The one thing they hadn't spoken about and yet one of the most exciting things to happen for Mina's self-esteem. Claire waggled her eyebrows as she bit down on the chocolate chip cookie, dying for the response she was sure she would get.

"Like I was made for it."

CHAPTER 34
Alexander

Days away. He was days away from being alone with Mina in acompletely different state. He would have her all to himself and he couldn't fucking wait. As far as the weather was concerned, it wouldn't be a complete one-eighty, but it had been a long and hard Colorado winter. The fact that he would be able to see her with a couple less layers on was adding a pep to his step with each passing minute.

He was grateful he didn't have to travel this week so he wouldn't be rushed to pack and then repack, but he was also swamped with work. The Super Bowl season drove up alcohol sales, who would have guessed, and now he had been racing to finish up work to take their vacation this holiday weekend.

The vibration across the desk filled him with instant dread at yet another work call weighing down his already busy day, until he saw the name flash across the top. *Speak of the devil.*

"Hey gorgeous. I was just thinking about you. I can't wait to get out of town and have you all to myself." He heard her sniffle and then felt his stomach drop with concern. "Mina? What's wrong? What happened?" With an asshole ex of this caliber, any number of things could go wrong at a given moment and he was on high alert.

"I'm so sorry," she broke out into a sob.

Sorry?

"Sorry for what? Baby, what's going on?" He was also on guard for her to drop him with the next sign of trouble. She had skated around the idea when she first mentioned her ex, but with every new antic her ex carried out, he was always fearing she would jump ship.

"We can't go. I'm so sorry, Xander." He knew something would happen. It was just too good to be true to ride off into the sunset with this woman, but she needed to know he was here for anything.

"It's going to be fine, I just need to know what happened. Are you okay?" She sniffed and gathered herself on the other end of the phone.

"It's Evan. He's threatening me again with trying to take Sophie and said he would use the trip and your arrest against me."

With his grip on the phone tightening, he had to remind himself that they had to work smarter, not harder. He had to figure out a way to make this asshole pay without screwing things up for Mina and Sophie.

"Baby, calm down. It's okay." Saying it out loud wasn't just for her at this point. He didn't realize he was white knuckling the armrest of his chair until he looked down in frustration. He had to take his own damn advice and it didn't feel good to swallow this pill.

"What did he tell you? Start from the beginning, and don't worry. We will figure it out. There will be other trips. No need to get worked up, baby." There would be other trips, and there really wasn't any need to add more stress to her anxiety riddled nerves from the douche. The poor woman could never catch a break with that guy.

"He called me and asked me how you were doing now that you were out of jail. Said he wanted to make sure you were staying out of trouble and that I wasn't getting involved with someone who isn't a good influence on our daughter."

What a fucking piece of shit. Talk about the ultimate cock block. The man was getting more and more crazy by the day. But then again, Mina had warned him.

"Then he said that he knows I'm going on a vacation soon and that he should move our court date up and tell them about how I'm off galivanting with strange men when we have a little girl at home. He said he could get full custody if he brings it up to the judge."

Her biggest fear was losing Sophie and the asshole knew exactly how to pull her strings.

"All right, now hold on. I'm not some strange man, and what you do in your free time is your business, not his. But," *I can't believe I'm about to say this.* "I understand. He makes threats, and at this point, I really don't know what a judge would say, considering how he has cronies all over this town." *The asshole would use anything against her.*

Her family had been right. He wanted to keep her in his life at any cost.

"We will plan another trip. It's really no big deal." It was killing him, but he knew there was no point in fighting it right now. They would need to regroup and figure out this mess.

"You promise you're not upset? I really am so sorry for all this, Xander." He knew she was upset, mortified and any other emotion she wasn't numb to feel at this point. The man kept coming, and to her defense, she kept trucking along.

"I'm not leaving no matter what. I meant what I said the very first day. I'm done looking, crazy exes and all."

She took a big breath, and he could hear her relaxing on the other end of the phone. This was how it had been lately. It seemed like he always needed to reassure her that he wouldn't leave her like that asshole did. He wasn't sure how long it would take to convince her, but if he had to, he would spend the rest of his life proving that she was worth staying for.

"I am worried about him calling you, though. Has he called other times to talk about me or threaten you about our relationship?" He should have asked more often. He should have been more attentive. He knew that she had heard about the arrest. The town was small and people talked, but he tried to minimize the gossip as best he could. He slammed his fist into his desk at the idea of him being so preoccupied that he didn't think to ask more questions and make sure she wasn't being harassed anymore.

"Just one other time." She paused. The silence made him tense every muscle in his body at the thought of him calling his girl. "He told me you were in jail and then kind of asked if I wanted to be back together with him."

His vision blurred as rage ruptured throughout his body. The armrest screamed in protest as he tried not to mangle the damn thing.

"But I let him have it, then I hung up."

He muted the phone and took another punch, this time landing his fist into the wall adjacent to his desk. The wall puckered under the pressure, pieces falling to the ground before he clicked the mute button off. "I'm glad you told him off. I bet you feel a bit better doing it, and maybe he will get the hint sooner rather than later." The words felt like sand in his mouth.

The fact that he just told her he was proud she told off her sleazy ex was bullshit, and they both knew it.

She shouldn't have to deal with him anymore, and Evan wasn't slowing down. The jerk was just gearing up.

"Thank you. I don't know why you want to stay and deal with all this. I have so much baggage, Xander. I don't know if it will ever get easier." He knew she meant it, but he was dead set on fixing the problem. Although beating the 'baggage' to a pulp was preferable, he would have to think of a more lawful way of dealing with it. More lawful and more strategic. For now, he would relish the fact that he still had time off work and could see Mina on nights when he didn't have Amelia.

"I don't care if it gets harder, baby." After taking another deep breath, he felt like he could function again without murdering someone. He just wanted to see her. "I have another couple hours of work to do, but then I can take some time off to grab dinner if you're free." He was hanging on her words these days, constantly waiting on her approval for dates and times.

"I don't have Sophie until he drops her off around seven tonight. Dinner sounds incredible."

"Alright, I'll swing by and grab something on my way out and bring it over to your place. Sound good?"

He prayed to God she didn't mind eating in because every moment he was with her was filled with a blind territorial need. They both had schedules and time with their kids that took them in different directions, leaving him a mindless caveman. She could eat dinner, but he only craved one thing.

"Dinner over here sounds perfect." She held onto the last word like she wasn't finished. Like she didn't know what else to say. "Thank you. For everything, Xander."

He couldn't help the greedy grin. "I'll see you in a few hours, baby."

He leaned back in his chair and stretched out his neck. The long days hunched over an office desk always sucked worse than travel ones. At least then, he was moving around and seeing different things. Being confined to his office felt like a small prison when he had to chain himself up there for hours.

Baby.

He called her baby all the time now. Like he was some love-sick puppy using terms of endearment that had never crossed his lips, let alone his mind, before her.

Everything felt so right that it should scare the bachelor in him, but none of it did. Not her little girl, not her ex and not the fact that most of his friends and her family felt like it was all too fast. He was so ready to leave those bachelor days behind. It all felt like the pieces of his life had fallen into place, and he had someone to finally be his person.

Dealing with the asshole could wait a day or two. He just needed to finish up work so he could go see his girl.

CHAPTER 35
Mina

"Enough is enough! You are worthy, and you are worth this." She looked straight ahead and took a deep breath.

"This is so stupid." She didn't want to talk to herself in a mirror like she was on a shrink's couch, but drastic times called for drastic measures. "You need to stop being such a little bitch and acknowledge all the shit you have gone through." Motivational speaking was not in her future, but she was all she had at the moment. "He loves you. Enjoy it." She paused and took another minute to look hard in the mirror. Besides the random water spots she missed this afternoon while cleaning the bathrooms, she liked what she saw.

Better yet, she liked who she saw. Maybe for the first time in years. Her long, wavy hair looked shinier than it had before. The way it fell down her back gave off some golden hues that she hadn't seen since she was in high school. Maybe she just stopped noticing or caring, but here they were, loud and proud. Her cheeks held a slight pink to them and looked a bit more plump. She had always had full cheeks, but the year that the cheating came to light and divorce had slimmed her down to an unhealthy weight and had made her naturally round cheeks all but disappear. She smiled and took them in, dimple and all. They were back, and she loved it. She was back, and she loved it more than anything.

The doorbell rang, and Lupe lost her shit like it was her fucking job.

"Lupe! Calm down. It's Xander." She hurried to the door and scooped up Lupe as she grabbed the handle with the other hand. She needed to somehow train her not to hate the world, but she would have to put that training session on the back burner for now, or forever.

She opened the door expecting the blast of cold air from the Rockies to hit, but something else did first.

"Mommy!" Sophie barreled into Mina and wrapped her arms around her legs.

"Baby! What are you doing here so early?" That was the understatement of the century. She shouldn't be surprised that Evan would pull something like this. She was just shocked he was able to ruin her plans when he most likely wasn't aware she had any.

Speak of the devil.

Sophie didn't enter the house on her own like she normally did for drop-offs. Evan came in behind her, looking like an innocent lamb while Mina was well aware he was anything but.

"Hey, M."

My old nickname. He was pulling out the big guns with old habits now. She wasn't sure if he thought he could pull on heartstrings with that one, but he was about to find out he was sorely mistaken. Those days are dead and gone. The little lamb he was playing at was nothing more than a wolf under the mask.

"Evan… hey. What's going on?"

In the past, she would be quite concerned with a situation like this. She was always naïve to his tricks when it came to Sophie. Naïve or afraid, either way, it had always worked, and she always fell into another trap. But tonight, she wasn't in the mood to take the bait.

As they shuffled awkwardly inside the house and away from the front door, Sophie let go of her legs and started to take off her jacket and head for her room.

"Soph, don't you want to say bye first?" She was really hoping Evan would be on his way quickly, but her hopes were dashed when he looked intent on taking a seat.

"Actually, I was hoping we could talk for a couple of minutes. I told Sophie we needed to talk before I left. Just us two."

She smiled weakly and felt the tiniest cheerleader in the world doing the saddest "yaaayyyy." If Claire were here, Mina would wait until Evan turned his back to her so she could put an invisible noose around her head and make a ridiculous face just to show how shitty this was and to make her laugh. But Claire wasn't here, and this situation was really that shitty.

Xander was due any moment, and her ex-husband was sitting in her living room like this was a casual occurrence. As if he normally reclined on her sofa and made small talk with her in private.

It's turning out to be a great fucking night.

She sat down on the adjacent loveseat with her legs tucked under her and a pillow across her chest like a shield. Then she just waited for him to start what was sure to be either an awkward as fuck conversation or something more along the lines of infuriating.

"So I just wanted to say-"

It was all he got out before the doorbell rang, and Lupe started to lose her mind again. He looked at her and then at the door in confusion, little flickers of understanding flaring up behind his eyes.

"Are you expecting someone?" Maybe she should write a comedy instead of a romance novel.

"Cousins are here?" Sophie ran from her room and bolted to the door like her feet were on fire, *because, why wouldn't the night get any more dramatic?*

"Sophie wait!" But it was too late. Xander looked down at Sophie with wide eyes and then at Mina on the loveseat. From his vantage point just outside the door frame, he couldn't see Evan on the couch. A few more inches, then the night would certainly get more interesting.

"Hey Sophie." The intonation in his voice held both curiosity and a playfulness as he tried to smooth over whatever mess he just walked into.

Mina took a quick second to glance at Evan. "I did have plans for the next couple of hours but you didn't ask before you showed yourself in."

She got off the couch and walked to meet Sophie and Xander at the door before the whole house dropped thirty degrees. "Come on in Xander. I would like you to meet Evan. My ex-husband."

Xander walked into the small space and the walls instantly felt like they were closing in. Mina was pretty sure Xander was thinking he would be halfway to her bedroom right now rather than standing in the living room with these two crashing the party, but being the gentleman that he was, he reached his hand out for Evan to shake.

"Alexander McCade. Nice to meet you." Evan popped up and pretended that he wasn't part of the arrest bullshit.

"Hey man, how's it going?" As he rose from the couch, Mina watched as Evan puffed his chest out and tried to look larger than he actually was, like an alpha trying to claim his territory even though he was clearly out of his.

While Evan spent hours at the gym obsessing over himself, Xander was naturally built. He filled up space and had muscles probably given to him by his Greek God ancestors. Maybe she was biased, but she didn't give a fuck. She was team Xander.

"You remember Princess Sophie." Mina gestured to the little

lady now standing at her side. Sophie beamed up at Xander. She loved him. He had gotten more and more bold about chatting with her, and she was in awe of his humor and his knowledge of everything little girl.

Xander squatted down to her level, "How could I forget my pickup line buddy? Bring it in, princess!" He held out his arms and she ran into them.

Mina smiled at their affection while she was positive she saw Evan flinch at the adoration his daughter showed Xander. As Sophie closed her eyes to give Xander a squeeze, Evan looked over at Mina with his eyebrows on the ceiling. She looked over at his with a cool and calculated expression.

"Has she mentioned Xander at all? They talk every time I pick up the kids for Beth and Jared. Or maybe the fact that his daughter is friends with Claire's oldest."

Confusion now crossed his face as he watched Sophie turn and run down the hall, yelling that she had something to show Xander.

"I'm not the stranger you want to paint me to a judge, am I?" Evan stood awkwardly, not knowing what to say. When he finally opened his mouth to speak, Sophie ran back with a unicorn stuffie in each arm and started to chat with Xander about how much Amelia would love the black and white unicorn and when she would finally be able to have a real playdate on her own with her.

They talked for a couple of minutes while Mina and Evan looked on. She knew he was fuming but couldn't say a damn thing because it would show him as the jealous and manipulative father he was.

Xander looked up at the two stuck in their stare-off and broke up the moment. "You have to ask your daddy." It snapped Evan out of his trance and brought his attention back to his little girl.

"What's that honey?" Sophie popped up again and reached for Evan with puppy dog eyes.

"I asked when we could have a playdate with just Amelia. She goes to school with Stephanie, Daddy!" As he held her, he pretended to do some thinking. As if he needed reminding who his ex-niece was.

"Oh, I didn't know that. We will have to set something up now, won't we?" *Oh, I bet you'll get right on that.*

"Speaking of which," Xander interrupted. "I think we need to put something in the books for us." Evan looked like he had shit himself.

"Yes, daddy! How fun would it be for you to have a playdate too!" Soph may have liked the idea but Mina wasn't entirely sure about the two actually talking alone together. Although, after watching the interaction tonight, she was positive Evan wouldn't be able to keep up with Xander. He was smart and quick on his feet. Evan was just an asshole that was good at manipulating a situation when he knew your weakness, and Claire was right. He had nothing on Xander.

"How about tomorrow for some coffee?" She almost felt bad for Evan. He was backed into a corner, and he had completely put himself there.

"Y Yeah, sure. Coffee sounds great." He stumbled over his words before he gave Sophie a hug and walked towards the door to let himself out. He was officially the odd man out of this happy little family, and it looked like he finally took a hint. "I hope it's cool if I duck out early tonight. We can talk a different day, it's no big deal."

He was running with his tail tucked between his legs like he needed to retreat to his goons for some backup on how to handle the situation.

"Absolutely. And now that you were here when Sophie and Xander officially met outside of the pickup line, we can meet up to talk at any of their playdates or when he comes to hang out over here too. I know we've always kept things pretty cordial and somewhat distant, but maybe Mindy wants to meet Xander, as well. You know, so she has a face to a name when Sophie brings him up."

The smile was plastered across her face, and she was loving every minute of what it did to Evan. Leave it to him to forget about his fiancé.

"Sounds awesome." It sounded anything but awesome judging by the tone of his voice.

"I'll give Xander your number to have in his phone and you guys can decide on a time for tomorrow." Another awkward head shake and goodbye for Sophie and he was out the door like a bat out of hell.

She turned back toward the living room after locking the door behind him and stared at the two loves of her life. "And then there were three."

CHAPTER 36
Alexander

The night hadn't gone according to plan, but it was one of the best nights he could have imagined. He was missing his girl, but having Mina and Sophie to himself was a blessing in disguise. Watching them in their own little world was a highlight he never knew he needed. The conversations they held, the mannerisms they shared, and even Sophie's bedtime routine was a peek into their relationship.

He waited quietly in the living room when the melody of Mina's voice carried through the house as she sang a bedtime song for Soph. Her soft voice, like the soundtrack to his life, was the most beautiful sound he had ever heard, and he found himself asking questions he didn't know the answers to.

How did I get so lucky?

How did we get here?

What song would she sing to Amelia?

What a difference a couple of months could make. How quickly his life had gone from mundane movements between time with Amelia to full of color and vivid in every detail in ways he hadn't ever thought nor dreamt of. The one he had just witnessed included. The little parts of a day he never knew he needed in his life. Needed so badly that it made his skin burn when she wasn't touching him or made his days dull when they couldn't all be together. Like he never knew loneliness before they met, but now the thought of her not being behind every corner or roped into every conversation just felt foreign. It felt dull.

After her song had ended, he heard her quiet footsteps coming down the hall before she found her spot next to him on the couch and cuddled up against his chest. They finally had a minute to talk in private, but it was the last thing he wanted to do. He had already realized why Evan would want to get her back, but now it was painfully clear why he was going to such lengths to attempt it.

Every moment with Mina drug him further and further into a need and obsession for her. He understood Evan's torture, but he was the one who fucked up while Xander caught the biggest break of his life. He would forever be indebted to that man for being such a narcissist. The thought made him laugh but it pained him simultaneously. If it wasn't for a simple choice that asshole made, he wouldn't have found his way to Mina, and that, was a painful thought.

"I'm so sorry about tonight. About Evan."

He hated this part. It always ended up this way. She had fears or her ex caused some type of drama, and she always ended up doubting things or apologizing for all of it. He didn't want to hear any of it as he pulled her in closer, shifting her weight so that she straddled him. Face to face, and nowhere to hide.

"Stop apologizing. I'm going to start getting upset if you keep on taking responsibility for that dick just because he duped you into marrying him a long ass time ago." She tried to bury her face in his chest, but he held her chin and made her face him again.

"I mean it. We are in this together." He searched her face, and couldn't understand why she kept on trying to hide from him. Unable to look him in the eyes like she was about to start crying.

"I just feel like I didn't warn you enough. I didn't want to tell you that he had started following me a long time ago, probably to keep tabs. I just thought it was always about Sophie. I didn't know he would go this far. I didn't think it was actually about me and that they were right..." Her voice trailed off to nothing but a whisper.

"What do you mean he was following you? And let me make this clear, I'm not mad you didn't tell me because you feel some deep sense of guilt about having a crazy ex you need to protect me from. I'm mad he's fucked up enough to stalk you, and you feel the need to hide it. How long has this been going on?"

He knew he shouldn't project his anger, but the woman wasn't allowing him to take care of her while simultaneously allowing an asshole to scare her.

"And Jared and Claire knew?" Her face winced at the mention of her siblings, and it was obvious the guilt had sprung up yet again. "So they knew. Why didn't any of you call the cops or do something about this? About any of the harassment?"

She tried to swing her leg over and right herself, only to have him grab it, holding her firmly in place. "Stop trying to run away from this. You have to tell me. You need to let me in."

Now he was the one who felt a pang of embarrassment as

she seemed to open herself up to everyone else without allowing him the opportunity to help.

"It's not that easy. He's a fucking cop, Xander. Who would we tell?" She looked at him as agony blurred her brown eyes. "Who do we run to for help? It's a small enough town, and half the people here are his buddies or under his thumb in some way."

He hated to admit it, but it was the same truth he realized the other night. It was a pretty small town, and he was a fucking cop. She and her family were just trying to survive without adding drama to their already eventful past. The realization hit him again, but now he felt like a dick for pushing it.

"Hey, I'm sorry, okay?" He wrapped himself around her and let her sink into his embrace. "I get it. I promise I do." He did understand. He just couldn't stand the idea of her being harassed at any point in her life, but especially now that she was his. "I just get territorial. That asshole doesn't have the right to bug you. Not in the past and especially not now." Holding her face in his hands, he brushed the tears away as she looked up at him with defeated eyes. "I'm going to fix this, okay? I'm going to make him stop."

He kissed her hard as if willing her to believe in him. He didn't know how he was going to do it, but for this woman? He would willingly walk through hell to figure it out.

They rested there, tangled together, with his lips firmly planted on hers as she nodded in agreement. Breathing in and out, until they let their lips rest and their foreheads keep their connection.

So much had happened since they hung up the phone hours before, but they found their way back to each other as if they had always been fighting on the same team.

"I won't share you, Mina. That man will have to find out the hard way, and I have every intention of teaching him." With her legs firmly tucked by his thighs, he moved his hands to wrap around the swell where her legs met her backside. Slowly, he groped and kneaded her ass and thighs, letting his thumbs caress the erotic fold of her hips. He kept one hand on her ass, keeping her in place while the other found purchase gripping the root of her hair, pulling her head back and exposing her delicate neck to him.

"I don't care what it takes, Mina. You're mine." Using his tongue to tease her while nipping at her skin hungrily. It said everything without him saying a word. As he cradled the back of her head with one hand, he used the other to pick her up and place her underneath him on the couch. He couldn't handle being this close without grabbing or kissing, or fucking under normal circumstances. But with tension and her ex trying like hell to get her back? He was feral with the need to show her who she belonged to.

He couldn't stand the thought of another man sniffing around and thinking he had a chance. Not with this woman. His woman.

The natural scent on her skin was an aphrodisiac, and he could spend the rest of his life nestled in the crook of her neck, letting his hands roam over her perfect body. She was flawless. Every bump and indent needed his touch and every inch of skin needed his kiss. He couldn't keep himself from becoming this way around her. His drug of choice for the addict inside him. She consumed his day, his thoughts, his everything, and yet it was never enough.

Leaving her neck and trailing kisses down her collarbone, he replaced his hands with his mouth and sucked and teased her nipples until she was panting and whispering his name. Her hands slid into his hair, and he felt her tug as he continued on his path down the length of her body, like she was hanging on for the ride. Every kiss and nip along the way was met with a pull of his hair and a greedy thrust from her hips, begging to feel more, needing to feel more. But he wasn't in any hurry to stop exploring.

He locked eyes with her as he licked the inside of her knee and pushed both legs over his shoulders. "Do you know how much I crave the taste of you?"

He groaned as his tongue slowly slid into her. "Always so fucking wet for me. Do you realize how good you taste?" His eyes bore into her as he made a show of slowly sliding his tongue into her, tasting her. "Fuck, baby. I've had a lot of pussy, but I've never tasted anything like this." When he went back down for a deeper kiss, he wanted her to feel his words. He wanted her to know he wasn't just saying she was the best. He wanted her to scream his name so she would never forget how fucking obsessed he was with her pretty cunt.

The slow licking morphed into sucking and pushing a finger into her wet slit. She had to put her face back into the blanket to muffle her moan when he added another. Using his fingers in tandem with his tongue, she was losing her mind. Legs shaking and hands gripping his hair, he knew she was getting close.

"Come for me, baby. Come on my tongue, and then I'll let you come on my dick." The speed and pressure took hold of her and he felt her grip change just before she let out a muted cry. "Oh my God, Xander. I'm gonna…" She couldn't finish her words before he could feel her pulsing beneath him, moaning into the blanket and gripping the sheets.

He gripped her thighs and took it all. Taking his time as she exploded beneath him. "Fuck baby, I could eat this pussy for breakfast, lunch and dinner." Somehow, with his head buried between her legs and her post-orgasm high starting to slow, she seemed shy as her cheeks burned with a deep crimson that wasn't there mere seconds ago.

"Do you still get uncomfortable when I talk like that?" It was cute that she was so innocent. She was *his* innocent.

"Maybe…" She threw an arm over her face, but he caught it before she was able to hide from him. He settled his weight between her thighs and framed her face with his hands. Brushing back any loose strands that came between them. He didnt want any more hiding.

"What part of it? The part that I salivate just thinking of your pussy or that it's literally the best I've ever tasted?"

It may make her feel uncomfortable, but he couldn't help what came out of his mouth when he was around her. He'd always loved going down on women, but this woman? She was truly something else.

"All of it?" She looked so embarrassed, and he couldn't hide his grin. He was loving every second of her shyness. Of course, she would feel insecure. He hated what that asshole did to her, and with his past extracurricular activities, she was bound to feel inadequate.

"I don't know how you don't believe me. I'm a goner, baby. Have been since the day I first saw you." He drew her in even closer, placing a gentle kiss on her forehead before resting his head on hers for a moment. Just like they had started.

"All that said, baby, I don't know if I can be gentle tonight. I haven't been able to properly fuck you the way you deserve, and with this weekend out the window, I'm not sure I can be a gentleman. Your pussy is just that good." He meant every word.

She peppered kisses on his neck and around his square jaw before meeting his lips and giving them a little nip as he had done to her before.

"Then don't be." Her voice was hoarse. "I'm yours, Xander."

Hearing her say those words was all it took for him to lose control. Since the moment he laid eyes on her, he wanted to prove that exact statement. Prove that she was the one he's been searching for his whole life. Love at first sight, whatever bullshit words he never believed until he saw her for the first time.

"Fuck baby, that's all I've ever wanted."

CHAPTER 37
Mina

"Hey ho bag." Claire was her usual chirpy self.

"God, stop yelling at me. Some of us didn't get a lot of sleep." Being a mother was her greatest gift and all she had ever wanted to be. But being a mother also meant that the tiny little miracle she gave birth to decided when it was time to wake up and take on the day. After a second cup of coffee, her five am wake-up call was still haunting her two hours later.

"Why is your voice so shitty. It very much matches your attitude, I must say." She could hear Claire sip on what she presumed to be her first coffee of the morning. "Why didn't you get any sleep, Mina?" She hung onto the question like she didn't know the answer when she absolutely did. She just wanted to make her say it out loud.

"Because I'm a slut who can't keep my legs closed, Claire. Is that what you want to hear? I'm lucky Sophie is watching Wild

Kratts right now, or she would be able to look down on me as well."

"Ahhhh!" Mina immediately held the phone out in pain. She wasn't sure arms length would be enough for the octave her sister was reaching. She rubbed a heel of her palm into her eyes, and begged.

"Oh my God, Claire! Please stop the loud noises. I seriously can't. I'm pretty sure the man fucked my brains out, and I literally don't have the cells to support the kind of noise you're throwing at me."

"Seriously, I love this so much. You're in the I-can't-fuck-enough stage!" She giggled some more and let out a sigh as if she was looking back on memories. "I remember those days. They were awesome."

They are awesome, she thought. But life in this stage requires a lot of coffee and willpower now that she has a little lady to tend to. "I still can't get over this whole damn Hallmark movie," Claire said. "Seriously, sis. You go, girl. Get all the action you can with Hot Dad. Everyone is wishing they could."

It did feel good, and she wanted to let herself have this moment. Everyone wanted to land him, and by some miracle, she had him all to herself.

"Claire," she couldn't wait for her reaction to this one. "Xander walked into the house last night right as Evan was dropping Sophie off early."

The line went silent.

"All right…I'm officially obsessed with your life. Spill the beans."

Mina filled her in while they both downed their coffee. It was filled with ooohs and ahhhhs and ended with a "well shit."

"The man put him in lock up mere days ago," *a bit longer, but who's counting?* "And Xander still managed to invite him out for coffee and managed to be the bigger man."

"First of all," Claire cut in. "Xander is the bigger man. You've seen him naked and told me so yourself." *It's true*. "Second, there is no way in hell that the asshole makes it to coffee. What would he be able to say to Xander? We both know he's a damn coward."

Of course, that was the truth in this whole matter. He really was a coward with everything he did. A coward who didn't want to face marriage issues, a coward who ran off before coming back to play daddy, and now a coward because he didn't want to face his replacement.

Her phone buzzed in her ear and she cursed her late night once more before checking who texted her. A third cup of coffee should just be injected straight into her veins at this point. She looked down at the screen with relief or possible frustration, she wasn't sure but at least she didn't have to deal with extra drama today.

"Well, we don't have to wonder what Evan would say. Xander just texted me that Evan told him he couldn't make it this morning, but that he would love to reschedule sometime soon. Of course."

"Wow. Shocker. Asswipe didn't want to meet Hot Dad for coffee." Claire was starting to get more and more creative with Evan's names while she remained a die-hard fan of Hot Dad comments. Xander may never have a real name to her, but she wasn't sure she cared if Claire stuck to Hot Dad.

"I know that him being an asshole isn't new to any of us, and now it's old news for Xander, but have you told him everything? Like why he finally backed off for a while during the divorce?"

Mina had told him almost everything. It was the most stressful thing in her life besides the actual shit Evan was putting her through—the idea of being completely honest with Xander about what transpired between them. The ugliest part of her marriage would be put on the table. Everything from her past and her fears combined. Laid bare before him to do with what he pleased.

She knew Xander would do nothing but support her, but she also knew he was protective, and she was tired of being treated like the little glass sculpture that needed to be handled with care.

She went through hell and had to face a lot of those moments alone. She was able to do this, she just wasn't sure how yet.

"Not yet. He knows it got physical, he knows about the stalker vibe he gives off, but he just doesn't really know what happened the last time he was at the house before the divorce." The poor man believed that the worst of it was the stalking, she couldn't imagine what his reaction would have been when they were alone in the house together had he known the whole truth.

"The man deserves to know, Mina." Deep breaths on both ends of the line were all that could be heard. Claire must have needed to calm her nerves just as much as Mina did. She was her other half, after all. "But you're also entitled to your secrets and your own hardships. It's no ones business if you don't want it to be, Mina." She knew she didn't have to tell anyone. "Xander hasn't exactly been forthcoming involving matters with Evan, even if he had good intentions about it."

It was true but like she said, it was also true that he did it to try and prevent her any future stress. He was always thinking of her, just like Claire and the rest of her family. Always in her corner. Like he had always fit right into her family without preamble.

Just like with everything else in her life, Claire had been the first person she called when it had happened, and she was positive that she immediately called his father so he could let him have it before things went further. She always thought, with time, she would get the courage to report him, but when her courage finally resurfaced, she just wanted the asshole to leave her alone and she wanted to forget any of it ever happened. She didn't want to relive the ugly parts of her life when, at long last, she was starting to get back little bits of the woman she used to be.

She wasn't sure if all the therapy in the world could help her go back to that last day at the house. All the what ifs and knowing it could have been so much worse. But none of that leveled with the fact that Xander had a right to know. If this relationship crumbled, she didn't want to know that it fell because she was too afraid to speak up again.

"I know you're right. He deserves to know everything. He constantly tells me he's all in, and here I am, floundering with one foot out the door because of these fucked up secrets." Claire was right, her life was a fucked up romance novel, full of twists and turns.

"I'm glad you decided that's the route. Let me know when you tell him, or if you need help. You know where to find me." She did. She always knew Claire would be there for her and knew her sister would talk her off any ledge or through any storm. It just didn't make what came next any easier.

The weeks went by in a wave of normalcy for them. Whenever Amelia was with her mom, Xander was a permanent fixture at her house once Sophie had gone to sleep. The playdates with the girls increased in frequency, and they started to play house as a little family from time to time.

Having Jared and Claire's girls as a small buffer to what their little family could be. Family dinners and playdates at the park were their getaways by day although they both made sure to keep their time with their girls at the top of their priorities. Even his ex, Lauren, started meeting up with her every now and then at Amelia's request when she wasn't with Xander.

It was so strange to meet with an ex of his, and yet so normal it seemed routine. This woman would be in her life if she was lucky. She found herself curious about every detail, even if it meant running into Robert, Lauren's new husband. The man gave her an uneasy feeling and his stares lingered a bit too long, but she wasn't going to go down that road when there were bigger issues at hand.

She was sure the man had heard of her, other than him being a police officer as well, the look on his face told her so. The one that she noticed behind the cocky eyes and when everyone else wasn't looking. He was just like Evan, she was sure of it. But it was a problem for another day.

They split their focus between their girls and work, so late nights become their afternoons. Like clockwork, he would drive down her street and she would lock Lupe away as to not wake up Sophie. Once she opened the front door and he hit the front porch, they were instantly a mess of hands and tongues, trying to feel and taste every square inch of each other as if each night could be their last.

The tension with her ex seemed to hit a steady plateau, but she knew it could only last for so long with a man like him. A man that thrived on tension and sought out spectacles like he lived for the fallout of his wrongdoings. Like he would allow them some slack on their leash only to pull them back, shocked and grappling with what to do once he grew tired of watching their happy lives grow together.

Besides the stalking, the tug on their ever-shortening rope came in the form of headlights glaring through Mina's front windows one evening. Even with her blinds shut, the bright lights filtered through her living room as if someone had flipped a switch for the sunrise, interrupting their stolen moments together and making Mina feel naked to the world again. Proving, yet again, she didn't have as much control over her life as she thought.

The harsh lights stayed there long enough to prove a point, before backing out of her driveway and down the street, just out of reach. As if he could time it perfectly, it was always an interruption, and whoever it was wouldn't stay long enough to get caught. By the time Xander would get his jeans pulled up and make his strides for the door, he was only ever able to catch the blinding lights backing down the drive and pull away with a stranger inside. The windows were always too black to make out a face, and the authority of the position was always apparent when they knew they couldn't do anything about it.

That evening was no different when the lights flared into the room, illuminating their bodies and sending Xander into a fit of rage. It wasn't that Mina didn't care about what was happening, but she had grown used to harassment with the prospect of her not being able to change anything.

"That mother fucker!" Xander threw on jeans, and raced for the door. If he hadn't looked so damn delicious, maybe she would have tried harder to stop him, but shirtless and disheveled Xander was always her favorite. He threw open the door, Mina hot on his heels wrapped up in a blanket and perched in the doorway.

"Xander!" Whisper yelling seemed ridiculous when trying to call after a half-naked man running full sprint down the street, but it was all she could do as she tried to grapple with what would actually happen if he caught up to them. *What would he even do?*

As if the situation couldn't get more awkward, Lupe decided her geriatric hearing was on point and started running after Xander and the suspected threat.

"Lupe!" Again with the whisper shouting. The shit show was on full display to anyone taking out their trash and she was just hoping a bear didn't decide to join in on the action.

Thankfully, the cruiser sped away before Xander was able to catch up to them, but not before a loud whistle could be heard coming from the driver's side. The sight of Xander, fuming and shirtless halfway down the street as Lupe lagged behind should have her worried, but she couldn't help but laugh.

He turned toward her house after shouting, "FUCK," as loud as he could, then took a couple of deep breaths. Lupe finally made it to his side as he scooped her up and walked back up her street, toward the mountain and back to her. She had never seen anything so sexy and hilariously frustrating in her life.

CHAPTER 38
Alexander

The hand on his chest twitched as he groggily remembered where he was. They often fell asleep together, but he always set an alarm so he could be gone before Sophie woke up.

He looked down and felt like a stalker. He could stare at Mina all day, or in their case, all night. From her dark hair draped over her bare back, to her long dark lashes dusting her cheeks. She was his exotic paradise. All mocha with hints of golden from her skin to her hair. But tonight, like many nights, she was restless. He knew it didn't just have to do with the damn spectacle they put on just before midnight down her street. He knew it was so much more than that.

She moaned in her sleep with fear rather than pleasure and he watched as her brows pinched together. Her head on his bicep kept turning inward as if turning away from something while the hand on his chest flexed into a fist.

He had never mentioned it to Mina, but he was well aware of the terrors that haunted her in her sleep. The nightmares she hid from him that came back to remind her of the past. Of what, he still didn't know, but they frightened her often enough. He knew that no one could be as strong as she was without having a weak moment, and true to form, she only allowed herself to be weak when she was tucked away from the world.

Tonight, was different, though. She talked this time, and the words that came out made him want to kill someone. With her shying away from the dream that tortured her, she kept turning deeper and deeper into his arms while telling someone "no." Begging and pleading someone to stop…doing something...to her, he assumed.

"No…no…" The room was quiet except for her desperate prayers. "Please stop. Please, please.…" Her whispers came out terrified as he could hear a tremble in her hushed voice, and it tore him apart. He wanted to be a gentleman. He always pretended to be sleeping when she would wake herself up, so she could have the privacy she so desperately protected. He wanted to give her that much of her independence. He really wanted to wait until she was ready to tell him what had happened in the past, but he was done waiting. He needed to know what she was battling alone so he could make sure she knew nothing would ever be able to get to her again.

She startled herself awake after what seemed like hours of being stuck in her terror. Although it was minutes, she was damp with sweat and out of breath. It came in shaky waves that sounded like a muffled sob, like she was trying to regain control. He could feel the perspiration on his arm coming from her forehead and the tears slide down his bicep as she tried to stay stock still as best she could while she steadied herself.

But this time, instead of pretending to be naïve to what had just played out, he reached his other arm around her so she was trapped in his warmth before he placed his lips on the top of her head. It wasn't sexy and it wasn't possessive like before. He just hugged her hard and kept himself there until he felt her sink into his body, relaxing and realizing the cat was out of the bag.

"Have you been here before when this has happened?" She asked quietly. He couldn't help but love this woman more than he already did. She sounded so innocent, her voice so hollow with the question.

"Yeah, I have. Been here for a lot of them." She lay there quietly in his arms, breathing softly and rhythmically now. "Mina," he wasn't sure how to go about this. "I've tried to let you have your time and space." *Am I being supportive or pushy?* "But I need to know what happened. What's going on in the dreams that makes you so afraid? Is this all tied to that prick?"

He wasn't questioning it anymore, he knew he was being pushy at this point. But he couldn't wait for more night terrors or more ways for that asshole to harass her. He had to know what happened between them.

The room stayed quiet. It was practically pitch black with a distant streetlight barely leaving shadowy outlines along the wall, adding a sense of discreetness to her confession. Something he was sure she wanted and needed in order to get through this.

She didn't face him. Just picked up from where she had left out the details before. "Remember I told you he would come around the house looking for sympathy to take him back?" Of course, he remembered. It rendered him speechless on their first date, but instead of admitting it made him seriously consider killing a man, he went with, "Yeah, I remember."

"Well, the last time he stopped by the house, he took things too far."

Taking another deep breath, she took the silence as her cue to keep going. "He um…He." Time seemed to stand still while she gathered her thoughts and he waited with bated breath. *Fucking hell, what did he do to you?*

"He grabbed me and held me down. Sophie was watching a little cartoon, and he thought she wouldn't notice if he pushed me onto the floor behind the couch." He had to fight the urge to flinch after the statement, knowing it may be the first of many that would shock him. "He held me down and then groped me on the outside of my clothes before he um." Her breath was shaking, just like her body. "Before he shoved his hands into my yoga pants."

She didn't continue for a bit. Not until he asked her.

"What did he do after that, Mina?" He knew what she was getting to but he could still feel his stomach start to roil with disgust. The man was a fucking coward, and he wanted nothing more than to see if he liked being held down while he beat the shit out of him.

"He held my arms with one hand and used the other to take them down my legs." A nervous laugh broke out from her trembling body. "It feels so stupid how easy it was for him. He used his knees to keep my legs open and then used his free hand to grope me and then put his fingers inside of me." This time she went quiet. The memory still haunted her, and there was no way around it.

There was nothing to do but hold her tighter. None of this was okay, he just wanted to make sure she knew he was here to help her through it all.

"The pain of his knees on my inner thighs was awful. The feeling of his fingers shoved inside me made my skin crawl." She paused and he prayed to God he didn't make it further.

"But the things he said to me…" When she couldn't go on this time, he felt more warm tears streak his bicep and felt her body silently shake in his arms. He's never hated a person more in his life than he did right then. For the past shit he did to her and for making her relive that moment every time he was around her. She should feel safe in her own bed, her own home.

"He said I was his. Only his." A sniffle and more tears followed. "Said that I would never escape him. He tried to undo his pants while he told me that I would only be his. But Sophie came around the couch, and he crashed his body onto mine so she couldn't see anything. She started asking why I was crying." He had heard enough, and he was positive it was killing her to confess it all.

"Come here." He pulled her on top of him, so she splayed out on his chest and straddled his hips. He wanted her as close to him as possible. He wanted to hide her away from the world. He just wanted to her. End of story.

They lay there for what seemed like forever. Her in his arms, and him trying to will away her silent tears. "I'm sorry I'm just telling you all this now. I never meant for it to take so long for it all to come out."

He tried to ease her turmoil but when he tried to tell her to stop, she kept going. "I didn't want to say it because he made me feel so weak. How easy it was for him to hold both my hands above my head with just one of his was humiliating. I finally realized my size in a way that terrified me. In that moment, I didn't know what he would do but I knew there wasn't a damn thing I could do to stop it." Her words hung in the air. "It terrified me."

All of it made so much more sense to him. When he looked closely at her life, all of the little things started to add up. How she acted around Evan, how she didn't trust anyone, looking over her shoulder everywhere she went and even the security doors and cameras in her own home. It was as if a big siren went off in his head and he was angry with himself for never piecing it together sooner.

He held her in his arms until her body slipped into a peaceful sleep. Only then, did he slide her off his chest and tuck her in with extra blankets. Making sure Lupe snuggled up next to her nice and close.

He walked through the house with ease and suddenly felt bad for Amelia. This little cottage at the end of the street had felt more like a cozy home than his house ever had. He wanted nothing more than to scoop up Amelia and tuck her in right next to Sophie. Like nothing would feel right until they were all able to be under one roof, and he could make sure all his girls were taken care of and felt safe. *My girls.*

With one last look around the living room and a final glance at the picture wall, he gathered his stuff and opened the front door, making sure not to wake the ladies. He had a plan now, and he didn't give a fuck if that meathead wanted her back. Evan wouldn't stand between them anymore and wouldn't be able to so much as speak to Mina without his permission. *There's a new man of the house, and this one isn't a fucking coward.*

Sitting in the parking lot before sunrise, he wondered if he should have shown up at Evan's house instead. He was positive he could have looked up the address for that prick but then thought better of it for legal purposes. It wouldn't do him any good to get himself locked up and give him free rein to terrorize Mina. *Work smart, not hard.* Especially with a manipulative son of a bitch like him. So, here he was. Sitting in his truck before the sun came up in a lonely parking lot. Waiting for the man of the hour to show up.

As the sun peaked over the trees and made its way up and over the mountain, people filtered in and out of the station, changing shifts. But it wasn't until just past seven in the morning that he watched the scumbag saunter up to the door, scrolling his phone, no doubt thinking that he could avoid his texts for the rest of the day. The assholes inflated ego had him believing that Xander wouldn't show up in person, but he was about to find out just how wrong he was. *Now or never.*

Opening the glass doors, he was met with a front desk receptionist. The hallway behind the woman was wide and opened to a bullpen area with countless desks and computers, filled with officers writing up paperwork or about to leave for their beats. He spotted his target just before asking the receptionist if he would be able to have a private conversation with Evan.

The woman walked back to the bullpen full of desks, and he noticed how the men all interacted with one another. The way they cracked jokes and carried on, acting like best friends. All of which could pose a challenge for him in terms of credibility, but he didn't give a fuck. He didn't care which asswipe was part of Evan's little clique that took pleasure in harassing and stalking Mina. He just wanted to end his shit once and for all.

The woman made her way to Evan and pulled him aside, making him aware that an individual had requested his attention. The guy had the gall to look down her shirt as she was filling him in, even giving her a wink when she noticed. *Fucking piece of work.*

Once the name passed her lips, he saw the pinch of his eyes before they went back to normal. His fears having gone into hiding. It may have been quick, but Xander saw it. He was afraid. The woman continued on and he returned his gaze to her chest as she finished up their little chat. If this was his behavior in public, he could only imagine what went on behind closed doors.

He took a moment to look up from his desk and send Xander a sideways smile, waving him over and leaning back in his chair. He did his best at intimidating Xander the whole length of the walk, chatting with his desk mates, never losing eye contact. By the time Xander took a seat adjacent to his workspace, Evan had decided to make it a party and invite some of his buddies over for the conversation. Xander also noted how he had decided to change positions, choosing to sit at the edge of his desk so he could look down on Xander rather than look up.

Xander normally towered over him and most of his cop friends who now stood around the desk, hands resting on their bulletproof vests, trying to look more dangerous and take up more space than necessary.

"Hey man, I was just about to text you back. A little anxious this morning, huh? Is there trouble in paradise?" Chewing gum and smiling wide, like the cocky bastard he was, Evan looked at ease with his buddies around him. A bully in the school yard who was nothing without his cronies.

"I came here to talk about what you're doing to Mina and how you and your buddies are going to cut that shit out." They all looked around at each other, smiling and scoffing at the presumed accusations about to come their way.

"We don't know what you're talking about. If you keep on getting in trouble with the law, we will have to keep arresting you. That's just how this works, man. No hard feelings."

He looked like a beefed up Ken doll. All charm and dripping with goodwill and manners, but he had already shown what he was like behind the mask. He was a coward who scared women to feel more powerful. A snake. *Men like him don't deserve women like Mina*. "And Mina is seeing things. I haven't been following her and neither have my friends. You both really need to get a life if all you talk about is me."

The group erupted into laughter. Cackling and nudging each other with elbows, like they just scored a touchdown at a college football game. They were all beaming grins and looking down on Xander, expecting anger. But it never came. What they didn't realize, was that Evan just fumbled and it may cost him the season, or in his case, his upper hand.

"That's strange because I never told you that Mina worried about being followed." The group of men slowly quieted down. "And neither did she." Evan's eyes narrowed on Xander as the smile slowly slipped off his face. He wanted to fuck with them, but now he was going to pay.

Xander held his smirk as he looked up at the man now fuming, nostrils flared. “Your stalking habits are beside the point. I actually came to talk to you about something else entirely. A certain time when you tried to rape Mina and got interrupted by your little girl.”

The mask was off and all manner of civil conversation would be thrown out the window. *You fucked with the wrong woman.*

Evan grabbed Xander by the collar and shoved his back to the desk, seething at the comment. His friends all jumped up to pull their friend off of Xander, and the whole station seemed privy to their private conversation now. It took captains and security to pull the men apart and feel comfortable with their little chat continuing.

Once everyone had settled down, one of his friends leaned forward, telling Evan they would give the men some space as the rest of them cleared out faster than if he had shot a round off inside the building.

“Alright, asshole, what do you want? I’m all ears but if you ever talk about-”

“No, you listen to me.” Xander interrupted. “You’re lucky that it’s up to Mina if and when she will charge you for the assault and attempted rape. It will also be her choice if and when she wants to get a restraining order on you for stalking and intimidating her. So, you better listen, you piece of shit, because I’m done being nice. You will stay away from her. You will only see her or speak to her as long as it regards Sophie. If you so much as breathe wrong in her direction, I will fucking beat your ass so bad they won’t be able to put you back together. Consider this your one and only warning, because besides getting your ass beat, the charges would ruin you for good. I’m glad you decided to keep a little audience because now they all know about what kind of man you really are. You’re a fucking coward, and now you're done."

Both men remained frozen in place, letting the words between them settle into an understanding. Evan didn't say anything and he didn't need to. The expression on his face spoke volumes as he stood just before Xander, head down, focused on the desk as if a reading his termination papers. His jaw tensed and his lips pursed. Most likely seeing his defeat laid out before him and Xander had never felt more satisfied with anything in his life.

Evan didn't look up from the desk as Xander rose to leave. Didn't even so much as speak a word, just nodded to himself with a grimace as he continued to look down, apparently coming to terms of the new reality that he was doused with. Xander had made it down the hall and just past the front desk before he turned and called to Evan, making sure he had the full attention of the irate man across the room.

"You were wrong with what you told her. She doesn't belong to anyone but herself. She decides what she wants and who she wants."

His smug smile pulled at his lips. "And considering all the late night drive-byes, we both know it sure as hell isn't you."

CHAPTER 39
Mina

It wasn't even six in the morning before Evan started texting her. *Xander didn't waste any time.* She was interested to see how their meet up would go and when it would happen, because she was sure, considering the annoyance in Evan's texts, the meet up was going to happen come hell or high water. With the fresh knowledge he was given last night, Xander seemed more eager than ever. One cup of coffee wouldn't cut it today. *No way in hell.*

With that sentiment, she poured herself the first of many, then nestled next to a shivering Lupe on the couch. The weather out the front window looked frosty, and she curled in on her cup even more, scratching Lupe behind her shivering ears. She was positive that she should enjoy the calm of the morning because there were little time bombs about to go off at any moment.

By late afternoon, the house had been scrubbed clean, and Sophie had officially made every craft in her thousands of kits.

Mina was a wreck. No call from Xander and no more texts from Evan. Claire was at work, and so was Beth. She was on her own with this shit.

"Mama? Can we go get some ice cream tonight?" Sophie was helping her hold onto the little bit of her sanity she had left today, that was for damn sure.

They spent the rest of the anxiety-filled afternoon cooking along to music and then driving a couple of blocks over to grab some ice cream. It may have been March, but the weather was still sporadic and freezing in the evenings. She didn't need to add frozen fingers and toes to their list of problems for today, although thawing them out could serve as another good distraction.

At some point during bath time, Xander texted that he would be heading over as if it was any other night. As if he hadn't left her hanging all day while she tried to figure out what went on between the two men. If they even met up. Evan never texted her back after his early start and texts asking her to keep her boyfriend on a leash, which only set off more alarms for her. Had they met up, and he was scheming? Had they talked it out? With Evan, only the former seemed plausible.

When the time came, Xander pulled up to her house after Sophie was asleep, just as he said he would, but walked up to the door like a man possessed. He took her in with his eyes, as he always did when she stood in the doorway and waited for him to approach, but something was different. He seemed more intent. His eyes looked sinful in the low light as he went straight to her mouth, his hands grabbing anything he could get to. She had no problem being naïve that they had much to talk about. No issue with going along with the best form of distraction possible.

His fingers in her hair gave her goosebumps down to her toes, and the way he groped her ass was rough, almost painful.

She was sure he would leave purple prints as evidence of his lust. Even how he picked her up and guided them to the couch showed no hint of gentle attention. Tonight, he was the other side of the coin. The rough side of Xander that reeked of sex and control. The side that blew her mind and made her feel worshipped with the same hand. All of it was delicious. There was no other way to describe life with Xander.

He pushed them onto the couch and started to pull up her nightgown that had already gathered around her thighs, groaning when he realized she wasn't wearing panties. She was a whore for this man, and she was so far gone she was never coming back. *Fuck the questions. They can wait.*

Half an hour later, they were a tangle of limbs and a panting mess. It was the most hurried and frazzled she had seen him, as if he had been driven mad staying away today. Perspiration clung to their bodies and they hung off the couch, trying to catch their breath together. As they tried to readjust themselves, she wrestled her hair into some semblance of calm as he continued with his post-sex ritual of showering her entire body with kisses and rough massages, taking the time to literally worship her in a more delicate, intimate way. It was insane to her. She had never been treated like royalty in her life until she met this man.

"Why wasn't sex this fun before I found you?" She was completely serious, even if she had her playful tone attached. She knew the answer right after she thought about the question. She loved him. More than she ever believed she could love another person.

"Maybe the movies weren't a bunch of bullshit, after all." She giggled and nestled herself under his arm as they found their rightful places on the couch, lying astride one another. "Sex is seriously mind-blowing when you love someone."

She could feel him smile down at her and feel the extra squeeze of his arms around her body.

"Mina Washington, did you just say you love me? Out loud... and on purpose?" *Goddamn, this man and the technicalities.*

She rolled her body over to rest on his chest slightly. She was guessing he wasn't going to let her off the hook for this one. Only once had she let it slip.

"Yeah, Alexander McCade. I did." His grin split even further, and he crushed them together where they lay. All sweat and smiles. It wasn't as if he didn't know it. But she had hoped that he felt it from her. She had never been good with words. The introvert in her always kept her feelings from overflowing, and the scars on her heart had permanently erected walls to protect her.

He gripped her ass with his hands and pulled her so their mouths were level, kissing her deeply. She could feel the scruff on his chin chafing her further, but she didn't mind. This man was everything she never expected and everything she had always wished for, all rolled up in one.

"Thank God." He let out a sigh and took a moment to nestle and inhale her neck. "I kept convincing myself that you felt it enough to overcome some of that bullshit your ex was putting us through. But I was worried he would scare you off." He lifted her chin to make sure her eyes were on him. Had her full attention. "Thank you for loving me." The look on his face so pure, she couldn't help roll her eyes, not wanting the attention.

It felt like she was being sliced right down the middle by this man. No place to hide. Everything was out there, and it was terrifying once more.

"Oh yeah, sure. I'm not the one with the nickname 'Hot Dad' at the parent pickup line, complete with adoring fans. You've told me before that you're just an average Joe but that's bull. I may not understand why you picked me, but I'll take it. I'll take you any way I can get you."

His eyes bore into her, incredulity marking the edges of his mouth. "You still don't get it, do you baby? You're it. My days and nights, my highs and lows and everything in between. I've been looking for you my whole life." He swiped a stray hair from her cheek and placed it delicately behind her ear. She couldn't believe this man was real.

"Now." He had set her hair in order and rubbed her bottom lip nonchalantly. Waiting for the more serious topic at hand. "What was your day like? I'm sorry I got so wrapped up in work."

She knew he was playing coy with her simply from Evan's texts. "No way. You first. You either talked to Evan, or you guys scheduled something. I've been dying all day." She rested her chin on her hands, finding comfort in the middle of his chest.

He played with her hair as he gazed at her on his chest. Smiling and looking painfully handsome. "I decided to talk with your ex at the police station since he kept trying to avoid my texts or calls." Judging by the amusement on his face, she could wander to guess that her eyes looked like they were attempting to bug out of her head.

"You talked to him already?" A huff of air coming from her lungs proved that she was still in the room and in the conversation. "What did you say to him? What did HE say?" No one has ever stood up for her like this, but she wasn't sure why she ever doubted that Xander would. He nodded his head, slowly, those piercing eyes unreadable.

"I thought it was time for him to understand the way things will be going from now on." He cleared his throat and went back to rubbing the base of her skull with his hand. Even her scalp got the attention of this man.

"Honestly, I'm a little worried you'll be upset with me, but I want you to hear me out." His hands moved from massaging her scalp to her shoulders, moving his focus up to the ceiling as if he couldn't face her. She wasn't sure why he seemed so nervous when he sought Evan out for the conversation.

"Him and his little cronies didn't seem to get the message that their version of fun is harassment and that we wouldn't be tolerating it anymore." He paused before continuing, letting out a deep breathe. "So, I told him that I knew about the attempted rape." He looked down at her through pained eyes. He looked as if she had punched him in the gut.

"I'm so sorry. I know it wasn't my place to say it, but I didn't see any other way for him to stop running his mouth or for his little dirtbag friends to see him for what he really is. A fucking coward."

He probably wasn't expecting her to huff out a laugh after his confession, but she couldn't help it. She had always wanted to gather her courage and tell someone, anyone outside of her immediate circle, but she never could. After long enough, she figured people would cast her as the scorned woman and think she made it up out of resentment. He just took the rug out from under Evan, and she couldn't believe it. In front of his friends no less.

He noticed the incredulous look on her face and took it for what she hoped he would. "You aren't mad?"

The question seemed silly to her now. She could never be mad at him. He was perfect even when he thought he was at fault. "Mad? How could I be mad that you made him listen? Xander, I'm amazed that you had the nerve to go in there and stick up for me. Stand up to a cop and his buddies for me. In the damn station!"

He grabbed her face and kissed her senseless again. His relief being her reward as she basked in the attention. The heart this man had kept inspiring her to take that leap long before tonight. She wasn't just smitten, she was head over heels for this man. He was everything she wanted and feared. Everything she hoped for.

"Thank God you're okay with it." He set her back to rest on his chest as he went on with the story. "After I told him, the others scattered, and before I left, I made sure the whole room could hear me when I told him that you are none of those things he whispered in your ear that day. I told him you get to choose who you want and it sure as fuck wasn't him."

She wrapped her arms under his chest, sealing herself to his body.

"I'm sorry no man has done this for you before, but I hope to be the last one who ever gets the privilege of defending you. I love you, Mina."

CHAPTER 40
Alexander

One Month Later

"A fried green tomato and grits all in one day? I think these ladies are getting a proper introduction to the South if you ask me." Mina looked happy, and Xander felt completely full. Full of love, full of happiness and just plain content. That's what he expected when he planned this trip for their family. *Family*.

Nothing was official, but he had his plans, and he didn't need a piece of paper to make them feel like a family, anyway. These three girls in front of him were his life. After the little scene he caused at the police station, Evan tried to put a stop to the relationship in different ways, but it was obvious he knew defeat when it was laid out in front of him and his colleagues. He didn't have a say in their lives anymore because they had an ace up their sleeve.

Xander wasn't sure if Mina was ever going to press charges or if she ever cared to go back down that road, but they had the threat to make sure he kept himself in line. It was everything they needed to make him cut his shit and start backing off. Nothing was perfect, but the fact that they could start acting like the family they truly were was all the progress they needed.

"I think we just need some fried okra and a ghost tour in a cemetery to seal the deal for me." Mina wagged her eyebrows as the girls squealed. *Who knew all my girls would be into creepy shit?*

"Yeah, yeah. I think you girls just like to watch me freak out. It's your entertainment these days and being outnumbered is starting to wear on this old man."

Mina faked a pout before adding. "Yeah, but you like being outnumbered and we love our old man." The girls each got up to give Xander a hug before Mina rounded the table and gave him a kiss, whispering promises for being a good sport. He would go to any of those haunted places, and she knew it. He was so over the moon for this woman, she could ask him to dress up and be part of the damn vampire tour, and he would ask where the fake fangs were.

"All right, let's get out of here and wander through one of those creepy cemeteries or churches you guys talk about." He faked a grumble because this was all part of his plan, anyway. It felt like everything had finally come together.

The girls giggled and twirled as Mina spun them around in a dance just walking down the street. They do the same little dance and song every new place they went just to make it special. She made everything special.

As they wandered down the street along the uneven sidewalk and vine-covered gates, he saw his cue, and asked his girls if they wanted to check out the historic church on their way back to the hotel.

"I'm pretty sure I saw some headstones in the back just through the gate over here. You're allowed to thoroughly freak me out again if you want." He joked, but he couldn't deny that even the cemetery at this church looked charming. It was why he chose it. The way the greenery grew over each headstone. Mixing moss and grass between the rambling and jagged walkways. The way the vines fell in between the trees and Spanish Moss draped the fencing felt like being transported into a different time. It cast a spell on him, that was for sure. He was hoping the landscape would cast a spell on Mina as well.

They slowly wandered through the walkways and knelt before graves. Taking in years and names as if they knew the inhabitants. Their ages, their engravings. All of it led the girls to wonder about what happened to the people occupying each grave.

It was mesmerizing watching his girls be fully immersed in the history around them and, hopefully, the history that was about to be made.

While looking at the name of a certain gentleman's grave, Sophie and Amelia traced the stone, giggling about something before a loud shout was heard through the whole cemetery. "BOO!" Another scream, loud enough to sprout new grey hairs on his head, rang out through the tiny cemetery.

"I got you!" shouted Stephanie. The look of shock on the little girls' faces was priceless, and they weren't the only ones. Mina's mouth hung open, a mix between a smile and confusion. Then a group of others came in through the opposite gate wearing their Sunday best. Mina looked around at the familiar faces.

"What are you all doing here?" The grin on her face never faded as she took in friends and family in stunned laughter.

"We wanted to check out creepy churches with y'all," Claire said with a Southern drawl. Just like he had planned, her shock gave him a moment to gather himself.

Just the right amount of time to get down on one knee and pull out the tiny box he had been hiding for weeks. The ring Mina had never intended to ever get from a man but a ring that Xander was dying to see on her finger. The idea of her wearing his ring just did things to him. And now, it was about to become a reality.

As Mina doled out hugs and shared happy laughter at the chain of events, she was about to hug Claire when she turned and found Xander.

As everyone grew quiet, he cleared his throat and looked around, then up at Mina. For being so damn sure of his decision, he had never been so nervous to ask someone a question. Holding open the box containing her solitaire oval ring flanked by two little gold bands he had made for the girls, he looked up at her. Her hands flew to her cover her mouth, and he could see her eyes grow glossy.

"Mina, I know you don't believe in rings, and it's only because of the failures of one man." He took a breath, trying to steal his nerves. "But I do. Because I know what our rings could mean, I know that I'm dying to see you wear my ring because I'm dying to be your husband. From the first time I fumbled my chance with you, to the time I made you cut the line to talk to me, you've turned me into a man possessed. I've never believed in love at first sight, but I knew the second I saw you that I had it all wrong before. I've been searching my whole life for love, but I never thought it could come close to what I found in you."

The tears in her eyes spilled over.

"You love to bake and cook, and I promise to be your permanent taste tester. You live for creepy things, and you're a night owl while I swear, I've gotten heart palpitations with each scary movie you've forced on me, and despite your best efforts of converting me, my body still wakes me before five a.m., reminding me how different we are. You always tell me I'm the sun to your moon and the light to your dark, and I realize you couldn't be more right. You balance me in everything I do and everything I am. You're the love of my life, and I promise to prove that love every day of this life and the next if you let me."

Looking over to Sophie and Amelia, he adds. "You three girls are my whole world, and this is all I've ever wanted. So please do me the honor of being my wife, Mina. Say you'll be mine forever, and I promise you, we can get through anything this life throws at us."

He didn't have time to add anything else before her lips were on his. Crashing into him in the most honest form of an answer he knew he would get.

"Yes!" She repeated in between kisses and hugs as he lifted her into his arms and kissed her right back. Their families cheered loudly, and even the priest on standby was all smiles and smitten with the crowd. It was everything she had told her sister she had wanted, and although Xander wasn't sure she would remember, the smile on her face as they danced the night away proved she did.

Small and intimate. Just friends and family, the people who held her up when she and Sophie couldn't have done it on their own. Claire and Xander had spent the entire previous month planning and prepping to make it a perfect day for Mina, and they didn't fail.

As he reached over to scoop up Sophie while Mina danced with Amelia, Xander thought back to all the times her ex had made their lives a living hell and the fact that he most likely would keep on doing it. He knew what Mina was worth and understood why the guy would never stop trying. He knew he couldn't fault him for that.

She was worth chasing.

She was worth fighting for.

She was worth everything.

Acknowledgements

There are many people I want to thank for encouraging and supporting me while creating my debut novel. First, I want to thank my amazing husband and kids. Their patience and support was everything to me. My husband pushed me to learn and tackle each new hurdle while my kids were my biggest cheerleaders.

Thank you to my parents, who always taught me to believe in myself and to chase after my passions.

Thank you to my Under the Covers Book Club beta readers! I couldn't have done this without you ladies pushing me to improve. Your honesty made the story better with every little Post-it note you stuck on every page! The books we read and the moments we share are cherished and valued more than you know!

Thank you to my fellow indie authors for taking a chance on a stranger and giving their time and energy to my questions!

Finally, thank YOU, the reader, for taking a chance on an indie author. Thank you so much for picking up this book and reading Mina and Xander's story. I hope this is the beginning of a beautiful friendship. 😉

About the Author

Summer Adams lives in the sunny South West with her husband, kids and dogs. She loves to travel with her family, has an addiction to reading and loves a good coffee shop anywhere she roams. If she isn't reading the current pick for the Under the Covers Book Club, she can be found in their backyard with one of her little sidekicks. Her love for all things romantic keeps her mind buzzing with stories and her computer busy with work!

Follow Summer on Instagram at
summeradams_author.

Watch for Summer's next book in the Kings
Ranch Series
Luck of the Irish

www.ingramcontent.com/pod-product-compliance
Ingram Content Group UK Ltd.
Pitfield, Milton Keynes, MK11 3LW, UK
UKHW042004190726
13854UKWH00005B/2165